SHATTERED LIGHT

RYAN D GEBHART

Other Books by

Ryan D Gebhart

The Jewel of Life

Splendor of Dawn

Hidden Within

Fading Lights

Burning Desire

Spires of Arenthyl

Memories of Twilight

Shadow of the Lost:
A Novel in the Jewel of Life Series

Shattered Light

Part Seven

of

The Jewel of Life

Ryan D Gebhart

Hardcover ISBN 979-8-9853738-5-1

Paperback 979-8-9853738-6-8

Distributed by Ingram Publisher Services

Printed in the United States of America

Cover design by Fiona Jayde Media

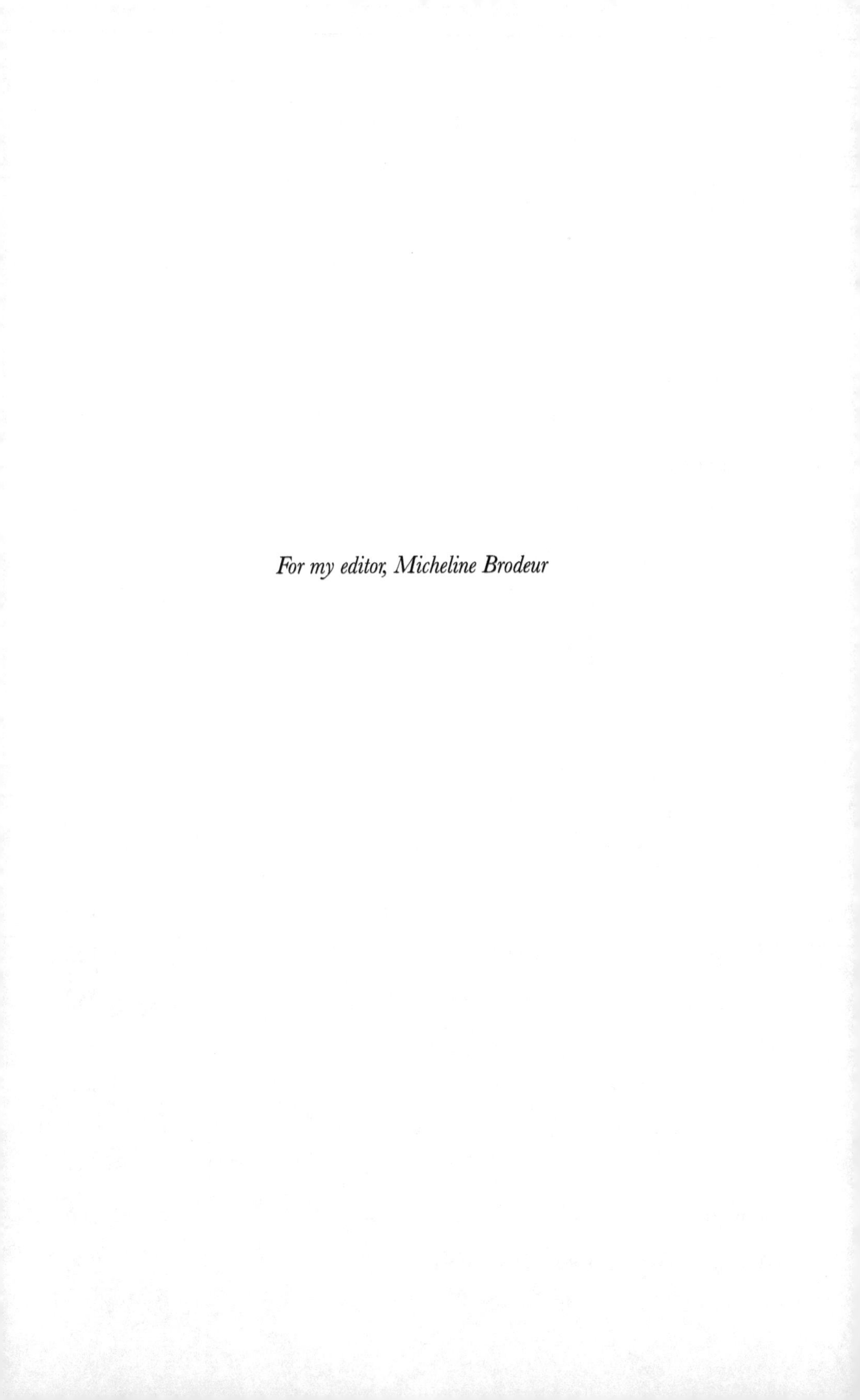

For my editor, Micheline Brodeur

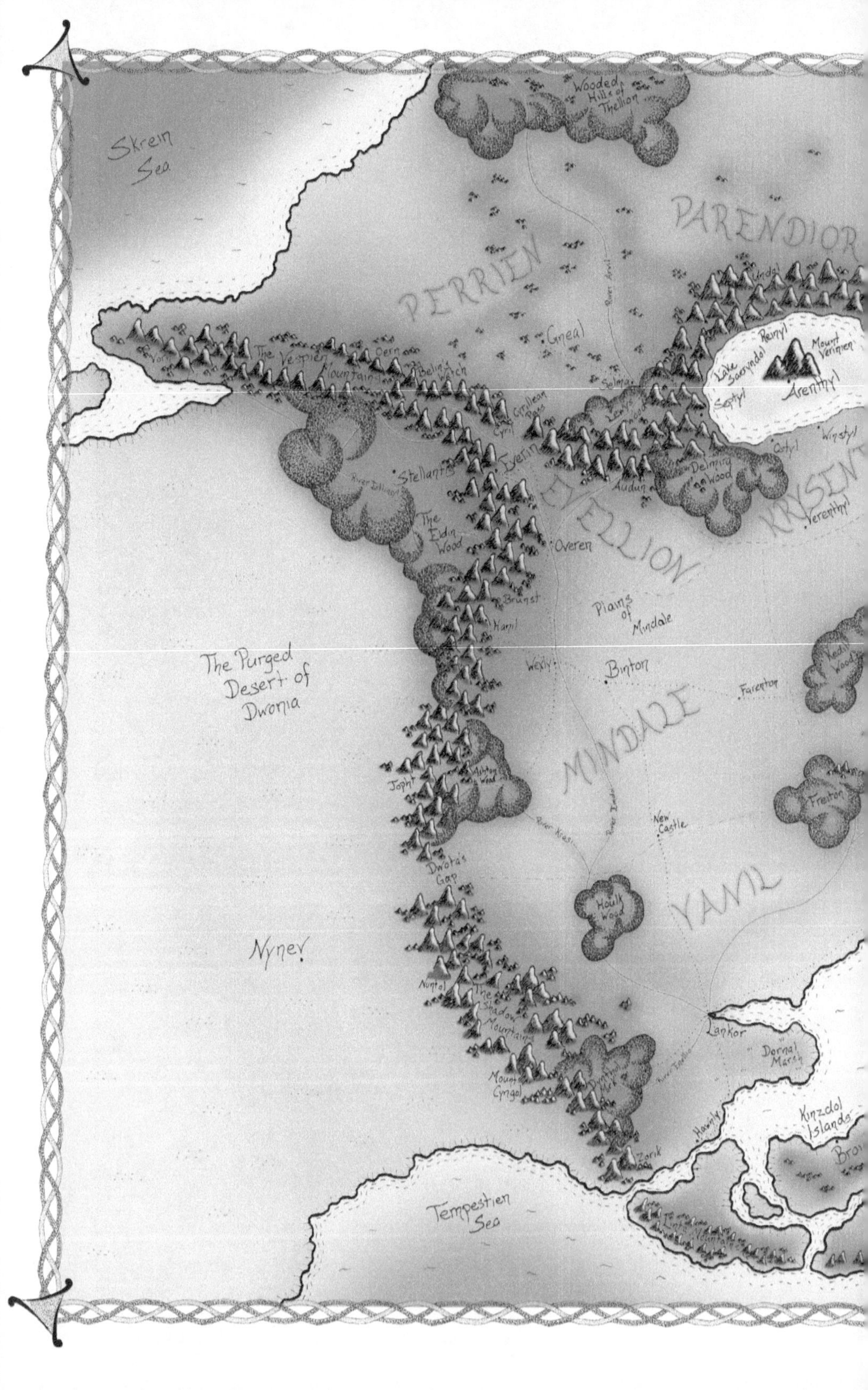

Skrein
Sea
Wooded
Hills of
Thellion
PARENDIOR
PERRIEN
River Anvil
Gneal
Undgil
Reinyl
Mount
Verinien
Lake
Socryndel
The Vespien
Mountains
Oern
Beling
Welch
Solma
Arenthyl
Sotyl
Grillean
Pass
Cyril
Delmiry
Wood
Cotyl
Winstyl
River Delliner
Stellante
Everin
ELLELLION
Lewys
Audun
Verenthyl
KRYSINT
The Eldin
Wood
Overen
Brunst
Plains
of
Mindale
Harnil
The Purged
Desert of
Dwonia
Wexly
Binton
Farenton
Medlin
Wood
MINDALE
Jopht
Ashton
Wood
Frenton
River Kriest
River Tralse
New
Castle
Nyner
Dwota's
Gap
Houlk
Wood
YANL
Nuntol
The
Shadow
Mountains
Lankor
Dornal
Marsh
Mount
Cyngol
Dimbhen
Mrk
Kinzdol
Islands
Harnly
River Trelleur
Zorik
Brow
Tempestien
Sea

The Unarian Sea
River Bethyl
The Laudien Mountains
Galvarith
The Illumined Wood
Ceurenyl
Erithel
Lucillia
Mount Saecrien
Kweil Aitch
Roselan
SORENTHIL
Myrium
Ruins of Quellion
Peran
Daerinth
Plains of Orithil
GISTORIA
River Merien
RSIZ
Dead Wood
Mendil
Brief
Eddle Port
River Reifen
TIEL
Harding's Crossing
Nairin
Josque
Ja'mare
Iryniem Bay
Jahro Islands
Suderri
Jadien
Map of the Continent
EKLEAN
Inscribed in Ink
by the Hand of
RDG
N
W E
S

The Price to be Paid

Ithendryl sat alone in her study, taking a brief respite from her responsibilities, which, by right after Faerndryn had died, should have passed to their son and his wife. An aryl was composed of a wedded pair, to best serve all their people. But with Faerndryn gone and her youngest son captured, Ithendryl was left to rule alone. Despite the long and drawn-out war with the Erynien Empire, she could not believe that her Faerndryn was no more. The suddenness of his ending was painful and had left her scarred inside.

Eliel, her phoenix and constant companion, nuzzled her cheek, sharing her grief.

Thank you, old friend, Ithendryl conveyed, her heart aching with fear for Eliel. She didn't want her phoenix to suffer the fate every other phoenix had. Who among them were left? Were Eliel and the thousands-of-years-old egg that had yet to hatch the last free phoenix? Ithendryl and Eliel were the last bonded Phaedryn. Erynor's dragon had eaten the others, killing the elf and preventing the phoenix's rebirth. The hope of their people now rested in the unhatched egg.

Moving to the window, Ithendryl frowned at the war barges surrounding Arenthyl. She missed the peaceful waters of Lake Saeryndol—of how they used to be. The Erynien Empire had defiled those waters and blood spilled into them in a near constant flow while elves drowned beneath the surface, the bodies left to decay rather than transition to

Lumaeniel. Her heart ached; outside, her people were dying defending Arenthyl against the Erynien Empire and there was nothing she could do to stop it. It was happening across all Krysenthiel, every city under siege.

Not for the first time, she regretted crafting Ceurendol. She and Faerndryn had thought the Jewel of Life would bring an end to war and death. How wrong they'd been. They had never anticipated the reaction of the Cyndinari elves. How could they see themselves as gods to the mortal races? What had led them to their destructive and twisted path?

Haunted by dismal thoughts, Ithendryl was sure she would never learn the answer. She sensed her time was ending, a kindness she had not expected from Anaweh. Had Faerndryn also known he was about to die? Or had his brutal death been as shocking for him as it was for her?

Holding her grief, she steeled herself when she felt a presence enter her study. "You should not be here," she said, turning slowly from the window to face the uninvited elf, noting the distinctive scar on his face.

"My father sent me. I'm sure you've learned that refusing him is in no one's best interest." The Cyndinari smiled as he spoke, the scar pulling his features into more of a grimace. Prince Erethien Meriden, Erynor's eldest son and heir strode across the office. Ithendryl could see in the way he carried himself that he had never been refused anything or anyone.

"How did you get into the palace?" Ithendryl tapped her connection with Eliel, prepared to bond.

"I must say, I've always found Luminari architecture to be quite subdued. The humans named you high queen and you did nothing to augment Arenthyl or Aerodhal to display your dominance over the lesser races."

"Our views of governance are quite different."

"Clearly. Pity most of the humans on this wretched continent have denounced you and now bow to my father as emperor."

"It's hard to fault them for changing their allegiance after you destroy their homes, drowning thousands of people in a single catastrophic wave."

"An example had to be made of Lankor. You give us little credit. We've helped the Yanileans rebuild their city."

"With dorthl so they may never touch the erendinth. That stone does not belong in Teraeniel."

"Well, they did anger my father and he isn't quick to let go of grudges. Besides, if they are wise, they will be stronger for it."

"Why are you here?" Ithendryl was done with this conversation. It would go nowhere.

"I'm here as a courtesy," Erethien drawled, bored, scratching at his scar. "This war will end today, and your people will become slaves. My father might have spared the Luminari this fate—elves should not be slaves—but you did make yourselves mortal and dependent on a jewel, so he is less bothered."

"You came here to tell me that?" Ithendryl raised an eyebrow. "You're no closer to pulling down Arenthyl's gates than when the war started."

"You will flee your cities, abandoning their protection." He said it so matter-of-factly, that Ithendryl had to believe him. "But no, that is not why I came to you. Your people *will* be slaves and there is no way for you to alter that course. However, my father does have compassion. The descendants of your now mortal elves might be offered their freedom again, *after* my father tires of them—after the Lorenthiens and Phaedryn are long forgotten. It would be a shame if Krysenthiel were to be destroyed and for the Luminari of tomorrow to not know your meadows of kryseniels or the shade of your kirenae trees or even the touch of lumaryl." Erethien lingered at a vase of kryseniels, tracing a petal. "My father has a heart. He does not desire your culture to be erased."

"What are you saying? Speak plainly."

"That you could preserve Krysenthiel. My father has no desire to destroy elven beauty." His lewd gaze suggested he merely recognized lust, not true beauty.

"Erynor's view of beauty is quite different from our own. If he valued beauty, he would not have started this war, causing so much death."

"You gave him no choice. Don't forget, he had wanted to work together."

Ithendryl glanced out the pointed arched window. Krysenthiel had been marred by war for centuries now. Its meadows had been trampled and muddied, but the kryseniels would regrow in time. Like the Luminari, the flowers would survive this war. "What do you propose?"

"You have a choice. You can let Krysenthiel die or you can preserve it in ice."

"You expect me to freeze the entire aryldom?"

"If you don't, Teraeniel will never know the aroma of a kryseniel or the golden blossoms of a kirenae tree in spring. You can either freeze them or let them wilt, never to return. The choice is yours and yours alone. This war will end today, and either way, you will not live to see tomorrow's dawn." With that, Erethien left Ithendryl's study.

She had no idea how he had managed to get into the city, let alone into her study in Aerodhal. Wards protected Arenthyl from those wishing to cause harm to any Luminari. Of course, Erethien hadn't come to harm Ithendryl or the Luminari. If his mind hadn't been free of such intention, he wouldn't be able to enter.

But what Ithendryl could not understand was why he thought the war would end today. Erynien legions might surround every Krysenthien city, but they could not break through the walls and wards. The Luminari had enough stores to ride out this war. Still, seeing Erethien inside Aerodhal was troubling. Had they found a way past the wards? Although, he had said nothing of the legions breaching the walls. Instead, he claimed the Luminari would flee their cities.

Troubled, Ithendryl left her study, Eliel following her in search of the First of the Guardians, a position that had seen more elves bear the title over the past century than there had been in the thousands of years since the order had formed. While Ithendryl did not think this war would end today, neither did she take Erethien's threat lightly. Contingencies had been in place since before Faerndryn's death and several had already been carried out. The principal one was the separation of the seven lucilliae that formed Ceurendol. Only three remained in Arenthyl.

She'd given the violet jewel to the Aldinari to protect. Erynor had vowed not to harm them if they stayed out of the war, which they had. There were so few Aldinari as it was. Not even Erynor wanted to see any Aldinari elves die. The yellow jewel was in the possession of the Druids of Kweil Aitch. They would take it into Somnaeniel the moment it looked like Arenthyl might fall and hide it away in Kweil Aitch.

The third and final jewel in Arenthyl, Ithendryl would protect with her dying breath. The red lucilliae was the heart of Ceurendol. It held the virtue most prized by the Luminari, the very attribute that had first drawn the phoenix to Kien and Kiara and inspired the Luminari to create Ceurendol in the first place.

Love.

But there was another contingency Ithendryl had to see to. She reached the First of the Guardians in Aerodhal's map room where Trealyn was rubbing his eyes. *When did he last sleep?* She conveyed to Eliel.

"Ei'terel." Trealyn bowed, respectfully as he caught sight of her.

"Cousin," Ithendryl replied fondly. Trealyn was one of the few Lorenthiens who had not been killed in the war. Ithendryl's youngest child was still alive, as were his children. He might be Erynor's prisoner, but he was alive. Her other children had all perished at Erynor's command. "I need your selection of the hundred Guardian knights to be sent away in secret, abandoning this war to protect the phoenix egg."

"Are you certain now is the right time? The city is surrounded, but the walls remain strong."

"I fear the window is closing."

"I'll have them report to you first thing tomorrow morning."

"They must leave with the egg at once." Ithendryl's heart ached at sending the egg away. Every Lorenthien aryl had safeguarded the egg since Kien and Kiara Lorenthien had entrusted it to their successors. Ithendryl, who had married into House Lorenthien, would be the first to send it away. She prayed it would be safe and survive the war if she would not. Faerndryn's mother had impressed upon her the importance of protecting the egg. Ithendryl had worried she would not be up to the task, but then Eliel, the phoenix who had laid the egg, had bonded with Ithendryl.

"What are you not telling me?" Trealyn asked.

"Prince Erethien came to my study unannounced. He told me the war would end today."

"That's preposterous. How could he enter Arenthyl, let alone the palace?"

"A mystery I wish I had the answer to."

"Ithendryl—Ei'terel—our cities cannot be breached. We've taken every precaution. Mosquitos can't pass over the walls if they so much as desire to bite a Luminari elf."

"Peace, Trealyn. I do not see a way Erynor could end this war today, but neither will I risk the egg falling into his hands."

"Understood." Trealyn left a lot unsaid, obvious in his furrowed brow. He pivoted toward a strong, formidable-looking woman who had approached while they spoke. "Ei'terel, might I introduce Jeanne Darkel."

"Ei'terel." Jeanne placed her right hand on her chest and bowed. Ithendryl offered the same gesture in response, shocking Jeanne because Ithendryl had just acknowledged Jeanne as her equal. Rarely did an aryl take the time to fully *see* another person. "You honor me."

"Your task will decide the fate of our people," Ithendryl said.

"Jeanne and her company of Guardian knights are aware of the assignment and will leave at once for our citadel in the Laudien Mountains, west of Septyl. Erynor has yet to discover it as we haven't led any operations from there," Trealyn said.

"When you reach the citadel, you must destroy its seguian portal,"

Ithendryl said.

"What if we're needed here?" Jeanne asked, alarmed.

"One hundred Guardian knights cannot alter this war's outcome. Your task is more important than what happens here. Our future rests inside the egg. An unsung light will sacrifice everything for our people," Ithendryl replied prophetically.

"Yes, Ei'terel. We will stay with the egg until it hatches. The egg will remain a secret." Jeanne bowed and left the map room to gather her companions.

Ithendryl scratched Eliel's chin. Eliel's connection with the egg was deeper than Ithendryl's. While Ithendryl worried about the fate of her people, Eliel worried about her child inside that egg. She had had the egg thousands of years ago when still bonded with Kiara, and the love Kien and Kiara shared between them had spilled over to their phoenix who had produced a rare phoenix egg. Ithendryl hoped there was still time. Erethien's threat weighed on her.

"Be prepared, Trealyn. I worry how this day will end." Ithendryl turned to leave.

"Would you like an escort?"

"Do not spare Guardian knights for my sake."

"There isn't an elf in this aryldom who would see you left unprotected, especially if Erynor's vile offspring has discovered a way into Aerodhal."

"Thank you, Trealyn. But I order your Guardians to remain at their posts," she said, overstepping her authority to directly command the First of the Guardians. Only the Guardian Senate could do that. But it had disbanded after so few senators had chosen to remain in Arenthyl.

She left the map room to go see the red lucilliae—to prepare herself for what was to come. The Life Immortal of the Luminari was held in that jewel and it was intended to be shared. She and Faerndryn had vowed that no harm would come to the lucilliae. They would protect it. As she walked through Aerodhal, she heard bells ringing and horns blaring outside. She hated the thought of hiding inside the palace as Luminari fought and died protecting Arenthyl.

Two elves stood guard at Ceurendol's chamber, stepping aside for Ithendryl to enter, leaving her alone with the jewel. Afraid of what was to come, she prayed.

Glimpses of potential futures came to her. She felt pain and suffering and sought a way to avoid it. She found none. Nothing she could do would stop or alter it.

"How were we so mistaken?" she asked.

A flash of light followed, and Uriel was with her in the chamber. "The fault is not yours to bear, Child of Luminare."

"But surely we could have avoided so much death. So many innocents gone too soon."

"Anaweh will welcome them into Lumaeniel. If this war hadn't happened and Ceurendol never wrought, Ramiel would have used other avenues to corrupt the hearts of the living."

"To escape the Void?" Ithendryl asked.

"Just so. Krysenthiel will ever draw his attention. He can only escape if Verakryl dies."

"And what's to happen if we lose this war? The Guardian Senate has disbanded; the senators have fled to their home nations, scattered across Teraeniel. How are we to stand united if Erynor rules Eklean and kills the Tree of Life?"

"Not even I can see that answer. Use your sight. There is more than pain and suffering in the Luminari's future."

Ithendryl sighed and closed her eyes. A storm of anguish came first. Centuries of slavery under a lash clouded her vision. She pushed past the pain and saw the violet jewel return to the Luminari, the smallest seed returned to grow. Freedom and joy followed, with a promise of more. A child of her own house would bond with the phoenix in Eliel's egg. The lucilliae would be reunited and the Luminari would remember what they had lost. But only after the Tree died. The price the child would pay once Ramiel returned to Teraeniel caused a tear to spill down her cheek.

"The cost is too high. How could we ask such of a child?"

Before Uriel could answer, swords clashed outside the chamber and the irythil vanished as Cyndinari forced their way in. Ithendryl was all that stood between them and the red lucilliae.

"Where are the others?" a Cyndinari asked, glancing at the jewel.

"Far away from here," Ithendryl said.

"It matters not. We only need the one." Erethien stepped close to Ithendryl and whispered in her ear, as though to prevent the others from hearing. "Have you made your choice?"

Ithendryl and Eliel bonded and their wings flung outward, pushing the Cyndinari away from the lucilliae. "You shall not have it," she said.

Erethien, still close to her, smirked. "You could have survived this war. My father so longed to have you as his consort. It was the last thing Faerndryn heard when he died."

Erynor might have said that, but those were not the last words her Faerndryn had heard. Her voice had filled his mind and heart in that moment. They had restated their vows to each other. Ithendryl wished she, too, could hear his voice one more time. The gift of the elves was ever to accept Anaweh's call to Lumaeniel, a gift which had been stolen from so many Luminari. And now, Ithendryl feared death herself. She felt icy metal slide into her chest. She had not seen Erethien draw the knife, but she felt it and weakened, her life fading.

"You have a choice to make." Erethien left the knife in Ithendryl and walked to the lucilliae. The Cyndinari formed a ring around it as Ithendryl watched, helpless. They chanted in a language older than High Aelish; a tongue once used by Ramiel, rumored to now be spoken exclusively by the dwarves in the Shadow Mountains.

Ithendryl watched the world twist in on itself around the lucilliae; its vibrant ruby hue warped as tenebrys spilled out from the Cyndinari. A woman's laughter reached Ithendryl—a voice she recognized. Erynel

Meriden.

"Hello, Grandmother," Erethien said as the supposedly dead Sha'ghol stepped out of the shadows, followed by other twisted spirits. The Cyndinari surrounding the stone screamed as fallen anadel leeched onto them—changing them.

"Ah, sweet Ithendryl." Erynel disregarded Erethien as he fought to maintain his autonomy from the Deurghol. "My Shroud will claim your aryldom entirely and nothing shall remain. Your fruit will spoil and your flowers will wilt under my Shroud. And any anacordel foolish enough to enter *my* domain will die as they breathe my death."

The Shroud spilled out of the red lucilliae. With a burst of unexpected strength, the icy knife still between her ribs, Ithendryl wielded lumenys. The wield was too powerful for the impaired Cyndinari; she flung them out of the chamber and sealed the doors behind them. Those doors would not open until Ceurendol could be restored.

Ithendryl felt the poisonous mist that was the Shroud, somehow part of Erynel. Having no idea how to combat it, she reached outward. Already, her people were fleeing Arenthyl, running from the ever-expanding Shroud, their only haven the war barges. Erynor would capture and enslave the entire Luminari population. "Forgive me," Ithendryl whispered to the empty chamber, then tapped into the entirety of Krysenthiel; she would preserve it. She felt the ice form over every tree and flower and blade of grass. She felt the water of Lake Saeryndol slow as it too froze. Too late, she sensed another freeze in the water.

Locked away in the lucilliae's chamber and bonded with Eliel, a chill consumed her.

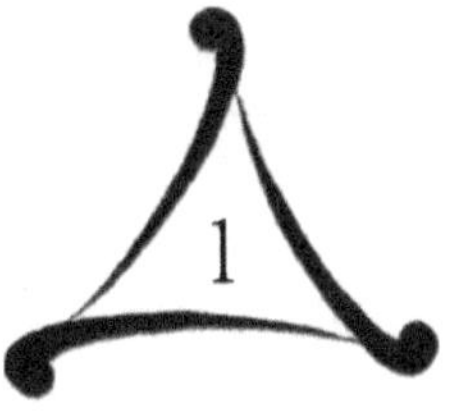

Prophecy

Devlyn blinked, waiting for his eyes to adjust to the dark and for the ghosts in Binton's throne room to vanish. Ellendren tugged his wrist, pulling him out of his shock and back to his senses. He'd felt the world shatter when the lance pierced the Tree of Life's roots far below Lake Saeryndol, killing the Tree. It should not be possible. The Tree could not be dead.

He could still feel the verathn first wrought by Kyrendal from one of the tree's sprouts and later corrupted with tenebrys. His mind stung, as though someone was screaming at a glass-shattering pitch.

The pain lanced through him. Devlyn barely recognized Ellendren as others poured into the throne room to find Cairn dead; the chief-king's specter lingered above his corpse. It was not the only specter, and an eerie silence hung in the room, impossible to ignore.

"Devlyn!" Ellendren screamed, trying to reach him through his haze. He was still bonded with Aliel, but their sight was greatly diminished. Neither could he see the spiritual light every living being gave off. Their inner lights were doused—diminished and drowned by the Void.

The Light was gone and the Tree was dead.

Ellendren screamed again, this time finally reaching him. He blinked, then looked away from Cairn's ghost. Despite the darkness holding the space hostage, he could see Ellendren and the others. Dozens of Dwonian deserters filled the throne room, surrendering their spears.

Viren, Alex, Rusyl, Tye, and Falthion were behind Ellendren, and Jaerol and Liam stood beside him.

"Devlyn, we have to go," Ellendren said frantically.

He nodded, saw Viren's expression and knew there would be no argument. They were not safe here. The Tree was dead and the dead roamed Teraeniel. But they could not simply retreat. Alex and the Thellish forces were still here, as were the Mindalean forces who had pledged themselves to Thellion and the Dwonians who had crossed Dwota's Gap to end Cairn's reign. He could not leave them to fight this nightmare alone. Could the Void be fought?

"What will you do?" Devlyn asked Alex.

"Return to Elothkar once the Ashtons sit on Mindale's throne. They're more than capable of restoring the peace here, but I fear peace is the least of our concerns now," Alex said, avoiding the specters.

"Right." Devlyn looked at Viren. "Is there anyone else that needs to go to Arenthyl?"

"Velaria and Yelaris will likely return to Septyl," Viren said, and as though summoned, they hurried into the throne room. Velaria looked just as frantic as Devlyn felt.

"We're here, and we should leave at once." Velaria strode forward but stopped beside Alex. "Be strong, Alexander. Much depends on a unified Thellion. Eklean will ever be at her weakest when human kingdoms war with each other. Hate must not triumph."

"Surely, you don't expect me to conquer the continent. Myranda will remove my head if I even suggest Sorenthil joining Thellion."

"It is not for me to say how human kingdoms unite," Velaria said. She touched Alex's arm in farewell. "You could not have chosen a better bride. Treat Diana well."

"I will. I promise."

"Are we ready then?" Velaria asked.

"I shudder to imagine the state of Arenthyl," Ellendren said.

"Then we should have already left," Velaria said.

"Liam, Rusyl, and I will stay. Someone has to watch the Dark Flight," Jaerol said.

"From a distance," Velaria added; it was not a suggestion.

"Of course," Jaerol tipped his head, acknowledging her order as Chair of Azurelle.

The small group returning to Arenthyl formed a circle, holding hands. In the blink of an eye, Mindale's throne room faded, replaced by Aerodhal's throne room in Arenthyl. A great crystalline dome rose above, but no light poured through. The Crystal Throne, wrought of lumaryl and known to have its own inner light, had dimmed. The lumaryl walls of Aerodhal still held light, but they too had dulled as the throne had, as though an oil had spilled over everything.

A startled elf noticed the arrivals and ducked out of the throne room.

"We need to call a chamber meeting with the aryls at once," Ellendren said, taking command of the situation. They had to do something—anything. "The presence of the Seven Chairs would be invaluable."

"I'll alert the other Chairs, but I think it would be prudent to ensure that Arenthyl's protections are secured first," Velaria said.

"Do you fear an attack?" Devlyn asked.

"Dozens of dragons of the Dark Flight are just outside Krysenthiel's border. They are waiting for something," Ellendren said.

"Waiting for something?" Devlyn repeated. "We need to send word to the aryls of Verenthyl and the Delmira Wood. Jeanne has the bulk of the Guardian knights in Verenthyl on reserve. They need to be notified that the Dark Flight could be planning an imminent attack."

"They're likely already expecting it," Viren said.

"How do you mean?" Ellendren asked.

"Erynor's tactics are not new to the Guardian knights." Viren shifted his weight and Devlyn gleaned an uncomfortable memory, too foggy to decipher.

"What will he do?" Devlyn asked.

"He will not be idle. It's clear that he only distracted us and pulled us away from Arenthyl to kill Verakryl. I can't imagine what lengths he took on Ramiel's behalf to kill the Tree of Life." Viren sighed, exhausted and worried. "Cairn and Mindale were a diversion. He knew the lucil-liae would keep us abroad. But I also wonder if Ramiel played a part in Aldinare falling from the sky."

"You think the Evil One permitted Aldinare to escape the Darkness that had consumed it?" Velaria let the question linger.

"What would it have mattered? The Void is all around us. Aldinare was given a brief respite, but the Void now covers all Teraeniel," Devlyn said.

"Do we know for certain that it covers the entire world? Has it even covered the entire continent?" Ellendren asked, pacing. "The Void was supposed to be a small realm of non-existence, tucked away. Surely it couldn't consume everything the moment it was freed."

"It does seem weaker, stretched thin to cover more territory. Think of the stories of when the Darkness stole the Skylands from us. We haven't seen any tenebrys lightning yet," Velaria said.

"And traces of Light remain, if muddled," Ellendren said.

"Do you think the Void is concentrated in a specific location and its effects are oozing out from that one place?" Devlyn asked.

"That's my assumption. Life on Teraeniel will die if consumed by the Void. But I also fear its influence will expand. Wherever Ramiel has chosen to exert his presence in our world, that presence could strengthen and spread like a disease," Velaria said.

"The Shadow Mountains then," Devlyn said.

"Very likely. But none of us should journey there to confirm it. The risk is too high and we know too little." Velaria held her chin in concentration.

"Is there a way to contain it?" Devlyn asked, desperately seeking a solution.

"The Shroud had clung to Krysenthiel and only Ceurenyl was free of its disease. The Light within the temple had kept it at bay, denying it entrance into the city. But I do not know how we could replicate it. It's possible that only the ei'ceuril have that ability, given their connection and devotion to Anaweh," Velaria said.

"But Verakryl is—" Ellendren bit back her words. "Verakryl was Anaweh's physical manifestation on Teraeniel. Weak or not, the Void has also consumed Somnaeniel, so the path to Lumaeniel is blocked."

"There are too many unknowns, and the enemy is on our door-step," Velaria said, her small smile gone.

"We are not just dealing with the Erynien Empire now though," Viren reminded.

"The Void beasts." Devlyn shared a worried look with Ellendren.

"Krysenthiel never had to defend itself against their likes before. Only the draelyn know what it is to suffer their assault," Viren said.

"They won't be alone. The rest of the Deurghol will be freed as well and I doubt they'll require a body to sustain them in Teraeniel now," Devlyn said, terrified by what the corrupted anadel who had pledged themselves to Ramiel and abandoned Anaweh's designs were capable of.

Overwhelmed, Devlyn tried to prioritize what had to be done first. He had yet to see the full potential of the Dark Flight. For all he knew, they could easily level Verenthyl and burn the Delmira Wood. He began to visualize the city to shift there and warn the Guardian knights.

No. The Dark Flight had been around the last time Erynor had raged his war. While the Luminari elves had never been able to defeat those dragons, neither were the dragons capable of leveling Krysen-thiel's cities. Devlyn hated to consider it, but Verenthyl and the Delmira Wood would have to manage without him. The Delmira Wood was still frozen, and its trees still slept beneath the ice. Devlyn hoped their current state would protect them.

He thought back to what Velaria had said about Arenthyl's defens-es. Before they could do anything, they had to ensure that the defenses would hold. He worried that the wards were tied to the Tree of Life and if so, they were gone. "Viren, is there a way to know if the wards still stand?"

"I am no wielder. Arenthyl's wards are old and beyond my expertise."

"Would the Aldinari know?" Ellendren asked.

"I doubt anyone alive is more familiar than they are," Velaria said.

As they made to leave the throne room, Jeanne strode in, accompanied by Toryn and Byron, her squires who would one day become Guardian knights. "Thank the Light you've returned," Jeanne said.

"We need to know if our defenses still stand. Are the Aldinari familiar with the ancient wields?" Devlyn asked, relieved to see Jeanne. There wasn't any time for pleasantries.

Jeanne turned to Toryn. "Go to the Aldinari at once; we need one of their ei'ana familiar with Arenthyl's defenses." Toryn left without question, Shroudsbane sheathed at her hip.

That left their group to pause. Devlyn wanted to go to the Aldinari himself. If he was moving, he was doing something. Now, all he could do was wait. Not a moment ago, he had felt overwhelmed with everything that had to be done. Ellendren took his hand, feeling overwhelmed as well and both withdrew from their phoenix.

Where the throne room had been dark before, the darkness now felt heavier. He had no idea whether Arenthyl's wards could keep the Void at bay. The Void had severed them from the Light, but could its poisonous disease seep through? Would the Void change the Luminari like it had changed the Aldinari? Would those without any protection from the Void's effects become deranged? How much time did they have? And the Luminari weren't the only ones in danger. The majority of Eklean's population were humans and their cities had no such protection. What would happen to them? There had to be a way to contain it.

Devlyn knew he couldn't march an army to the Shadow Mountains without a plan. He didn't even know if containing the Void was possible. This wasn't only his problem. All Teraeniel had to come together to devise a solution.

Toryn returned, accompanied by an exhausted Arlyn and an Aldinari.

"What's happened?" Devlyn asked, not expecting his uncle.

"The Light has vanished from the cathedral. It could have been too freshly restored to survive Verakryl being killed, but I fear the Light might have vanished from the Temple of Ceur as well." Arlyn looked at his fingers, crestfallen.

"How is that possible? Was it dependent on the Tree?" Devlyn asked.

"I cannot say. I'd have to go to Ceurenyl to know, but I am needed here," Arlyn said.

"We'll need all the help we can get." Devlyn turned to the Aldinari. She looked familiar but he hadn't spoken with her before.

"I am Naer." She bowed formally. She had not been stripped of her Life Immortal, and Devlyn found determining her age impossible. She appeared to be in her prime, but that could easily range from four hundred to several thousand years.

"Do you know how the wards work and do they derive from the tree?" Devlyn asked.

Naer stepped forward and pointed to Devlyn's verathn. "Your verathn grew from a seed of a verathel, yes? Can you still use it?"

Devlyn didn't know. He hadn't tapped his verathn's power since the Tree had died. He tried now, pressing into aerys, and pulled more strength from his scepter. It supplemented his wielding just as it had done before. His verathn had not weakened. "Yes, I can. Are the wards similar to verathn?"

"Yes and no. Like verathn, they were wrought and strengthened by the Light. But they are not the Light. Just as we were created with that spark of Life, we still exist despite the Tree's death. Krysenthiel's wards were wrought from Verakryl and lumaryl, but they are rooted in the lumaryl. I do not know if they will hold against the beasts freed from the Void, but they should not be altered with the passing of the Tree. Do know that without access to the Light, we will not be able to replicate them. We will not be able to extend this protection to other cities," Naer said.

"Can we do nothing for them?" Devlyn asked, anxious.

"*Two sons of Light I shall birth. Alone one shall rule. When the Age of Shadow returns and the Darkness engulfs the Light, the last bird of Light shall hatch as a new sun rises. The lesser brother shall give his life and the glory of the Light shall shine from Arenthyl to reach every crevice darkened by Shadow,*" Velaria recited Lucillia's prophecy.

Devlyn had not thought of that prophecy for a long time. He didn't want to confront what it meant—what it demanded of him. Did Lucillia mean for him to die to save the world? Was his life all that could stop Ramiel? A tear slipped from his eye, mirrored by Ellendren, and that sense of overwhelming dread returned.

He couldn't simply sacrifice himself. What good would that do? He'd be dead and Ramiel would still be here. His heart quickened and he felt everyone looking at him. What did they expect of him? Velaria had told him the prophecy years ago. Everyone had thought he would have to become an ei'ceuril to give all of himself to save the world. The alternate interpretation ended with him dying. He felt their expectations fall heavily on his shoulders. The darkness crept further into him, rooting in his chest.

"Devlyn," Ellendren said, barely a whisper.

"I need to be alone, I'm sorry." He turned to leave. There was nothing he could do right now.

Ellendren watched him walk away, Aliel hovering above him. Her heart ached. She knew the prophecy just as well as anyone. She had never imagined she would live in the days Lucillia had foretold. Nor had she anticipated falling in love with the elf named in the prophecy. She could not lose him.

Instinctively, she touched her belly.

"You have kept a secret from me," Jeanne said, now focused on Ellendren.

"It was only a hunch when we left, too early to name. I confirmed it while we were away."

"It is good that you are bringing about an heir," Jeanne said.

"Surely you don't think Devlyn has to…" Ellendren couldn't finish. She wouldn't let herself say the word, afraid she would see no other way to defeat Ramiel.

"Ithendryl had the power of sight, and she knew a sacrifice would have to be made. She sent me and the other Guardian knights away to ensure the phoenix egg was protected until it hatched. Ithendryl did not share what she saw, but many in Aerodhal at the time overheard her fretting about the sacrifice that had to be made. No one here wants Devlyn to die, least of all at Ramiel's bidding. But he is a Lorenthien, and with you, the Exalted Aryl. We will stand by your choices and support you both. But we also trust you will not doom the world to suffer under Ramiel."

SOLACE

Outside the throne room, Devlyn took a deep, steadying breath. He held it for a moment, feeling a dash of anxiety crawl through his skin as his heart fluttered. Eyes closed, he placed his hand against the too-dull lumaryl wall to support himself. He felt as though he would collapse at any moment.

He had no idea what he was supposed to do or what was expected of him. Well, he did know the latter. The world expected him to give his life to save Teraeniel. The path to Lumaeniel was blocked and the dead would linger here as ghosts in a Void-laced Teraeniel. There would be no peace for the dead, no Light, only an endless wandering, ever lost.

Devlyn could still see the expression on Cairn's face as he had died and had realized that he had been wrong—that he and his forebears had been deceived. The first and only chief-king had glimpsed what awaited him in death when the dagger had pierced him. And it was nothing. So long as the Void claimed Teraeniel, the newly deceased would wander.

Teraeniel was not a place for the dead. They neither belonged here nor did they belong in the Void. Ramiel's deceptions had rooted in the minds of many, and they believed there was no path in death beyond the Void. As they died, they allowed Ramiel's deception to burden their spirits, weighing them down to the Void as thralls.

Devlyn *had* to do something. But according to the prophecy, all he could do was die.

He took another deep breath. He couldn't let anyone see him like this. Fortunately, news of his and Ellendren's return had not spread far yet so the corridor outside Aerodhal's throne room was blessedly empty. That would not last long. He had to get away from the public's eye; he needed to go somewhere safe, somewhere he could let himself collapse without scrutiny.

He bonded with Aliel in a flash, a now-rare illumination within the Void. The world was still dark, but some color did return to his sight. He went to a nearby room where there was a balcony and leapt off the ledge. Arenthyl spread out below as his wings carried him over the city. Darkened spires and domes reached upward and the city appeared as though it suffered an incurable disease and was dying. Would it die with the Tree of Life? Would all life cease to exist now that Verakryl had been slaughtered? Could Ellendren give birth to new life without the Tree?

Angling upward, he flew behind the palace and up the southern slope of Mount Verinien to the cavern that contained the now-dead Tree of Life. He landed on a shallow outcropping before the cave mouth. Still bonded with Aliel, he wielded a globe of light to further illumine the dark cave, but it did little to help. The darkness felt more oppressive the deeper he went, as though it swallowed the unwelcome light.

Hours passed before the cavern expanded to the voluminous space that had once glittered in the light of Verakryl; once, the Tree had overpowered the little light that Devlyn had brought.

"You know," said a small voice, "Verakryl was not always part of Teraeniel. Only when Ramiel had betrayed Anaweh and was banished to his Void did the Tree grow, its roots separating the Void from Teraeniel."

"Verinien?" Only one person resided in the mountain named after him.

"Before the Great Blessing and before the days of Verakryl, Anaweh walked among us, just as you and I do and as anadel are known to. Anaweh imbued the Tree with Life at its creation, and the Tree became as much Anaweh as the Creating Light in Lumaeniel and the Breath in Somnaeniel."

"But the Tree was killed." Devlyn looked back at the dried-out husk. It had been a vibrant, living, crystalline tree only a day ago.

"The Tree's death had been foretold, or have you forgotten?" Verinien cocked an eyebrow. "When all the other Children chose to age, and only my sister and I remained as we were, Anaweh blessed us. We were told two great mountains would rise for us to reside in. Anaweh would also reside inside each mountain, not as we had known the Creating Light, but in a different form. Saecrien and I were asked to be caretakers, a task which we have been honored to have. But we were also told that a day would come when the Tree would die and the world would fall into Darkness. Our mountains would be torn down, their contents rejoined for Life and Light to return."

"Saecrien mentioned something about her Waters returning Life to the Tree." Devlyn recalled the crystal-clear waters hidden in Mount Saecrien.

"Just so, but the mountains still stand."

"Would Saecrien know how to bring the Tree back to life?"

"She was told as much as I. It's possible for her to have figured out how to do so, in the very long time we have been separated."

"What about the anadel? Surely the irythil, Sariel, Lord of the Land, could bring down mountains." Devlyn's mind whirled as he tried to envision a solution for reviving the Tree.

"And who are you to command Sariel to do anything? Even the dwarves do not demand such of Mundi."

"Wouldn't Sariel want to help revive Verakryl?" Devlyn asked, now doubting himself. Ramiel was also one of the seven irythil who had brought about the creation of Teraeniel and he had betrayed Anaweh's designs to become a lord of chaos and death. Had the other irythil had a change in confidence? The only irythil that Devlyn had met was Uriel, who was said to be most like Anaweh.

Devlyn left Verinien with more questions and doubt than when he had arrived. He hadn't expected to find any answers in the cavern with the dead Tree, but neither had he anticipated the situation becoming more complicated.

He flew back to Aerodhal and sought out Ellendren. If anyone could unravel the puzzles in his mind, it was her. Through their bond, he sensed her practicing jienzu on a terrace off their private quarters. Wasting no time, he didn't bother going through Aerodhal's entry hall and the entire palace, but rather flew directly to the terrace that bowed out from the spire they lived in.

Ellendren's back arched, one leg rooted to the floor, while the other followed the curve of her body and pointed upward. She took a deep breath before releasing the form, then turned to face him. His anxiety and burdens melted away as he hugged her. Simply being with her seemed to resolve everything, even if nothing actually was.

"How's Verinien?" she asked, knowing where he had gone.

"Troubled, and even more so, troubling." Devlyn withdrew from Aliel, and the grey haze of the Void thickened. "There might be a way to revive the Tree."

"Truly? How?" She dabbed the sweat from her brow.

"Remember the Child I met in the Illumined Wood?"

"Saecrien?"

"She watches over some sort of sacred water that might be able to revive the Tree. Verinien says the Tree's death was foretold in the Elder Days."

"Who could have made such a prophecy?"

"Anaweh."

Ellendren blinked, digesting the revelation. They had both heard the legends of the Creating Light walking among the Children on a young Teraeniel, but neither had considered Anaweh speaking with them. "How can we transport this water?"

"Verinien said that both mountains would have to be brought low."

"Mount Verinien is Teraeniel's largest mountain; it can't simply be torn down," Ellendren said aghast.

"And Mount Saecrien isn't much smaller. Elle, how would we go about destroying mountains? Are we even capable of that?"

"I don't know. Perhaps the Sophillium might hold a solution."

"I could make a quick trip to Septyl and ask Kevn." Devlyn leaned against the balustrade.

Ellendren nodded in response. "If you go to Septyl, I should go to Ceurenyl."

"Why Ceurenyl?"

"We need to find out the extent of the Void's damage with the Tree now dead. Our assumption is that Anaweh's presence has been completely eradicated from Teraeniel. I fear that not even the Chamber of Light was spared."

"Couldn't we send someone else, Elle?"

"We could also send someone else to Septyl." Ellendren smiled as she wrapped her arms around him.

"Fair," he laughed, pulling her in tightly. For an all too brief moment, he forgot they were the Exalted Aryl of Krysenthiel and all those other titles. The responsibilities and tragic events they had to deal with slipped away, leaving them simply Devlyn and Ellendren who loved each other.

Ellendren rubbed his back, her fingers making his skin tingle.

The relief didn't last. The floodgates in his mind opened, his anxiety returning in a storm surge. Their shared love couldn't banish Ramiel or the Void or revive the Tree of Life. He held onto Ellendren tighter, as though she was a raft and only she could keep him afloat. "I'm scared, Elle." He broke down as she continued to rub his back. The weight of Lucillia's prophecy returned. He buried his face in the crook where her neck and shoulder met.

"Me too."

"Elle, the prophecy, the one about me…" He couldn't finish.

"I will not lose you. Do you hear me, Devlyn Lorenthien? I will not raise our children without you."

"Children?" His eyes widened.

"Twins. I felt them when the Tree was killed. Two echoes inside me."

"Elle, what are we going to do?" He was torn between his elation that they were going to be parents of twins, and the current state of the world their babies would be born into. He lifted his head and looked into her golden eyes.

"This isn't the first time we've confronted a challenge, nor will it be our last. I won't pretend to understand Lucillia's prophecy about you giving your life to return Life and Light to the rest of the world, but I refuse to believe that it requires your death," Ellendren said with more conviction than Devlyn had ever heard from her. "For now, we focus on what we can control. You'll go to Septyl and I'll go to Ceurenyl. We'll find out what we can and how to keep our people safe. This problem is not ours alone to solve. Representatives from every continent have been flocking to Arenthyl, even before the Light went out."

"When do you think we'll be able to open the Guardian Senate?"

"I imagine shortly after Alexander and Diana's wedding. The Ja'mare seafarers who took our messages to the various nations across the world had agreed to wait in dock until the representatives were ready to travel to Arenthyl. They have the fastest ships in Teraeniel, and with any luck, enough representatives will be here by the time we've returned."

Devlyn nodded, forcing himself to be positive just as Ellendren's attendant, Pevrel, came onto the balcony. She curtsied to them both before saying, "Ei'terel, Ei'denai, the aryls have gathered and request your presence in chamber."

"What could they want?" Devlyn asked, more to Ellendren than to Pevrel.

"I cannot say," Pevrel said, assuming Devlyn's question was for her.

"Right," Devlyn said as Ellendren splashed water onto her face.

"Pevrel, do I have time to bathe and change into something more suitable for the aryls?"

"They're already in chamber, Ei'terel. They did not insist you rush, but several did seem impatient," Pevrel said, apologetic on behalf of the aryls. She slipped a shawl over Ellendren's shoulders.

"Very well; shall we?" Ellendren said, holding her arm out for Devlyn as her escort.

"We wouldn't want to keep the aryls waiting. No doubt they expect details and answers about what has happened," Devlyn said, leaving the balcony with Ellendren, arm in arm.

They moved through the feigned privacy of their residence in the palace, passing a multitude of elves who saw to their every need. They had made it a rule that nothing official was to occur in their residence. The rest of the palace was large enough for them to carry out their responsibilities as the Exalted Aryl of Krysenthiel. The residence felt as though it was a palace in its own right, but it was only a single spire. Viren waited in the entry hall to their private residence, a hall majestic enough to be the entry to the grandest of castles, and not just a portion of Aerodhal.

A shadow of relief crossed his features, quickly replaced with irritation. "I wish you wouldn't fly off without a guard, more so now than ever before."

"I'm sorry. I needed a moment alone," Devlyn said.

"A moment alone could be your last."

Viren was right. Devlyn could not afford foolhardy exploits that would put him in harm's way. If he wasn't careful, a Deurghol, Sha'ghol, shadow elf, dragon, or any number of Void beasts could kill him or kidnap and deliver him to Erynor or Ramiel. "I won't do it again, I promise."

"Mhmm." Viren stepped aside, clearing their path. Four guards in starched tabards bearing Krysenthiel's sigil of seven golden kryseniels blossoming around a larger kryseniel in the center stood at attention outside the residence, their swords sheathed.

Many more elves and dignitaries went about their business as Devlyn and Ellendren passed into the public sphere of Aerodhal. Both Jeanne and Viren had reservations about how public the palace was—anyone could walk in. In their opinion, it mattered little that the Exalted Aryl were Phaedryn. A cloaked dagger or arrow would still kill them.

Torches never before needed now lined the corridors, a reminder of recent events. Krysenthien cities weren't supposed to require torches and braziers, for lumaryl walls glowed in the lights from the day and through the night. But the Void had doused the sun, moon, and stars. How were they to defeat someone capable of killing the Tree of Life and banishing the Light?

More guards waited outside the aryl's chamber; it seemed that all the high aryls had brought their own protection to Arenthyl. When the doors parted to let them in, the commotion from within poured out. The aryls were already thick in debate and only noticed the new arrivals when Devlyn and Ellendren were halfway to their seats.

Naesiv coughed to clear his throat. "Ei'denai, Ei'terel," he said ceremonially.

"We do not have time for ritual," Silvia interrupted.

Devlyn held his breath, dreading the all but guaranteed berating that was to follow in how he and Ellendren had allowed the Tree to be killed. Devlyn didn't know how he was supposed to defend their actions to not only the Luminari aryls, but also to the Eldinari and Aldinari aryls that were present. Would a smaller chamber be easier to navigate? "Forgive us, we should have been here, we should have been aware that an Erynien legion had been tunnelling beneath Lake Saeryndol, in search of Verakryl's roots. If we had known, we would have never left Krysenthiel and gone to Aldinare and Nynev, and then to Binton to relieve the city of Dwonian deserters and retrieve a lucilliae." Devlyn feared he was rambling.

"Don't be ridiculous," Enoria said, cutting him off, just as impatient as Silvia had been with Naesiv. "Every aryl here stood by that decision. You did retrieve the orange jewel, yes?"

"We did. It's in its shrine now," Devlyn replied, confused. "And we met Aldarch Gael and overthrew the chief-king. House Ashton now sits on Mindale's throne and has joined Thellion."

"That's all fine and well, but that is not why we are here. None of us are thrilled that the Tree was killed and neither do we fully understand the repercussions. The lack of light is more of an inconvenience, promising trouble if Ramiel has truly been freed and the Void released across Teraeniel," Binoral said.

"If not for Ramiel and the Void, why have you called us to chamber?" Devlyn asked, curious about Ellendren's silence.

"Because we have just learned that Ellendren is with child, and is possibly carrying House Lorenthien's heir," Fyona replied.

"And worse, she took part in a battle while pregnant," Silvia said severely.

"It is still early," Ellendren said, Devlyn sensing her irritation at being referred to as though she were not present. Impressively, she concealed it and maintained her dignified mien. "I was far from the frontlines; guards and ei'ana surrounded me at all times. I could not have been safer."

"That's all fine and well, but these are dark days that have only darkened. We would like a Crimsyn ei'ana to stay by your side and monitor your health to ensure a smooth pregnancy, Ei'terel," Ciraenth said.

"I am grateful for your concern, all of you." Ellendren offered a warm smile to the aryls. "But my chambers will be crowded enough with others fulfilling the same role. It is our custom to have trusted friends at our side during pregnancies."

This was news to Devlyn. When had Ellendren had time to reach out to anyone?

"And who are these trusted friends?" Binoral asked.

"Abbie Wintyr has been a dear and invaluable ally."

"The druid?" Zara asked.

"Yes. Fyona Orendi and Danielle Aerquin will also stay with me throughout my term."

"Oh," Sylvia commented. Devlyn saw Ellendren's smile. She knew Sylvia would support her if it brought Danielle and her son, who was guaranteed to follow, to Arenthyl.

"Our granddaughter would be a welcome guest in the palace," Valerie said, beaming.

"Queen Myranda and the three of us were inseparable at Gwilnor. Trethien also, of course," Ellendren said.

"Our son is unlikely to stay at Gwilnor if Danielle leaves," Toral said, giving Sylvia a sideways glance.

"When will your chosen companions join you?" Sylvia asked, ignoring Toral's point.

"Abbie is already here in Arenthyl. As for Fyona and Danielle, I intend to visit Ceurenyl to find out what has happened at the Temple of Light. I'll arrange for them to meet me there," Ellendren said cheerily.

"Surely, someone else can make that trip," Therrin said.

"It would be a comfort to see my brother. I'm sure you can understand," Ellendren said.

"Given the vulnerability of your house and your tendency to place yourselves in mortal danger," Ciraenth glanced at the other aryls nodding in support, "the aryls would feel more at ease if one of you stayed in Arenthyl when the other found a need to leave, the Thellish wedding being the exception, of course."

Devlyn debated challenging Ciraenth's preposterous proposal. They were Phaedryn. Were they expected to remain locked away in a palace? Surely, the aryls understood that they were needed in this fight. Before he could object, Ellendren said, "Agreed."

Devlyn struggled to keep his jaw from gaping. Ellendren squeezed his hand, sharing her thoughts. To his shock, she was of the same opinion. *Besides, they have already agreed on it. We would have been outvoted*, Ellendren shared. She stood, clearly thinking the session had ended.

"One other thing," Silvia said, as though to remind Naesiv of something he had forgotten. Devlyn grimaced at yet another demand. "The Thellish wedding is of great concern to us, the travel arrangements in particular."

"Surely you are not recommending we skip it," Ellendren said, her tone crisp.

"As preferable as that might be considering how vulnerable the journey will make us, no." Naesiv exhaled deeply. "But the arrangements decided before the Tree was killed now seem imprudent."

"I would argue they are more critical now. Eklean needs to see us. We can't hide away in a castle, while the rest of the continent is ravaged by Ramiel and his agents," Ellendren said.

"Surely you must understand the danger you're putting yourselves in. If either of you were to die, let alone both of you, the end of House Lorenthien would doom us to a new age of Darkness with Ramiel as our lord," Naesiv said.

"What would you recommend?" Devlyn asked. As much as he disliked what the aryls were insinuating, he didn't have the stomach to recklessly condemn them.

"Jeanne will organize a guard, Guardian knights and their bonded dragons included, for the journey north but let us not waste any time returning south. Travelling all that distance once is more than enough for people to see you along the road."

"Very well."

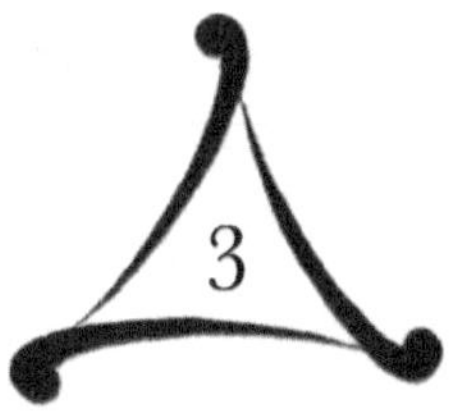

DIPLOMATS

Devlyn glared at one of the many missives on his desk, its wax seal unbroken. He tapped the polished wood surface, likely sung from the Delmira Wood and the sleeping kirenae trees there.

Nestled beside the rolled parchment was an orderly stack, every wax seal broken and the contents absorbed. Feline eyes stared from the seal of the offending parchment as he picked it away. Lucid ink flowed across the parchment when he unfurled it.

Another invitation.

Devlyn was exhausted. He had only just returned to Arenthyl, the city full of emissaries demanding to know why the sun had gone out and the dead walked. He wanted to believe they all had come in good faith but naiveté was a luxury he couldn't afford. He considered sequestering those whose loyalties were to the Erynien Empire, ideally in a cell. But no, every emissary that would join the Guardian Senate was given proper accommodation in a sixth-tier palace.

The most surprising arrival was Aorinol, a Daer senator. Aorinol was not old enough for the shock of platinum hair that contrasted with his ebony skin. Like every other Daer Devyn had met, Aorinol had elongated limbs, making him two heads taller than most elves. The hair and stretched limbs were due to the Daer Sorcery dabbling in experimental magic in a past millennia.

Aorinol's invitation and the broken panther seal hung between

Devlyn's fingers.

"You can't ignore him forever." Ellendren strolled into his study as though it were her own, Abbie trailing her.

"Would you like to go in my stead? After all, we're the aryl." Devlyn offered the scroll.

"*I* wasn't invited," Ellendren said. "Besides, I'll be leaving for Ceurenyl shortly."

"What do we know about this Aorinol?"

"Only that he's a Daer senator. According to his ship's travel log, he came directly from Daereneth."

"How is that helpful?" He raised a skeptical eyebrow, invitation still in hand.

"Aorinol has had no interaction with the Daer colonies already here in Eklean."

"You don't think he's innocent of their crimes, do you? The reports of forced slavery in their colonies are impossible to overlook."

"It tells me that the Daer Empire is more complex than we'd originally thought."

Abbie scoffed. "Complex? What's so complex about an empire bent on enslaving anyone they encounter, anadel included?"

Devlyn smirked at the assessment. "You think they still practice their Sorcery?"

"I don't think; I know. The druids in Ja'horan say they never stopped, not even when outlawed. Their Chronicle Stones hold the truth of the Daer's wicked ways." Abbie's low opinion reaffirmed Devlyn's own position on the Daer. Could they really trust an empire that caged anadel for its own benefit?

Ellendren cleared her throat. While he knew the Daer troubled her, she would undoubtedly be looking at the situation differently. Ellendren would never cast off a people or civilization, regardless of their crimes. She was already considering how they might ease the Cyndinari elves out of the Erynien Empire when it fell. The empire might be evil, but that didn't mean its citizens were. "I'm of the opinion Daer senators act independently of each other; it's not like they have an emperor or king to rein them in."

"And how does that benefit us?" Abbie asked, arms crossed.

"If we find favor with one, we could find favor with more. We cannot fight the Daer and those aligned to Ramiel at the same time," Ellendren said.

"You expect to make an ally of the Daer Empire?" Devlyn asked, aghast.

"I expect *us* to bring all creation together to defeat our common enemy." Ellendren turned to leave, glancing back over her shoulder. "He's expecting to see you within the hour."

"I never said he asked to see me at the eighth hour."

"I'll see you when I return." She smiled and left the study, her lierathnil gown adorned with embroidered citrines cascading down her back.

Devlyn left his desk and walked to the balcony. He had thought he was getting better at calming his mind, but exhaustion and weighty burdens plagued him. Expectations from others multiplied with every passing hour. The coming days promised endless meetings with domestic and foreign dignitaries. Not only did he and Ellendren need to be brought up to speed on the state of Krysenthiel during their absence, they also had to open the first session of the Guardian Senate.

Grabbing his lierathnil robe, Devlyn draped the silky fabric over his tunic. Ellendren insisted he wear the gold and violet lierathnil when meeting diplomats. They couldn't afford to show loyalties to one kingdom over another by wearing a certain color. Instead, they both wore Krysenthiel's colors, ever reminding the dignitaries who they were. Once his outer garment was fastened, he considered retrieving his crown. Crowns were more proper for ritual and official meetings as the Exalted Aryl, not the Prelate of the Guardian Senate. *What better way to remind them of who I am than wearing the Exalted Aryl's crown?*

Quiet your thoughts. Ellendren's voice filled his mind.

She had to be on the other side of the palace by now. Distance mattered little to them since the Seraph had declared them wed. Their minds, hearts, and bodies were connected, even as he felt new life quickening in her. He felt her precise location; she was talking with someone she felt comfortable with. A vision of Jeanne and Abbie blossomed in his mind's eye.

He walked to the standing mirror to make sure his outfit was proper enough for Aorinol. His hair was slightly tussled, with strands of golden-brown, ebony, silver, and bronze woven throughout. He was undeniably a child of Luminare, but his unique hair, shared only by his sister marked him as an elf of all four Skylands.

Gold eyes looked back at him. He tried to remember what his eyes had looked like before his connection with Aliel had brought about the gold color. The green that faded to silver was now only a memory for the Luminari, the color having changed as Lucillia's buildings returned to the Illumined Wood. They had regained the elven silver eyes, appearing as though starlight had been captured there. Only Devlyn and Ellendren had a different light shining from their eyes, a gift shared among the Phaedryn.

"Ei'denai." Viren bowed with his palm over his chest as he entered the study. "I was asked to accompany you to your meeting with the Daer senator."

"By Ellendren or Jeanne?"

"They shared the same opinion, as do I." Viren wore his ribboned armor, common among the Guardian knights, with his verathn sheathed at his waist.

"I'd rather not argue with either."

"Smart." Viren smirked and led the way through the impressive kirenae door of their residence and into the expansive corridor. Unconsciously, Devlyn squared his shoulders and corrected his posture as he left the residence.

The quiet Devlyn had enjoyed for a brief hour in his study faded as hundreds of elves bustled about the palace. A mix of soldiers and nobles, and elves in service to both rushed about, quickly acknowledging him with formal bows even as they went about their duties. Devlyn was still young, but they either knew him on sight or by the gold and violet lierathnil with Krysenthiel's crest. And if his outfit didn't alert them, the phoenix flying over his shoulder did.

He was still uncomfortable with others treating him so formally. *I wonder if Alex is used to it.* Devlyn smiled as an image of Alex hollering at someone to stop gawking at him came to mind.

Eventually, he walked into the immense entrance hall and down a grand double curved staircase. It felt miniscule in the space yet perfectly proportioned. Although the palace was wrought entirely of lumaryl, there was a great degree of differentiation in the stone and only the walls were a vibrant semi-opaque gold. The staircase was more sculptural, and its lucid form felt alive, as though it had paused in a formal dance within the grand space, frozen in time for others to use and enjoy.

Devlyn and Viren walked out onto the plateau-like plaza at the front of the palace, like the bow of a large ship. The plaza had two levels, separated only by three deep stairs, encompassing the upper landing. Two curved ramps stretched from the lower plaza like open arms, with pointed arches along the sloped path toward the gate dividing the highest tier of Arenthyl and the sixth tier.

Twenty additional palace guards joined Devlyn and Viren. Devlyn thought they were unnecessary but he would never win an argument to go without them. Kryseniels blanketed the gardens, the golden lotuses filling his sight before he passed through the gate into the sixth tier.

Aorinol resided in a palace traditionally occupied by representatives of the Daer Empire. Apart from the Qien Dynasty, the Daer Empire was the only nation to span an entire continent. Because of such esteem, they were entitled to accommodations fitting their status and influence in Arenthyl. The Daer's palace was a vast complex, rivaling the largest of Eklean's castles to accommodate their dignitaries and supporting staff.

The streets in the sixth tier were crowded with richly clad elves, humans, and dwarves going about their day. Ogres and giants were unlikely to come here, but they did have the right to representation if they chose. Devlyn was troubled over those who had not responded to the invitation. The merpeople, Charrenese, and Qien would be pivotal members of the Guardian Senate. That they had yet to send any representatives to Arenthyl was troubling indeed.

Following the gentle bend of Arenthyl's winding streets, Devlyn reached the Daer embassy. It was an extensive palace that still held a faint glow from the lumaryl stone, but not as bright as it had been before the Void snuffed out the sun. Two women stood at the entrance, looking down on everyone due to their incredible height. Neither wore armor, but they were dressed in a white garment, a veil of the same color shielding their faces.

Viren spoke before Devlyn had the chance to introduce himself.

"Ei'denai Devlyn Lorenthien of Krysenthiel is here at the invitation of Senator Aorinol Penauld of the Daer Empire."

"The senator is expecting you," said the woman on the left.

Devlyn blinked twice. *She's a wielder.*

Shield your mind. The reminder from Ellendren felt expected.

The woman who had spoken opened the door to the palace but did not enter.

Only Devlyn and Viren went into the building, leaving the other knights with the two women outside the palace. Ellendren had told him when they had begun meeting emissaries that expecting the knights to enter a foreign diplomat's residence would have been seen as aggressive.

The entry was lit with additional torches just as at Aerodhal, and the subtle transcendent light of lumaryl made him feel at ease. His shoulders loosened even as he noted that a third veiled woman dressed in white waited in the center of the entry.

"The senator is expecting you, Ei'denai." Before Devlyn could respond, she turned and walked through the hall expecting him to follow. Her elongated legs moved oddly, as though she was too tall for her own limbs.

Devlyn and Viren trailed the woman. Devlyn was curious—what did these women know of wielding? They would not have suffered the same fate as Eklean and Septyl had with the loss of Balance between kien and kiara wielders. Were Daer men equally capable of wielding? The Ei'ana of Septyl would want to investigate Daer wielders further, particularly in the ways they had strayed from Septyl. Alex and Abbie's warnings about the Sorcery nagged at him.

The wielder led Devlyn and Viren through several corridors and spacious rooms to a balcony where Aorinol sat at a table with two chairs, standing as they came out.

"The Exalted Aryl of Krysenthiel, Ei'denai Devlyn Lorenthien." The wielder bowed and moved to stand behind Aorinol.

"It is a pleasure to finally host you, Ei'denai. Your city is most illuminating."

"The pleasure is mine, Senator." Devlyn pressed his hand over his heart and bowed slightly. It never hurt to show respect to a diplomat.

"Please, have a seat." Aorinol waved at the free chair, ignoring Viren entirely.

"Thank you," Devlyn said, taking the seat facing Aorinol. "I must admit, I received your invitation with some surprise." Devlyn calculated how far he could push for a candid reply.

"Are you sure my presence in Arenthyl did not stir more than just surprise?" Startled by the direct comment, Devlyn held back a gulp. "Pardon my manners," Aorinol said with a turn of his head. "Menthel, please bring the urshin tea." The wielder left the balcony.

"Given the aggression of Daer forces in Eklean, your presence was not expected," Devlyn said.

"I can only imagine how that might be interpreted. It has been a long time since Daer has interacted with Eklean, so I'll overlook the ignorance. But please understand that the four senators involved in colonizing Eklean act independently. The larger empire has withheld any blessing of such—aggression—as you called it."

"Am I to understand Daer senators act without consensus?"

"It's rare for us to act as a unified empire," Aorinol replied, confirming Ellendren's theory. "We have always been free to pursue our own endeavors. Jendie, Hivln, Koth, and Panor come from assertive provinces; Hivln more so."

"You understand their aggression reflects on the entirety of the Daer Empire?"

"Yes, which is partly the reason I desired to meet with you. I hope to sway that misconception, and also speak of this Guardian Senate. As I understand, it once incorporated peoples of every land and race, intent on shepherding peace in the days after the elves came from the sky to discover how humans did little but wage war, particularly here in Eklean."

"Slavery will not be tolerated by the Guardian Senate." Devlyn felt his blood begin to boil. Everything he had learned of the Daer's culture involved slaves of conquered lands.

"They live a fine life, better than most of the peasants I've heard of in Eklean; some even hold rank in the households they serve."

"Yet, it is nonnegotiable."

Aorinol held Devlyn's gaze then let it go as a lighter expression replaced the seriousness when the wielder returned with two cups of tea. "As to the other Daer senators already in Eklean, they are beyond my control. Only a unified consensus in the Daer Senate can enforce them to halt their advances and release their property. Until that happens, if it happens at all, the empire will remain in its inactive state. The only time we've ever done anything remotely similar is when we demanded that Senator Reth relinquish his recent acquisition over a Charrenese noble."

"What of the Sorcery? Is the Daer Senate as divided in opinion over what the Guardian Senate outlawed when it was last in session?"

Devlyn asked.

"You are well informed," commented Aorinol. He sipped his tea.

"I understand it's common knowledge in Charren, Daereneth, and Ja'horan." Devlyn knew this from having been told by Abbie, Alex, and Kevn.

"We are far away from there though." Aorinol took another sip, his eyes on Devlyn. "And what would you like to know about the Sorcery?"

"Whatever you can tell me. My understanding is limited to the subduing of an anadel to a sorcerer's will."

"You assume it's another form of slavery, yes? In truth, it is not dissimilar to the Phaedryn." Aorinol gave the faintest glance at Aliel. "But the Phaedryn did not extend their gift to the entirety of their nation. Every Daer benefited from the Sorcery's advancements and we were all changed by it; our bodies grew taller, stronger even, and our hair whitened."

Devlyn blinked at the comparison. Aliel was no slave and he nearly interrupted Aorinol to say so, then reconsidered and asked, "When did this physical change occur?" Their elongated proportions were noticeably different from other humans'. Were they still human or were they something different now? Had they made themselves into a new race?

"Before you elves migrated from the Skylands, but not before our ancestors first met. Some of our historians claim ancient Daer were inspired by Phaedryn who came to Daereneth. Like Eklean, we were ruled by warring kings in those days. But no Daer has bowed to a king since we became who we are today; we are all each other's king."

"To what degree is the Sorcery still practiced?" Devlyn asked, careful with his words.

"Officially, it is not practiced, and every senator is unified in denouncing it." Aorinol fished in a pocket and retrieved a globe of swirling light. "But unofficially, every senator has heirlooms and familiar ties with the Sorcery."

"I see." Devlyn cautiously took in the talisman as he took another sip of the urshin tea. The meeting went on as they discussed the Void and Devlyn couldn't decide how he felt about Aorinol. Was he trustworthy? Everything he said was through the lens of the Daer Empire, built and sustained through slavery of both anacordel and anadel. Were the veiled women wielders or sorcerers?

"There's something else I would like to ask before leaving," Devlyn said as he returned the empty cup of tea to the table.

"How else might I enlighten you?"

"As Charren's immediate neighbor and friend, do you know why their representatives have not made the trip to Arenthyl?"

"Rumors of internal strife and regicide have reached the Daer Senate. The continent of Ogren has seen a rise in ogre aggression. Charren is the last human kingdom with a foothold there. I'm sure whatever is preventing them from sending representatives is related to one or all of those issues."

"What happened to the other kingdoms?" This was the first time he'd heard of them. No one had mentioned other human civilizations in Ogren. So much of that continent remained a mystery, as were Ja'horan and Daereneth. How could they reestablish the Guardian Senate when he knew so little of the world? Fortunately, a visit to the Sophillium was in his near future.

"Slaughtered by ogres, their cities sacked and burned. The Daer Senate thinks pockets of resistance remain in Ogren, but most of the refugees have fled to Charren, and others have found their way across the channel to Daereneth."

Devlyn was afraid to ask how the refugees had reached Daereneth, fearing they were now enslaved.

"Do know, you would be a most welcome guest in the Daer Empire. We would love to arrange a visit. You see, not every senator can simply abandon domestic interests, but every senator is eager to meet you."

"Why is that?" Devlyn wasn't sure whether he wanted to know the answer.

"To see how different we are. A long time has passed since we've encountered an elf bound to a phoenix."

Devlyn's skin bristled at the suggestion of binding Aliel against his will. He couldn't burn any bridges with the Daer and might have need to go to Daereneth one day. "If time allows."

"Very diplomatic of you." Aorinol's smirk seemed to imply things Devlyn couldn't begin to guess at.

VACANT

Due to the forced agreement to a number of conditions presented by the aryls, one of which was that Devlyn and Ellendren could not travel independently and at the same time, with rare exceptions, meant that while Ellendren went to Ceurenyl, Devlyn had to wait before going to Septyl to ask Kevn's help in his capacity as Grand Librarian of the Sophillium.

Devlyn and Ellendren had agreed that visiting the Temple of Ceur was the more pressing of the two meetings. They had no idea whether the Light had gone out everywhere. Neither wanted to consider what it would mean if the Light was gone from the temple, but they needed to know. So Ellendren and Abbie, along with Prya and Liara, shifted from Arenthyl to Ceurenyl. To Jeanne's delight, Prya and Liara had insisted on staying with Ellendren as her guardian.

Before she could adjust to her new surroundings, a familiar voice called out excitedly, "Elle!"

Although Abbie, Liara, and Prya spun around to defensively confront the speaker, Ellendren easily recognized the voice, and turned to see Fyona in Gwilnor's grey robes, trailed by Danielle and Trethien, their hands clasped.

Fyona rushed to embrace Ellendren, her haste making Ellendren's protectors uneasy despite Ellendren casually hugging Fyona back. "It's good to see you, Fyona," she said. "And you too, Danielle and Trethien."

Danielle hugged Ellendren next, but Trethien hung back and simply nodded. He seemed more relaxed than Ellendren had ever seen him. "I see you got my letter."

"We did, and of course we'll accompany you," Fyona said.

"Myranda will be livid she's missing out," Danielle added.

"We could hardly expect her to leave Sorenthil to see to my wellbeing," Ellendren brushed her hair behind an ear.

"I'm not sure what she would dislike more," Danielle said. The three women laughed, well aware of Myranda's priorities.

"Are you certain you can miss classes? I don't want to interrupt your studies for my sake," Ellendren said.

"They've been interrupted just fine without your help. The new Chancellor, Myrah Glaeda, is trying to normalize Gwilnor now that the Tenebrae no longer have control over it, but everyone knows Gwilnor won't return to normal until the Void is dealt with," Danielle said.

"Can't exactly focus on studying with the Evil One returned," Fyona shrugged.

"And you, Trethien? You've only just returned to Gwilnor," Ellendren said.

"We both know why I returned and it wasn't to study." Trethien's fingers entwined Danielle's. The sight made Ellendren smile. "Besides, I'm sure my mother will be thrilled to have me back in Arenthyl."

"She did seem pleased when I mentioned bringing Danielle to Arenthyl."

"I apologize in advance," Trethien said to Danielle.

"You've yet to meet my parents and grandparents. You might want to withhold any apologies until they have their way with you." Danielle's eyes sparkled.

"Well, I'll come back after meeting my brother, unless you prefer to join," Ellendren said.

"We'll wait here. We wouldn't want to impose," Fyona replied for all of them.

Ellendren walked to the front of the temple with Abbie, Liara, and Prya. Seven temple knights stood in the alcove, the temple's only official entrance. There were of course hidden passages and other secret entrances into the Temple of Ceur, but as far as anyone in Ceurenyl knew, there was only one way into the temple that loomed over their city.

Ellendren had always seen the temple as a beacon of light, illuminating the city with its opulent white, almost silver, stone. On a sunny day, the temple often appeared brighter than the sun as it reflected not only the sun's rays but emitted its own inner light. But now, while the masonry walls remained a brilliant white, they appeared darker in the Void's presence. The stone looked sickly, as though it had absorbed a poisonous oil. She prayed that that wasn't the case.

Could Anaweh even hear her prayers now? Were they completely alone, severed from the Creating Light?

Ignoring that thought, she passed into the always-dark corridor leading into the Chamber of Light. At least the Void had not caused this. Ellendren had crossed this space hundreds of times while studying at Gwilnor. Her reflection marched with her along the highly polished stone columns on either side, Tariel providing just enough light. *It feels wrong*, Tariel conveyed.

I sense it too. Ellendren held a small seed of hope that the Chamber of Light was unchanged.

Seven knights waited at the end of the corridor. They saw the phoenix and recognized Ellendren as the Exalted Aryl. While Ceurenyl was part of Krysenthiel, the temple knights answered only to the Ceurtriarch. "Who wishes to enter the Light?"

"Ellendren Lorenthien." Titles were not needed when entering the Chamber of Light. "I am not worthy to enter into such splendor, but by the will of Anaweh, the Creating Light." Abbie, Prya, and Liara repeated the phrase. Ellendren held her breath as the knights opened the door. Every other time she had come to the temple, a blinding light had issued the moment the doors parted. She had shielded her eyes during her first visit with her parents and said a prayer for them now. Had they been able to reach Lumaeniel in death or did they linger behind as ghosts?

Distracted by her thoughts, she didn't at first register any change. The doors were open but the searing light was gone. And while the space was darkened, lit only by torchlight, she saw clearly across to the other side, something she had never been able to do before. The beam of Light in the center had always obscured her vision, making it impossible to see the far walls. That beam was much more than light though; it was a gateway to the Empyrean Sphere, a bridge to Lumaeniel. Few who stepped into the Empyrean Sphere ever returned to Teraeniel. But those who did returned with the ability to wield lumenys.

As she had feared, the Light was gone. Tariel cooed sadly. The entirety of the dome above was visible. The circular space with its many balconies and robust columns felt empty without the Light that had filled it for thousands of years. Dozens of people walked aimlessly through the Chamber of Light; some prayed, others gawked at the loss of Light. Tariel was now the brightest source here. The torches and candles felt misplaced.

The Chamber of Light had dozens of ancillary chapels around the large drum, but only three ways led out of the chamber. Ellendren had just entered through the most used portal for visitors, the other two reserved for the temple's residents. One led to the temple's cloisters, where ei'ceuril and temple knights lived, and the other led to the Ceurtriarch's quarters.

Ellendren crossed the space, no longer having to walk along the perimeter to stay out of the beam of Light. Two temple knights guarded the door to the Ceurtriarch's quarters. She hoped her brother was inside and able to speak with her. One of the knights shepherded Ellendren and her companions inside, leading them through the vestibule and into a reception room. It was one of the few spaces Ellendren had been permitted to see in the Ceurtriarch's quarters. In truth, she had no idea how extensive the space was. It could be limited to a few chambers, or more likely, resemble her own residence in Aerodhal, akin to a spacious palace.

Before Ellendren could sit, Jehn, Aaron's secretary, joined them, attired in the customary white ei'ceuril hooded robe. "Welcome to the Temple of Ceur, Ei'terel. Do you seek an audience with Ceurtriarch Aaron Roendryn?" he asked. There was a clear note of fatigue in his voice.

"I do; forgive me for not arranging a meeting ahead of time." Ellendren didn't comment on the house Aaron still identified with. Kaela would be irate when she heard.

"No trouble at all; these are unprecedented times." Jehn turned to leave.

"You should sit," Abbie said, gesturing toward the sofa.

Arguing with Abbie was never a wise choice, so she sat on the stiff sofa without complaint. Abbie sat near her, but Prya and Liara remained standing by the door. Ellendren thought they were being overprotective. What harm could come to her in the Temple of Ceur? People couldn't wield in the temple. But that was before the Chamber of Light had gone dim. The temple wards were all connected to the Light.

Curious, she surrendered herself and embraced kiara. She felt the wondrous power flow through her, the elemental erendinth at her control, then she embraced aerys, attempting a simple wield with air. Her hair whipped in her face in response. Shock jolted through her. She had just wielded in the temple.

"I understand why Ceurtriarch Daeryn implemented the protective wards to eliminate wielding in the temple, but they should have never been wrought," Liara said, her ruby eyes alight. Even in her smaller form, Liara was very much a dragon. "It is not natural to sever people from the erendinth."

"What about the kien wielders who could not control their wielding?" Abbie asked, clearly having little sympathy for them.

"Balance would not have been lost if the ward had never existed," Liara said.

"Ceurenyl could have met a similar fate to Septyl if those precautions hadn't been taken," Ellendren countered. She couldn't say whether Ceurtriarch Daeryn had made a mistake all those years ago.

"Perhaps." Smoke wisped out of Liara's nose as she huffed.

"Nothing can be done about a choice made fourteen hundred years ago," Abbie said. The room fell silent, and Prya smiled at Abbie. While Ellendren felt safe in their company, she was beginning to fear the dampening of her voice in their company. She might be the Exalted Aryl, but her safety was in their hands.

"Hello, sister," Aaron said. His white lierathnil robe was resplendent and embroidered with many symbolic patterns.

"Aaron," Ellendren said, relieved to see her brother again.

"Please tell me you've learned something about the Light vanishing. I would've come to Arenthyl sooner, but my time has not been my own since it vanished. There was no warning here. The sun was bright that day, and the sky a clear blue. I felt something tear—no, shatter, in my heart. Then everything went dark. The sun was doused and the sky turned a dark grey with unending storm clouds. When I went into the Chamber of Light that first time…" Aaron stopped, lost for words as he gazed toward the door leading to the chamber.

"I saw. I can hardly believe it myself," Ellendren said.

"Elle, the Light has been part of the temple since its founding. People whisper in the streets that Anaweh has abandoned us."

"The Creating Light would never abandon creation to be swallowed by the Void," Ellendren said, also fearing people would come to that conclusion.

"A small pocket of ei'ceuril wise ones and archstewards claim it's a sign that I'm not fit to be the Ceurtriarch. The same ones who opposed my elevation in the first place. This time I fear they might be right." Aaron slumped into an armchair.

"And do they expect a new Ceurtriarch to be capable of returning the Light?" Ellendren raised an eyebrow. She looked forward to the next generation of ei'ceuril, capable of wielding kien with control. The men in the temple had been isolated for too long. The ei'ceuril were needed outside the temple walls, protecting others from Ramiel and the Void.

"I'm not as skilled as Kevn when it comes to hearing other's thoughts, but I agree with your sentiment about the male ei'ceuril here. Our long isolation has poisoned us. We should be actively working with the ei'ana and you and Devlyn to find a solution in eradicating the Void."

"Are you still able to wield the Light? I mean that special form of lumenys that is so much more." Ellendren didn't know what she hoped to learn or how it would benefit them.

Aaron did not answer, but a flame of light appeared between them. The Light was alive and Ellendren could feel it burn in her chest, connecting to her heart. Light and color returned to the receiving room, and Ellendren almost forgot the Void waited outside this small light's influence.

"In truth, anyone can learn to wield it. Naturally, it's easier for trained wielders to learn. There are many wise ones who have debated over the centuries whether it was a gift that ought to be shared. There are records from before the elves had to abandon their Skylands that touch on it. I really need to thank Kevn for his research."

"I'll make sure Devlyn conveys your gratitude when he visits Septyl." Ellendren fixed her gaze on the light between them, wondering whether she might be able to replicate the wield. "How do you mean anyone can learn to wield it? I was always under the impression that only ei'ceuril were capable of it."

"Anyone who spends time in contemplation and is in tune with their inner self can manage it. You can feel it within yourself, can't you? The Creating Light placed a living Light inside each of us. Our spirits, our *ana*, are part of Anaweh. We are all linked to the Creating Light, since a part of that Light resides in us all. The Light in the temple might be gone and the Tree dead, but Ramiel would have to exterminate every anacordel and anadel to eradicate Anaweh from our world."

Ellendren wondered how they could use this against Ramiel and the Void. Was it possible for every anacordel and anadel to bond, tap the Light within themselves, and overpower the Void? She knew Ramiel was powerful, but surely he had his limits when faced with the entirety of creation. But it wouldn't be the entirety of creation. The Erynien Empire had freed Ramiel. Had they known that they would have also unleashed the Void? The Cyndinari were elves of the high sun; surely they were suffering just as much as the other elven kins in its absence.

"Can you show me how to tap it?" she asked.

"It's not really something that can be taught. An ei'ceuril will spend years of quiet contemplation before they manage it."

"Years?" Ellendren couldn't spare a day, let alone years. If she wasn't meeting dignitaries she was strategizing how to defeat the current threats against creation.

"Afraid so. You should know, many ei'ceuril have refused to leave the temple, including archstewards. I've named a new archsteward for Elothkar and he's already set up residence there, taking two dozen ei'ceuril to assist him. Elothkar was easy though. There hasn't been an archsteward there in thousands of years. I was free to choose a new candidate who was willing to travel."

"Do they not realize they may be their city's only defense against Ramiel and the Void?"

"They've been in the temple too long. I considered waiting them out, but that was before the Light vanished. Everything has changed now. My advisors and I have drafted a resolution. Any ei'ceuril unwilling to travel to their post will be released from their responsibilities and titles."

"They'll hate you for it." Ellendren smiled.

"I'm sure they will. But they also made a vow to serve."

"Have all the archstewards learned to control their wielding?"

"Yes. I made it a priority over the past few years. Only the most stubborn ei'ceuril have refused and they no longer have any official responsibilities. The archstewards fought the mandate but came around when I threatened to strip them of their titles."

"A helpful bargaining tool. Do you think they'll bend again?"

"I hope so. We can't continue to isolate ourselves. Not now."

"The ei'ceuril might not thank you, but the people of Eklean certainly will."

"I'm happy to hear it."

"Out of curiosity, who did you name as the archsteward of Elothkar?"

"Another crusty old man. Clara was not pleased. She's been urging me to balance out the ei'ceuril leadership."

"Smart woman," Abbie said. Ellendren restrained herself from commenting on how many old men were archstewards and wise ones. Aaron laughed nervously, seeming to notice he was the only man in the room.

"I also couldn't help but notice that you haven't adopted House Lucillia." Ellendren had not missed Jehn naming Aaron as a Roendryn nor did she intend to let it pass.

"I thought it would be better for me to not be attached to an aryldom, especially one with Kaela at the mantle."

"Few are as capable a politician as she."

"And that is precisely what worries me." Aaron laughed.

"Not changing your name is a political act, Aaron. It could sow dissent, signaling your disapproval. Some of our less savory cousins might try to use that to their advantage."

"I believe our sister is more than capable of controlling her house and our relatives."

"But you will consider changing your name, yes?" Ellendren made it sound like a question. She couldn't order her brother, the Ceurtriarch to do anything.

"If you insist," he replied, clearly understanding that it wasn't a request.

Ellendren concealed her smile. She needed Kaela to be a cunning politician. While Kaela and her house were now Krysenthiel's stewards, Ellendren had also chosen her to sit on the Guardian Senate to represent the Aryldom of Arenthyl. Ellendren would not waste her sister's talents, and she had experience beyond a common elf, having once been a *guest* of the Yanilean.

UNITY

Velaria and Yelaris followed Kevn to another sophilliae. A solution had to be hiding in one of them. Velaria had been preparing for Ramiel to break free of his prison since she was a student wielder, but it was difficult to accept that he now roamed the land. What horrors would he unleash on Eklean and the rest of Teraeniel? Already, the dead were visible, unable to transition to Lumaeniel. Their ghosts floated by, ignoring the living.

As though the ghosts weren't issue enough, the Purged Desert of Dwonia had expanded past Dwota's Gap, claiming large swaths of Mindale and Yanil. The plains had dried all the way to Binton, the grass brown and dead. Unlike many of her sister ei'ana, especially those who were human, she didn't believe it was normal. They'd said there was nothing unnatural about a drought, but Velaria had her doubts. After all, her instincts were the only the reason she was still alive.

Yelaris was just as worried about the desert as Velaria, and when she wasn't patrolling the skies, she was here in the Sophillium helping Velaria research the growing desert. "Did you find anything?" Yelaris asked. Sophilliae required an enormous amount of time to absorb, especially for those unattuned to them.

"Nothing explaining how the desert has the ability to expand."

Kevn returned with another sophilliae. "This one might prove useful."

"Does it offer a solution?" Velaria asked.

"No, but it does offer some insight into Eklean. Our continent is unique compared to the others. It reflects the state of the larger world, people included, as though the land itself is alive."

"How can a continent reflect the state of the world?" Velaria asked.

"It'll be easier to understand if you see it for yourself." Kevn offered her the sophilliae.

Velaria closed her eyes as she touched the glassy orb. There was no way to prepare for what one might see from any given sophilliae. Some contained entire languages, some offered stories from a certain perspective, while others delved into dense theories and applications of the erendinth. The Sophillium was a treasure trove of knowledge thought lost forever. That they had regained access to it was a great boon to Septyl and the larger world.

Not knowing what to expect from this sophilliae, Velaria was startled as she was rushed away by a wind that caught her and flung her into the sky. At first glance, she saw only water; the sophilliae told her it was the Unarian Sea. Its waves covered everything. The waters receded and land formed in a recognizable landmass: Eklean.

She looked down on Eklean and saw the continent in its entirety. Yelaris couldn't fly high enough to view the whole continent at once. But there Eklean lay, as though Velaria looked down on a map sprawled out before her. The Illumined Wood was immediately recognizable, as was the Purged Desert. She watched as the two seemed to fight each other. When one expanded, the other shrank, almost as though they danced. The forest grew and covered all the land east of the Vespien Mountains and even pushed west past Dwota's Gap.

It didn't last. There was no sense of time and Velaria couldn't say whether several years had passed or a thousand. Eklean hummed as the two extremes went back and forth. They settled into how Velaria recognized them now; the desert had grown larger and pressed past Dwota's

Gap. Eklean's lush meadows and fields were brown and dead as the Purged Desert pushed further east, encroaching on the Illumined Wood itself. But just as the forest had receded when it had pushed past Dwota's Gap, so too did the desert retreat and the forest expand once more.

Velaria observed the sea expand, seeming to claim Eklean as waves rushed over the Illumined Wood. The waters swallowed the entire continent, but it did not seem destructive. There was nothing violent about the Unarian Sea. But swallow the continent it did. Just as there was only water when the vision began, so too was there only the Unarian Sea at the end.

The vision faded and Velaria came back to herself and the subtle lighting, blinking from the change. Yelaris took longer to withdraw from the sophilliae. The more often one absorbed knowledge from a sophilliae, the less time the process required. Kevn was already absorbing another sophilliae. She worried he was going to exhaust himself if he continued at his current pace. While all Septyl benefited from Kevn's role, she worried it would see him to an early grave.

"Another prophecy?" she asked.

"I think it's more of a reflection," Kevn replied.

"And the sea claiming Eklean?"

"Nothing lasts forever. But I imagine that won't happen for a very long time, if ever."

"Kevn, where did the names for the sea, forest, and desert come from?" Velaria asked.

"I've never heard of them referenced as anything else. It's possible they've had those names from the very beginning."

Velaria considered that. Had the names come from Anaweh? The vision alluded to Eklean being much more sensitive than she'd ever imagined, as though the continent was alive, just like any cordel, anacordel, or anadel. But how could a continent be living? Were all the continents alive or just Eklean? Lost in her thoughts, a mental nudge from Paurel brought her back. She was gentle in her reminder that the Seven Chairs were to sit in council together.

"Forgive me, but the other Chairs are waiting for me."

"Of course."

Velaria wondered when he last stepped outside Septyl. Not that they could enjoy the sun any longer, but the air was still fresh, even if the Void had consumed the entire world. She had meant to tell him to take care of himself but already late, she hurried out the Sophillium and made her way to the Chamber of the Seven Chairs. Septyl's corridors were gloomy and depressing without the sun spilling through their crystalline vaults. Ei'ana still walked about the palace-city's corridors, but she saw that many went in pairs now, and some were even accompanied by knights.

The events that had unfolded at Gwilnor with the Tenebrae School still haunted the ei'ana. A sense of distrust had permeated the city. Only the Eldinari ei'ana were spared that sense of dread. They had known that Razcul, calling himself Danyol, had been a Cyndinari. But they had also known that to expose him was to jeopardize their chance at eradicating the Tenebrae School. As it was, the Tenebrae Chair was still at large. Velaria worried about what sort of mayhem Nadia Desuani would be creating. More concerning was that she might be hiding among them, either here at the palace-city or at Gwilnor Academy. Nadia's escape from Gwilnor weighed on Velaria.

She wanted to hunt down the woman she had once trusted as a mentor. That she was also responsible for the death of Velaria's parents only added to the betrayal. Nadia was undoubtedly gathering her Tenebrae sisters. Whether their loyalties belonged to Erynor, Ramiel, or themselves remained a mystery. What Velaria did know was that they would not hide forever.

At the Chamber of the Seven Chairs, Velaria took her place on her throne-like seat. Everything about this chamber had been replicated at Gwilnor Academy. Truly, when Velaria had first come to the original here in Septyl, she'd thought she'd been transported back to Gwilnor.

The other Chairs had already taken their seats and were waiting for Velaria.

"Forgive my tardiness; I lost track of time in the Sophillium."

"An easy thing to do. Did you learn anything?" Paurel asked.

"The Purged Desert expanding into Mindale and Yanil concerns me," Velaria said.

"Do you think it's connected to the Void?" Selenya asked. The Albien Chair spent just as much time in the Sophillium as Velaria did. Selenya had directed her School to learn as much from the forgotten sophilliae as possible. The Albiens hoped some secret knowledge might be hidden there to solve their current challenges.

"Remotely, perhaps. Kevn thinks Eklean physically responds to the state of the world. If that's the case, the expanding desert is not a good omen," Velaria said.

"Concerning, if true," Paurel said, glancing at Phendien. He didn't comment but appeared deep in thought. "If it is a reflection, then our only recourse is to improve the state of the world. Our first and foremost priority is to rid Teraeniel of the Void and Ramiel. We have a responsibility to protect this realm from those who would threaten its existence."

"Ramiel's return should not have been possible," Loretta said.

"Yet the Tree is dead, and ghosts roam, visible to all," Velaria said.

"I still haven't seen any ghosts. Are we certain they aren't just rumors?" asked Ira, the new Arantiulyn Chair. Her seat had proven a dangerous one to fill. One predecessor had been killed and the most recent had been stripped of the title once it was discovered she belonged to the Tenebrae School.

"Septyl was sealed for over a thousand years. Anyone who died here when the city fell would have transitioned to Lumaeniel long ago," Phendien said.

"Let us pray history doesn't repeat itself," Agnelle said.

"I saw them firsthand in Binton. Everyone who died in battle lingered afterward, unable to find their way to Lumaeniel," Velaria said.

The experience was still harrowing. She feared waking up to find a ghost watching her. Septyl might be protected with wards, but she couldn't stay behind its walls forever. The ei'ana were needed in this fight for the living.

"Debating whether they exist will get us nowhere. We must plan on how we're to meet these challenges," Paurel said.

"In battle, of course," Ira said, as though there was nothing more obvious. As the Arantiulyn Chair, she was known as the General and was responsible with leading the Septyl knights. She might be the newest Chair, but Ira was a seasoned ei'ana intent on rebuilding her School's reputation.

"We can't just march to the Shadow Mountains, nor can we simply offer ei'ana to the Guardian Senate to use as they will, assuming Devlyn and Ellendren manage to resurrect that body," Selenya said.

"Agreed; we must determine what our role in this conflict is to be," Paurel said.

"Why wouldn't we offer our services to the Guardian Senate?" Agnelle asked.

"We can't expect others to give orders to ei'ana, Guardian senator or not. We must be the definitive leadership of Septyl, as the Chairs have always been," Ira said.

"If we don't acknowledge the Guardian Senate's authority, why would any other nation lend their army to them? If we don't stand as an example, no one will follow," Velaria said.

"This is not the first time this chamber has heard this argument," Phendien said, quieting the others. "Septyl fell the last time. Thousands of ei'ana died. If I hadn't been in the Eldin Wood, I too would have perished. Erynor brought Septyl to her knees. Today, we face Erynor *and* Ramiel. If we do not come together, history will repeat itself."

"Phendien, what would you recommend we do? Should we maintain our autonomy or allow the Guardian Senate and First of the Guardians to direct us?" Paurel asked.

"Neither. We are the Seven Chairs of Septyl. We cannot allow others to make demands of ei'ana. But there is a middle ground. Jeanne Darkel is no fool; while she is no leader of ei'ana, she will know how to best utilize us on the battlefield. We remain independent from any nation but answer the call to serve Teraeniel, as is our duty."

"So, we cooperate with the Guardian Senate," Paurel said.

"And if we disagree with their choices?" Selenya asked.

"The Luminari elves stripped their aryldoms of their military when they founded the Guardian Senate, as a show of good will to the other nations. Those who remained soldiers were brought into the newly formed Guardian knights. From their inception, they were to answer only to the Guardian Senate, an oath they hold to this day." Phendien took a breath as he paused. "We are not Guardian knights. Our actions are our own, but if we're to defeat Ramiel, the Guardian knights will need our full cooperation. A single plan of attack must be taken."

"You're right. There can't be two separate battles on the field. We'll be stronger together," Ira agreed.

CHANGED HEART

The lumaryl map in Aerodhal's map room was remarkable. Unlike the lierathnil maps Devlyn had grown accustomed to, this map was sculpted of lumaryl and could show any part of Teraeniel with a flick of the wrist. Viren and Jeanne stood to either side of him, while several advisors under Jeanne's command also hunched over the map table.

The recent addition of Ramiel's fortress on Mount Cyngol stared up at them, goading them. Jagged spires thrust up like lances. Darkness clung to the fortress, seeping out like a disease.

Today wasn't about looking south, but north. The journey to Elothkar should be relatively simple, but Jeanne had insisted on meeting to discuss the safest route since she would not be joining the wedding party. Fortunately, most of their adversaries were now to the south, having been driven out of Thellion. Before Jeanne could address the logistics, Ellendren joined them, her expression grim. Abbie, Danielle, Fyona, Prya, Liara, and to Devlyn's surprise, Trethien, followed her in. "How are preparations?" she asked. Tariel flittered to the upper reaches of the space to join Aliel.

"Moving along quite well. We should be ready to leave after I return from Septyl. The aryls have already been notified to rendezvous in Reinyl," Devlyn said.

"Splendid. I'm afraid my trip to Ceurenyl was less optimistic. As we feared, the Chamber of Light has gone dim, though Aaron did provide a glimmer of hope," Ellendren said. Jeanne perked up. They could use any benefit they could find. "He was able to summon the Light."

"How? We've been cut off from Lumaeniel," Devlyn said, astounded.

"From Lumaeniel, yes, but not the spirit that resides in us all," Ellendren said.

"Can we use this to protect ourselves from the Void?" Devlyn asked.

"I asked that but Aaron did not know. Perhaps Kevn will have the answer," Ellendren said.

Devlyn nodded as he looked at the map, before turning to Jeanne. "Is there anything you need of me before I go to Septyl?"

"We can handle the remaining preparations in your absence," Jeanne said.

"I'll return as soon as I can." He kissed Ellendren goodbye, briefly greeted and farewelled the newcomers from Gwilnor, and left, Viren following. They passed through the palace, Aliel's light providing much needed warmth to the dark, cold corridors, heading to the library, one of the few places in the palace that had a seguian. All the others were at the docks, outside the city walls.

The library had four levels, with a continuous balcony opening onto the reading room from each one. Devlyn, Viren, and Aliel went through the impressive space, lit by hundreds of wielded orbs. None of the small lights could reach the vaulted ceiling that had previously illumined the space. Dozens of elves filled the library, all in quiet study. Despite the Sophillium and its sophilliae being once again accessible, tomes and scrolls weren't entirely abandoned.

The seguian to the Sophillium had its own chamber off the reading room and was locked and guarded. Jeanne hated that there was a seguian inside Aerodhal. She didn't care that it only went to another library; to her it was an easy way into the palace. The guards quickly unlocked the grate and in a single step, Devlyn, Viren, and Aliel crossed from

Arenthyl to Septyl.

Aerodhal's dim library was replaced by a dark haze. Unlike the rest of the world now confronted with perpetual darkness, the Sophillium had always been dark. There weren't any windows and the lumaryl walls and roof acted differently here. Rather than illuminating the space, they cloaked it in shadow and mystery. Globes of various sizes hung as though suspended by invisible strings. The voluminous space was difficult to move around, not because it was congested, but because one couldn't get a sense of direction. Devlyn saw two columns stretch up into the dark haze but couldn't tell what they were supporting—they simply disappeared, like the walls here.

Devlyn passed an ei'ana holding a sophilliae, her eyes closed. He had never considered how odd it would look for someone to find him absorbing information from a sophilliae. She looked as though she had fallen asleep standing up.

"I wouldn't disturb her if I were you," Kevn said from behind Devlyn. "I presume you're here to learn if there's a way to fight the Void."

"Afraid so. It's nice to see you again, Kevn," Devlyn said, offering a smile.

"You as well, my friend," Kevn sounded and looked tired. "Our ancestors never fully understood the Darkness that had claimed their Skylands, only that it was somehow linked to the Void. It wasn't just linked to the Void, it was the Void made manifest in Teraeniel."

Devlyn walked with Kevn and Viren; Aliel hovered nearby. Devlyn could already sense where their conversation was going. Only the Aldinari had remained on their Skyland and they had paid a heavy cost in doing so. "The aldarchs were able to protect their sanctums, extending that protection to their cities. Do you think they would help us?"

"Can you protect every city across Teraeniel? What about villages, towns, and farming hamlets?" Kevn sighed, his exhaustion evident. "I don't think we can look at this defensively."

Already frustrated, Devlyn balled his hands into fists. "Can nothing be done?"

"The oldest tomes in Gwilnor's library describe creation entering the Void. Ramiel was the first irythil to bring an erendinth into the Void. Despite its similarities to the Void, umbrys had an immediate effect on it. The Void that had been Ramiel's home and prison since the Elder Days is not the same Void that he first interacted with."

"What are you suggesting?" Devlyn asked.

"It's only a theory, but I wonder how the Void will change if the erendinth were funneled into it, like they were when Teraeniel was first created."

"With the Void now covering Teraeniel and Somnaeniel, isn't that already the case?"

"Perhaps—perhaps not. I'm imagining an incredible torrent, not only to push the Void back, but to alter it as it was altered before."

"Who's capable of harnessing so much power?" Devlyn asked.

"The ones who have already done it."

"The irythil?" Devlyn balked. He had met Uriel, and that was only when the Lord of the Stars had sought out Devlyn. How was he supposed to not only contact Uriel, but also the other six irythil who had brought the erendinth to create Teraeniel?

"And the dragon flights," Kevn added. "Along with the anadel accompanying the irythil, the dragons were the ones who physically shaped our world."

"I haven't the faintest idea of how to reach out to the irythil, but I know where the primuses of the dragon flights are. Although, I fear the dragon flights will be occupied by the Dark Flight."

"Is their Primus still imprisoned?" Kevn asked.

"The Qien Empire has sent no information to suggest otherwise."

"Good. There's enough evil in the world without Tolvenol being freed. I'll start researching how to approach the irythil and whether it is even possible."

"Thank you, Kevn."

"Is there anything else I can do for you?"

"I spoke with one of the Children recently, the boy who had lived beside the Tree of Life all these years." Devlyn debated what to say, still undecided whether Verinien's instructions were literal or figurative. "He said something impossible."

"Nothing seems out of the realm of possibility these days." A wry smirk appeared, a flash of the younger and carefree Kevn Devlyn had first met at Gwilnor all those years ago.

"What about tearing down a mountain? Two mountains."

"What did you just say?" Kevn asked, his tone strained. "What exactly did the Child say?"

"That the mountains would have to be torn down for Life and Light to be returned."

"Tear down the mountains," Kevn repeated slowly, seeming to puzzle out the phrase. "I wonder—" Without finishing his thought, he darted toward a sophilliae. He seemed to know precisely which one he needed, despite them lacking distinguishable features. Devlyn, Viren, and Aliel chased after him; losing him in the poor light would be all too easy.

Kevn briefly closed his eyes then left that sophilliae for another. Devlyn didn't have the chance to ask what he was looking for. Kevn scurried from orb to orb across the Sophillium. How could he navigate the space so well? Devlyn could barely see ten paces ahead.

Kevn held one sophilliae longer than the others, eyes closed and brow furrowed. Suddenly, he gripped Devlyn's wrist and brought it to the sophilliae's glassy surface.

Devlyn was transported to a lush valley, a chain of mountain ridges only just visible in the distance. Devlyn recognized them, although his vantage point was different from what he was accustomed to. He looked around to place himself, but everything was different. Lake Saeryndol and Mount Verinien were nowhere in sight. Storm clouds formed a ring about the valley, hungrily seeking to consume the fertile land. Devlyn recognized those angry clouds. They were the same that threatened Ter-aeniel in the present.

A being of great light walked past, neither male or female, but something else and somehow both. The light prevented Devlyn from seeing their face, yet he somehow saw it, and it made him want to fall to the valley floor and lie flat before the Creating Light. But he had no control over what he saw or did; this was someone else's memory preserved in the sophilliae.

"I will die here," Anaweh said. The Creating Light's voice was meeker than Devlyn had expected. This was the most powerful being in all creation—the very being who caused creation. "Many eons will pass, and this world and its people will look different when that time comes, but I will die, and my own children will cause it. Anaweh's gaze flicked toward Devlyn, or rather whoever's memory Devlyn was looking through."

"Who would want to kill you? *How* could someone kill you?" a Child asked—Saecrien. Devlyn hadn't realized she was here, as was her brother, among many others, all of them elves by appearance. But this was before the Great Blessing, when these people had become known as elder ones, the elves' common ancestors who had never ventured out of the valley.

Anaweh smiled, gentle and loving. "A choice is to be made. I offer all my children this choice. Their choices will define them and forever change them."

"Will you punish those who left the valley and those who have murdered others?" an elder one asked familiarly. Devlyn was surprised how easily everyone spoke to the Creating Light. He'd always envisioned Anaweh to be an all-powerful monarch, making those who approached tremble in fear. But the people here spoke to Anaweh as they would to a loved and caring parent or sibling.

"Our choices are only punishments if we decide they are. Ramiel has chosen the Void. The creatures he's twisted with hate will join him there. But my anacordel will remain here in Teraeniel. This realm belongs to you, and you can do with it as you please. Not all your choices will be for the betterment of Teraeniel, but they will be yours. Few will remain as they are now, for even those who have remained here in the valley have made choices that bring change."

"I don't understand," said a woman holding a man's hand. Devlyn recognized Thien immediately, which meant the woman had to be Loren. The progenitors of House Lorenthien.

"Oh, Loren, your love will change much in this world, and it might even save it. From your line will one be born to consume the Darkness—a vessel to contain it, until they bring it into my Light. Only love will allow the Darkness to pass." Anaweh pulled away from the gathered crowd, then turned to the Children. "Verinien, a mountain shall grow from this place, and within it shall I stand, but not as I stand and walk now. Saecrien, a second mountain will grow in the Illumined Wood. In it will be an empty basin, though it will not remain empty. Many tears will I cry in the eons to come, brought on by my children harming each other, forgetting who they are. The basin will fill and overflow with my tears. You both must guard those mountains until the day when they must be brought down. Only then will Light and Life return to Teraeniel."

Anaweh stepped further away, and the anacordel were pushed back in a sweeping arc. The act wasn't forceful, and it appeared as though no one had moved, but a great distance now stood between the anacordel and the Creating Light, whose form transformed into a large crystal tree. The tree's branches were heavy with crystal fruit and the entire tree emitted the same wondrous light that Anaweh shared while walking. The Light issued outward in a thunderclap and the dark menacing clouds vanished in the wind. Then the ground shook, lifting the tree as the valley deepened. The valley swelled toward the tree in waves as it rose to form a large mountain.

Water pooled into the valley, flooding it as hundreds—thousands—of dragons came to the frightened elves there. A red dragon landed beside the person whose memory Devlyn was viewing. "Come, Kynol min Othstrin, I will take you to your new home. A lake will claim this valley and those who have remained here all these years are to be gifted the Skylands," the red dragon said.

Kynol nodded and climbed onto the red dragon's back and they flew away. Devlyn sensed Kynol's thoughts about whether he would see the valley again. A lingering thought remained—how could Anaweh die? Did the Creating Light have a weakness?

Devlyn blinked and stepped away from the sophilliae. He had just witnessed the Great Blessing when Anaweh had banished Ramiel and his beasts to the Void and all the separate races were distinguished. Anaweh had blessed their choices and desires, sanctifying them. Elves, dwarves, humans, merpeople, centaurs, giants, fauns, and goblins had all been set apart that day, taking on a form that most closely identified with their desires. Even Ramiel had been given what he wanted. Despite everything Devlyn had just seen, the owner of the memory overshadowed the vision.

Devlyn had met Kynol min Othstrin in Binton. The Mouthpiece of Ramiel was the undisputed leader of the Sha'ghol. He could still hear Kynol laughing when the Tree of Life had died, and the Void spilled into Teraeniel. That was a very different Kynol than the one from this memory. How were they the same person?

"That didn't quite explain how the mountains are to be brought low, only that they would be." Kevn interrupted Devlyn's inner thoughts.

"Did you recognize Kynol?" Devlyn asked, distracted. He couldn't move past how someone who had spoken with Anaweh had betrayed the Creating Light for Ramiel.

"I did. He must have offered his memory to Sophie before he and the other Sha'ghol first went into the Void. I wonder what happened to him."

"Can we trust this memory?" Devlyn asked, fearing the Sha'ghol could have tampered with it to his advantage.

"I believe so. It supports what we already know about the Great Blessing and Verinien has verified the necessity of bringing down the two mountains."

"Do you think we'll find anything here about how to do so?" Devlyn asked, daunted by the enormity of the task.

"I'll keep looking."

"Thank you, Kevn." Devlyn turned to leave but had no idea how to find the seguian that would take him back to Arenthyl.

"This way," Kevn said lightly.

MASTER

Erynor Meriden, Emperor of the Erynien Empire, rightful sovereign of the elves and all living beings, knelt at his Master's feet, his thoughts guarded. Only the foolish thought freely in the Master's presence. On either side of Ramiel stood his mother and Kynol, the rat. Erynor had only known Erynel as a ghost. She still had power beyond measure; the Shroud had been her doing after all. But the Shroud was gone and the Tree was dead. In their absence were the Void and the Master.

Ramiel had yet to acknowledge Erynor since he had pressed his forehead to the dorthl floor. Erynor had never bowed to anyone in his long life, not even to his parents. His father was locked beneath a volcano on the other side of the world, and his mother had died giving birth to the draelyn son she had so desperately desired, even knowing it would cost her life. Her elven frame could not withstand giving birth to a dragon's spawn, the Dark Primus' son no less.

"Rise." Kynol spoke for their Master. Ramiel's Mouthpiece made Erynor's skin itch. He hated the man and knew the sentiment was mutual.

Erynor did as commanded, his knees creaking as he stood. "You honor me with your summons," Erynor said, expecting some sort of gratitude for fulfilling his obligations. He didn't look at Kynol, but at Ramiel, who ignored him.

"Gratitude?" Kynol scoffed. He must have caught his thoughts. Erynor reprimanded himself for being so careless. "Our Master might be eternal, but you promised his freedom fourteen hundred years ago. Your obsession with the Luminari nearly cost him that freedom."

"We could not kill the Tree with them in the way."

"You begged for an empire, then lost it. A frail woman was your undoing, and she wasn't even a Lorenthien. She was a nobody who slipped through your fingers because you let the Luminari live. Your life was spared by our Master's mercy alone. Twelve hundred years you made him wait, regaining your strength just to slither out a cave on your belly like the worm you are." His Master loomed over him, seeming to grow larger with Kynol's every word. "Why should our Master spare you? Your own mother desires a body. Perhaps she could put yours to better use."

"Master, I have served only you."

"While you aim for the rest of creation to serve you as their emperor," Kynol said.

"All I have done is for you." Erynor trembled before his Master. Death was but a breath away. He could practically taste it.

"You've chosen this corrupted Teraeniel over the pureness of the Void. Too many have grown weak or betrayed our Master. Even Yloran has stolen back the weakness that our Master freed her of."

"Master," Erynel complained, clearly not wanting to be counted in Yloran's company.

"You should have stayed in the volcano and left your son to Tolvenol," Kynol snapped.

"The dragon would have devoured him," Erynel said.

"And we would have been spared your son's incompetence!" Erynel recoiled, cowering.

"What would you have of me?" Erynor asked, head bowed in defeat.

"Too long has your father been trapped under the Qien volcano.

Direct his flight to free him."

"What of the monks?"

"They are useless without the jade dragons. You have done one thing right in petrifying them. I suppose you aren't an entire failure."

"The Jade Flight would have never met their fate if Tolvenol had raised Erynor instead of the Cyndinari elves," Erynel squeaked, defending her decision to let them raise her son.

"Was your opinion requested?" Kynol asked. Neither he nor Ramiel looked at her, but the threat hushed Erynel once more. "Who's to say Tolvenol wouldn't have been a better influence? Few have reason to hate the jade dragons more than he. In our Master's absence, he thought to become a god, a mistake which cost him his freedom."

"When would you have me order the Dark Flight to free their Primus?" Erynor asked, carefully phrasing his question. He had other plans for those dragons.

"Since when did our Master issue commands and entertain a delay?" Kynol hissed. The dark shroud around Ramiel thickened, threatening to consume anyone who stood too close.

"An Erynien legion draws near Cor'lera. I intended to have the dragons assist them and return the weapon the village conceals—a weapon capable of killing a dragon."

"You would delay our Master's plans, again?"

"They could burn the village to the ground in quick order, then fly to Qien after."

"Your obsession with that lethien village will be your undoing. There is no weapon there," Erynel snapped.

"There is. It will undo us all."

"You worry about Lucillia's prophecy," Kynol said, sneering in concert with Ramiel. "Let me worry about the younger son she named. I assure you, he won't be a threat much longer."

"But the weapon is in Cor'lera. Ythinor has foreseen his doom there. Something of great power is still there!" Erynor's voice rose frantically.

"The Dark Flight will leave for Qien—today. You are forbidden from ever crossing the Laudien Mountains. Is that clear?"

Erynor swallowed hard. This was a mistake. How could Kynol and Ramiel not see it? The weapon in Cor'lera would be their downfall if they didn't seize it for themselves.

"I'm waiting." Erynor flicked an agitated glare at Kynol's impatience.

"Understood." Erynor lowered his gaze, fists clenched.

"Excellent. Your son will remain here, lest you become tempted to disobey our Master."

"Erethien's place is in Broid as my heir."

"Erynor, don't be a fool," Erynel said.

"His place—*your* place—every elf's place is where our Master says it is. Now leave. Our Master tires of you." Ramiel recessed, more ethereal, as though no longer fully in Vasknir.

Erynor ignored Kynol's smug expression and looked at his mother. She had never been there for him; when she had been given the Shroud, he'd wished she had not been granted access to Teraeniel. "What are you waiting for? You heard our Master. Be gone!"

"What of Erethien?"

"What of him? He has his body and autonomy to himself again. The Deurghol don't need him as a puppet any longer. He is free to do as he wishes here," Erynel said.

"Vasknir and Tosk are filled with ghosts and anadel. This is no place for the living," Erynor said.

"Our Master gave you an order. Leave. Go salvage our reputation with him. Do not ruin this for us."

"Mother. Kynol," Erynor spoke in farewell.

"Nadia, come forward," Kynol said as Erynor retreated. "Have you found a way in?"

Erynor didn't hear the rest. What did it matter? He wasn't part of the Tenebrae's schemes. She might be an elf but she did not know immortality; she was weak like the rest of them.

He left the cavernous great hall that would have been a throne room had Ramiel need of a chair. Ythinor waited in a courtyard, aware of their Master's command. The dark dragon dipped his head for Erynor to climb aboard, while the dragon Erethien had flown here growled in his companion's absence.

"Our Master orders you to take the rest of your flight gathered in Mindale to free your Primus."

The dragon sent back images of the rest of the flight in Broid. Erynor responded by kicking Ythinor's sides. They were in the sky above Tosk and Vasknir in a heartbeat. The other dragon waited only a moment longer. Their Master had made it clear he would not tolerate any delay. Grateful that the dragon did not ask about the dragons in Broid again, Erynor directed Ythinor home. They flew over the Void city, crossed Dynthol Mirk, then flew over Yanil. Erynor scowled at the reminder of its current Yanilean. The treacherous man would answer for sending representatives to Arenthyl to serve on the renewed Guardian Senate. They would all pay and bow to their rightful emperor or burn.

Ythinor sent images to Erynor, inquiring about the weapon in Cor'lera.

"I am forbidden to cross the Laudien Mountains. We will wait for our father to be freed, but after, the village will burn in your flames. I remain the Erynien Emperor and I will have my weapon."

A VOICE ON THE WIND

The erendinth coursed through Devlyn as he rolled his shoulders and transitioned into another jienzu form. The sun had set and the caravan travelling to Elothkar had halted for the night. A mix of Guardian knights and ei'ana formed the security force ensuring Devlyn and Ellendren's safety. Most frustrating about the security demands was Jeanne's request that they not fly during the trip.

After hours inside a carriage, he had been relieved when they had finally stopped. He couldn't afford to stop training, needing to practice the new forms Jeanne had taught him. Unlike those he already knew, these were best geared toward carrying a staff, or in Devlyn's case, a scepter. He gripped his verathn, straining his body, mind, and spirit in the next form.

He had doubled the time he spent training since the Tree had been killed. How could he not? Ramiel was free and the Dark Flight lingered in Mindale. What chance did he have in surviving a fight against either if he couldn't even stand against Erynor? He vividly remembered his first and only interaction with Erynor and Ythinor; he had been lucky to have escaped with his life.

When he had fled Ceurenyl on Yelaris shortly after first enrolling at Gwilnor Academy, Erynor hadn't considered Devlyn a threat worth pursuing. Since then, Devlyn had defeated a Deurghol, barely surviving the confrontation. And that had been when they required a host. Now that the Void had been loosed on Teraeniel, the Deurghol—anadel pledged to Ramiel—no longer required a physical host. They could roam Teraeniel in their true forms, without a corporal body.

Contorting his body, a slow motion to train his muscles and not injure himself, he felt a breeze catch in his hair. The trees surrounding him bristled in the wind. His skin prickled and he breathed in, wondering where this wind had come from. What had it seen?

Further opening his inner sense, he extended his awareness to it. Did the wind and air have a consciousness like trees, soil, and stone? He had never considered it a question worth pondering. All he knew was that it was linked to aerys, just as stone was linked to terys. The air current was vast and despite the gentleness of the breeze, it stretched on for leagues in every direction, mingling with other air currents. The wind seemed to register that Devlyn was studying it.

"Hello?" Devlyn tried. Could the wind hear him?

The wind lessened, and Devlyn assumed it had passed. Just as he was about to fall into another jienzu form, the wind whipped about him again, more fiercely. He looked around, wondering what to expect. His hair fluttered in the breeze, just like the leaves and grass. The wind strengthened and whipped into a misty form, speckled with leaves and petals to give it shape.

"Odd for an elf to reach out to me," the airy form said.

"Forgive me, but what exactly are you?" Devlyn asked as courteously as he could.

"Hah! You elves care only for lumenys anadel, as though you could live and breathe without the others."

"You're an aerys anadel?" Despite his bond with Aliel, direct interaction with anadel was rare. During his novitiate in the Illumined Wood, he had come across many nymphs, anadel linked to terys. "Do you have a name?"

"Every wind has a name. Some are greater than others, as are the air currents that guide the lesser winds."

"Is every wind an anadel?" Devlyn asked.

"Just as every star is a lumenys anadel. I am Kespus of the East Wind, Eurnos."

"It's a pleasure to meet you. I'm Devlyn Lorenthien."

"A Lorenthien? I had a great fondness for Thien and Loren. They sought Eurnos' council often in those early days on Luminare, fearful the Skyland would fall from the sky." Kespus laughed, not in mockery, but playfully. "Their children played in my breezes. I can still hear their laughter pealing across the meadows."

"You knew my ancestors?"

"Oh yes, but the elves, once they were confident that Luminare would not plummet to the land below, sought our guidance less and less. We became invisible once more, forgotten. I believe Kiara could sense us, but she never reached out as you have now. Your people's devotion to Auriel and Uriel has blinded you to much of the world."

"How do you mean?" Devlyn asked.

"Until now, you had no idea that every breeze was an aerys anadel moving through the world. And we are not the only anadel forgotten by the elves."

Devlyn wondered about Kevn's theory of the creative anadel being able to help against the Void. How many anadel were around without anyone realizing? He had interacted with Dwonia—was Dwonia a terys anadel? "If the winds are anadel, are the great land masses terys anadel?"

"Yes and no." Kespus' form fluttered. "Anadel are not physical beings. We are soul and spirit. We do not have bodies—your *cor*. Terys anadel are often hidden deep in the ground, influencing and guiding when required. Ramiel's tenebrys anadel, corrupted and twisted by the Void, have long fought against terys anadel, seeking a release from the Void. Aquaeys and ignys anadel suffer a similar struggle. The ground quakes, volcanoes erupt, and tidal waves follow as they clash.

"And now that Ramiel is freed?"

"Hatred does not die quickly. The tenebrys anadel will only fight harder now that they are freed, seeking retribution. They resent the terys, aquaeys, and ignys anadel for restraining them. It is when the quakes, eruptions, and tidal waves stop that we should be really scared."

"Because tenebrys anadel would have defeated the others?"

"Correct."

"Would anadel fight against Ramiel and the tenebrys anadel?" Devlyn asked.

"It is not for me to decide, but the irythil. The Tree of Life is dead; the Void blocks our path to Lumaeniel," Kespus replied.

"But will they?"

"I cannot say, but they are in council."

"They're deciding now! Where?"

"Why do you think the Meridean Conclave and all the merpeople have been secluded in the Bowl of Theniel all this time?"

"The irythil are meeting at the Bowl of Theniel?"

"The Meridean Conclave await Theniel's direction. The irythil do not gather in the Bowl of Theniel, but there is a portal there to the irythil's thrones. Every irythil has such a portal."

"Could you take me to Lerathel's portal?"

"A mountain in the west quakes. Tolvenol will soon darken the sky," Kespus replied, brushing aside Devlyn's request.

"The Qien monks hold him captive," Devlyn argued. He didn't want to believe Tolvenol could be freed. They had enough enemies.

"You believe the monks can stop the Dark Flight from freeing their Primus?" The anadel spun about. "Already, they fly west across the winds. Their journey will be slow since aerys anadel fight against them."

"They're flying to Qien now?" Devlyn asked, disheartened.

"A messenger brings news. Seek out the irythil after you warn Qien. Find a way to wake the Jade Flight. They imprisoned Tolvenol before, and only they know the great wyrm's weakness."

"Is there no way to stop him from escaping?"

"You would have to defeat the Dark Flight. Nothing will stop them from freeing their Primus now that Ramiel is freed."

"You expect us to let him escape?"

"How many will die in the attempt to prevent it? Are you willing to make that sacrifice? Only the Jade Flight knows the Dark Flight's weakness. The Qien monks can restrain Tolvenol, but do not have the strength to subdue him once freed." Kespus' form fluttered, the petals and leaves defining his form falling away in the breeze. "Light be with you, Devlyn Lorenthien." The wind settled and Kespus was gone. How far could he travel in a single day? What would he see?

No longer wanting to practice jienzu, he grabbed his shirt from a nearby tree limb. His torso slick with sweat from the exercise, he hesitated before putting it back on. Viren and his dragon Falthion waited nearby, and Viren asked, "Were you talking to someone?"

Devlyn sensed his protector's anxiety. "I assure you, no enemy snuck past you. Are you aware the winds are anadel? In the same way the stars are and who knows what else."

"My studies, many years ago, touched briefly on the anadel of the other erendinth but never indicated their forms," Viren said as they returned to the carriage. A smile tugged at Falthion's lips. As a dragon of the White Flight, he had an intimate connection with aerys and by extension, the aerys anadel. Before he could offer any insight, a horn sounded from the caravan.

Devlyn's gaze shot to the sky. A Guardian knight and her dragon flew out to investigate while Prya and Liara hovered above the caravan. Falthion shifted to his larger form but stayed on the ground, his claws digging into the dirt, ready to fly at a moment's notice.

Opening his awareness, Devlyn broadened his senses. A dragon approached the Luminari caravan. Alarm pierced him and he bonded with Aliel in a flash of golden light before identifying the incoming dragon as Rusyl, with Jaerol and Liam on his back. His shoulders slackened. They must have seen Devlyn's lighted form near Falthion, for they sped toward him, joined by the Guardians. The white and blue dragons land-ed with a thud and greeted Falthion. They stayed in their larger forms, alerting Devlyn that whatever danger they perceived had not passed.

Liam embraced Devlyn. "It's good to see you again, brother. You too, Elayne and Viren."

"It appears giving you two lessons wasn't a complete waste of my time," Elayne said, a smile tugging at the corners of her mouth. "This is Kanastil." The white dragon offered a low rumble, followed by images of greeting.

"A pleasure," Jaerol said, clapping Devlyn on the back as he nod-ded to Elayne and Viren.

Devlyn forced his best smile. Kespus had alerted him to the tidings Jaerol and Liam brought. "Please tell me you haven't returned to bring news of the Dark Flight moving west."

"You already know. How?" Jaerol asked.

"It doesn't matter. We must inform Jeanne," Devlyn said, ready to shift back to Arenthyl.

"*We* are going to Elothkar." Ellendren walked past the dragons, joining the group. "Hello Jaerol, Liam, and Rusyl. It's good to see you safe and well."

"The Dark Flight is going to free Tolvenol," Devlyn explained.

"I know." Ellendren had been aware of his conversation with the anadel. "Which is why I think it would be best if Jaerol, Liam, and Rusyl take the news directly to Jeanne. Once they do, they can fly to Elothkar with her plan."

"Elothkar," Devlyn said mostly to himself. "The place will be packed with world leaders."

"What are you suggesting?" Ellendren asked.

"Why not ask Jeanne to come to Elothkar? I'm not sure how much time we have to spare, but surely, we'll be in a better planning position with so many leaders in one place."

"This would be a matter for the Guardian Senate to decide." Ellendren pointed out.

"Which hasn't opened yet. Too many representatives are missing. But all the elven aryls are attending the wedding, as will many human monarchs. With Evellion's close ties to the dwarves, there's bound to be matriarchs and patriarchs present too." Devlyn wanted to shift directly to Elothkar so they could begin planning how to deal with the Dark Flight and Tolvenol. Just considering Tolvenol darkening the already Void-laced sky sent chills down his spine.

"There's one problem." Ellendren looked from Jaerol and Liam to Rusyl. "How will Jeanne get to Elothkar?"

"Should one of us shift to Arenthyl and bring her?" Devlyn asked.

"The aryls will be furious. We're to stay with the caravan, a precaution I agree with."

Devlyn bristled at the impositions they had agreed to. As the Exalted Aryl, he had never expected to be so limited. But the thought of either he or Ellendren being alone in a surprise attack nagged at him. Ellendren was right and the rules had been suggested to keep them both safe.

"Falthion will go," Viren said, the large white dragon looming behind him.

"Are you sure? You've only just been reunited," Devlyn said.

"He won't be gone long." Viren patted Falthion's leg and the dragon arched his back and launched into the sky.

"We'll see you soon. Dragons can move much quicker than a carriage," Jaerol said as he and Liam climbed on Rusyl. The blue dragon quickly joined the white dragon already in the sky.

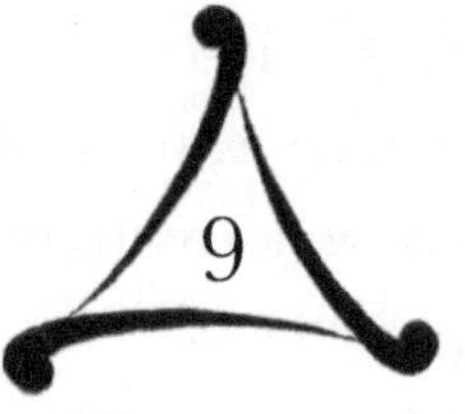

Elothkar

Devlyn looked out the carriage window and into the dark forest. Because of the Void, the Luminari caravan travelling north toward Elothkar had to wield globes of light, supplemented by fiery torches. The sun was at its highest, but the Void prevented its light and warmth from passing through. Devlyn missed the sun's touch and knowing that the Dark Flight was on their way to free Tolvenol, he needed that warmth now more than ever.

Torchlight and wielded light filtered through the trees of the Wooded Hills of Thellion, making the ilithae trees appear ominous. Guardian knights and ei'ana accompanied the caravan, ensuring no harm came to any of the aryls. Devlyn and Ellendren could defend themselves, but even they would not risk travelling without added protection.

While they shouldn't have anything to fear from this forest in the heart of Thellion, Devlyn repeatedly glanced out the carriage window, uncertain as to how far he could see. The Void had changed everything. He felt as though he could no longer rely on his instincts or senses. Any number of beasts could be hiding in the Void's shadows, waiting to strike.

A ghost passed through their carriage. He sucked in a breath, holding back a curse. Ellendren held his hand, sharing in the discomfort. He had lost count of how many specters he had seen since the Tree of Life was killed.

"It wouldn't be so bad if they made a noise. Something to alert to their presence," he said.

"I feel sorry for them," Ellendren replied, compassionate for the silent dead. "Their way to Lumaeniel is blocked and so many have been adrift in the Void, only to return now and wander Teraeniel, lost."

"We'll figure something out. We'll find a way to rid Teraeniel and Somnaeniel of the Void." Devlyn tried to sound confident, not just for Ellendren, but also for himself. Even if the irythil couldn't give him any reassurance of how to manage it. The carriage rolled along the bumpy path and Devlyn forced himself not to look out the window again. "More and more emissaries are arriving in Arenthyl to represent their people. We should be able to open the Guardian Senate soon. Teraeniel will come together and stand against Ramiel and the Void."

"We still haven't had any word from the merpeople," Ellendren said. "The Meridean Conclave has been isolated for years now—ever since Ferinn organized the merpeople and Jahro seafarers to come to the Sorenth's aid after Queen Karina was murdered."

"Would they abandon us to fight this war without them?" Devlyn asked, recalling what the aerys anadel had said about them waiting.

"I don't know. I'll be glad to learn if you're able to reach the Bowl of Theniel." Ellendren sighed, then smiled down at the slight bump of her stomach.

Devlyn feared he would have to leave Ellendren. Someone had to warn the Qien empress and then possibly find a way to the merpeople. An overwhelming urge to protect Ellendren during her pregnancy loomed over him. She was still in the early stages and the bump was still mostly unnoticed except by those who looked closely. But that did not mean it was a secret. The entire Krysenthien court had learned of it, which meant the entire world knew of it.

Ellendren wouldn't be alone though. Abbie, Danielle, and Fyona would be with her. They took their responsibilities seriously—a little too earnestly for Devlyn's taste. He didn't mind any of them, but they were present more than he cared for. He couldn't remember the last time he had a waking moment with Ellendren alone. Fyona typically took the early shift and woke Ellendren for a checkup every morning. The added company was not how Devlyn envisioned starting his days. Their zealous supervision made Ellendren's attendants appear negligent and Jeanne Darkel like a push over.

Devlyn tried to gentle his frustrations. Like so many other Luminari elves, Abbie, Danielle, and Fyona easily accessed their inner senses and if Devlyn wasn't careful, they might hear a rude thought directed their way. "They don't need to tap their inner senses to know your feelings," Ellendren said, amused and ever aware of Devlyn's mind. "You're not exactly a closed book, my love."

"Fyona could have made herself scarce this morning," he grumbled.

"She worries how the travel will affect my health."

"Then we should have just shifted from Arenthyl to Elothkar. We could have saved an entire month's worth of travel."

Ellendren placed a hand on his thigh, sensing his tension. "The people of Eklean, not only those in cities and palaces, need to see us. We need to give hope to villagers and farmers too."

"I suppose, but I think Aliel is insulted I'm riding in a carriage."

Not insulted, merely amused, Aliel conveyed. Aliel and Tariel flew above, looping about. With Falthion gone to Arenthyl, only the two phoenix and two dragons patrolled the skies.

"On another note, are you sure it was wise to leave every city in Krysenthiel without their aryl?" Devlyn asked.

"They could not miss this wedding, and neither could we afford to go a month without meeting in chamber with the aryls. Our evening sessions during this trip have been critical. Besides, each city has a chain of command in place; they're hardly defenseless. If anything happens, Kaela will notify us immediately and we'll return without hesitation. Not that she's forgiven me for having her stay behind while we attend a royal wedding. I'll never hear the end of it, but she's the one who fought so hard to become our steward."

At last, the forest thinned, and Elothkar came into view. It was remarkable. Brilliant limestone and granite made up much of the city, reminding Devlyn of Everin. The palace, rising above the city in the distance, was all that had remained before people had returned to the long-abandoned Thellish capital. Although Aewen had instructed ei'ana how to wield the city walls, much of the city had been reconstructed through more traditional means. Masons and architects had accomplished a remarkable feat in under two years.

As impressive as the city was, Devlyn wondered how much more the aldaryl-laced city could be appreciated if the sun's light could reach it. An oily haze of grey clung to everything. The Void didn't obscure his sight like fog but dulled everything. The sun still rose and set every day, the stars and moon were visible at night, but their light could not reach Teraeniel or its inhabitants.

Thellish knights stood at Elothkar's gate, wearing tabards that reflected the Thellish flags and banners above. The silver-winged horse stood proudly on a white field. Each knight also had a second sigil, showing which Thellish province they belonged to. The knights bowed to the Luminari procession before stepping aside for them to enter the city.

Once past the gates, a flurry of banners and flags lined the streets of Elothkar. Most prevalent was the Thellish sigil, but it was accompanied by the white eagle of Evellion, the grey stallion of Perrien, the brown ox of Mindale, the most recent addition to Thellion, and a flag Devlyn had only seen fly in the wind once before at Cor'lera. Rising with the same importance as the other sigils was Parendior's purple doe on a beige field.

Devlyn had once believed that the now deposed Perrien Council had had every such flag burned when they had annexed Parendior a century ago. Turning to Ellendren, he smiled at seeing Parendior's recognized status, and asked, "Have you ever seen it before? Parendior's crest?"

"You know my education before Gwilnor encompassed a thorough history of Eklean that wasn't curated by the deposed Perrien Council." Ellendren kept her head level as they processed through Elothkar. "Have you never seen it before?"

"Only when I accidentally shifted to Cor'lera to escape the Tenebrae ei'ana at Gwilnor. No villagers flew it when I was growing up there; Perrien had a tight grip over the village. The flags must have been tucked into trunks and passed down in secret through the generations."

"It's a miracle Parendians managed to maintain their identity while the Perrien Council ruled over them."

The horses pulling their carriage trotted into a large plaza in front of Elothkar's royal palace. Buttressed spires with immaculate gilded domes rose over the castle's halls and keeps, all constructed from a pale grey, almost white marble and granite, embellished with aldaryl. Unlike most castles Devlyn had visited, this palace had not been built as a fortress. There was no doubt in his mind that it would hold against a siege, but the architecture contained more elven influences than the sturdy robust forms often associated with human architecture. Slender piers and buttresses rose from the ground, weaving into the masonry, allowing for large arched windows and doors. Five flags flew on every spire and turret, the largest flag bearing the Thellish crest and standing above the smaller banners of Evellion, Mindale, Perrien, and Parendior.

The celebratory banners concealed most of the city's ongoing construction as the buildings rising from Elothkar's ruins tried to mirror the palace. The architects and builders from Everin had focused on completing the buildings along the main boulevard to the palace, giving the sense of a complete and vibrant Thellish capital. The palace looked as though it too had only just been built and not eight thousand years ago.

Devlyn reminded himself to straighten his back and level his chin as he hopped off the carriage with Ellendren; hundreds, if not thousands, of Thellish citizens would be appraising them as the High King and High Queen of Eklean. Ellendren was a natural. She had presented herself as a leader her entire life and needed no reminder.

Thellish knights pulled the heavy gates open. Alex strode forward at the head of a procession to welcome the elves. The Thellish entourage followed the straight line from the castle to the opened gates, banners with the silver-winged horse on the white field flapping in the wind above them.

Devlyn quickly noted an intricately woven crown on Alex's head, mingling with his sandy blond hair. It was not the first time he had seen his cousin don the Thellish crown, but it always startled him to see Alex in his official capacity as the King of Thellion. Granted, Alex likely felt the same whenever he saw Devlyn as the Exalted Aryl and High King.

Protocol demanded several procedures, but once Alex passed through the gate, both he and Devlyn ignored them all and embraced each other.

"Oh, is it good to see you!" Alex grinned broadly as he squeezed the air out of Devlyn's lungs. Alex had always had more muscle mass than Devlyn, but thanks to jienzu, Devlyn's leaner muscles answered the friendly squeeze just as hard. "You remember Diana, of course." Diana stood back with the rest of the Thellish court, frowning at Alex's breach of protocol. Devlyn could sense that Ellendren felt similarly, as she too hung back until it was clear Devlyn and Alex wouldn't return to formalities. Devlyn thought he saw the two women share a look of understanding regarding their companions before each stepped forward.

"You must be elated about the ceremony," Ellendren said. "And the city looks beautiful."

"Thank you. I still have no idea how Lady Aewen managed to keep the palace from crumbling to ruin with the rest of Elothkar. The forest had encroached everywhere but the castle, as though guarding it. When we were restricted from felling any of the trees that had dominated the city, our architects and masons nearly lost their patience with Lady Aewen," Diana said.

"Of course," Ellendren said. "They're ilithae trees from Aldinare.

Felling them would have swiftly ended Aewen's friendship."

"So we've been told. But to our surprise and delight, the forest simply retreated from Elothkar one morning. The remaining trees either formed manicured parks and gardens or lined the streets. Since then, masons have been busy rebuilding. If only you could have seen it before the Light went out." Diana said, holding back a frown.

Alex rubbed Diana's back comfortingly. "I'm sure Devlyn and Ellendren have deliberated plenty on how to fix things. Let's not let the Void further darken our wedding."

Horns pealed across the city and shouts of "Dragons!" echoed through the streets. Devlyn spun at the warning but saw only two dragons above, one white, one blue. He grinned. "Looks like Rusyl and Falthion were able to bring Jeanne Darkel after all," Devlyn said.

"I thought she wasn't able to make it." Alex's flat tone was answer enough as to how he felt about the First of the Guardians attending his wedding.

"Matters occurring after your wedding, I'm afraid," Devlyn said, squinting toward the approaching dragons; they weren't alone. Two much smaller creatures flew beside them, and if they hadn't been beside the dragons, Devlyn would have mistaken them for birds. But they were much too large for birds. Smaller than dragons, yes, but not that small. Sharpening his sight, he saw they had talons as forelegs and paws for their hind legs. Devlyn's heart raced—griffins! Could it be Eolwn and Leithel? Had Wyn succeeded in his quest to bring Alethea back from the Void? Devlyn held back his hope, his heart hurting with the memory of the Void swallowing Alethea.

The dragons and griffins descended toward the palace gates. Devlyn's heart thumped so loudly in his chest, he wouldn't be surprised if the entire city heard it. Rusyl, Falthion, and the griffins were easily recognizable the closer they came. Restraining himself from opening his inner sense to learn their news, he waited for them to land. The dragons thudded onto the plaza, Jaerol and Liam on Rusyl, and Jeanne and Toryn on

Falthion. The griffins hovered, waiting for the dragons to settle. Devlyn's eyes widened when he noticed two elves on Leithel. His vision narrowed on the white hair of an older elf flowing in the wind, contrasting with her warm skin.

Alethea!

His eyes glistened with tears as he sank to his knees. *She's alive.* The thought ricocheted through his mind until that was all he could think of. He hadn't let himself hope her survival was possible. He was surrounded by voiced exclamations from the Eldinari aryls as they recognized their esteemed and former aryl. Mental exclamations reached out to Alethea, all just as pleased as Devlyn. The riders dismounted and his heart ached anew. They were all alive. Wyn and Aren had embarked on an impossible journey into the Void. The likelihood of rescuing Alethea, let alone surviving, had been miniscule. He pulled Wyn into a tight hug.

"You did it. You actually did it." Devlyn and Wyn held the back of each other's head, gripping each other's hair as their foreheads touched.

"Not without a cost."

"What cost?" Devlyn frowned in concern.

"Another time. This visit to Elothkar is to be celebrated." Wyn forced a smile, acknowledging Alex.

"It's good to see you again, Devlyn." Aren clapped his shoulder.

"You too, Aren." Aren's appearance was still jarring. Without his black wings and shadowy form, he looked like every other Luminari elf, golden-brown hair and all.

Alethea hung back, hands clasped behind her back. She was far from young, but she seemed older now than she had before. Devlyn had never seen her weary or exhausted, but now it seemed she longed for rest. "Hello, Devlyn."

"Alethea." Devlyn's heart pounded in his chest, overjoyed at seeing her.

"You've been busy since I last saw you." She grinned, banishing some of her weariness as she turned and embraced Ellendren, their foreheads touching. "Congratulations."

Both Wyn and Alex's eyes widened as understanding dawned on them. "By the Light, you have been busy," Alex exclaimed. Diana smacked the back of his head and Wyn stifled a laugh.

"How are the preparations for the wedding going?" Ellendren blushed, shifting the conversation.

"Hectic! Who knew organizing a wedding to include three, now four, separate kingdoms would be so cumbersome. As you know, each Thellish province has retained their standing and right to rule while bowing to the Thellish crown. So, they all expect equal representation. Fortunately, the new Mindalean king and queen have been lovely," Diana said.

"Daphne and Henry Ashton are delightful," Ellendren said.

"I still can't believe you invited those traitors from Torsil," Alex said.

"House Carvil is a direct descendant of Thellion. To withhold an invitation would have led to all-out war."

"We're already at war with them," Alex grumbled.

"Their families would never forget it. And once this war is over, Eklean will be in political shambles, so it's best to begin diplomacy before we start pointing fingers at each other."

"Torsil did lay siege to Myrium," said Devlyn, remembering the desperate state of Sorenthil shortly after Aren had murdered their queen in full view of her people. Granted, Aren hadn't murdered Karina as an agent of Torsil, but as Ramiel's thrall.

"Yes, and King Gordon and his court will be held accountable. We cannot think in a span of short years though. We must look at foreign relations with an eye open to the centuries to come," Diana said.

"I think we'll get along just fine," Ellendren said. Devlyn recognized that smile all too well.

"Well, I think we've been outside in the dark long enough. Shall we abandon these formalities and head into the palace?" Alex asked, then waved to everyone assembled before turning around, forcing his own entourage to turn on their heels. He spared a glance for the dragons before they jumped back into the air to provide added security.

"Agreed. Is there a place where the aryls can meet in chamber?" Jeanne asked, clearly cognizant of why she had been asked to join them.

"We should be able to find a hall big enough," Alex said, gesturing everyone inside.

An army of attendants awaited the elven aryls and their entourage in the grand entrance hall. While the aryls met, members of their houses would see to their accommodations.

A boy tugged at Alex's sleeve and whispered something.

"Will they never relent! Don't they know I'm getting married!" Alex pushed his fingers through his sandy blond hair. "Bloody Daer! Tell Karl I'll be with him momentarily."

The boy's gaze lingered on Devlyn and Ellendren as he skipped past the gathered attendants, disappearing into a corridor.

Devlyn offered a weak smile to Alex and he and Ellendren followed Diana through the palace. A surprising amount of artwork adorned the corridors, portraits and statues which could not have been commissioned and completed in the brief time since the castle had been repopulated. "Where did all this artwork come from? Has it been here all this time?"

"Lady Aewen safeguarded much of Thellion's treasures. There's still some debate over whether Elothkar or Alexandria should be the Thellish capital, but for now, they'll stay here in Elothkar, as will the court. If the capital and everything here does move to Alexandria, that palace will likely be just as grand as this one in time. Aewen oversaw the erendinth architects she had trained in the lost art who wielded that palace into existence. She ensured that it resembled this palace and appeared properly Thellish. Even the material is the same. Where she excavated it from, I'll never know."

"Remarkable," Ellendren said.

Devlyn marveled at the ancient artwork, miraculously preserved from the stains of time. It was also the first time Devlyn had heard any reference to erendinth architects being trained again. He wondered if there had been a specially trained group of ei'ana that had overseen and wielded the marvelous elven cities in the past. There had to be.

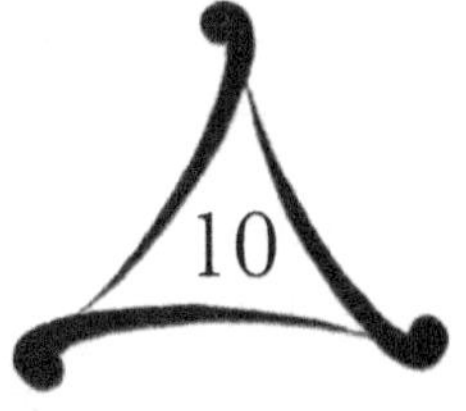

DRAGONS

The aryls filed into the long hall, three times as tall as it was wide. Devlyn, Ellendren, and other aryls took seats at the table. Many still had to stand, given how many aryls Krysenthiel now had. Aliel and Tariel stayed close by; Thellion might be an ally but there was no telling what daggers hid in the dark. Jeanne splayed out a lierathnil map on the table for all to see and placed a dragon figurine over the Plains of Mindale.

"Thank you all for agreeing to meet following our arduous journey to Elothkar," Ellendren said with a warm smile. "You have all been briefed on the Dark Flight's movement and what that might mean."

"Do they truly intend to free Tolvenol?" Enoria asked.

"Their trajectory certainly suggests so. The Dark Flight bided their time in Mindale near Krysenthiel's border for reasons unknown to us. After the Void was freed on our world, we feared they would strike Krysenthiel. But Jaerol, Liam, and Rusyl, after monitoring them at great personal peril, reported their western course." Jeanne moved the figurines along the path that Jaerol had described.

"I have it under good faith that the winds are fighting them, slowing the dragons as much as possible. But make no mistake, they will reach their destination," Devlyn said. He didn't mention Kespus, unsure how the aryls would react to him talking to an aerys anadel.

"We believe they're currently crossing the Purged Desert of Dwonia." Jeanne again moved the dragon figurines over the sandy expanse.

Devlyn followed an invisible line west, relieved the dragons had ignored Eklean's cities. What city could stand against a unified assault from the Dark Flight? A single dragon could wreak havoc and cause insurmountable destruction. He hoped the dragons of the other flights would come to Teraeniel's aid. They had to—they were just as much a part of this world as anyone else. What sort of future would they have if Ramiel lorded over Teraeniel?

Devlyn wanted to see what else would be in their path and swiped his hand across the lierathnil map. The Vespien Mountains moved to the edge of the map and the Misty Sea came into view as Dwonia also moved to the side of the map, Qien now filling it. A large mountain stood at the continent's center, the prison for the Primus of the Dark Flight, held captive by the continued attendance of the Qien monks. Only once had they failed to restrain the powerful dragon, and that day had seen the conception of Erynor, son of the Sha'ghol Erynel Meriden and Tolvenol himself. Erynel had sacrificed herself to bring a draelyn of the Dark Flight into the world. In return, Ramiel had promised her Krysenthiel.

"We cannot allow Tolvenol to be freed," Jeanne said, palms pressed on the table. "Tolvenol's return will be just as detrimental as Ramiel's return has been. He is not only the Dark Primus but Ramiel's most loyal general. He directed the Void beasts in battle before they were locked in the Void."

"What do you recommend?" Devlyn imagined going to Qien was now all but unavoidable. Empress Qien Wei had to be warned at the very least.

Jeanne hunched over the map, her gaze fixed. "As Guardians, our responsibility is to the whole world, not only Krysenthiel. The threat Tolvenol poses is too great to ignore. We must ensure he doesn't escape, for all our sakes."

Devlyn expanded the view of the central regions of Qien. Four cities surrounded the great volcano that was Tolvenol's lair and prison. Beishi was north of the volcano, Dongshi to the east, Nanshi in the south, and Xishi to the west. People had only flocked to those areas after the four central monasteries had been established and the Dark Primus, who had long terrorized the continent, had been subdued by the jade dragons and monks. Unlike the Temple of Ceur and the city of Ceurenyl, the monasteries were all set apart from the nearby cities that shared their names.

Glancing back at the dragon figurine, he realized the Dark Flight would raze the monasteries. Nothing would stop them from freeing their Primus. Not knowing the full capacity of the Dark Flight, he feared they would be unstoppable without help from the other dragon flights. How many people would die if they attempted to thwart the Dark Flight's attack? Devlyn leveled a hard look at Jeanne. "We aren't ready to confront the Dark Flight—we won't succeed without the other dragon flights."

"You would suggest we abandon Qien to suffer the Dark Flight and Tolvenol alone?" Jeanne arched a brow in disappointment.

"We need to warn them so they can prepare, but Tolvenol will only be defeated if the Jade Flight is woken."

"And how would we do that?"

"I think the merpeople know. Perhaps not how to wake them, but they would be familiar with the sea drakes who betrayed the Jade Flight, causing their enchanted slumber."

Jeanne spun around, back straight and arms crossed behind her back. "Are you certain the Jade Flight knows how to defeat Tolvenol? Once the Dark Primus is released, he will gain momentum and will be more difficult to defeat."

"Do you see an alternative? We cannot send Guardians to a fight they cannot win," Devlyn said.

"Perhaps an offensive plan," Silvia offered.

"How do you mean?" Fendryl asked.

"Simple; kill the beast before he's freed. Stop his momentum before it can escalate." Silvia looked across the table, daring the aryls to offer a better suggestion.

"You think no one has tried that before?" Naerelle asked, a stunned expression on her face. Devlyn caught a wisp of the Eldinari aryl's thoughts regarding the apparent youth of their Luminari counterparts.

Jeanne nodded to herself, contemplative. "A small group with the right weapon might succeed where no one else has." She paused and waited for Elayne and Toryn to join the table accompanied by Kanastil in her smaller form. The white-haired dragon bonded to Elayne was still much larger than anyone else in the hall.

"Three Guardians cannot kill Tolvenol," Therrin said.

"Shroudsbane is eager to remove more of the Void from Terae-niel," Toryn spoke with confidence, shifting her weight to clasp the hilt of her now-famous sword.

"Would we send three Guardians to certain death?" Aegian asked, clearly uncomfortable with the idea.

Devlyn felt Jeanne looking at him, smothered by Ellendren's anxiety. They had both been preparing for the very real possibility of Devlyn returning to Qien. They did not have the luxury to wait for a full host to travel to Qien; even a small party on dragon back would take too long. The Dark Flight had had a head start and would free Tolvenol before they even reached the neighboring continent.

"I'll go," Devlyn said simply. He squeezed Ellendren's hand. If they could kill Tolvenol before the Dark Flight could free him, they could save thousands, if not millions of people. "When do we leave?"

"Are you sure?" Jeanne asked. "This will be dangerous."

"We should go to Zhongshi first. Empress Qien Wei should be consulted," Devlyn said.

"Other than Viren and Falthion, is there anyone else you would take? I don't envision this mission being successful as a large undertaking. Getting an army into Tolvenol's lair, even while he's subdued, will not end well."

"Agreed. If we fail, we make for the Bowl of Theniel."

———————————

Ellendren hugged herself in the privacy of the chambers they'd been provided, her back to Devlyn. This plan was rash, and he knew it. She had glimpsed his conversation with Kespus during the journey north. If not for her irrational and death-seeking husband, the aerys anadel would have consumed her thoughts. But no, despite Kespus telling Devlyn he could not kill the Dark Primus, he intended to go into the belly of a volcano and try.

She was furious. How could he not consult her first? But what she hated most of all was that he was going without her. The aryls wouldn't tolerate Ellendren going into such danger while pregnant. They didn't even entertain the possibility while in chamber. They were content to let Devlyn recklessly enter Tolvenol's lair.

"We have to try," a solemn Devlyn said. "If we fail, I'll be able to shift everyone to safety."

Ellendren remained quiet for a time, letting the silence fill the room. "I will not lose you, Devlyn Lorenthien," she said at last. "I want you to shift out the moment it is clear you cannot defeat Tolvenol while he's subdued. I want you to keep our bond open the entire time. The instant you try to block me, I will shift to your side, be damned what the aryls demand of us."

"I promise." Devlyn reached out to her, but her back was still to him. Looking at him right now was too difficult. He knew how she felt—she allowed her emotions to flow through their bond, assaulting his psyche better than any verbal berating.

"Elle." His voice was tender—vulnerable. Her shoulders slackened and she turned to face him. "I'm scared too," he admitted.

"I know." She fell into his arms and he held her tight. Then she cried.

"I'll come home to you; I promise."

"Of course, you will." She said it aloud, mostly to convince herself. "Take Jaerol, Liam, and Rusyl with you."

"You don't think our group is already big enough?"

"Rusyl is known to the merpeople, and we still don't know what has become of Ferinn since he was summoned by the Meridean Conclave. Myranda has expressed concern over his wellbeing."

Devlyn remembered what Ferinn was to Myranda's mother. He nodded, recalling how fiercely Ferinn had fought to protect Myrium from being razed by Tieli, Torsillian, and Dwonian armies at the command of the Erynien Empire. The presence of shadow elves had made that battle particularly frightening. If only shadow elves were all he had to worry about now.

A Vow

The tailor poked and prodded at Alex's wedding garment. That the final alterations had to be completed while he wore the blasted ensemble was a nightmare. There was only one person's fingers he wanted carefully moving about his body today, and they were not the old tailor's.

Already in a prickly mood, Alex leveled a glare at Wessex, one of the few former Perrien councilors he had employed after liberating Perrien from its wretched council. Wessex had had a minor role but also had a wealth of knowledge about Perrien and its messenger birds.

"What do you mean, you haven't heard from them?" Alex asked. Wessex had assured Alex they would have no trouble maintaining lines of communication with Oliver and the Thellish force who had sailed to Charren to support Sanjin's claim to his throne.

"I'm afraid it's worse than that. I believe the birds are being killed before our messages reach their intended destination," Wessex said.

"How long have you suspected this?" Alex bit back a curse, accusations building in his mind. He'd come to an agreement with Senator Koth to ferry some of his army across the sea. Despite Alex's insistence that slavery would not be tolerated, not one man, woman, or child had left the newly formed, and begrudgingly tolerated, Daer colony. Alex regretted striking a bargain with Koth from the moment he'd left the Daer senator.

"Since the first birds didn't return. I thought it was simply the toll of the long flight."

"Are you telling me we've had zero communication with Oliver since he and a whole bloody battalion boarded Koth's ships?" Regrettably, Alex lost his temper and shouted. He knew he shouldn't have trusted Koth. The slimy senator had played him for a fool. Part of Alex wanted to saddle Dennion and fly to the Daer colony on the Skrein Sea's coast to get a straight answer. But Diana would never forgive him. Neither would the many monarchs and nobles who had travelled to Elothkar for the explicit purpose of witnessing the royal nuptials. No, Koth would have to wait until after the wedding. Besides, Alex doubted he'd be able to peel his wedding garments off himself. He winced as another pin pricked him.

"That's correct, Your Majesty." Wessex avoided looking at Alex as he spoke.

"Dismissed," Alex growled, suffering yet another pinprick.

Alex wished he could dismiss the tailor as easily. But the tailor answered to Diana and his mother. Both women knew he wasn't to be trusted with today's attire. He would have selected comfortable, loose trousers and a tunic that breathed if he had been given the choice.

Wessex still stood before him. "What else?" Alex asked, irritated.

"Jenyd of House Tarneth, advisor to Senator Koth, is at court. He's made it known that Koth wishes to expand his colony."

"I'm sure he would like that. Might as well hand over all Perrien to satiate his appetite."

"Your Majesty?"

"A joke." Alex rolled his eyes. "When does the illustrious advisor wish to meet?"

"He seemed rather impatient. I told him you're getting married today…"

"Let me guess, he's waiting outside my chambers," Alex said, glancing over Wessex's shoulder. "Send him in and be off. Find out why our birds aren't reaching their destination!"

"Of course, Your Majesty." Wessex hurried out the room, clearly eager to be away from Alex's disappointment.

Jenyd ducked through the doorway, alone, splaying his long fingers and dipping his head in greeting. Alex recalled he had a way with words, particularly when it came to twisting them to suit his ambitions. "I was told of Elothkar's wonders from a past age but never dared to dream they had survived Thellion's collapse."

"Thellion grows stronger with every passing day."

"I heard you brought a failing kingdom into your fold." Jenyd glanced from Alex to the tailor, then out the window. "Still, land is land. The Daer have a certain proclivity when it comes to expansion. Perhaps our people are not so different. We were once humans too, after all."

Alex had forgotten the Daer had once been human. Easy to forget considering their bodies had evolved to something very different, only an echo of humanity remaining in their features. Elves resembled humans more than the Daer's stretched-out proportions did now.

"I have every confidence Queen Daphne and King Henry Ashton will return Mindale to its former dignity." Alex suffered the formal small talk, even as the tailor's wrinkly fingers continued in their relentless task of pricking every sensitive area of his body. "Tell me, have you received any communication from your empire? News of other Daer senators and their ambitions in the south are quite worrying."

"Senator Koth's interests are independent of his fellow senators'," Jenyd said.

"So you've mentioned." Alex wasn't interested in Koth's interests, though he did doubt their sincerity. "That's not what I asked."

"Why the curiosity about Senator Koth's correspondence with the larger Daer Senate?"

"Call it diplomatic reasons." Alex didn't like how easily Jenyd saw through his questions. Could the Daer perceive another's thoughts as easily as elves? He shouldn't have entertained a meeting alone, not without Diana, wedding day traditions be damned.

"Suppose I believe you and take your interest in strengthening the bonds between our empire and your kingdom as genuine, what should I expect in return as Thellion's friend and ally?"

"You expect something in return just for letting me know whether Koth has received correspondence from Daereneth?"

"Everything is a transaction." Jenyd smiled, enhancing his too-small head for his elongated limbs.

Alex didn't like how he said that and liked his venomous smile even less. What else did this slimy man hope to own? Before Alex could ask what Jenyd wanted, the door opened, and Devlyn entered unannounced, Viren trailing behind.

"I apologize, I wasn't aware you were in a meeting," Devlyn said. Alex highly doubted that.

"Ah, you must be the elf-king I've heard so much about." Jenyd's full attention fell on Devlyn like slime.

"Devlyn Lorenthien." He pressed his palm to his chest and bowed in his weird elven fashion. Alex was of course accustomed to Devlyn adopting everything elven since they had left Cor'lera together, but he still thought a handshake was more than adequate. What need was there to imply that he saw the entirety of another person. That certainly wasn't a greeting Alex ever thought appropriate. He certainly didn't want people seeing his inner workings, physical or mental.

"Jenyd of House Tarneth." He splayed his hands, just as he had done earlier. Alex didn't know which greeting he thought was more bizarre. Perhaps the Daer greeting was to show that he didn't carry a dagger or some other weapon. Not that Jenyd needed a weapon since his words were just as bindingly deadly.

"I hope I didn't interrupt anything important," Devlyn said. Alex caught the caution in his tone and smiled. He trusted the Daer as much as Alex did.

"Merely curious whether Senator Koth has managed to maintain lines of communication with the larger Daer Senate," Alex said before Jenyd could add his own spin.

"Can't imagine why he wouldn't. Senator Aorinol tells me he's had no issue maintaining contact with Daereneth," Devlyn said as he took a seat on the couch. Alex beamed a grin. Thanks to Devlyn's timely arrival, he was spared from striking another bargain he'd regret.

"I was not aware Senator Aorinol Pennauld had made the voyage across the sea," Jenyd scratched his chin.

"Well, now that that business is concluded, is there anything else I might help you with, Jenyd?" Alex asked.

"As it happens, yes," Jenyd said. Alex wanted to kick himself. Too overjoyed with Devlyn's presence, he'd forgotten Jenyd had sought Alex out in the first place. "The original reason for my coming to see you. Senator Koth has expressed a concern over the sudden disappearance of the sun. He wonders whether the newly planted crops will take root."

"A misfortune that we can all agree on. I trust you're aware of the Guardian Senate being called into session to deal with that very issue," Devlyn said.

"Rumors—whispers on the wind—but nothing more," Jenyd replied.

"Aorinol has come to Arenthyl intending to sit on the Guardian Senate to represent the Daer Empire. I trust you understand how much power that gives him as the sole representative for such a numerous people," Devlyn said, maintaining eye contact with Jenyd.

"Abundantly. One can never know if these new institutions will stand the test of time. As you know, the Daer Empire has survived thousands of years. I'm sure the other Daer senators were simply unsure whether this Guardian Senate would endure a second bout. We all know how it fared the first time. Now, if you'll excuse me." Jenyd left without further question.

Alex glowered at the tailor as they waited for the Daer's footsteps to fade before asking Viren to shut the door. "That is quite enough fussing with this blasted outfit. You're dismissed."

"But Your Majesty…"

"Leave us." Alex didn't leave any room for discussion and the tailor gathered his threads and needles and bowed out the room. "Finally." He sighed, leaning against a sturdy table. He was afraid if he sat something would come undone and he'd have to suffer the tailor all over again. "Odd that Jenyd left so quickly."

"How do you mean?" Devlyn asked.

"He wanted something, but you told him something he didn't know."

"I admit, I feared Aorinol wasn't being completely honest with us. Even if the Daer have little faith in the Guardian Senate, that only Aorinol was sent makes me wonder whether he's keeping the rest of his people from knowing." Devlyn frowned, clearly considering something. Alex wasn't sure if he needed to meet this Aorinol; he had enough Daer to deal with in Thellion. "Out of curiosity, why did you want to know if Koth had contact with Daereneth?"

"Because I haven't received a single report from Oliver since he and a battalion sailed on Koth's bloody ships to Charren."

"Still? It's been well over a year, hasn't it?"

"Yes, hence my concern," Alex grumbled, teeth clenched. "To make matters worse, an advisor fears our messenger birds are being killed before they can deliver our messages. Diana will be furious, but I fear the only solution is travelling to Charren myself after the wedding."

"At least you won't be the only one upsetting your wife by leaving." Devlyn pinched the bridge of his nose.

"And where are you going? Back across the Misty Sea?" Alex was more than happy to talk about Devlyn's marital trouble than consider the soon-to-be rocky start of his own marriage.

"Yes, actually. As we speak, the Dark Flight flies west to free Tolvenol."

"And who dare I ask is Tolvenol? Isn't Ramiel being freed bad enough?"

"He's the Primus of the Dark Flight and would-be general of Ramiel's Void beasts."

"So, a delightful dragon."

"And Erynor's father."

"Splendid." Alex scratched an itch.

"If it's any help, I can take you and a small party to Charren before going to Qien."

"That would be ideal. Diana might even forgive me if what would have been months of travel occurred in a single day." Alex wanted to hug Devlyn. Diana would still be furious with him for wanting to leave so soon, but the kingdom would be in her very capable hands while he found out what was happening to his soldiers across the sea. "But you'll have to make a fuss about it for me. Make it seem like I had to convince you."

"Dare I ask why?"

"Consider it a wedding gift to get me on Diana's good side before leaving."

They laughed at the suggestion. "Forgive me, it's your wedding day; I only meant to see you before the ceremony to congratulate you and offer a drink to calm the nerves. Light knows I could have used both before I married," Devlyn said, pulling a bottle of Cor'leran Blue from his robes. "Just a glass—or two. I'd rather avoid earning Diana's ire on her first day as Thellion's new queen."

"You're so wise." Alex beamed and pointed to wine glasses on a nearby table.

"Are you ready to marry Diana?" Devlyn asked as he poured the ice wine.

"Very. It's hard to believe our engagement has stretched so long. I partly expected Evellion to withdraw from the treaty."

"The dukes would never stand against Queen Lara."

"Not successfully," Alex said with a wink. "Hopefully the former Duke of Overen rots in a cell under his mother, the reinstated duchess' capable watch."

"To Queen Lara and her daughter, your soon-to-be bride and queen." Devlyn lifted his glass and clinked Alex's.

"I can't believe the day has finally come." Alex thought back to the first time he had met Diana. That visit to Everin would have been memorable in its own right. Both he and Devlyn had answered Evellion's call for help, beating giants and his uncle's army, sent by the Perrien Council who answered to Erynor.

"A lot has happened since that battle." Devlyn followed Alex's thoughts. That he could do so was troubling, but anyone who lingered in Alex's mind too long did so at their own peril, especially on his wedding day. Devlyn seemed to recoil at Alex's pent-up longing for Diana. "We'd better get you married and quick."

Alex laughed, knowing what Devlyn had gleaned from his mind, intentionally or not. He finished his drink and he and Devlyn left his quarters, Viren trailing them. Did he follow Devlyn *everywhere?* Alex wondered.

Viren cleared his throat in answer.

"No one said listening to my thoughts was advisable. Can every elf do that?" Alex asked. He quickly decided he didn't want any elves near his bedchamber following today's ceremonies.

"All living creatures are capable of it, not just elves. And believe me, if I was able to shut out your thoughts, Alexander, I would," Viren said.

Alex paused when they reached the chapel where he was to be married. He'd been distracted by the thought of elves hearing his every thought and hadn't realized they had crossed the entire palace so quickly. Thellish knights stood guard and guests flowed past to take their seats. Devlyn clasped Alex's shoulder. "Ready?"

Nodding, Alex stepped into the chapel in what felt like a brave step. How many other men had done the same? His life would be forever bonded to another. He walked to the front of the chapel where Aaron stood, nodded to the Ceurtriarch, then turned to face the guests. His mother, father, and siblings smiled at him. Devlyn had joined Ellendren. Human monarchs, elven aryls, and several dwarven matriarchs and patriarchs filled the chapel, accompanied by countless Thellish nobles. Velaria had even made the trip to see him married. The kings and queens leading Thellish provinces sat at the front. Lara took her seat with a small boy, Amryian, and her younger daughter sitting beside her, no longer the child that Alex remembered. An empty seat was left where Evellion's royal family sat, presumably for the late king. Alex was saddened by the thought that Diana's father couldn't see this day, one of many casualties in Erynor's war.

Memories and dreams rushed through Alex's mind as he waited for his bride, then his mind blanked when Diana stepped into the chapel. Alex couldn't say whether her presence had silenced the guests or whether he could no longer hear them, nor did he care to dwell on it. All he cared about just then was his bride. The problems of the world slipped away. The war, the loss of Light, the ghosts, the Daer, and all too many other worries were pushed to the recesses of his mind as Diana walked toward him.

They were soon holding hands while Aaron said prayers for them. Alex heard none of it but managed to repeat oaths and vows when asked. The entire ceremony passed in a blur. Before he knew it, he was kissing his wife. The crowd cheered and congratulated the newly married couple. So surreal had the entire experience been that he wondered if he had been dreaming.

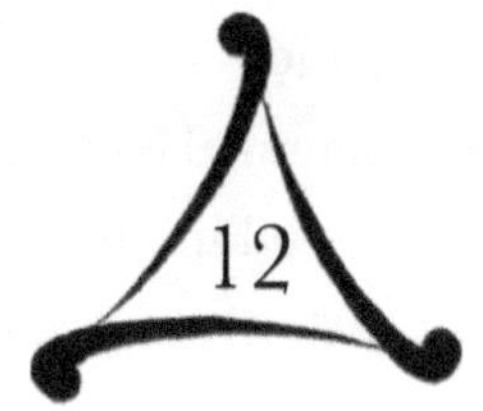

A Thellish Affair

Devlyn smiled across the elongated head table in Elothkar's palatial banquet hall, where family and guests celebrated the marriage of Alex and Diana. The treaty following the Battle of Everin was finally ratified, formalizing Evellion's union as a Thellish province. Flowers of every color filled the hall, arranged in ornamental wreaths and garlands with streamers of silver, blue, and green intertwined, representing the colors of Thellion. Large ice sculptures greeted guests as they entered the hall, the most prominent a winged horse. But there also were ice carvings of eagles, horses, oxen, and does throughout the hall, symbolizing the renewed Thellish provinces.

Queen Lara wore a diamond brooch in the shape of Evellion's white eagle, resplendent on her blue velvet gown; her daughter's brooch was a silver-winged horse. A retinue of Evellion's nobles and generals had journeyed to Elothkar with their queen, each bearing their kingdom's sigil. Even the grieving Duchess of Cyril had made the journey to see her niece marry.

Diana led Alex around the banquet hall to greet each and every guest. All the northern and central kingdoms had sent representatives. Yanil, Tiel, and Jadien had stayed away, perhaps terrified at what a unified northern Eklean meant. Minor nobles from Torsil had come, but despite being invited, King Gordon refused to show his support, likely fearing Erynor's retribution. Devlyn didn't even have to open his awareness to Ellendren to know that she would only leave the banquet once she'd learned all she could about southern Eklean's loyalties now that Erynor's true plot to free Ramiel had been revealed.

Queen Myranda of Sorenthil, King Irvienne of Briel, and King Leonard of Gestoria were present, each fully supporting Thellion, if not encouraging its expansion to pause and remain in the north. None seemed eager to be swallowed by another kingdom, ally or not.

Pushing his empty plate away, Devlyn stood, the table now largely vacant as most who had been sitting there were already dancing. Devlyn looked around the banquet hall for Ellendren. He would most likely find her talking with a noble or Myranda.

As he walked along the perimeter, someone reached for his arm. Turning at the gentle touch, Devlyn saw an elf with silvery hair flowing down her shoulders. Looking into her silver eyes, Devlyn smiled back. "It's a pleasure to see you again, Lady Aewen."

"You have accomplished much since we last met. Aldinare might not sail among the clouds any longer, but my people are free. I hope they enjoyed the sun while they were able to."

"I hope they will be able to feel the sun once more," Devlyn said.

"As do we all." Aewen grimaced, as though thoughts of the Void and its origin caused her pain. "I do not wish to dwell on such as he. May Vespiel guide us in Anaweh's Light. Ever will she mourn at his meddling with Aldinare and what he did to her children."

"Are you saying he's responsible for the loss of the Skylands—for the Darkness?"

"Indirectly. As I am sure you know, the Darkness that consumed our Skylands is the Void. If the Cyndinari had not sought that which is forsaken among the Shadow Mountains, even in our pride, we would not have lost our Skylands. The Aldinari elves would not have been consumed by the Darkness for all this time nor would Vespiel have had reason for her unending tears."

Aewen moved to leave, blinking then gazing at Devlyn again. "If you'll excuse me. Today is a day for celebrating, not dwelling on the Void."

"Thank you for your time, Lady Aewen." She offered a weak smile and left the banquet hall and festivities behind.

Devlyn looked across the space, mystified by this conversation. Merriment filled the room; it was impossible to find anyone not enjoying themselves. Despite his heavy heart at Aewen's words, Devlyn wanted to return to the celebration.

"Why so grim?" Alex scanned the room then slapped Devlyn on the back. "There'll be no melancholy on my wedding day; Diana will have my head! Come, I'm sure Ellendren is dying to dance with you." Alex yanked Devlyn forward, nearly pulling his arm from its socket and pushed him into the crowd of people dancing in the center of the hall.

"You really are incorrigible!" Devlyn shouted over the music which was much louder here.

"My mother is the incorrigible one; you wouldn't believe her involvement in planning this wedding. She still hasn't forgiven me for not bringing her to Everin with us, which, mind you, was under siege by her brother. Once she heard that Diana and I were engaged, she spent the entire time planning and organizing. She practically levitated when she learned the ceremony was to be held here in Elothkar."

"I noticed she even managed to acquire Walei's candies."

"She had them shipped all the way from Ceurenyl now that she knows his source. She wasn't entirely thrilled to discover they're elven in origin, but she's warmed up quite a bit since she left Cor'lera. Old Ents hasn't though, he outright refused my invitation." Alex lowered his voice before adding, conspiratorially, "From the sound of it, he's in loads of trouble with the ei'ceuril; locked himself up in the abbey school and won't permit students to return."

"Is that so?" Aaron was suddenly beside Devlyn.

"Ah, Ceurtriarch," Alex stuttered, embarrassed at being caught gossiping.

"What can you tell me of your uncle? He's been a thorn in my side," Aaron said, hesitating, voice low. "I have reason to suspect he's a steward of shadow."

"I'd be shocked if he wasn't. Remember how he treated you, Dev?"

Devlyn flinched at the reminder of growing up at the abbey school. "I'd rather not."

"We should discuss him more before I leave," Aaron said and pulled away.

"Right." Alex shrugged. "Have you and Ellendren discussed tomorrow?"

"Not yet, but it's not like I can hide anything from her. Have you talked to Diana?"

"Not yet. Didn't want to ruin a perfectly good day." Alex smiled nervously.

"If only there was another way to find out what has happened to Sanjin and the others."

"The Kilnae Del supposedly have ways of communicating across large distances, but Sanjin couldn't leave his mage."

"Solving the problems of the world?" Ellendren asked from behind, accompanied by Danielle, Fyona, and Myranda.

"What do two men know about saving the world?" Myranda asked, a laugh in her voice.

"It's been known to happen before," Alex said.

"On Teraeniel?" Myranda asked, eyeing Alex skeptically.

"Can't imagine where else," Alex said.

"A mystery indeed. Almost as confounding as your union with Diana." Myranda smirked.

"That's not the only impossible union I've heard rumored. Tell me, *Your Majesty*, how did you manage to court a prince of a kingdom that no longer exists?" Alex pried.

"The same way Ellendren and Diana managed it, of course. With my superior intellect and wit, I yanked Gestoria from the forgotten sands of history and willed them to exist once more." The four women laughed while Alex smacked his head.

Ellendren turned to Devlyn, her eyes locked with his, blinking only twice. Whatever Alex and Myranda said next, Devlyn did not hear. Ellendren's hand grasped his own. Her fingers felt delicate, an odd thought since he knew her to be anything but.

Leading him away, Ellendren took him to an exterior balcony that looked over Elothkar. The still night air caressed his skin, his lierathnil a thin barrier to the elements, yet wondrously capable of keeping him warm in the night's chill.

"I caught some of your conversation with Alex earlier," Ellendren confessed.

"What do you think we should do?"

"None of the Charren representatives have reached Arenthyl and only one Daer representative has made the trip. I understand that their continents are far away, but I'm worried something sinister is happening. I also believe Charren and its Kilnae Del will be powerful allies. I can't say the same for the Daer Empire and its Sorcery."

"But?" Devlyn could hear the hesitation in her voice.

"I worry this might be another distraction. The Dark Flight intends to free Tolvenol. They could have already for all we know, and if so, they'll return to Eklean with Tolvenol at the Evil One's behest. Shortly after that, he'll lead the Void beasts against those who reject the Evil One. We both need to be in Eklean when that happens. We'll have to have this conversation with the Guardian Senate, but we will only suffer destruction and a loss of civilian life if we don't take the fight to them when the time comes. Cities will crumble if Void beasts are allowed to siege them."

Devlyn took a deep breath, knowing Ellendren was right. "We'll stop them."

"I hope so. You'll have to leave Alex in Charren, no matter what awaits him there. It's the only way you'll reach Tolvenol's lair before the Dark Flight."

Devlyn nodded, uncomfortable with the idea of abandoning Alex on another continent that neither of them had been to before. Stopping Tolvenol from being freed was a better use of his time than going to Karithel. And even that distracted him from the task of pulling the two mountains down to revive the Tree. But what option did he have?

Ellendren looked past the city and into the ilithae trees that the Aldinari had planted when Thellion had fallen. Her fingers loosened in Devlyn's as she squinted into the dark horizon.

"What are you looking for?" he asked, no longer thinking of Charren.

"Tariel and Aliel are somewhere out there; they're quite fond of each other."

"They must be learning much from each other. Tariel has only known Lumaeniel, while Aliel has known only Teraeniel."

"I think there's more to the story." Ellendren smiled.

Devlyn's mind wasn't on the phoenix. A mischievous smile crept to his lips. "Remember the last time we were alone on a balcony at a feast together? You said something along the lines of people making assumptions about us."

Ellendren blushed. Turning from the ilithae trees, she looked into his golden eyes. Hints of silver lingered in her irises, but the golden light of the phoenix had largely overwhelmed them. Devlyn tried not to grin like an excited boy looking at the woman dreams were made of but knew he had failed miserably.

Stepping closer, Ellendren left room for only a finger between them. She touched her growing belly. "I think they're beyond assumptions."

Unable to restrain himself, Devlyn narrowed the gap, the distance but a memory as his lips met hers. Time slipped away, and he no longer recalled where they stood. Everything concerning him moments ago no longer weighed down on his shoulders.

"You do realize that when the balconies are lit, everyone inside can see you through the windows, which are quite large, mind you." Wyn walked past a slender column entangled with ivy.

"Right." Ellendren pulled away from Devlyn, leaving enough space for two people to pass between them. A single hand rose to her lips, as if to hide any evidence.

"Well, I guess there's no room for assumptions anymore," Devlyn said, looking through one of the large windows Wyn had referred to. Dozens of people pretended not to look, but their quick movements in the opposite direction revealed that they had seen the entire exchange.

"Oh, how embarrassing," Ellendren said. "I want to bond with Tariel and disappear into the night."

"You might have an opposite effect in that dress; it's not lierathnil," Devlyn said.

Ellendren glared daggers at him.

"I'm certain there isn't a single guest who doesn't know your intentions," said Wyn, a slight laugh in his voice.

Straightening, Ellendren resolutely ignored the windows and the wedding guests inside pretending not to look. "Well, we might as well return as dignified as possible. Try not to slouch."

Devlyn huffed a laugh. He hadn't realized he was slouching. Once brought to his attention, he straightened his spine and squared his shoulders, standing taller.

"Better," Ellendren said, still frazzled as she tried to regain control.

"Indeed; the Exalted Aryl in the flesh," said Wyn, clapping Devlyn on the back.

There was no purpose in disguising their relations when returning to the banquet hall, and Devlyn and Ellendren grasped each other's hands. Devlyn felt nervous sweat slicken her palm.

No need for that; they can watch me kiss the love of my life all day if they want. Devlyn shared his thoughts with Ellendren and hopefully only Ellendren.

As if I'd let you kiss me for an entire day. Imagine how chapped our lips would get, Ellendren shared back.

A small sacrifice, Devlyn shared, sending several other images to make her blush.

Ellendren squeezed his fingers, and he felt her smile through their bond. Devlyn saw Alex's grin from across the room. Diana was with him and from their panting, they'd just been dancing.

"Don't worry, no one saw a thing. I made a royal proclamation that no one should look out the windows," Alex stifled a laugh.

Diana slapped his upper arm. "You did no such thing! I can't believe I agreed to marry you. Please forgive my juvenile husband."

"But you did marry me, and you just called me your husband," Alex said, grinning more broadly and wolfishly than when he had seen Devlyn and Ellendren return from the balcony. He wrapped his arms around Diana's waist.

"And don't you forget it." Diana's expression softened to a warm smile, quickly fading when her eyes shifted to Devlyn and Ellendren. "Now apologize to these two lovebirds!"

"I'm sorry for noticing that you left the banquet hall together and continuing to see you from the corner of my eye and for yelping like a schoolboy when I saw you get close to each other and I'm especially sorry for when you finally did kiss, taking way too long to initiate if you ask me…"

Diana slapped him again, audibly harder this time.

"Ow! I'm trying to apologize." Alex rubbed his arm dramatically. "As I was saying, and I'm especially sorry for excitedly hollering 'they're kissing!' for everyone present to hear." Alex wore the most innocent expression Devlyn had ever seen him muster. Not even when they were caught sneaking treats from Vine's kitchen as children had his expression been so irreproachable.

Devlyn felt his cheeks blush a violent red, thinking they must match

Ellendren's cheeks, which not even a sunburn could rival.

"Wyn ruined the moment though; he strolled outside just after my excited declaration, interrupting your special moment, and you two stopped what you were doing and leapt apart as though one caught fire. You can't blame your cousin for getting excited when he sees you displaying your affection."

"Oh, I could blame you for many things, Alexander; Thellish king or not," Ellendren said, now squeezing Devlyn's fingers so hard he was beginning to lose feeling in them.

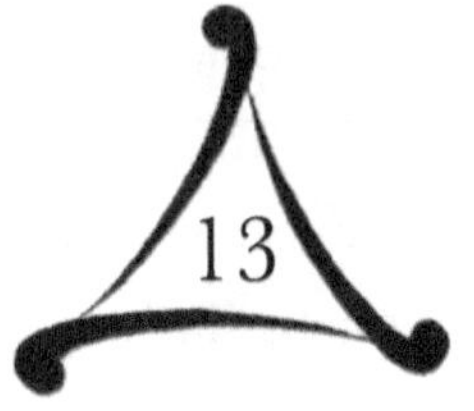

FACADE

Most of the elven entourage huddled around Ellendren, ready to return to Krysenthiel, while another group held hands, waiting for Devlyn to shift them to Charren. Alex was glad Wyn and Alethea had agreed to join him and Aen to find out what was happening there. Aen was particularly ecstatic, for going to Charren meant he finally had his own winged horse. Devlyn wouldn't stay in Charren though. He would continue on to Qien with Viren, Jaerol, Liam, Elayne, and Toryn, accompanied by the dragons, Falthion, Kanastil, and Rusyl.

Alex didn't envy their task. Tolvenol was more likely to swallow them whole before they could kill the old dragon. Alex shared a parting smile with Diana. She wasn't pleased with him leaving the morning after their wedding but understood the necessity of uncovering what was happening in Charren. Their smiles shared yesterday's bliss, both the public ceremony and more private night. Like her mother, Diana was strong and would be a remarkable queen. Thellion would thrive under her leadership; it might even prosper more from his absence. He ignored that last thought when Devlyn bloomed in light as he bonded with Aliel. The transformation still caught Alex off guard, especially now that their sources of light were limited to torches.

He watched Devlyn and Ellendren share a parting smile of their own before they both shifted their groups. The pale granite courtyard they had been standing in disappeared, replaced by a dense jungle on the southern tip of Ogren. Sanjin had told Alex that the entire continent was now under brutish ogre control, every human kingdom on the continent other than Charren having toppled. Shifting to Ogren was risky, but it was safer to come here than to scope out Karithel from Daereneth. For all they knew, the Daer were behind the silence of Prince Sanjin, his hippogriff riders, and the Thellish force led by Oliver.

In the humidity, Alex's skin slickened with sweat. He tore off his overcoat; his tunic would be drenched regardless. What he wouldn't give for trousers that breathed!

Alethea touched Devlyn's face. "Be safe. Be strong."

"And don't be stupid," Wyn added.

"What he said," Alex said, with a wry smirk. He liked Wyn. There were worse partners to be stranded with. The griffins scratched the ground, their dark eyes scanning their surroundings.

"I could say the same of you." Devlyn clapped Alex's shoulder. "Reach out when you're ready to return."

"We will," Alethea said. "Farewell."

A flash of light followed, and the rest of the party vanished with Devlyn. Alex was grateful they had brought their flying mounts with them, but even so, leaving the continent would be no easy task without a Phaedryn to magically shift them. Diana would be irate if he had to waste needless months travelling north from Charren, through Glacien, then back south to Thellion.

Not knowing what dangers they might encounter, Alex gripped the hilt of his sword, but kept it sheathed; Aen copied him. Alethea and Wyn no doubt had their senses open. Alex didn't like the idea of being caught by surprise in an unknown land. He peered through the jungle, trying to see, but the foliage was so thick, his eyes were useless. Worse, the jungle was far from still, with countless animals moving through the trees. The birds singing from above didn't help.

"Have you found anything?" Wyn asked.

"What's there to find but trees? We've only just got here," Alex said.

"It's like the Illumined Wood. I'm surprised humans were able to settle in it," Wyn said.

"I thought it felt familiar," Aen said.

"You can sense it?" Alethea asked.

"Only that it feels familiar."

"What sort of elf-magic are you going on about?" Alex asked.

"Simply being aware of your surroundings. You might try it some-time," Alethea said.

"I'm plenty aware of trees," Alex said, just as an arrow whistled past him, striking the bark of the nearest tree. He yelped and whipped out his sword.

"We mean you no harm," Alethea said, as though she spoke to a friend.

"You say that easily enough yet appear in our forest by neither wing nor foot." A ring of centaurs closed around them, all with nocked arrows on taut bowstrings.

"We were brought here by a Phaedryn who can shift between loca-tions. We came from Eklean," Alethea said.

"Phaedryn are not known to us, but the Daer Sorcery is. Do you also imprison anadel in talismans, stored away for your abuse?" the cen-taur who had first spoken asked.

"I am Alethea Lenwyn. Wyn Lierafen and I are children of Eldin-are. And they are Alexander Vaerin, King of Thellion, and his squire, Aen Finamarc. We practice no Sorcery. The phoenix, Aliel, chose to bond with Devlyn Lorenthien. I'm sorry you missed them. They won't be coming back to this spot."

"The Lorenthien name is not unknown to us." The centaur tow-ered over the group, approaching Alethea and Wyn. "But we better re-member Lenwyn and Lierafen from long ago. I am Deothoril," he said. The centaurs lowered their bows.

"Eldinare still floats over Ogren, watching down on this special forest," Alethea said.

"You've been here before?" Alex asked.

"Long ago. The Eldinari almost migrated here, but the humidity would have been unkind to our Stellendae trees."

"Why have you come to Ogren? It is not safe, especially for anadel," Deothoril said.

"We've come to find soldiers in my service, as well as find out what's happening in Karithel," Alex said.

"Why is Ogren unsafe for anadel?" Alethea asked.

"The Daer poach anadel for their Sorcery. The deeper one goes into the forest, the safer it is for them. But as you know, anadel are not meant to be limited to one area. They need to roam and move about the world. Odd things happen when there are too many in one place and too few in another," Deothoril said.

"How is it safer the deeper one goes into the forest? Don't ogres control those lands?" Alex asked, getting a chuckle from Alethea. "What's so funny?"

"What do you know of ogres?" Deothoril asked.

"That they burned every human kingdom and settlement here," Alex said confidently.

"Those humans once lived in small tribes with and in communion with the forest, ogres included. That changed when the Daer arrived on our shores. The tribes were appropriated into Daer society. They built cities and felled swaths of the forest to do so. The ogres and centaurs watched in agony. But they did not attack any humans until it became clear they were harvesting Ogren for anadel. The human kingdoms, save Charren, poached anadel for the Daer Sorcery."

"That's horrible," Wyn said.

"Indeed. The Daer will enslave anything that lives," Deothoril said.

Alex suddenly grew nervous about the Daer colonizing Eklean. He'd spoken with some of them, and while he didn't necessarily trust them, he hadn't gleaned any ill intentions from them either; certainly not an intent to poach anadel. But neither had he known to explicitly ask.

"So, you're saying the ogres are the good guys?" Alex balked at the notion.

"They fight an endless war with the Daer Empire and their Sorcery," Deothoril said.

"Fine. The Daer are slaving bastards. We already knew that. What about Prince Sanjin and those with him? Where's my bloody army?" Alex said.

"A Charrenese fort overlooking the coast isn't far from here, an outpost of Karithel. You'll find your army there. As for the prince, he likely returned to Karithel," Deothoril said.

"Will you take us to the outpost?" Alex asked. He needed to know what had happened to his soldiers and friends.

"I can but know that I do not know who controls it." Deothoril said.

"Are you suggesting my army could be captive?"

"It's possible. The outcome could be worse if the Daer or their allies hold it."

Alex didn't like that. Was Charren ally or foe? His only interaction with Charren had been when Sanjin and his entourage had come to Eklean to find allies. He now worried whether the need for allies was less to fight off the Daer and more to secure Sanjin's place at court.

Deothoril alone took them through the jungle. The rest of the centaurs vanished back into the trees, there being no need for them all to escort the small group from Eklean. Alex grumbled about what he would do if he learned his soldiers were being sold off as slaves in Daereneth.

At times, it felt as though they were going deeper into the tangled mass of trees and vines. After a few hours, the trees thinned and Alex could just make out a fort in the distance. The closer they came to it, the better he was able to see its defenses. Although the walls looked sturdy enough, they had a slight outward curve and thinned as they rose. Presumably, it was to stop anyone from scaling them. Deothoril stopped at the jungle's edge. "It is not safe for me to leave these trees."

"And we're to assume it's safe for us?" Alex quipped.

"Regardless of who holds the fort, you'll be more welcomed than I."

"Why is that?" Wyn asked.

"We centaur are known allies to the ogres. Even Charrenese do not fully understand the ogres' role in protecting the anadel here. They only see ogres as monsters who slaughter humans without understanding why," Deothoril said. Alex held back another quip.

"May the miervae you guard grant her fruit and shade for all the days to come," Alethea said, pressing her palm to her chest then bowing.

"You honor us, Alethea Lenwyn." He dipped his head.

"People of every land and race gather in Arenthyl for the Guardian Senate. Teraeniel would benefit if representatives of your clan and the ogres could sit on that body," Wyn said.

"The stars have long sung of anacordel returning to the lost valley. I'll relay your message to the ogre chiefs."

"Thank you, Deothoril," Wyn said as the centaur vanished into the jungle. The group left the shade of the trees and approached the fort. The gates were sealed, and no guards patrolled outside its walls. Alex thought that odd. Even in wartime, gates were only shut at night or when under siege.

"Is anyone there?" Alex called out impatiently.

"Who goes there?" The Parendian accent was unmistakable.

"Your king, come to find out why I haven't received any reports, not even a message that you reached Charren," Alex called.

The gates swung open to a busy yard where Thellish soldiers, all in short sleeves and sweating in Ogren's humidity, practiced swordplay, archery, or hand-to-hand combat. Those who weren't training busied themselves with upkeep and repairs around the fort.

A man dressed in Charrenese style emerged from the castle. He did not hurry to greet the newcomers but walked slowly, evidently to avoid sweating although his silky black hair was damp with it. "I am Tenir al Fosi. What brings you to Castle Mavarre?"

"I am King Alexander of Thellion and I wish to speak to Sanjin, Oliver, Reia, and Sara."

"I apologize, but His Highness is not here, nor are the general and ei'ana who accompanied him," Tenir said.

"And where have they gone?" Alex asked.

"To Karithel, of course. It was my understanding that His Highness sought to claim his father's throne," Tenir said.

"And when did they leave for Karithel?"

"It must have been six months ago, at least."

"And you haven't inquired about not receiving any reports from him?" Alex grumbled.

"The late king's advisor regularly sends me updates. He relays that His Highness and guests are quite comfortable."

"And why did I have to come all this way to find out they are *comfortable*? I have not received any messages from them." Alex asked, his patience strained.

"I cannot say why. Perhaps the distance is too great for messenger birds."

Or to lure me here. Alex didn't like this. Tenir's responses offered no elaboration. The gate had already closed, despite no immediate threat. "Why keep the gate shut?" Alex asked.

"Ogren is not a hospitable land. Ogres are known to attack and burn any human settlement they come across."

Alex looked about the yard again, suspicious. The soldiers seemed well fed and healthy, but none made eye contact with him. He scanned the yard, tallying the soldiers present, then frowned.

"I sent a force four times what I see here. Where are the others?"

"I don't know what you're referring to."

"There's the lie," Alethea said.

Alex unsheathed his sword, its tip a finger away from Tenir's throat. "Where are they?" Alex asked, slowly and deliberately. He spun around. "Where are your comrades?" he shouted to his soldiers in the yard.

The faux training stopped and a hush fell over the fort. No one spoke, although some seemed to be straining to speak. "Their minds are troubled, tortured with threats. But I wonder whose lives are being threatened? The soldiers present here or those missing?" Alethea asked.

"The fort is largely empty," Wyn said.

Tenir's right eye ticked nervously as he seemed to seek an exit. That meant he was alone.

"Where are they?" Alex pressed, his teeth clenched tightly. Wherever they were, they were undoubtedly prisoners.

"There you are," Alethea said to herself, then raised her voice to address Alex. "You can tell your soldiers here that I've found their companions in the mines below this fort. No harm will come to them now by betraying Tenir."

"You heard her," he hollered, the tip of his blade still at Tenir's throat. "Who ordered you to enslave my army in your mines?"

Sweat beaded at Tenir's temple as he fumbled in his robe. Alex glanced down quickly and saw a crystalline object. Intricate silverwork tied the crystal together, forming a beautifully crafted infinite spiral. Despite its beauty, Alex couldn't help imagining it as a cage.

"You have no power here," Tenir said, his lip twitching into a smirk.

"What is it you hold?" Alex kept his sword at Tenir's throat.

"Power." Wind exploded outward from Tenir, throwing Alex back. Their mounts panicked, whinnying and rearing in the volatile wind, as soldiers ducked and covered their eyes. This wasn't the first time they had witnessed this power. Alex didn't care to ask if Tenir was wielding or doing whatever it was the Sorcery did. He didn't think this had anything to do with the mages of the Kilnae Del since the arcane gems they used had colors associated with them.

Alethea and Wyn were unaffected by the blast, although their hair whipped about their faces. Tenir clearly saw them as his true adversaries, not the king with a sword and a bad temper. Alex sought Aen and found him pressed to the ground, hands over his head. Debris mixed with dirt flew about, stinging Alex's eyes. Not wanting to interrupt the elves' magic, Alex crawled toward Tenir, sword in hand. Tenir still gripped the talisman; whatever magic he accessed flowed from it. Alex surmised he would be powerless without it. He just had to separate it from him.

A daunting task considering the gale.

Elbows scraped on dirt as he crawled, each forward movement harder than the last. The wind intensified the closer he drew to Tenir. Unsure whether he'd be able to stand to properly to strike, Alex slashed his sword at Tenir's calf. Tenir screamed as blood seeped into his robe.

He spun on Alex, fury in his eyes. He still gripped the talisman, knowing he was defeated or dead without it. The gale focused anew on Alex, giving slight relief to the others. Eyes on Tenir, Alex barely heard the snap of a bowstring but saw the arrow slice through Tenir's wrist causing him to scream in agony, dropping the talisman. The wind stopped at once. Alex looked about and saw Aen standing by his winged horse, bow in hand.

Wyn wielded dirt and stone to contain Tenir, a prisoner in his own fort.

Tenir looked back spitefully. "He will end you," he snarled.

"Who?" Alex asked but another arrow barreled into Tenir's throat before he could answer. Alex spun toward Aen, but the boy's bow was hitched over his shoulder. "Who did that?" Alex demanded as Tenir slumped forward, dead; his ghost drifted out of his body. The soldiers in the yard looked confused. No one had a bow nor had anyone seen who shot it. Whoever it was wanted Tenir dead before he could reveal his secrets. That didn't bode well for Alex. Another enemy was hidden among them.

Wyn released his wield and Tenir's body slumped to the ground. Alethea picked up the talisman. "So, the Sorcery has been adopted in Charren."

"Do you think he referred to the Evil One?" Wyn asked.

"Doubtful. There is another player here," Alethea said.

Alex glanced across the yard. "Well, whoever it is, they're not here. And if they intend to pay us a visit, I'd prefer this fort in a more defensible position and no longer a slave camp. Who's next in charge here?" Alex yelled so everyone could hear, ignoring the present threat of Tenir's killer.

A man with a bruised eye stepped forward. "I'm Second Lieutenant Kam Seirsen. The first lieutenants and captains are all in the mines below."

"Are the mines dangerous?" Alex asked.

"I can't say, Your Majesty. None of us here were taken down. Tenir wanted anyone who came looking to find us healthy and busy at our posts." Kam said, scowling at the dead captor.

"Well, let's be sure that the next bastard who tries to inspect this fort finds it fully staffed and capable of repelling any threat."

"Understood, Your Majesty."

"Find out what's being mined and if we can use it. I want every soldier down in those mines released and whatever injuries they might have seen to."

"What about the others?" Kam asked.

"What others?" Alex asked.

"Tenir was overseeing the mines and its slaves long before we arrived."

"Have them all brought to the surface and cared for. We need to find out what's been happening here."

Mountainous Rage

Monumental, red-lacquered doors, ornately carved with serpentine dragons, flowers, and people, towered before Devlyn. He had visited Her Radiance's Palace of Celestial Bells once before and knew better than to shift inside the palace, and certainly not into any of the gardens, lest he ignore Qien's customs again. In his defense, Kai had chosen the location to intentionally get Empress Qien Wei's attention. She was not a woman to be summoned, least of all in her own palace.

The small group from Arenthyl had been brought directly to the throne room, as though the Qien had been expecting them ever since the sky had darkened and the dead became visible. The bronze bell above them bonged thunderously as the large doors scraped open.

The throne room was just as Devlyn remembered it, although now he knew the hundreds of jade statues twining up the columns were living dragons, frozen in place. He marveled at what the throne room must have been like with the dragons awake, moving about the columns. Extra braziers filled the room, adding light and warmth in the absence of the sun.

Devlyn led the others forward, while Aliel fluttered about the tall columns, shining his own light onto the frozen dragons, bringing forth an inner light in their eyes. The largest of the dragons was at the far end of the hall, and atop the massive, sinuous Guanxi sat Empress Qien Wei, resplendent in imperial gold accented with reds.

Kneeling at the clawed feet of her dragon throne were Di in orange and Kai in red, their heads shaved.

"We welcome you back to Qien, Devlyn, Aliel, and guests," the empress spoke. "Our representatives are enroute to Arenthyl to take their place on the Guardian Senate. What more do you request of Qien? Our resources are stretched thin as civil wars grip our empire."

"Thank you for welcoming us to your illustrious court. Your Radiance honors us. I'm afraid I bring ill tidings. The Dark Flight flies to free their Primus, Tolvenol. They will burn every monastery to achieve their goal."

Wei's lips thinned. "How can you be certain?"

"We have tracked their movement west. It won't be long until they cross the Misty Sea," Jaerol said, head bowed. Liam and Rusyl bowed their heads as well.

"A Cyndinari." Wei settled her gaze on Jaerol. "Are We to believe you betrayed your people and emperor?" Her distaste for traitors was clear.

"The Erynien Emperor has long been a disciple of the Evil One. I pray the rest of my people realize what they have done before it is too late," Jaerol replied sincerely.

"We have no reason to doubt the Dark Flight's motives now that the Evil One is freed and plagues Teraeniel with his Void," Devlyn said, bringing the conversation back to why they had come to Qien.

"We trust you did not come here just to warn us."

"We intend to go to the volcano and kill Tolvenol before the Dark Flight can free him."

"The Great Dragon cannot be killed. The jade dragons and Qien monks of old would have done the deed if it was possible."

"We must try, even though we do not expect to succeed." Devlyn paused at the admission. "If we fail, we will make for the Bowl of Theniel. We believe the merpeople might have some insight in waking the jade dragons."

"And why would you assume the merpeople would know where my people have failed?" Wei's tone took a dangerous edge. Devlyn couldn't tell whether she disliked the merpeople or whether her animosity reflected Qien's failure.

"Because the merpeople have long fought the sea drakes."

Wei's nails dug into her throne. "You would do well to remember not to speak of the betrayers in this hall."

"I apologize, Your Radiance." Devlyn dipped his head. He couldn't anger the empress any more than he already had. "The merpeople's proximity to the *betrayers* might hold the answer to waking the jade dragons. If the Jade Flight truly know Tolvenol's weakness, we must wake them."

A silence passed. Devlyn didn't know what else to add. He feared Wei would further isolate her dynasty. Even if the jade dragons were woken, would she command them to remain in Qien to end the rebellions striking up across the continent?

"And if you fail and cannot slay the Great Dragon—as you fear will be the outcome—how are we to defend ourselves against the Dark Flight?" Wei asked.

"They will know to target the monasteries. They will slaughter every monk that now binds Tolvenol."

"We see." Wei glanced sadly at her son. "Qien will fracture. The hundred kingdoms will name it my failure and inability to reign if the Great Dragon is released and the monks slaughtered." She stepped down from her dragon throne. "If *I* do not return, my death will alleviate some of the harm. Our dynasty might survive, but not if I remain behind our walls. Be strong Qien Di; you will make a great emperor." Devlyn's eyes widened at her decision.

"Mother—you can't." Di's voice cracked.

"I must. If we fail, the monks must release their hold over the Great Dragon, so they might fight another day. Send missives in Our name to the monasteries of Beishi, Dongshi, Nanshi, and Xishi that they are to empty in three days. Ensure they preserve as many relics and scrolls as possible. If the Great Dragon is freed, he will not look kindly on the places that held him captive. The adjacent cities are also to evacuate." She turned to Devlyn. "The jade dragons must be woken. Promise me you'll find a way."

"I promise, but that doesn't mean I'll let you die." Devlyn didn't know what else there was to say. The empress had just said she was joining them and would all but march to her death.

A small bell rang somewhere and dozens of attendants rushed into the throne room. The empress extended her arms. There was a moment of hesitation from the attendants, but they didn't question the silent demand. They unravelled her imperial robes, then removed her crown and placed it on the dragon throne. Beneath the heavy robes, Wei wore a simple red outfit, similar to Kai's monastic garb. She squeezed Kai's hand. "Thank you for coming home." Then, she cupped her son's face. "Be strong—our dynasty depends on you, as does all Qien."

Di nodded, blinking back tears as his mother approached Devlyn. "It's time," she said, taking command of the situation. Symbolic though her change of garments had been, it altered little in Devlyn's view. She was still very much Empress Qien Wei. Like her attendants, Devlyn knew not to question her.

Devlyn and Aliel bonded, flooding the room in light. Viren, Jaerol, Liam, Elayne, Toryn, and the three dragons in their smaller forms came forward and joined hands after Wei took Devlyn's hand, forming a circle. He closed his eyes and visualized the volcano and one of its smaller vents leading into the core.

The throne room with its many columns vanished, replaced by a black sky and smoke spewing out the volcano. "Is it safe to go in?" Toryn asked, gripping her sword tightly.

"There are few places more dangerous." Wei stepped forward, and the others followed.

Devlyn and Aliel remained bonded, their light providing little help as they entered the cavernous tunnel. Its volcanic walls were glassy black, but there were no reflections as the dark walls drank in the light. The group quietly went further into the cavern, barely daring to breathe.

Wei strode forward, back straight, resolute in her decision to kill Tolvenol or die trying to save her dynasty. The volcano was massive, and it felt like they had walked for hours, as the temperature steadily rose the deeper they went.

The darkness shifted when the tunnel opened to a large cavern. A red glow from lava barely illuminated the all-consuming darkness and explained the unbearable temperatures. Sweat clung to Devlyn's body and his breathing labored, each breath feeling as though it might be his last.

Peering around the large cavern, Devlyn looked for Tolvenol. He had assumed the dragon would be easy to find. Tolvenol was said to be one of the largest dragons in existence. It was not like they could miss him. Several tunnels split off from the cavern and Devlyn feared they'd never find the dragon in the maze of volcanic tunnels.

He tapped his inner sense. He felt the volcano first. It thrust outward after eons of eruptions, beginning before the Children first woke. It was still active and would continue to expand; judging by the insufferable heat, it would erupt soon. He realized they were only halfway to the volcano's core. The maze of tunnels and caverns were extensive and only became more tangled. If they weren't careful, they could easily find themselves lost here with no hope of escaping. Only Devlyn could shift out of the volcano at will. The others had to rely on him to get them out alive; splitting up would prove disastrous.

Sensing the fires churning in the volcano, Devlyn wondered if any ignys anadel called this place home. Would they respond to him if he called out to them? Feeling like he had limited options, he sought out an anadel as the group crossed the large cavern. They couldn't afford to stop. There was no telling when the Dark Flight would reach the first monastery.

"Foolish to enter a mountain of fire." The group paused at the crackling voice just ahead, its owner not revealing herself.

"Show yourself," Wei commanded.

"You might be Empress of Qien, but your authority does not extend to my kind."

"What are you?" Wei asked, her voice iron-like.

Devlyn sensed the being. "You're an ignys anadel."

"Why did you call out to me?" A fiery form appeared before the group.

The others stared at Devlyn, their expressions clearly showing they thought he was mad for possibly alerting Tolvenol of their presence. "How do we reach Tolvenol's lair? We'll get lost without help."

"You're already lost if you think you can defeat the Dark Primus in his lair. Even when subdued, he is beyond your ability. Leave this place with your lives while you still can."

"The Dark Flight is heading here to release him," Devlyn said.

"And you aim to kill him before they do."

"Will you help us?"

"You are a fool to try—only the jade dragons know Tolvenol's weakness."

"Yes, I've heard."

"Then why are you here and not seeking a way to wake them? You will not strip the Evil One of his greatest general without their help."

"We must try first. Qien will burn if he is freed," Wei said.

Smoke billowed about the ignys anadel, turning red as fire blossomed. "What do you fear for more? Qien or the Qien Dynasty, Empress?"

"To care for one is to care for the other. Qien has only known peace when the hundred kingdoms are united under our dynasty."

"Does Qien want your peace?"

"Civil wars are already here. We cannot afford to be divided in these dark days."

The ignys anadel seemed to consider Wei's words, her form smoldering like a hot coal. "The Evil One desires a fractured Qien. I will show you the way but know that you will not succeed today." The anadel led them across the cavern and into one its offshoots. Their path split many more times and the already unbearable heat intensified. Devlyn dabbed again at his forehead, his sleeve damp from the repeated action.

A low hum tickled his ears. It started so softly that Devlyn hadn't picked it up at first. Now, it sent goosebumps across his skin, not so much a hum but a rumble; the sound of a giant beast asleep. "Does anyone else hear that?" he asked.

"We are close," Viren said in confirmation.

The ignys anadel vanished. What did an anadel have to fear from a dragon? Devlyn had known this would be dangerous, but he now realized he hadn't fully comprehended how foolish this expedition would be. He felt Ellendren's mental agreement.

The tunnel opened to an enormous cavern billowing with smoke. The smell of sulfur hung in the air and Devlyn again wondered how soon this volcano would erupt. The ground fell away in abrupt black cliffs, mingling with the red glow of lava below. The rocky terrain of hardened lava rose and fell. Devlyn peered through the smoky haze, but even with his Aliel-sharpened sight, he couldn't see any dragon here.

The rumbling had been at its loudest just before they entered the volcano's core, but now the only sound was the crackling and bubbling of the lava as the pressure in the core intensified. The group huddled closely, keeping their eyes peeled for the Dark Primus. They stayed near the exit, not wanting to become trapped in Tolvenol's lair by some trickery.

A deep laugh filled the cavern, hanging in the air, prideful and hungry. "Do you know how long it has been since I last feasted? And what a feast it shall be—elves, dragons, an empress, and a phoenix."

Devlyn's head snapped about as he searched for the seemingly invisible dragon. He could sense the mighty dragon's presence, so overwhelming he didn't have to tap his inner sense. Then, the ground shifted. His eyes widened as he realized anew just how foolish this mission was. They weren't standing on hardened lava, but on Tolvenol! The dragon's scales rippled as though to relieve an itch.

A head, larger than most buildings, lifted from the lava where Tolvenol lay. Large black eyes reflected the small, terrified group who had thought they could slay a dragon.

"Ah, the woman demanding my seed told me about your kind— elves who learned to bond with anadel. Tell me, how is my son? Erynor, I believe she named him. I was promised he would dominate the world and end your kind." The group remained quiet, too scared to speak. "Well?" Tolvenol snarled impatiently. "I've been asleep for a very long time. I feel the eons that have passed, and I also sense my flight coming to release me. Now answer my questions before I feast on your flesh and bones." His tone snapped at the end, fire gurgling in his throat.

"An egg was hidden, kept secret," Devlyn stuttered. He tried to steady his voice, but Tolvenol's presence stripped him of that dignity. He was surprised he could speak at all. "The rest he slaughtered. He killed the elf and your other son, Ythinor, consumed the phoenix."

Tolvenol purred, licking his lips in hunger. "I'm sure the lumenys anadel were delectable. And how ever prophetic of my children."

"How do you mean?" Devlyn squeaked.

"We will devour the Light, and in creation's place there will only be the Void. The Master will purify what Anaweh sullied. The Tree is dead. The fool turned into a tree for the sake of creation. And now the Tree is dead." Tolvenol roared in delight.

Coming to their senses, the small group backed away slowly. They had to get away. There was nothing they could do to fight this beast. Swords were mere needles beside Tolvenol. How had the jade dragons and monks subdued him?

"And where do you think you're going? You've only just arrived." Tolvenol's tail whipped from the far end of the cavern and slammed down behind them, blocking their exit. "Don't you want to witness my glorious return before the volcano ends you? I could quicken your death and end you myself, of course. But I do not desire to deprive you of witnessing true power. You'll have eternity to serve the Master once your meddlesome bodies melt away."

Peering around, knowing that they were trapped, Devlyn looked for any surface that was not the dragon. Shifting out of the volcano was their only recourse. But they would bring Tolvenol with them if they shifted while standing on top of him. Not that it would matter much. The Dark Primus would be free within a matter of days.

Qien needed those days to evacuate the monasteries and nearby cities.

"It won't be long now, my pets." Tolvenol turned away from them, and tenebrys-laced fire poured out his maw as he roared up at the sealed caldera. Confident there was nothing Devlyn and the others could do to him, Tolvenol ignored them.

"Everyone hold hands and on the count of three, jump," Devlyn said. They all nodded, Wei included, too terrified to voice a rebuke. Nothing would be gained by her death here. If Devlyn hadn't already forced himself to speak to Tolvenol he doubted he would have been able to speak now. His throat was raw and he coughed from the sulfuric smoke. They clasped hands in a circle, but Devlyn saw Jaerol had his sword free and eyed the dragon's scaly back. "One. Two." Jaerol thrust- ed his sword between two of Tolvenol's massive scales, wedging it deep inside. The dragon roared in agony as Devlyn yelled, "THREE." They jumped and just as Tolvenol snapped his teeth at them, Devlyn shifted them away to just outside the volcano where they had entered.

Soot covered everyone and they coughed, trying to expel toxic gases and sucking in fresh air. They could hear Tolvenol roar from within, shaking the ground. The entire continent likely heard the promise of his return.

"Is everyone okay?" Elayne asked, once the violent roar settled. Jaerol's sword sheath was empty.

"We have failed." Wei looked back into the volcanic tunnel, defeated. "I will not return to court as empress."

"Qien needs you. This war is only just starting," Devlyn said.

"Qien Di will take the throne as emperor. If I return, the hundred kingdoms will hold me accountable for Tolvenol's release. They will turn away from the Qien Dynasty and either try to claim my throne or divide the continent into fractured dynasties, returning us to a warring people. Our culture will be lost as we destroy ourselves faster and more viciously than even the Great Dragon would."

Devlyn stood stunned until Elayne spoke, her voice hard. "You cannot roam the wilderness alone and I don't take you as one to simply give up."

"Come with us to the Bowl of Theniel; help us wake the jade dragons. Retake your place on Guanxi, not in a throne room, but in the sky," Devlyn said.

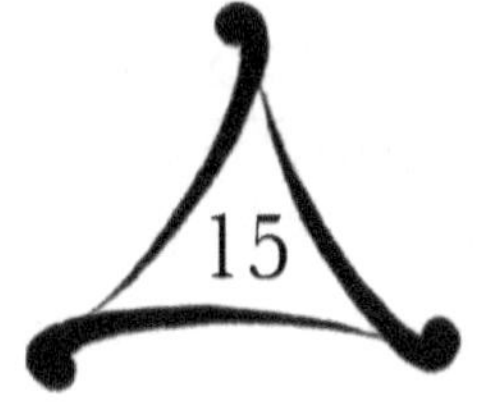

UNWELCOMED

Devlyn shifted the small party to the southwest coast of Qien. They stood on a sandy beach and looked across the ocean, squinting toward the horizon. Waves lapped the beach, their rhythmic and calming sound making Devlyn want to lie down and rest, if only for a moment. Going into Tolvenol's mountain had left them all tired. They couldn't stop to rest though, not now.

Only Wei didn't face the ocean. Instead, she looked east as though she could take in the entirety of her empire. She claimed she was no longer empress, but Devlyn had difficulty imagining her as anything but. Her posture and bearing declared her identity better than any throne would. So long as Qien Wei breathed, she would be Empress of the Qien Dynasty.

Toryn came up beside him, thumbing her sword hilt.

"How are you holding up?" Devlyn asked.

"I should have done as Jaerol did and stabbed the beast," she said.

"Knowing it wouldn't have killed it?"

"Not yet at least." Jaerol and Liam approached the group, nodding to Elayne and Toryn. "Next time you or whoever has to confront that beast of a dragon, be sure to look for my sword, wedged between his scales."

"You want me to retrieve your sword for you?" Devyn asked.

"He wants you to capitalize on the puncture," Elayne said, smiling at Jaerol proudly. "I wish I had thought of it myself. I doubt we'll have another opportunity to create such a vulnerability again."

"I had a good teacher," Jaerol said.

"I'm glad to see you both took those lessons to heart. With any luck your sword will be known as Dragonsbane," Elayne said. Kanastil snarled. "Dark-Dragonsbane," Elayne amended.

"I would like my sword back when this is all said and done," Jaerol said, mostly to Devlyn.

"I would as well," Viren said, sharing a rare smile. "So, do we have any idea how we might cross this ocean and reach the Bowl of Theniel? There's no telling how far we'd have to fly."

"Flying would be easiest, but its location is a bit of a mystery. Only the merpeople know the Bowl of Theniel's location. All we know for certain is that it lies somewhere in the ocean between Qien, Ogren, Daereneth, and Ja'horan," Devlyn said.

"That's not exactly encouraging, is it?" Jaerol said.

"A port city is not far from here—Dozha." Wei had been quiet until now, reflective. "If not for the rise in terrain we'd be able to see it. It's why I recommended this location. It also happens to be the capital of this kingdom."

"Why not shift closer to the city?" Liam looked at the hills she referenced.

"Because its king has declared his kingdom an enemy of the Qien Dynasty."

"Oh. That's a good reason. How do they feel about dragons and elves with magic birds?" Toryn asked.

"Aliel is not a magic bird," Devlyn said.

"And do you want to explain your connection with a phoenix—an anadel—to enemies of the Qien Dynasty?" Toryn asked, before adding apologetically, "Ei'denai."

"She makes a fair point. It'll be difficult enough to explain our arrival as it is. A magic bird is an easier answer than letting them know you're a Phaedryn. And since the only two Phaedryn are the Exalted Aryl, it won't take much for them to figure out who you are," Viren said.

How do you feel about being a magic bird? Devlyn conveyed to Aliel.

It's better than riding in a carriage, Aliel returned.

"All right, so we pretend we're not who we really are. That still doesn't help us find the Bowl of Theniel. Is there a chance that we'll be able to hire a ship to take us?" Devlyn looked at his companions.

"The kings here have long boasted of having the most complete map of this ocean. They have claimed to have visited the merpeople's home. A cyclone wider than most kingdoms is said to prevent ships from passing. No ship that risked drawing near has ever returned. But it's rumored the waters within the cyclone are so calm you can see your reflection in them, as well as the merpeople's realm below," Wei said.

"Would this king tell us how to reach it?" Devlyn asked.

"Doubtful. Nor would he lend us a ship and crew to sail there, certainly not to me. I'll keep my face hidden in Dozha. Wei is common enough that you may still call me that but refrain from my full name. No one will mistake Qien Wei if they hear it. I'll act as your translator. My Dozhan could use refinement and they'll easily recognize my imperial accent, but it should suffice."

"Dozhan? Does every kingdom here have their own language?" Devlyn asked, as Wei started to walk away from the ocean.

"The more remote a kingdom, the more distinct their regional dialect is and the Dozhan peninsula is as remote as it gets. The monasteries all speak the imperial dialect, even those here. It's a necessity since the monks are from all over the dynasty and are expected to live communally with monks from other kingdoms."

Wei led the way, telling them more about the continent's varied cultures and languages, all united under the Qien Dynasty. The city wasn't far and the walking helped clear their heads after the recent confrontation in the volcano. The city walls were soon in view, a tiered castle safely behind the walls perched over the city. As they approached the city gate, a strong scent of fish assaulted their noses. Even if the ocean wasn't visible from here, there was no denying that this was a port city by the stench.

The guards at the gate appraised the curious party, noting the unfamiliar elves, three of them much larger than the others, a hooded Qien woman, and the phoenix. A guard said something, and Wei interpreted for him, "What brings you to Dozha?" The guards' eyes did not shift away from Aliel, worrying Devlyn.

"Tell him we're seeking passage on a ship to Charren," Devlyn said; it wasn't a complete lie, as he would have to return to Charren. Wei translated and Devlyn had difficulty identifying one word from another. He felt foolish for not thinking to absorb a sophilliae that contained the Qien language. He had visited the Sophillium before Alex's wedding, but at the time, he had not known he would be travelling to Qien.

"They want to know what your bird is and if you're willing to sell it," Wei said.

"Tell them I have no interest in selling…" he coughed, stopping himself from naming Aliel, "…my magic bird."

Wei told the guards Aliel was not for sale. Despite being the most powerful person in Qien, she adopted her role as a subservient translator remarkably well.

The guard pulled out a coin pouch and lobbed it up and down, eyeing Devlyn as though he was a fool to deny him. "I said no," Devlyn said forcefully, his raised voice attracting the attention of several guards from the gatehouse. That was the last thing any of them wanted, especially Qien Wei.

A guard hollered from beyond the gate. Devlyn couldn't understand what he was saying, but his tone implied he was upset. Hopefully he was only upset with the guard who was trying to purchase Aliel. Surely that sort of practice wasn't accepted. But the captain turned on Devlyn and started yelling at him. Confused, Devlyn looked at Wei. She shook her head and began speaking to the captain, likely explaining the situation. The captain wouldn't hear it, and instead smacked Wei hard across the face, making her stumble back, shocked at being hit.

The elves sucked in their breaths. This man, whether he knew it or not, had just sentenced himself to death. By her steady and serious tone, Wei said something threatening in reply. She might have tried to remain unknown, but she could not permit anyone to strike her. Devlyn realized that she was pulling the elemental erendinth into herself and wielding all four together in a wield Devlyn didn't recognize. She laced animys into it and threw the captain into the wall.

Her crimson hood fell back and the surrounding guards recognized her. Several fell to their knees, mumbling apologies and oaths to Qien Wei, despite their king's dissent. Although the regional dialect was different, Devlyn recognized Your Radiance, having heard the honorific in Zhongshi.

Banishing the meekness she had pretended, Wei spoke, using the more clipped imperial dialect, her voice steely. Devlyn still couldn't understand what she was saying, but she reclaimed her mantle of authority and the guards stepped into line. They opened a path for them to pass and Wei replaced her hood to cover her face. She looked back at the others, expecting them to follow her into the crowded city where carts creaked past and callers yelled their wares to potential clients.

"What did you say? I thought they wouldn't welcome you as empress." Devlyn asked.

"Even the Dozhan king wouldn't dare shun me to my face. Whether they like it or not, *We* are Empress of the Qien Dynasty," she said, her spine straightening with every word. Devlyn wondered if that meant she still saw herself in that capacity. "I told them the truth. The Qien monks won't be able to contain the Great Dragon. He will be freed, and we are on a quest to wake the jade dragons. I ordered them to tell no one and not follow us. I expect them to ignore both demands."

"And where are they following us to?" Devlyn asked. They weren't headed for the castle.

"I know someone who is frequently in port here. If luck is with us, she'll be here today."

"A friend?" Viren asked, staying close to Devlyn.

"To be determined. But she has a ship."

Devlyn didn't ask any more questions, following Wei through the city and toward the docks. Dozens of ships were moored in the harbor, sails folded, as others waited to dock. Wei paused, looked around, and went toward an impressive ship. She strode up the unattended gang-plank, trailed by the others, then knocked on a cabin door.

There was no answer and just as Wei was about to knock again, a burly man came up from behind them. "The captain doesn't like visitors," he said, in the Common Tongue.

"Tell your captain to make an exception," Wei turned and dropped her hood.

The man's eyes widened in recognition. "Your Radiance," he stuttered.

"Do keep that quiet. We are not welcome in this city," Wei said.

The man kept his head bowed. Anyone looking would know he was speaking to someone important. Devlyn hoped none of the guards from the gate had followed them.

"I've carried precious and occasionally illicit cargo before, but none come near to Your Radiance," a voice said from the deck above. A woman leaned over the railing, looking down at the party and Qien empress. "To what do I owe the pleasure, *sister*? Or would you demand I address you only as Your Radiance and risk being chased out of court again?"

"Qien Fei. We need to speak," said Wei.

"We already are. Or is there a ritual I've forgotten that's required to speak with you? It has been an awfully long time since I was last at court."

"Please, sister, it's urgent and we're running out of time."

"What is so critical that the Empress of the Qien Dynasty begs before her exiled sibling?"

"The Great Dragon will soon be freed."

"That's impossible. The monks contain him. Why would they release him?" Fei asked.

"He is also known as Tolvenol and is Primus of the Dark Flight. That same dragon flight is flying here as we speak. If the monks don't release Tolvenol first, the Dark Flight will raze every monastery," Devlyn said.

"And who are your informed elven companions? I had thought my sister had employed you as a guard, but I'm thinking that's not the case, is it?"

"I'm Devlyn Lorenthien, Exalted Aryl of Krysenthiel, High King of Eklean, and Prelate of the Guardian Senate. Liam and Jaerol are studying to become ei'ana. Viren, Elayne, and Toryn are Guardian knights. Rusyl, Falthion, and Kanastil are dragons of the Blue and White Flights. We've come to find a way to wake the jade dragons."

"Then why are you here in Dozha and not wherever you need to be to wake them?" Fei asked, her gaze lingering on the dragons in their smaller forms.

"Because we need to reach the Bowl of Theniel and you have a ship," Wei replied.

"You expect me to risk my ship and crew to sail for that wretched cyclone? If the waves don't take us, the merpeople will," Fei said.

"Ah, so you know how to get there. How soon can we leave?" Wei asked.

"You'll never change, will you?" Fei asked, arms crossed.

"You know I don't have that luxury."

Fei stared at her sister, her expression one of scorn tempered by a hint of something tender. "Is the Great Dragon's imminent release also the reason the sun and stars have gone out—an omen of some sort?"

"If only," Devlyn said. "We'll tell you everything you want to know, but we must leave at once. We're running out of time."

"And the ghosts?" Fei asked.

"It's all connected."

Fei seemed to consider again, then turned toward Wei. "I want my place at court restored, along with my holdings and an imperial income fitting my station."

"Your current station is one of a pirate," Wei said.

"You gave me little choice. I believe being named an imperial admiral would be more fitting. What is your decision?"

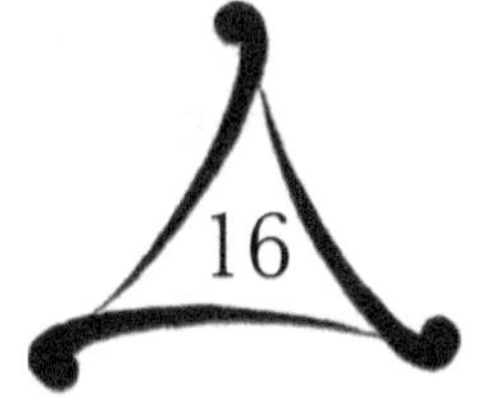

ROUGH WAVES

The Emerald's Kiss rode the waves toward the cyclone. Fei had agreed to the voyage, but only once Wei had accepted her demands. Since they'd left port, the imperial sisters had kept their distance. Despite the wind blowing east, the sails were full and carrying them impossibly southwest. Only a wielder could influence the winds. Tapping his inner sense, Devlyn saw the erendinth propelling the ship forward. Not just the wind; aquaeys also pushed the ship at an incredible speed.

Fei must have seen him staring at the sails. "Wei and I were both monks at one point. She was always more disciplined. It's likely why our father chose her to succeed him."

"I thought Qien monks weren't permitted to leave their monasteries."

"I knelt at Guanxi's claw when my sister took the throne. I had already left my monastery to serve as her protector. I appreciated it little better than living at Dongshi Monastery, but I did enjoy being back at court."

"Can every monk wield?" Devlyn had asked Wei a similar question when they had first met. She had told him their duty was to contain the Great Dragon. But now that Tolvenol would be freed, perhaps the monks could lend their strength in the days ahead.

"We are not ei'ana," Fei said.

"Kai became one."

"Is that where she disappeared to? I've heard a rumor she's returned." Fei looked up to the sails and wielded another gust of aerys into it. "I did learn a thing or two while I studied with the monks. Not every wielder must be an ei'ana; you should know that better than most."

Devlyn chuckled in response. While he was neither an ei'ana nor ei'ceuril, he had trained with both. But since he was a Phaedryn, becoming either wasn't appropriate. Ellendren still struggled with that. She had dreamt her entire life of becoming an ei'ana; she had even chosen Vyoletryn as her School. But that was before Tariel had bonded with her.

Whether Qien monks considered themselves akin to ei'ana mattered little. Devlyn didn't share the ei'ana philosophy that every wielder had to belong to the ei'ana or ei'ceuril. All that mattered was how well the monks could wield the erendinth and whether they would fight.

"What exactly are Qien monks capable of?" Devlyn asked.

"Would you like to find out?"

"Now?"

"Let's agree to not use ignys; I'm already risking my ship and crew by taking you to the Bowl of Theniel."

"Agreed."

She smirked then took several steps back. Her arms wove in a swift blur, each motion controlled and powerful. Her movements reminded him of jienzu. Of course, the Qien monks would know a form of jienzu, having been close to jade dragons. For a moment, Devlyn wondered if there were any draelyn in Qien.

Fei embraced aquaeys and aerys. The two erendinth twisted around each other in a tight spiral which she launched in a burst at Devlyn. He intercepted them and redirected them up, using Fei's momentum to strengthen his own wield of aerys and aquaeys.

A crowd soon gathered to watch. The crew cheered for their captain, while the elves watched quietly. Even Wei had come out of the cabin to watch the duel.

Devlyn studied Fei's technique, finding her a skilled wielder, her level of control one that he'd rarely seen. Her command over the erendinth was remarkable. Just as he was about to turn one of her wields against her, the sea turned violent and he lost his footing.

The entire crew who had come to watch were surprised too. Some managed to grab something near but others toppled over and slammed onto the deck.

Another wave crashed into the ship and Devlyn saw Fei and Wei both wielding. It didn't look like they had linked; rather each independently wove aquaeys and aerys into the ocean in hopes of gentling it.

The sea settled and Fei took a quick accounting of her ship and crew. Once certain they were all safe, she yelled at them to return to their posts and that they should have been prepared for a rogue wave.

"What do you think caused it?" Devlyn asked.

"Hard to say. Rogue waves aren't uncommon and without the sun and stars for guidance, it's near impossible to track a storm on the horizon," Fei said.

"That was no rogue wave," Wei said, hands trembling.

"What was it then?" Fei asked.

"That was from seismic activity. The ground will quake and the sea will churn in revolt as the volcano erupts." Wei gripped the railing to steady herself, looking toward Qien. "The Great Dragon is free."

"How can you be certain?" Devlyn knew the third day since leaving Zhongshi was fast approaching. The monks had either abandoned their monasteries, or the Dark Flight had destroyed them. Devlyn hoped as many had been able to flee to safety as possible.

"I might have failed my dynasty in not defeating the Great Dragon, but I am still connected to Qien. Ash rains down around the mountain. No one is fool enough to live near the volcano to suffer from the eruption, but no one lives far enough away so that they are safe. Not even my son in the imperial capital will be safe." Wei went back into her cabin, shutting the door behind her.

Devlyn shared a worried look with Viren. Tolvenol would not

remain in Qien. Ramiel needed his general in Eklean to lead the Void beasts. "How quickly can we reach the Bowl of Theniel?" he asked, a new concern in his belly. If he could safely shift to the Bowl of Theniel he would. But the Bowl of Theniel was said to be unpredictable, to say nothing of how the merpeople would react to his sudden appearance.

"It's difficult to gauge. The currents have been unpredictable, the surge we just experienced only adding to it. Before the sun went dark, I would say we'd be there in a month, and that's with wielding the wind and sea to favor us. But now, I can't determine how the currents are changed. Our voyage could either take us twice as long or even half the required time," Fei said.

"So we could be there in a couple weeks?" Devlyn asked, hopeful.

"Or two months." Fei squared her shoulders. "About our duel…"

"You're quite talented." Devlyn was glad for the distraction. He could do nothing to quicken their pace.

"As are you. When you agreed to not use ignys, I assumed you would be limited to terys."

"Why would I have been limited to terys?"

"Air and water are proper to women, just as fire and stone are proper to men. Only the empress is permitted to wield all four, as she ascends both. Do all wielders in Eklean wield all four elemental erendinth?"

"We do, along with the transcendental erendinth. Until coming to Qien, I had never heard of the erendinth being assigned genders or being proper to a man or a woman." Devlyn had long struggled with how people learned to wield the erendinth. He could never understand why kien wielders were naturally stronger with less control while kiara wielders naturally had more control but started off weaker. It didn't make any sense to him. The strongest people he knew were women and it wasn't something they had learned from a man, nor by being around kien wielders. But that dichotomy had destabilized the ei'ana and ei'ceuril since Erynor's last reign. Kien wielders had been locked away for their lack of control and kiara wielders couldn't reach their potential strength to teach the kien wielders control. The vicious cycle had continued for fourteen centuries.

Kien and kiara wielders also wielded differently. But why? Why did kien wielders press into the elemental erendinth while kiara wielders embraced them, and vice versa for the transcendental erendinth? Who had dictated that? Was it Anaweh's design for kien and kiara wielders to be so different?

The idea of balance, or harmony as the Qien monks referred to it, hung in his mind. A memory of Thien came to him. When Tenethyl had been attacked, Thien hadn't wielded the erendinth as Devlyn did. Thien had interacted with lumenys on a wholly different level and he hadn't been on the verge of losing control either. Thien was a second generation draelyn of the Gold House though. Surely his connection to the Gold Dragon Flight explained his grasp over lumenys. Was there something deeper than wielding the erendinth?

Devlyn had only been completely cut off from the erendinth twice, first when Queen Alesei of Tiel had locked him in a dorthl box then during his short stay in Lankor. It was as though he had vanished from Teraeniel entirely. While he couldn't interact with the erendinth when caged, he had been able to sense them. Was there another way to access the erendinth? He didn't want to consider it just yet, but what was he expected to do if he had to confront Ramiel in his dorthl-wrought fortress? He couldn't afford to be severed from the erendinth again.

"Ei'denai?" Fei asked, pulling Devlyn out of his inner musings.

"Sorry. I lost myself there for a moment."

"I'm no monk—not anymore—but the superiors wouldn't recommend doing what you just did on the open sea. Contemplation such as that is best reserved for stable ground."

Devlyn looked around but didn't notice anything different. "What happened?"

"Your spiritual energy pulsated off you, echoing through the erendinth. I've only heard stories of monks being able to do it. I'd thought the practice lost."

"But what exactly did I do?" He frowned, confused.

"What you did transcends wielding."

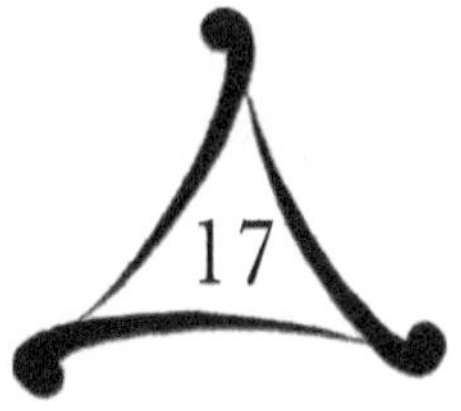

ENSLAVED

Alex pressed his palms against the desk, reining in his anger as best he could. If Tenir hadn't already been dead, Alex was wont to end his wretched life all over again. Not that killing the man would rid Teraeniel of him, for Alex had seen Tenir's ghost drift past the night before, among others who had been killed here, all now forever silent.

Hundreds of people had been brought to the surface from the mines. Men, women, and children had been enslaved for decades before being brought to the mines four years ago. The children had been born in captivity then forced to follow their parents' endless dig below the fort. Alex's heart ached for them. Most of them had called one fallen Ogren kingdom or another their home. Alex didn't know when those kingdoms had fallen, but surely the civilians didn't deserve this. They had all fled the ogre attacks, not knowing their rulers had caused the aggression. Castle Mavarre had offered them a haven before sending them down to the mines. None had been aware they'd escaped the ogre's wrath just to hand themselves over into slavery.

Alethea busied herself with healing anyone who needed it, many more than Alex cared for. Tenir had killed some of the Thellish soldiers to make an example of them. First the captains, then the first lieutenants. Tenir hadn't bothered to bury them and had forbidden anyone from doing so. Alex saw that those soldiers were given a proper funeral, grumbling that an ei'ceuril wasn't with them.

Frustrated that he hadn't learned anything since coming to Charren about Sanjin, Oliver, Reia, or Sara, Alex wanted to fly to Karithel to get a straight answer. His instincts cautioned against that. Something wrong was happening in the floating city. Sanjin wouldn't have postponed his coronation for so long. Someone had to be preventing him from ascending his throne. But why?

He needed more information before going to Karithel. The Daer Sorcery was undeniably involved. Tenir had been his only lead, and he was dead. They still hadn't found the culprit responsible for killing him. Whatever Tenir knew, his allies didn't want Alex learning of it. Worse, those allies, whoever they were, knew Alex was here. Whatever element of surprise he could plan for was gone. Not that Alex had a plan to begin with—he needed to know what was going on in Karithel before he could decide on anything. What he really needed was information.

He again looked past the castle walls, debating whether to hold onto the castle and mines beneath it. They were clearly precious to Tenir's allies, otherwise why go through the trouble of enslaving so many people? The bigger question though was why kill Tenir? What could he have possibly known that it was better for him to die than share that information? The mines must hold something precious to the Daer Sorcery. Tenir might have been Charrenese, but his talisman had been wrought by the Sorcery.

Most pressing to Alex was whether Tenir's allies would try to seize the castle and mines. The soldiers who had been spared the back-breaking work in the mines were certainly capable of defending the castle walls, but the others needed to regain their strength. They were in no condition to lift a sword or shield. Even a bow would be difficult for them to manage.

Then again, Tenir's allies might not care to take the castle and mines back. Alex needed answers. He spun about in Tenir's quarters. He had hoped they would provide some insight. They hadn't, of course. He opened the door to the adjacent hall to find Wyn playing a game with

Aen. Aen smiled, clearly enjoying himself as he moved a tile triumphant-ly.

Wyn's gaze flicked to Alex. The look unnerved him. He realized the elf already knew everything that had passed through his mind.

"I've already told you, elves don't intentionally eavesdrop," Wyn said, confirming Alex's suspicions.

"Yes, yes, you're simply open to your surroundings—visible and invisible," Alex said.

"Something like that," Wyn added without providing more detail.

Alex drew closer to see the tiles between Wyn and Aen, noticing seven colors. "Does each color represent an erendinth?" Alex had been around ei'ana long enough to make that connection. He wondered if it was a simpler version of the Erendinth Games students at Gwilnor com-peted in.

"More strategy than raw skill as a wielder," Wyn said, receiving a low growl from Alex at the unvoiced question. "Sorry. This game is largely intended for those who have yet to begin their formal studies with the erendinth."

"Yet you're still fond of it," Alex commented.

"Children learn it, but elders also play it. Alethea is brilliant at it. The more one understands the erendinth, the more successful they are. Certain erendinth have advantages over others, like water to fire. But that's just one tile against one tile."

Alex glanced at the tiles between Aen and Wyn and noticed that there were few instances where there was only one tile against one. "And dare I ask why you're teaching this game to Aen?"

"I think you already know that answer," Alethea said, entering the hall from the far side. "Dare I say you should probably learn it yourself?"

"I have no interest in returning to Gwilnor Academy, thank you."

"Septyl might accommodate a tutor, but not learning to control the erendinth is too great a risk. Aen, however, is of the right age. He's a bit older than Gwilnor prefers, but they did take you and Devlyn at a similar age."

"That feels like eons ago."

"Much has passed since then and more has yet to pass." Alethea's mysterious tone hung between them.

If Alex didn't know better, he would swear Alethea could see into the future. Perhaps she could. What did he know of this ancient elf who had lived on a Skyland? Ignoring those thoughts, he turned to Aen. "Would you want that—attending Gwilnor Academy?"

"Only if I can return to Elothkar and keep my winged horse."

Alex laughed. "You will always have a place at Elothkar. Who knows, if you study well, Septyl might make you their ambassador to Thellion."

"Would I still have a seat on your council?"

"Always."

"Good. I'd rather not get stabbed again because I can't wield. Queen Lara and Queen Daphne saved me by wielding." Aen moved two of the tiles and grinned at Wyn.

"I was waiting for you to make that move," Wyn said with a hint of pride in his tone. Aen's grin vanished when Wyn moved his tiles. "And that's game."

Aen flopped his head on the table and mumbled, "I thought I had you that round."

"It was a good move," Wyn said encouragingly.

Alethea whispered something in Aen's ear. He excitedly moved several tiles until Wyn's expression sank. "*That's* game!" Aen beamed a smile.

"I suppose it is." Wyn looked at the smattering of tiles, bewildered. "I've never seen that combination before."

"You didn't leave your quarters to learn a new game, did you?" Alethea and Wyn surely already knew the answer. Alex didn't want to consider how long it would take for Aen to do the same. That was a problem for another day. Alex wasn't a decade older than Aen, but he still felt responsible for him.

"There's too much we don't know about our situation here. It makes me uncomfortable," Alex admitted.

"And what would you like to know?" Alethea asked, her tone quizzical, not demeaning in the slightest.

"Where to start?" Alex scratched his head. "Who killed Tenir? What did they fear he would tell us? Are Sanjin, Oliver, Reia, and Sara enslaved or free? And what's happening in Karithel?" Alex also wanted to know how Diana was. He felt guilty for leaving her so soon after their wedding. If not for the circumstances, he doubted he would be able to forgive himself for it. Light, what would he owe her on his return? He caught Wyn's smirk and scowled in response. "And when are you going to tell me how to keep you out of my head?"

"Awareness is not an easy lesson. It took Devlyn years and he's far from mastered it. But I doubt that's your priority just now," Alethea said.

"If only it were then we wouldn't be on the other side of the world."

"Agreed." Alethea offered an understanding smile.

"So, how do we resolve what's happening in Karithel?" Wyn asked.

"Can we slip anyone into the city unnoticed?" Aen asked.

"Whoever is in charge would know," Alex said.

"But they likely also know we're here. Whoever killed Tenir is long gone," Wyn said.

"So, we just present ourselves to whoever is now running Charren?" Alex glanced toward the door, partly wanting to do just that.

"We do have an army," Aen suggested.

"But we don't know what we're getting into." Alex frowned. "We don't even know who we're up against."

"Only that they're involved with the Daer Sorcery," Alethea said.

"Do we know what they're capable of?" Alex asked.

"Anadel have immense power. You've seen Aliel's effects on Devlyn. Granted, Septyl has never studied the Sorcery, only condemned it.

All we know, depending on the type of anadel and where they fall in the hierarchy, a sorcerer is extremely dangerous."

"If only we could get a message to Oliver or sneak into the city," Alex said.

Before they could decide on one path or another, a soldier hurried into the hall. "A messenger from Karithel is outside."

Alex sucked in a breath.

"So, they do know we're here," Wyn said, fiddling with a game tile.

"It appears so. What does the messenger want?" Alex asked.

"He demands to speak to the foreign king who seized a Charrenese castle and valuable mine," the guard said.

"Did he mention Wyn and myself?" Alethea asked.

"No."

Good. They could remain in the castle with the soldiers and freed captives. "Stay hidden when I meet this messenger." Alethea and Wyn nodded and Alex followed the soldier out the castle and to the castle gate, Aen trailing behind him. "Is the messenger alone?"

"He is." The soldier stopped at the sealed portcullis.

A hooded man stood opposite, his face hidden in shadow. "You asked to see me?" Alex said.

"The king's advisor demands you answer for your war crimes against Charren."

"Why does the king not make such a request himself?" Alex asked. Wanting to be careful, he brought his time with Velaria and every other ei'ana to the front of his mind. They always managed to say one thing and mean another.

"Because a new king has yet to take Charren's throne." Alex caught a familiar tone in the messenger's voice. Aen must have noticed it too, for he stepped closer to look up into the shadowed cowl.

"And what's preventing a new king from ascending?"

"The advisor, Caspol li'Moren." The messenger removed his hood, revealing Prince Sanjin.

"Open the gate," Alex called, flooded with relief. The portcullis rose and Alex stepped out to embrace the prince.

"Hello, my friend." Sanjin returned the hug.

"What has happened here? Why were my soldiers enslaved in the mines below this castle? Where are Oliver, Reia, and Sara?" Alex was happy Sanjin was alive and well, but he couldn't stop the questions that had haunted him from pouring out.

"None of us are free in Charren," Sanjin said, shoulders slouched.

"But why?" Alex didn't understand. Who could prevent the heir from taking his throne?

"The advisor." Sanjin looked defeated. Always quick to smile, his scowl hardened his amiable features. This was not the same Sanjin Alex had had bidden farewell to.

"I don't understand." Surely an advisor couldn't be so powerful.

"Caspol li'Moren," Alethea said as she and Wyn joined them in the castle yard, "is the name of a Sha'ghol."

Alex knew precious little about the Sha'ghol, only that they were loyal to the Evil One.

"Is that what the elf is?" Sanjin asked. "I had assumed he was sent by the Daer to bring Charren into their empire."

"Why would you presume a Cyndinari elf was in league with the Daer?" Alethea asked.

"He belongs to the Daer Sorcery. Generations of Charren kings have managed to keep it out of Charren and now it's ruling the kingdom."

"Troubling. The Daer Empire might have a hand in this, but we can be assured that Caspol's directives aren't coming from your neighbors," Alethea said.

"How can you be so certain? Daer has always lusted for Charren."

"Sha'ghol answer only to one being, and their master has been freed," Alethea said.

"I see." Sanjin was unfazed by the passing shade of Tenir. "My father never trusted him."

"Smart man." Alex ignored the specter. "What are we going to do about Caspol?"

"Do? He's a Sha'ghol," Wyn said as though that was explanation enough.

"The Kilnae Del mages have ways to deal with the Sorcery, but not a Sha'ghol," Sanjin said.

"And what of all the mages?" Alethea asked. Alex wondered if a plan was forming in her mind.

"No one in Karithel trusts anyone right now. Mages and citizens are being killed left and right. Even the king died without reason," Sanjin said.

"Clearly Caspol is to blame," Alex said.

"Undoubtedly. But anyone who comes close to proving his crimes ends up dead. He will come for you. He knows you took this castle and he does not want to lose the mine below it."

"So, we fortify our position," Alex said.

"He has the entire Charren military at his disposal with whatever aid is promised from the Daer! I'd rather my friends not kill each other."

"What if ogres were involved?" Alethea asked.

"Ogres? They'll rip this castle apart stone by stone. They hate humans," Sanjin said.

"Only those who enslave anadel."

"You think they would help Charren?" Sanjin asked, aghast.

"I do," Alethea replied simply.

Sanjin paced. "They might deter an army from knocking on the castle gates. At least long enough to figure out what to do about Caspol."

Alex frowned at the impossible task ahead of them. "We'll have to figure something out. How difficult could it be to take down a Sha'ghol?" He forced an unconvincing smile.

"Until you do, I must return to Karithel. Caspol won't be happy if he finds out I came here in the messenger's place."

"That doesn't seem to have been advisable," Alex said.

"I had to know who had liberated Castle Mavarre. All we knew is that it was a foreign king." Sanjin gripped Alex's shoulder. "I can't tell you how relieved I am that it's you. Until next time, my friend."

BOWL OF THENIEL

The waters stilled and the Emerald's Kiss sailed through the sea like a knife cutting through butter, no waves or ripples created by the ship's passage, as though the water entirely ignored it. Fei had her crew at their stations, expecting to sail through a cyclone. She had said they were getting close and to expect a rough ride, but no cyclone appeared. Instead of stormy seas, the ocean was smooth as glass.

Aliel perched beside Devlyn at the bow. *Will you be okay going below the water again?* Aliel conveyed. The phoenix's light was the only illumination as a mist extinguished the torches.

Devlyn flinched at the memory of swimming beneath Lankor and nearly drowning. His chest tightened as though he could feel the watery depths pressing against him. *As long as there isn't any dorthl to disrupt my wield so I can breathe, I should be fine.*

The group from Eklean stood near Devlyn, unaware of his communication with Aliel. Wei looked off into the mist as a cautious Fei joined them at the bow.

"Is this how you remember the Bowl of Theniel?" Wei asked.

"I've never sailed here before—how reckless do you think I am?" Fei crossed her arms.

"Do we know what we're sailing into?" Toryn gripped her sword, expecting an attack.

"Only that it was given to the merpeople by Theniel," Elayne said.

Devlyn tapped his bond with Ellendren, letting her know they had reached their destination, despite not knowing how large the area was. They could end up sailing for another week or month for all he knew.

Good. You'll need to hurry back. We can't put off opening the Guardian Senate much longer, Ellendren sent back.

He shared a loving embrace with her then broadened his inner senses. He had no intention of sailing blindly through the Bowl of Theniel. They could easily end up lost or sail right out of it.

The ship moved forward, but oddly, Devlyn didn't feel any wind. The sails hung slackly in confirmation. What was pulling the ship forward? Curious, he brushed the water with his inner senses. He didn't feel any merpeople there—in fact he didn't sense any sort of sea creatures.

Before he could ask if anyone was there, assuming an anadel was guiding the ship, the bow lurched downward. Devlyn's stomach reeled at the sudden dive. He shared a desperate look with Viren, who clenched Devlyn's tunic, afraid they'd be separated. The frantic crew yelled out suggestions before the ship could take on any water. But whatever pulled them moved too fast and the ship dipped below the surface.

Devlyn pressed into aquaeys and aerys to create an air bubble around them, but he fumbled the wield when the ship suddenly lurched further downward. Soaking wet and without any clear options, he held his breath. Water filled his nose and he saw the terrified faces of everyone around him, many pinching their nostrils shut, desperately pleading for him to do something—anything. Heart racing, he tried to wield but the required erendinth slipped through his fingers as the ship sank ever deeper. Desperate, he tried to leap from the deck to swim to the surface. But whatever force was pulling the ship down also held Devlyn. The dragons might be able to escape the plunging force, but the deck was too small for them to transform into their larger forms.

Tiny air bubbles escaped his lips. Viren said something, somehow speaking despite being underwater, but through Devlyn's panic, it couldn't reach his ears. Did Viren know something? Against all reason,

Devlyn opened his mouth to ask what and found he could breathe. Startled, he gulped in the water and breathed it as though it was air. The others soon discovered the surprising phenomenon, and shouts of wonder swept across the ship.

"How is this possible?" Wei asked, moving her hand through the water as though she was swimming. Their clothes all floated about their bodies, weightless in the sea.

"The Lady of the Sea wishes it." Devlyn spun around to see a figure form in the water, floating above them and vanishing before anyone could ask anything of the aquaeys anadel.

The ship continued its dive. The lack of sunlight made it impossible to determine how deep they were going. No one on the ship spoke, silenced by terror that they were being taken to a watery grave. They had all expected the merpeople to come to the surface. Ships weren't designed to be hauled under the sea.

Soon, they could see a soft glow surrounding a city of turquoise and aquamarine structures. Devlyn took in the fabled city of the merpeople, unlike anything he had ever seen. He was used to towers with tapering, vertical walls. These looked as though the ocean currents had formed them, giving the city a fluidity that Devlyn had never imagined possible, let alone constructable. Like Arenthyl before the Void, the walls had a translucent quality and provided the dark depths with their own glow.

The ship neared the city where hundreds of merpeople swam about, not going into the buildings from the ground level when they could swim up to its highest reaches on the exterior.

There were no streets to walk on nor did they haul goods with carts. Instead, Devlyn noted heavy floating sled-like carts pulled by sea creatures. Where roads would typically fill the space between buildings lay a blanket of colorful and vibrant coral. Small fish of every color swam in and out of the reef, a city of their own.

Distracted, Devlyn finally noticed a group of merpeople headed toward the submerged ship. He broke into a grin when he recognized Ferinn. He had not seen the late Sorenth queen's consort since Ferinn had brought the Ja'mare seafarers and merpeople to Myrium's defense.

Ferinn and his group soon reached the ship, hanging just above the deck as they floated. "Welcome to the Bowl of Theniel," Ferinn said, noticeably the youngest of these merpeople.

"Thank you, Ferinn. It's nice to see you again. The last I heard, the Meridean Conclave had summoned you due to your actions in Sorent-hil," Devlyn said, much calmer now.

"We did," one of the other merpeople said. Devlyn realized this wasn't just a welcoming party, but the Meridean Conclave come to greet them directly.

"Aware of the state of the world, they decided my actions and leadership made me an ideal candidate to join the Conclave," Ferinn said turning to a woman with a kind and caring face. "Choral did not summon me to be reprimanded."

"I'm happy to hear that," Devlyn said.

"But you did not come here to learn of Ferinn's elevation, did you?"

"We did not." Devlyn cleared his mind before sharing their true purpose for coming here. "I trust you know Ramiel is free and the Void now strangles Teraeniel."

"Yes. We felt the Tree die and are also aware that Tolvenol has been freed. The seas tremble in his wake."

"The jade dragons battled Tolvenol and managed to subdue him long ago," Wei said.

"But only succeeded with the addition of the Qien monks." The merperson smiled at Wei, aware of her people's history.

"Just so, and since the merpeople have long fought the sea drakes who betrayed the jade dragons, we hoped you would know how to wake them," Wei confessed.

"Are you familiar with the Jade Flight's origin? As you know, they are not tied to one erendinth as other flights are," Choral said.

Devlyn shook his head.

"After Tenethyl fell, the dragons knew they weren't equipped to withstand Ramiel and Tolvenol. Each of the flights had a level of command over an erendinth, intended to help shape Teraeniel in the Dawn of Creation. A clutch of eggs, laid by Eilynol, Primus of the Purple Flight, was brought to a secret location in Qien. Tolvenol discovered the dragons' plans and made Qien his home, hoping to stop the threat. The Primuses of the White, Blue, Green, and Red Flights gathered around Eilynol's eggs, and poured their essences into them, granting their gifts. The clutch hatched as a new flight with control over five erendinth." Choral turned to Wei. "You should know how special your people are for the jade dragons to have chosen to bond with you. And you should also know that your first empress, after uniting the hundred kingdoms, never married." Choral waited for her words to sink in.

"I don't understand—how did she create a dynasty with a thousand generations of descendants if she didn't marry? Are you claiming I'm not of Qien Ji's blood?" Wei said.

"I would not make that accusation. But know that dragons fall in love and mate just as every other anacordel, although they rarely wed. Qien Ji died giving birth to her heir, and she made the father promise to watch over and protect their line as she breathed her last."

"Guanxi isn't just the imperial dragon." Devlyn gasped.

"—he's our ancestor," Wei finished, hand covering her mouth.

"Guanxi was among the first clutch of jade dragons. I believe you know the others."

"The monasteries—Beishi, Dongshi, Nanshi, and Xishi," Wei said.

"And one other. There was a sixth. Faoxi betrayed her clutch mates and was promised dominion over the seas. You were not wrong in coming to us, for we are likely the most familiar with the sea drakes given our endless war with them."

"How can we wake the jade dragons?" Wei asked.

"An amulet was wrought in secret and used to petrify her kin. Faoxi jealously guards it. To break its spell and wake the jade dragons, you must destroy it."

"How are we to manage that?" Fei asked.

"You will not be going alone. Faoxi must die."

Devlyn and the others were brought into a palace and provided rooms so they could rest. Viren stayed nearby but gave Devlyn his space. He still couldn't rationalize breathing underwater without wielding. All that mattered though was that the merpeople intended to launch an attack against the sea drakes.

Just as his eyes were about to close, a knock came at the door. When Devlyn opened it, Ferinn floated just outside. "Hello, Ferinn."

"Ei'denai." Ferinn dipped his head in greeting. "You should know the Meridean Conclave is waiting until we receive direction before sending representatives to Arenthyl to join the Guardian Senate."

"From Aquae or Theniel and the other irythil?" Devlyn asked, waving Ferinn in.

Ferinn appraised Devlyn as he entered. "I presume you've learned about the throncs?"

"An aerys anadel told me. He also told me there was a portal to the irythil thrones from the Bowl of Theniel."

"And you seek an audience with them?" Ferinn arched a brow.

"I don't see an alternative. We need their help to defeat the Evil One."

"They will not fight him head on."

"What if they know something that would help us?"

"Even if I do take you to the portal, there's no guarantee they will let you pass. Theniel could take offense at an elf crossing her portal and forever seal it. Do not offend her if you desire to maintain your friendship with the merpeople."

"I won't."

"Very well. Are you comfortable swimming or would you prefer to walk? That also applies to Viren and Falthion. I trust you have no intention of letting our friend out of your sight."

"Only when he wishes it, and even then, I might object," Viren said, Falthion beside him.

"Shall we?" Ferinn gestured to the balcony and led them out of the building. Devlyn's room was several stories above the ocean floor.

Ferinn's powerful tail covered in blue and green scales shimmered in Aliel's light in the otherwise soft aquamarine glow of the city. He had to stop several times for Devlyn and Viren to catch up. They soon came to the center of the city where the buildings formed an opening; the space had dictated how closely the buildings could press in. The coral reef only went so far into the clearing when the ground dipped, its depth hidden by a whirlpool.

"I cannot follow you. If you do not come out the way you went in, know that we will help Qien defeat the sea drakes and wake the jade dragons," Ferinn said.

"Why would we not return the same way we entered?" Devlyn asked, debating whether he should bring the others from Eklean with him.

"Who is to say what the minds of the irythil are? You might be needed elsewhere." Ferinn gestured to the whirlpool.

"I see. Will you let the people we came with know where we've gone?" Devlyn asked.

"Of course. Be well, Devlyn Lorenthien."

Devlyn, Viren, Aliel, and Falthion moved toward the swirling water and just as Devlyn thought he might have to breathe again, he stumbled forward into an ominous space. Seven distinct thrones faced each other in a wide circle, each throne too large for even a giant. Devlyn, Viren, Aliel, and Falthion stepped forward, hesitant in the overwhelming space.

"You should not be here." Devlyn spun to find a tall, watery form behind him. She was not as large as her throne, but Devlyn had no doubt that she'd be able to grow to that size at will.

"Theniel," Devlyn murmured, placing his hand over his chest, and bowing deeply in the elven fashion. "Please—we had to."

"Your reason for coming here is no secret to us, young elf, but that does not change the fact that you shouldn't be here," another voice from the other side of the room called. Its owner sat on a smoldering throne as fire emitted from his ethereal form.

Devlyn repeated the gesture of greeting to Kariel. The other thrones filled in. Leraeniel's windy form was barely visible, while Sariel's stony form appeared the most solid of the seven irythil. Gwynthiel had a nurturing, yet strong quality to her, and in the umbrys throne that once belonged to Ramiel sat the shadowy form of Remiel. Devlyn didn't know if the irythil, or anadel in general, had siblings or familiar relations, but Remiel would have been as close to Ramiel as possible. And last was Uriel, whose light transformed the space.

"Why have you come here, Devlyn?" Uriel asked.

"We know why he is here," Kariel said.

"Your soft spot for the elves cannot forgive this hubris. Imagine, an anacordel coming before our thrones—unsummoned," Sariel said.

"We should let him speak," Gwynthiel said in a confusing mixture of warmth and resolve.

Building his own resolve, Devlyn reminded himself of why he had come. He couldn't leave without at least asking. "Verakryl is dead and the Void has claimed Teraeniel; Somnaeniel is lost to us. You once went into the Void and filled it with creation. Can you do it a second time—to save Teraeniel?"

"Oh, child," Gwynthiel said, understanding. "Creation is already there. There is nothing else for us to bring into Teraeniel, for all that we are—who we are—is already present."

"Ramiel's Void is not the same as the void we had scattered before the first dawn. He's corrupted and twisted what he hid away from us and it became something else entirely," Remiel said, his tone melancholic.

"Can nothing be done?" Devlyn asked.

"You know what must be done," Sariel replied, reminding Devlyn of the prophecy that had determined his life from birth.

The impressive space shifted in vibrancy and Devlyn thought they might be expelled. He heard Uriel urgently say, "Quick, behind me." Trembling, Devlyn and his small party did as instructed.

As the space darkened, Devlyn felt something foreign enter. Crackling, negating lightning filled the center of the space, and standing among it was a figure composed of tenebrys. Ramiel had the form of a storm cloud as tenebrys lightning peeled off him.

"You have no right to stand here—begone," Theniel thundered.

"No right?" Ramiel kept his voice low but threatening "This space only exists because of me. Or have you forgotten who carved this pocket of existence out of the Void for our vanity?"

"You have lost your way and your place among us," Remiel said.

"And you think to have replaced me?" Ramiel strode to the anadel sitting on his former shadowy throne, so different from the tenebrys pouring off him now. "I had thought you understood true power, only to betray me and snatch this lesser throne of seven. What have any of you accomplished since creating Teraeniel? What have you inspired over the course of this world's existence?"

"More than you have a right to claim," Leraeniel said.

"Is that so? If not for me, only dragons and Children would walk this world. Nothing would have changed or evolved. I have made this world develop in ways Anaweh never dreamt of—too weak to realize this world's potential, despite creation's inherent flaws."

"You are the weak one, Ramiel. We all shared in the same vision and brought creation here. And you forsook that mission and warped it. We were to be guides to the Children and let them choose their own path, not force them down a path dictated by our own desires," Uriel said.

"We are gods to them! They will cower in reverence to me and forget you ever existed," Ramiel shrieked.

"We are not gods, Ramiel. We brought the erendinth here and guide the anacordel, but we are not their creators. We brought with us what was given to us. And what was given unto you is no longer recognizable. You have tarnished your gift," Uriel said.

"I have made what I am more powerful than you could fathom, *Lord of the Stars*," Ramiel sneered, spite and hate threaded through every word. "Your precious Light has no place in my domain. My Void will consume all. Not even Lumaeniel is beyond my grasp."

"You are a smoldering coal next to the sun that is Lumaeniel," Kariel said, his form ablaze.

"I had once hoped you would join me, Kariel. Imagine what we could have built together."

"My fires will burn you and this time, your beasts will not be spared. They too will burn."

"None of you are stronger than my Void. And you are a fool to stand against me. Do not think that your little elf and his pet bird can do what you cannot. They will suffer an eternal death."

Devlyn then felt Ramiel's gaze fall on him. A flash of light followed, and Devlyn woke with a start in a bed, sweat slick against his brow.

"Devlyn," Alethea said, relief flooding her voice. "You've woken at last."

He sat up in the bed. How was he here? Where was *here*? Had it all been a dream? "I saw him—the Evil One." His voice quavered, too scared to say Ramiel's name, terrified Ramiel might hear him and find him. Ramiel's gaze still bored into him.

"Yes. Aliel shared what happened."

"Are Viren and Falthion here?" Devlyn pushed himself up, but Alethea placed a hand on his chest to keep him in bed.

"They are here and resting, as you should continue to do."

Devlyn settled back into the pillows. "Where are we?"

"Castle Mavarre in Charren. You are safe here. Now, I must insist you rest. There will be time for answers later."

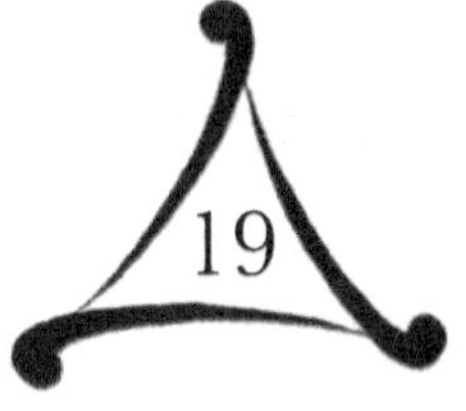

KARITHEL

Devlyn stood atop the fortifications, surprised to see humans, centaurs, and ogres working together to fortify Castle Mavarre. The recent liberation had mollified his temper after he had learned what had happened here before. Former slaves and soldiers would ensure they would never be taken captive again, even if it meant staying at the place of their captivity.

Devlyn wasn't alone in casting a wary eye toward the ogres. Half-giant and half-human, they were only half the height of giants, but that still made them twice as tall as himself and many more times as wide. Their bulbous limbs reminded him of old tree trunks and boulders, capable of uprooting trees and tearing down stone walls. He was glad to not be on the receiving end of their clubs. The freed slaves knew all too well what ogres were capable of. Granted, they couldn't have known that their lords and kings had assisted the Daer Sorcery in farming anadel. That ignorance was the only reason the ogres hadn't pulverized the freed humans from Ogren on sight.

The irythil had to know what the Daer Sorcery was doing. Was that why they had sent Devlyn here? Surely they didn't expect him to stop an entire order that had been around thousands of years. At least, not alone.

Aliel stayed close, his discomfort conveyed to Devlyn, just as when they'd met with Senator Aorinol. *I won't let any sorcerer near you.* Aliel cooed in greeting when Alex and Wyn joined them, both offering a brief nod to Viren and Falthion.

"How was Qien? Did you slay the dragon?" Alex asked too casually.

"Afraid not."

"Well, I hate to be the bearer of bad news, but there's trouble here too."

"Worse than Tolvenol?" Devlyn asked.

"A Sha'ghol," Alex supplied.

"Wonderful." Devlyn pursed his lips. That explained Charren's absence from the Guardian Senate. "Do you have a plan?"

"We were prepared to fly to Karithel, but then you arrived out of thin air. You have an uncanny way of changing plans merely by your presence," Alex said.

"And how have your plans changed because of me?"

"Well, we won't have to fly to Karithel anymore, now will we."

"How would you have gotten past a Sha'ghol?" Devlyn asked.

"Fortunately, we don't have to consider how epically that plan would've failed. Sneaking into the palace would have been the least of our troubles though. Sanjin says the Kilnae Del can overpower Daer sorcerers, just not Sha'ghol," Alex said.

"Do we have to deal with both?" Devlyn asked, not looking forward to fighting a Sha'ghol backed by sorcerers.

"Possibly. We have reason to believe Caspol is also a sorcerer. Must have learned their tricks at some point in his infernally long life," Alex said.

"Viren, if we manage to subdue Caspol, is there a means for us to hold him captive?" Devlyn asked, pinching the bridge of his nose. Having a Sha'ghol as a prisoner could prove valuable. What information might he know about the enemies' plans? Erynor had always been three steps ahead of them. There was no telling how unprepared they would be with Ramiel. Any edge would be invaluable.

"The Guardian Citadel has cells that can hold any wielder, even a Sha'ghol," Viren said.

"Good. When were you hoping to go?" Devlyn asked Alex.

"Yesterday. But that was before your timely appearance," Alex responded.

"I see, so now?"

"The sooner the better." Alex yawned, bored.

"Will Alethea stay here?" Devlyn asked, noticing her absence at what was no longer an informal gathering.

"Yes, she's helping the wounded," Wyn said.

"Good. She's likely the only person capable of keeping the peace between humans, centaurs, and ogres," Alex said, chancing a glance toward the congested castle yard.

"And Aen?"

"I'm coming," Aen said before Alex could answer for him.

"Promise not to throw yourself into any unnecessary sword fights," Alex said, concerned.

"Viren gave me some pointers. No one in Karithel can beat him." Aen beamed.

"You are not Viren, so please be careful," Alex said.

"I will," Aen promised.

"Should I use Sanjin as a marker to shift to?" Devlyn asked, the plan to leave at once seeming to have been decided. He couldn't blindly shift somewhere he'd never been or seen before. He needed an anchor.

"I wouldn't. He's being heavily watched. Oliver would be best. I doubt Reia or Sara would be keen about you using them for anything. Even if it is to save them," Alex said.

"Oliver it is. Is everyone ready?" Devlyn asked, surprised how readily he had been swept into this plan of action. A series of nods followed in response. He and Aliel bonded in a flash of light, then he reached out for Oliver, supplemented by Alex's memories of the man. He'd been around Oliver much more than Devlyn had been since leaving Gwilnor. Oliver's mind started in shock at Devlyn's unexpected touch. *Where are you? Show me where you are*, Devlyn shared.

Hesitantly at first, images of a stately bed chamber trickled into Devlyn's mind. With enough sense of place, he willed himself and the others there, immediately surrounded by the actual place in the images he had seen. Oliver stared in disbelief as Devlyn, Alex, Viren, Wyn, Aen, and Falthion stood in his bed chamber.

"How—*why* are you here?" Oliver asked, bewildered.

"A thank you would be nice," Alex said, inspecting the room. "After not receiving any word from you, I presumed, correctly mind you, that something terrible had happened."

"I beg your pardon?" Oliver looked troubled.

"Are you not aware that the soldiers under your care were enslaved by that Tenir fellow?" Alex asked.

"Enslaved? I've been in communication with them *and* you all along." Oliver gestured to a stack of parchment on his desk, all formal letters with Alex's seal.

"The handwriting is just as bad as his. Doesn't mean it's not a forgery, though." Devlyn examined the parchment.

"My penmanship is perfectly legible, thank you." Alex grabbed a handful of almonds from the bowl on the desk.

"My soldiers—we have to go to them," Oliver said, panicked.

"They're fine now. Well, not your captains and first lieutenants. Tenir slaughtered them to make them an example. I left Kam in charge of the fort," Alex said.

"Kam—he's a good man." Oliver frowned, clearly trying to fathom how he'd been duped.

"Did Sanjin not tell you anything?" Alex asked.

"He's been preoccupied with coronation preparations. I haven't seen him in months."

"Since when did a coronation require months of planning? Just place the damned crown on his head and be done with it." Alex said.

Oliver huffed, seeming to realize how blind he had been since coming to Karithel.

"Oliver, what's happened here? What sort of game is being played if they orchestrated a complex series of forgeries?" Devlyn asked.

"The Daer fleet brought us directly to Castle Mavarre, saying it would be a good base, seeing as our army couldn't necessarily march into Karithel, even if we were escorting Prince Sanjin. Tenir welcomed us like royalty. Sanjin and he embraced as old friends."

"That lying snake is dead—not at my hand," Alex added to Oliver's raised eyebrows.

"And since you came to Karithel?" Devlyn asked, bringing them back to focus.

"Sanjin and his court have been planning his coronation, just as I said."

"Alex, you don't suppose Sanjin would have betrayed us, do you?" Devlyn asked.

"I doubt it. He was overjoyed when Oliver, Reia, and Sara agreed to join him. He appeared as a prisoner when he came to Castle Mavarre in the guise of a messenger," Alex said.

"What of the ei'ana?" Devlyn asked.

"Sara spends most of her time in the palace's library. Wherever she found the time to learn Charrenese, I'll never know. Reia can often be found with the Kilnae Del, intent on unravelling their secrets, no doubt," Oliver said.

"Any chance they would pay you a visit?"

"Reia will likely stop by soon."

"Strategizing before dinner, are you?" Alex smirked.

"Something like that."

"Don't expect me to give her a more formal position at court than she already has. People will think Septyl is ruling Thellion rather than their king."

They didn't have to wait long before a soft knock announced Reia.

She came in without invitation, pausing in the doorway to take account of the new arrivals in Oliver's rooms. "I believe a letter would have sufficed," she said at last.

"Afraid not." Oliver handed over the stack of parchment. "All forgeries. Even the ones from Castle Mavarre."

Reia skimmed the pile, flipping through each page for some clue. "You're positive?"

"I'd know if I'd received a letter and wrote back. Wouldn't have travelled all this way if I had," Alex said flippantly.

"So, what's the situation?" Reia asked and Alex quickly repeated what he had just told Oliver. "Sanjin's advisor is a Sha'ghol? That would mean he was also behind the late king's untimely death and so many others'."

"Caspol?" Oliver asked.

"His features are always veiled but I thought he might be Cyndinari. He never leaves Sanjin. The mages keep their distance from him as though he's a rabid animal," Reia said.

"What do you intend to do with him?" Oliver asked.

"Ideally, take him alive for questioning," Devlyn said.

"That won't be easy. He has many supporters at court, though I doubt any know his true identity," Oliver said.

"No, but he might show his true colors with your arrival and the accusation that someone at court has been creating forgeries. Not to mention him murdering the late king," Reia said.

"You want to lure the beast out of its lair so it might better snap at us?" Alex arched a brow.

"Precisely."

"And what are you suggesting? Just waltz to the throne room?" Alex asked, his tone skeptical.

"Don't be absurd; need I remind you, Sanjin isn't the king yet. He'll be in the royal salon. And unless you want to stay here in Karithel for a month-long covert operation to uncover the truth, you'd best follow my lead," Reia returned.

"Neither Ellendren nor Diana would appreciate an extended stay here," Devlyn said.

"Both are intelligent women. Shall we?" Reia gestured to the door, clearly disinterested in delaying for an alternate plan.

"What could possibly go wrong?" Alex quipped before moving toward the exit. "Do you have a way to warn Sara?"

"She'll meet us there. After you, Your Majesty."

Alex pushed through the door, Devlyn close behind as the small group from Eklean walked through Karithel's royal palace. Rich and colorful marbles polished to a high, reflective sheen adorned the corridors, inlaid with intricate patterns. Accustomed to Aerodhal, Devlyn was surprised how empty the palace was. Where were all the dignitaries and staff responsible for ensuring Charren was governed smoothly? Surely, Caspol wasn't the only advisor to the crown.

A pair of guards stood at the entry to the royal salon. They recognized Oliver, Reia, and Sara who had joined them, but they hesitated at opening the doors for the larger group. The added presence of a phoenix fluttering over Devlyn's shoulder did little to persuade them. "And who seeks an audience with His Highness, Prince Sanjin al'Sanhir?" the guard asked formally.

"Alexander Vaerin, King of Thellion. And this is Devlyn Lorenthien, who has too many titles for me to recount lest you never open the doors," Alex grumbled.

"His Highness is not to be disturbed. He is busy preparing for his coronation."

"I doubt a chat with his allies from across the sea could prolong it longer than it already has been."

"He's not to be disturbed," echoed the other guard, gripping his sheathed sword.

"I would not recommend that," Viren said, mirroring the guards' grip. Before the exchange could heat up, the doors to the salon opened, revealing a surprised, yet delighted Sanjin.

"Alex? What are you doing in Karithel, my friend? You should have written! I would have held a banquet in your honor had I known you were coming," Sanjin said, embracing Alex, feigning surprise. "And Devlyn, so wonderful to see you. What brings you all to Charren?" Sanjin also embraced Devlyn, then whispered, "Beware the snake." He pulled away, grinning.

Devlyn's shock was reflected in Alex's face. Undoubtedly, Sanjin knew they were in danger.

A man stood beyond the doors, noticeably not Charrenese, or human for that matter, but Cyndinari. "Ah, Ei'denai Devlyn Lorenthien. What brings you so far from your reclaimed home? Has Erynel managed to retake Krysenthiel already? She never was known for her patience."

"I'm afraid we haven't been introduced," Devlyn said. Only a Sha'ghol would speak of Erynel Meriden so casually, confirming what Devlyn already knew of the elf.

"Where are my manners?" He purred and fell into an elven bow. "Caspol li'Moren." Tenebrys crackled from his fingertips, further darkening the salon. "I must say, I've enjoyed experiencing how resourceful the people in this hemisphere have been. The arcane gems are extraordinary, but it's the Daer who are most impressive."

"Capturing anadel and abusing their powers is hardly commendable," Devlyn said, ready to bond with Aliel at a moment's notice.

"I thought a Phaedryn would be impressed with what the Daer have accomplished. After all, is it really any different from what your kind have always done?"

"We've never enslaved phoenix. The only ones held against their will are the ones in Ythinor's belly."

"What a waste. So much power left on the table." Caspol's voice turned dangerous. "Where the Daer are superior to you Luminari is quite clear to me. They allowed their control over the anadel to not only change them, but they even allowed it to pass to their descendants, forever altering who they are as they took power." Caspol breathed deeply, electric static humming off his skin. He wasn't just wielding tenebrys.

Devlyn didn't fully understand what the Sorcery looked like when used, but he imagined it had the same corruptive nature as tenebrys. The only difficulty was that Devlyn didn't know which was more dangerous. Corrupting a metaphysical force in the world was one thing, but the Sorcery forced anadel against their will. It had not only physically altered the Daer, making them not quite human any longer, but it had also given them incredible strength.

"I will provide you one chance to leave Karithel. You see, I've grown quite fond of it and I care not what happens in Eklean."

"The Sorcery is outlawed in Charren," Sanjin said, clearly aware he could no longer pretend Caspol was innocent.

"Your father made some changes while you were away. You'll find that I can be quite persuasive. You can join your friends in Eklean or stay here. It matters little to me. I will be taking Castle Mavarre back though; ogres and centaurs won't stop me." Caspol rang a tiny bell, its tone sharp, crisp, and piercing. The sound of people stomping through the palace soon filled the corridors. Caspol blocked their way into the salon and the approaching guards, all loyal to the Sha'ghol, closed in behind.

"I will not betray Charren and forfeit the Charrenese to you," Sanjin growled threateningly despite the lack of a sword.

"Again, it matters little to me. You humans live such short lives as it is. But don't think I'll permit an heir to carry your name. Charren's royal line will end with you and Karithel will undisputedly be mine."

With those words, Devlyn bonded with Aliel and Wyn, Reia, and Sara embraced the erendinth; the others unsheathed their swords.

"You think to stand against me?" Caspol laughed. "Do not think for a moment that those are normal soldiers coming to apprehend you. I've made some allies in Daereneth since Erynor's previous defeat so long ago, and the Sorcery rarely fights with swords and spears."

Sanjin's eyes flickered, then he rushed to Devlyn's side. Caspol laughed again, presuming Sanjin wanted to flee. "Withdraw from Aliel when I give the word." Devlyn opened his mouth to protest, but Sanjin hushed him. "There isn't time to explain. Trust me."

Caspol's reinforcements soon closed in on them, blocking their escape.

"Last chance," Caspol teased, tenebrys crackling off his fingertips.

Sanjin thumbed a ruby and held it behind his back. "Charren will never submit to you, the Sorcery, or the Daer Empire. Devlyn—now!"

Devlyn obeyed Sanjin's command and withdrew from Aliel, the world darkening before an explosion of crimson light filled the corridor and spilled through the doors and into the salon. The sound of glass shattering filled the room. Caspol screamed and threw bolts of tenebrys without concern. The lightning thrashed everywhere, taking a guard in the chest. The Daer sorcerers who had come to detain them had also fallen to their knees, screaming in agony. Devlyn had no idea what Sanjin had just done with that ruby. Other than Caspol, the sorcerers were incapacitated.

Caspol continued to haphazardly wield tenebrys and just as a bolt lashed toward Sanjin, a cold darkness fell over Wyn and he stopped the bolt in its place. Devlyn stared in shock, realizing that Wyn had just wielded tenebrys. But this was not the time for an explanation; they didn't have that luxury. Caspol screamed and thrashed about as more bolts flew from his fingers.

"Bond with me," Wyn said. Reia and Sara were startled by the request, but did as Wyn asked, knowing they couldn't stop a Sha'ghol on their own. Devlyn too bonded with Wyn. He felt the negative erendinth course through Wyn, multiplying as he borrowed Devlyn, Reia, and Sara's strength. The tenebrys wields were pushed back into Caspol as he was forced to his knees.

"How long can you hold him?" Sanjin asked.

"Long enough," Wyn winced at the screams. The commotion soon brought the attention of the palace guard and the screaming died down.

A man garbed in robes pushed forward.

"What's happened?" he asked.

"The Daer Sorcery are here in Karithel. I doubt these are the only ones. And Caspol…" Sanjin choked on his words, "is responsible for my father's death."

"I see. You can stop tapping the arcane gem. The anadel are no longer prisoners to these monsters. Their talismans are shattered," the mage said.

"That's why you wanted me to withdraw from Aliel." The phoenix perched on a grateful Devlyn's shoulder as the crimson light died down.

"I didn't know how it would affect you nor did I want to test it."

"Thank you," Devlyn said, terrified that a power existed that could potentially shatter his bond with Aliel.

"Is there a way to contain the Sha'ghol?" Reia asked.

"We have ways of dealing with the Sorcery, but not wielders," the mage said. "The Daer are harmless now that they've been stripped of their anadel."

"Caspol will not escape the Guardian Citadel," Viren said.

"Can we go sooner than later? He's very strong," Wyn said, drops of sweat on his brow.

With the ruby no longer activated, Devlyn bonded with Aliel. "Will you stay here, Alex?"

"I refuse to let the bloody Daer tarnish my first visit to Karithel," Alex said. Devlyn suppressed a laugh. "You will come back for me though, yes? I'd rather not explain to Diana why I had to fly all the way back home."

"Of course. I'll see you at week's end." Devlyn, Viren, Falthion, and Wyn held hands, Viren gripping Caspol's shoulder. The chaos in Karithel's royal palace was immediately replaced with the quiet night of the Guardian Citadel. Devlyn didn't want Wyn to wield tenebrys any longer than necessary. Wielding it at all was too much.

Viren led them through the citadel and down into its foundations.

Lumaryl hummed a soft golden light in the night, the only time of day it appeared normal with the lack of sunlight. Defeated, Caspol went quietly and without a fight. Devlyn wondered if he was thankful to stop fighting. What sort of effect did fighting in Ramiel's name have on someone?

Caspol was soon behind thick lumaryl bars. Wyn released his wield, sighing as he did.

"Since when?" Devlyn asked, concerned.

"Since Aren and I went into the Void. I didn't intend to breathe it in, but the air was thick with it. I've been able to sense it ever since."

"And Alethea?"

"She wielded lumenys the entire time she was there; it could not touch her. I wish I had thought to do the same."

"Caspol might have killed us if you had."

TALISMANS

Alex spent his first full day in Karithel being treated to all the splendors the floating city had to offer. Sanjin had insisted after the Thellish army had finally been brought into the city. The prince and soon-to-be-king had promised to explain everything but was determined to conclude his delayed coronation plans before another threat emerged. Wearing a crown came with benefits when ensuring the kingdom's security.

As Sanjin busied himself with preparations, Alex sipped a spicy, yet deliciously fruity drink while half submerged in a steaming grotto. A host of Karithel's elite accompanied him there, but no one he knew by name. Oliver, Reia, and Sara were briefing and caring for the Thellish soldiers. Not that they really needed caring for any longer, as Alethea had already seen to their injuries.

Curiously though, after securing an alliance between the humans of Charren and the centaurs and ogres of Ogren, Alethea had decided to spend the day with Aen. Alex had a creeping suspicion it had something to do with elf-magic. So much for Aen becoming a knight. Alex hoped the ei'ana wouldn't pull Aen away to Gwilnor too soon. Aen had been an invaluable and loyal friend since they had left Cor'lera, leading a small militia to overthrow the corrupt Perrien Council.

It still boggled his mind that they had managed it, and now Alex was a Thellish king with the world's most beautiful woman as his wife and queen. Diana would have his head when she found out he had insisted on staying for another week. Especially since his day was consumed by being pampered by Charrenese royalty.

Unaware of the passing time, he looked up to see Sanjin come in. "I see you're enjoying yourself." Sanjin unabashedly removed the towel covering his waist, handed it to an attendant, then stepped into the steaming water. Clothing of any sort was forbidden in Karithel's grottos.

"At your command," Alex said, taking another sip of his drink. "I'll have to ask if there are any natural hot springs in Elothkar.

"A worthy endeavor, indeed."

"Have you learned anything new about the Daer infiltration?"

"I've sent a formal inquiry to the Daer Senate regarding Caspol li'Moren and his affiliation with them, along with the score of sorcerers who had accompanied him."

"And the Sorcery?"

"No good would come of accusing the Daer Senate of practicing it again. We know they do." Sanjin closed his eyes and dipped further into the water, his shoulders now fully submerged.

"What if they stage another coup or try to take the city?"

"I would like to see them try." Sanjin stood, water dripping off his lean figure as steam lifted from his skin. "Come, I would like to show you something."

"So soon? You only just got here." Alex did not want to leave the steaming water.

"We can't all spend an entire day sipping spiced wine while our appendages prune."

"Oh, very well." Alex followed him out of the water, toweled off, then dressed. He and Sanjin left the grottos to walk through the city.

The Charrenese showed no sign of how close they had been to bowing to a Sha'ghol. They went about their business, ignoring the blocked-out sun as best they could. The Charrenese didn't want to think of the shift of powers in Teraeniel and even fewer were aware of why the sun had been blotted out. Alex repeatedly reminded himself that it was Devlyn and Ellendren's problem. Aside from a unified northern Eklean, what help could Alex offer when beside the Evil One's intentions? His armies would be ready when called upon, but he didn't have any secret elf-magic to help return the world to its former state.

Sanjin stopped in front of high, impressive gates etched with gilded runes. He knocked and Alex thought the sound echoed more than it should, as though amplified by something unseen.

"Where are we?" Alex asked as the gate creaked open.

"The Kilnae Del's citadel. The magic here has always protected Karithel."

"Reia and Sara will be livid about you showing me this."

"The ei'ana do not need to have their fingers in everything." Sanjin gestured for Alex to enter. "And I must admit, the mages prefer your ignorance toward anything magical."

Alex ignored the jibe. The entry hall stretched back a long length and they went down halfway before they reached a grand stair. Sanjin continued to lead Alex through the impressive citadel until they arrived at a chamber with a shallow dome. An ethereal representation of Karithel floated in the center, glowing crimson.

"Karithel can only fall from internal sabotage," Sanjin said. "No enemy, not even the Daer Sorcery, can breach our defenses." Sanjin pointed at the large columns holding the arcane gems along the city's perimeter.

"They don't just keep Karithel in the sky, do they?" Alex asked.

"Charren's greatest discovery. We found only one mine with arcane gems. Since that discovery, we opened many more mines, none offering the same reward. Alas, Charren's success has always been in the Daer Empire's shadow. We've always known what they were doing to the anadel—subverting them to their will and trapping them in talismans."

"Yet you maintained an alliance with them?"

"Charren would have been absorbed by them thousands of years ago if we had not. The Kilnae Del only learned how to free an anadel from a sorcerer's talisman because of our proximity to them."

"So, you're saying it's possible to strip the Daer of their power?" Alex asked, intrigued.

"There are limits." A woman stepped forward. "I am Cali Mithr."

"Such as?" Alex asked.

"The Daer know we have this ability. Unlike the king's recent advisor, Daer sorcerers are wary of Karithel. They know better than to infiltrate us here."

"What about your forts and castles on the mainland? How long has Castle Mavarre been under Daer control?" Alex asked.

"Based on the accounts of the captives there, at least four years. About the same time Caspol appeared in court," Cali said, regret lacing her voice.

"Are we certain we've detained all the sorcerers in Caspol's employ in Karithel?" Sanjin asked.

"We can use the same arcane gems and purge the city of any talismans binding anadel. We can conduct the ritual at night when they are least prepared," Cali said.

"See it done," Sanjin said.

"Do note, Your Highness, that if we destroy the talismans, we won't be able to identify the culprits," Cali said.

"Stripping Caspol's allies of their most powerful assets is not enough. I want them identified and brought to justice," Sanjin said.

"It will be done, Your Highness."

"But why did the Daer want Castle Mavarre in the first place? Are the mines the only reason? Aside from serving as a base for slavery, why bother holding a fort in Ogren? It's not like ogres are hospitable to the Daer, nor the centaurs for that matter," Alex said.

"Unlike Daereneth, Ogren is still rich in anadel. The Daer Sorcery has all but ensnared every anadel on their continent. The ogres and centaurs will not tolerate them doing the same in Ogren," Alethea said as she came into the room. Cali seemed uncomfortable with the ancient elf being present in the Kilnae Del's citadel without invitation but said nothing. "Ever thirsting for more power, the Daer long to claim Ogren and Ja'horan for their empire, mining both for slaves, resources, and anadel."

"And Castle Mavarre, specifically? What were my soldiers forced to mine?"

"Castle Mavarre is an old mining site from when Charren underwent a mining frenzy. We thought it had the greatest potential. A mineral, not unlike our arcane gems, was found there. The Daer call it nethrin," Sanjin explained.

"The Kilnae Del tested the glassy crystals but could not unlock their secret. We abandoned the mine and used the fort for its original intent," Cali said.

"Having already mined quite a bit of it and having no use for it, merchants inquired if Daer would be interested in the nethrin. Now, my forefathers had no idea what the Daer would use it for, but the Daer agreed to purchase all that we had mined. This was long ago, when most of Ogren was governed by human tribes living in tandem with ogre and centaur tribes," Sanjin said.

"And what exactly is nethrin capable of?" Alex asked.

"The Daer would have recognized it at once; when crafted in a certain way, it's used to create their talismans to bind anadel. Nethrin has a very distinct presence," Cali replied.

"That is why ogres and centaurs have agreed to guard the mine, to prevent it from falling into the Sorcery's hands. The Daer will find resuming a mining operation there to be quite impossible," Alethea said.

"Thank you," Sanjin said. "I'm still wary of your account regarding the ogres. All my life I was taught to fear them. I've only known them to terrorize human kingdoms in Ogren."

"The Evil One would very much like to make them your enemy, but they have proven themselves incorruptible, and invaluable guardians of Ogren. So the Sha'ghol and Daer fabricated a story to conceal their own misdeeds in Ogren, to make them appear the victim to vicious ogre attacks."

"We were fools to trust the Daer's account," Sanjin said.

"You had no way of knowing the kingdoms the ogres sacked were controlled by Daer and mining Ogren for its anadel. The native tribes and kingdoms were either slaves or fully assimilated into Daer's world-view. But that is not why I came here. The mineral from Castle Mavarre is easily traced."

"What are you suggesting?" Sanjin asked.

"To find the remaining sorcerers in Karithel, we trace the nethrin directly to them." Alethea stepped closer to the illusion of Karithel and extended her hand; multiple blue dots appeared.

"Even here?" Sanjin eyed the dot inside the citadel. He turned on Cali. "Who's cell is that?"

Cali expanded the illusion until only the citadel was visible, further focusing on the individual chamber. "That's where our youngest initiates live. They can bring nothing from their previous lives to the citadel. I have no idea how one managed to get a hold of a talisman."

"I have a hunch," Alex said. "And I hope it is already locked in a cell in Arenthyl."

"Take us to this initiate. I have some questions for them," Sanjin said, moving to the door.

"And the others in the city?" Cali asked.

"Organize the city guard, provide as many mages as necessary. I want them rounded up before they have a chance to flee and infect the rest of Charren," Sanjin said.

"Of course." A ruby glowed in Cali's hand, presumably delivering instructions to the guard.

Alex, Alethea, and Cali trailed Sanjin, set on a warpath against the Daer Sorcery infesting his city. Alex imagined he'd react similarly if he discovered his people capturing and binding anadel against their will. They moved swiftly, as though Sanjin was worried the culprit would be alerted and flee. Upon reaching a certain corridor, Sanjin stopped and asked, "Which chamber?"

Cali knocked on an unimpressive door. A boy answered, confused at the arrival. He stumbled into a bow. "Your Excellency, Your Highness," he stammered.

"Bind him," Sanjin ordered.

Another crimson glow issued from Cali and the boy's arms were pinned to his side. "Why? I haven't done anything," he cried, panicked. More doors opened to witness the scene unfold.

"What's the meaning of this?" an old woman asked, pushing through the crowd, her hair a stark white against her caramel face.

"Sorry to bother you, Denil, but this initiate is accused of having ties with the Sorcery."

"Of what?" the boy cried, followed by gasps among the other initiates.

"Search his room," Sanjin ordered and the mages who had accompanied them filed into the small room. The sound of papers rustling and furniture shoved about issued from the room. The mages soon returned with a glassy object. Alethea proffered her hand and the mages waited for Sanjin or Cali to nod their consent, which they both did.

"It's all right—you're safe now," Alethea said to the talisman, as a purple line wove into the trinket before shattering. A wispy figure stood before them, shaking.

"It's her, not the boy," the terrified anadel screeched.

"Fool," Denil said, bringing her arms up as lighting forked from her fingertips. Alethea was too quick though. Before a single bolt could fly from Denil, Alethea wielded a torrent of aerys and Denil's arms were pinned to her sides.

"You?" Sanjin asked, betrayed. "You taught me."

"You were always a spoiled prince and you'll be a spoiled king."

"How could you? Why would you belittle yourself to the Daer Sorcery—and whatever you just started to wield?" Cali asked, enraged. The

Kilnae Del mage might not recognize tenebrys when wielded, but Alex did. Caspol must have shown those loyal to him how to not only harness an anadel's power through talismans, but also how to tap that corrupted erendinth.

"The Daer will always be our enemy. I am no traitor to Charren."

"Yet you insult me and dabble in the Daer Sorcery," Sanjin accused.

"It is only known as such because it originated there. The sun has gone dark and the dead walk. Why should we deny ourselves the power our enemy commands?"

"Enslaving anadel is not power, but weakness," Alethea replied.

"Do not speak to me elf—hypocrite. Your Phaedryn do the same. They take the anadel's power for their own and harness it. Your Phaedryn were once the most powerful beings on Teraeniel, becoming high kings and high queens, expecting us to bend to their whims. The whole world bowed to them and they would see history repeat itself."

"The world did not bow to Phaedryn but acknowledged them for bringing the world together in the Guardian Senate. And they do not enslave or bind phoenix to their will. They are an equal pair. One is not greater than the other," Alethea explained.

"If they truly cared about the world governing peaceably, then why isn't the Guardian Senate in neutral territory?" Denil asked.

"Enough," Sanjin said. "The Evil One is free and Void beasts can assault Karithel without warning and you want to prattle on about the two people doing everything imaginable to protect Teraeniel and its peoples? Take her from my sight. She's to be sentenced as a sorcerer."

The mages led the older woman away as she angrily thrashed in their grip.

"Please, return to your chambers. I think we've seen enough today. I'm sorry you had to witness that." Cali turned to the boy whose room had been ransacked. "And please, accept my apology for the mistake."

As the other initiates returned to their rooms, Sanjin asked, "How did you come to possess the talisman?"

"Denil gave it to me as a gift the other day."

"She likely didn't want anyone tracing it back to her once she learned Caspol had been captured," Alethea said.

As the others retreated from the initiates' corridor, Alex reflected on the anadel that had been caught in the talisman, his mind working.

"Intent on joining the Kilnae Del as an initiate?" Sanjin teased.

"No, but I wonder." Alex turned to Alethea. "The Evil One is an anadel, yes?"

"He was one of the irythil and remains one of the most powerful anadel in Teraeniel," she replied.

"Is it possible to use the nethrin below Castle Mavarre to create a talisman capable of containing him? There's a whole mine of it; surely we can make a talisman large enough to hold the big baddie."

"Theoretically, it's possible. But I do not know if it is the solution," Alethea said, seeming lost in thought. "Perhaps you should bring the idea to the Guardian Senate; doubtless the opening session will be focused on the Evil One."

Guardian Senate

Representatives from every nation, race, and culture filed into the Guardian Senate chambers. They had been coming to Arenthyl in a steady stream over the past several months, but once the Void had been released across Teraeniel, the missing representatives had boarded their fastest ships and set sail for Eklean. Conveniently, the Seafarers of Ja'mare had been docked in such cities. Even the merpeople had finally arrived now that the will of Theniel was known. Devlyn prayed their plans to attack the sea serpents in the Misty Sea would succeed. The world needed the Jade Flight in this war.

Jeanne shared a rare smile with Devlyn and Ellendren. "They are ready. Teraeniel is ready," she said, proud to see the day the Guardian Senate was finally called back into session. As a Guardian knight, she had made her purpose in life to uphold peace throughout Teraeniel, answering only to the Guardian Senate even when it had not been an active body.

Devlyn and Ellendren wore complementary yellow, nearly gold outfits, trimmed with pearlescent white. The lierathnil had many folds and layers and it lifted easily in the wind. They gripped their verathn scepters and Aliel and Tariel hovered above. When the doors to the Guardian Senate chambers opened, Devlyn and Ellendren stepped through and onto a high balcony where they removed their crowns for the entire assembly to witness. The Guardian Senate was no place for the Exalted Aryl of Krysenthiel, nor for the High King and High Queen of Eklean. Here, they were the Prelate of the Guardian Senate, and their unified voice carried no more weight than any other senator's.

The senate chamber was a heptagonal room, meant to symbolize the different races of Teraeniel. But despite the intended equal representation, humans, as the most populous race on Teraeniel, had a significant majority. They had come from every continent and nation to Arenthyl. The representatives from Charren were the last to arrive, having shifted with Devlyn, Alex, Alethea, and Aen that very morning.

All the world's leaders had received the Exalted Aryl of Krysenthiel's letter beseeching them to send representatives to Arenthyl. Teraeniel needed to bind in purpose to confront the approaching storm. Devlyn had understood the threat that Ramiel's return would pose but had never imagined the Evil One would pull the Void into Teraeniel and swallow their world in Darkness. From the accounts that he had studied, the Void was supposed to be a small pocket of existence. It should not have been capable of consuming Teraeniel.

Once they had taken their seats, Devlyn and Ellendren began the long and arduous process of recognizing every nation and its representatives. It was a ceremony performed only when a new representative joined the Guardian Senate. But as every senator was new, every anacordel in the chamber had to be acknowledged as a Guardian senator.

Hours passed before Devlyn finally recited the last name and the exhausted senators looked back at him and Ellendren. They all wanted to know whether the Exalted Aryl of Krysenthiel knew how to banish the Void from Teraeniel.

"As you know," Devlyn started, "the Tree of Life has been killed. The Erynien Empire has long been allied with Ramiel and has sought a means to release its lord from the Void, an endeavor that stretches back thousands of years, even before we elves lost our Skylands. When my ancestors settled in Arenthyl, they aimed to bring peace to the continent of Eklean, trapped in endless wars due to the collapse of Thellion. The idea of a body of representatives from every kingdom coming together took root; to ensure our intentions, Krysenthiel surrendered our military force to the rule of the Eklean Council, and later to the Guardian Senate.

"What began as a means for peace evolved when the Erynien Empire's intentions became known. The free people of Teraeniel can only confront Ramiel and the Void if we do so together. None of us will succeed if we strike out alone." Devlyn returned to his seat, Ellendren gripping his hand in support following his opening address.

Hushed murmurs swept through the chamber. None of what Devlyn said was new to anyone. Every nation had blamed the last millennia of troubles in Eklean on the Erynien Empire and had now sent representatives to Arenthyl to sit on the Guardian Senate. Their nations had felt the great loss when Krysenthiel had fallen to the Erynien Empire fourteen hundred years before. Balance between the nations had crumbled and the world's continents became isolated. Only the Daer sailed beyond their shores, but for devious reasons.

Wyn stood, chosen as the representative for the Lierafen aryldom. "I was in Ramiel's fortress when Verakryl was slain. I had gone into the Void with Aren Lorenthien to rescue Alethea Lenwyn, who'd been stolen into the Void by one of the Sha'ghol. The fortress is wrought entirely of dorthl and surrounded by a city called Tosk. In the Void, the substance was ethereal, yet somehow solid. Ramiel spent eons twisting its lance-like spires into the perfect weapon to pierce the veil that separated the Void from Teraeniel, which he was able to do when the Tree of Life died. With the Void unleashed, the fortress on the slopes of Mount Cyngol in the Shadow Mountains now looms in every realm save Lumaeniel."

Before Wyn could sit, a senator from Ja'horan asked, "What are the fortress' defenses? You were given an opportunity none of us will have again, not unless the Evil One is defeated."

"It's difficult to say. While we were in the Void, the fortress felt lucid, shifting at will. I don't know if it can do the same here in Teraeniel, but I wouldn't count on Vasknir being constant and predictable."

"What of the Void beasts? Have there been any reports of them crawling out of the cracks?" asked a Sorenth senator.

"Not yet," replied a draelyn senator from Tenethyl. "But Tolvenol, Primus of the Dark Flight and general of Ramiel's legions, has been freed from his long imprisonment. Undoubtedly, he will lead the Void beasts against us. When Teraeniel was young, before the different races took root and even with the dragons protecting us, Tenethyl fell to the Void beasts. If Ramiel directs them to destroy a city, it would be prudent to flee before they arrive."

"And where would you have us flee to?"

The draelyn senator didn't have a response.

"Is it this senate's belief that hiding from Ramiel is our best course of action?" Prince Donovan Orithil of Gestoria asked. "Gestoria has only just rejoined the world after rebuilding our kingdom from its ruins. We refuse to stand by and let either the Evil One or Erynor trample over us again."

"And what do you suggest?" Ange asked. She was both a Judge of Yanil and now a senator.

"I will not share strategy with a Yanilean who sold themselves out to Erynor," Donovan said, arms crossed.

"Peace, Senator," Ellendren said before Ange could retort. "Angennia is a Judge of Yanil. She and her order have long opposed Yanil's support of the Erynien Empire. We are here as allies with common purpose—our survival depends on it."

"Yet she is married to the Yaniliean's favored, and she herself has blood ties to the Yanilean," Donovan replied.

"I might remind you, Senator," Ange started, respectfully acknowledging Donovan as a senator here despite him being a Gestorian prince. Outside titles were not used in this chamber. "Women have less standing in Yanil than in other nations. Before the Supreme Judge of Yanil ended our exile, women had no voice beyond our husband's or father's. Women born of the Yanilean's blood lose their place at court if they do not marry a noble. Our rank and status is dependent on our husband's, even if he is a baker. Yes, my husband is favored by the Yanilean, and for all our sakes, let us pray he remains so if we hope to see Yanil return to how it was before Erynor destroyed Lankor with Nauto's Wrath."

A tense moment passed, then Donovan cleared his throat. "Forgive my outburst, Senator. My family has lived in hiding because of the Erynien Empire and those allied with them. Gestoria would welcome Yanil returning to our shared roots."

"Now that that's settled, do enlighten us on your vision for confronting Ramiel and the Erynien Empire," Ange said.

"We can't let the Void beasts reach any of our cities," Donovan replied.

"And how would you propose we stop even a single monster larger than most dragons, let alone all of them?" a draelyn senator asked.

"We too have dragons on our side—they've fought them before. There are wielders among us capable of incredible feats. We must take the battle to our enemies, lest we suffer the destruction of all our civilizations." Donovan returned to his seat amid an eruption into unorderly discourse.

"At the moment," Devlyn raised his voice to be heard over the commotion, "the merpeople, aided by Empress Qien Wei and others, are actively seeking a way to wake the Jade Flight. Only Tolvenol has ever been known to control the Void beasts, and the jade dragons know Tolvenol's weakness. If we can put an end to Tolvenol before he can rouse the Void beasts, we might gain a significant advantage."

"That, or the Void beasts will wander Teraeniel without direction, leaving a path of destruction in their wake."

"I'd rather a single Void beast than a horde of them directed at a city."

Deliberations continued with senators yelling out of turn. There did seem to be a consensus though—the Guardian Senate wanted Tolvenol removed from the field.

"Is there anything we can do to help wake the Jade Flight?" a Ja'horan senator asked, when the chamber eventually quietened.

"Her Radiance would welcome this body's assistance. She and the merpeople travel for the Misty Sea where the sea drakes have long dwelt at Erynor's command, ensuring Qien and Eklean remain divided. Any ship that has dared test those waters has never been seen again."

"Aldinare is close enough that we could reach the Misty Sea in time. The dragons who came to us recently have expressed concern for the Jade Flight and would see them awoken," an Aldinari senator said.

"Even if we devise a means to overpower Tolvenol, what's to stop Ramiel from commanding the beasts to do his bidding?" asked Princess Bernadette Haert, the Brieli senator.

"A fair point," replied Uon, the senator of Glyol Schtam. Devlyn hadn't seen Uon since the dwarven matriarchs and patriarchs had agreed to join in the resistance against the Erynien Empire. "But how do we defeat a being who fashions himself a god?"

"His Majesty, King Alexander Vaerin of Thellion, briefed me on a new discovery before this chamber was called into session," said a Thellish senator representing Parendior. "For those unfamiliar with the Daer Sorcery, they have a means of trapping anadel in talismans. His Majesty posited that we could fashion such a talisman to hold and contain the Evil One."

"The Daer Sorcery was outlawed by this very chamber when it was last in session," a Ja'horan senator said, swiftly followed by a chorus of agreements from other Ja'horan senators. The level of distrust between Ja'horan and Daer was plain as voices on both sides accused the other of slavery or barbaric traditions.

"Septyl maintains our stance against the Daer Sorcery." The Vyoletryn senator stood, and the chamber quieted once again; despite the world being divided and unreachable for fourteen hundred years, the Ei'ana of Septyl were remembered and respected. "However, Ramiel is by no means a typical case. Even Anaweh sealed the Evil One away in the Void to spare us his atrocities."

"Even if we're considering creating a talisman to contain Ramiel, we would need a vast quantity of nethrin to create the talisman," Aorinol said.

"You seem familiar with how these talismans are crafted," a Ja'horan senator accused.

"I'm merely commenting on the quantity required to hold an anadel who was once an irythil and has doubtless only grown more powerful since stripped of that role," Aorinol replied.

"As it happens, Charren is in possession of a mine that has vast quantities of nethrin," a Charren senator said.

"And how exactly would we mine and transport it here? To say nothing of creating what this chamber has forbidden," said a Ja'horan senator. "This chamber would benefit from more centaurs in attendance, as well as ogres."

"We do have ships in Daer to transport such a talisman," Aorinol commented, ignoring the inclusion of more senators.

"I would rather Ja'horan burn in fire than allow the Daer to hold such a weapon."

"And who do you imagine is going to make it and use it to bind Ramiel, dear Senator?"

The Ja'horan senator fumed but didn't retort.

"If this course is taken, I move that ei'ana be present at all stages of the talisman's construction and continue supervision when the Daer Sorcery are in its proximity. There should be enough ei'ana to overpower the sorcerers if needed," an Auburnis senator said, pulling her brown shawl tighter around her shoulders.

"If I might, Senator," Devlyn added, having recently experienced the Sorcery's capabilities. "As well as ei'ana, I recommend the Kilnae Del monitor the talisman's creation. They can free anadel enslaved by the Sorcery if threatened."

"A splendid idea," the Ja'horan senator said.

"How long will it take to mine this nethrin?" an Undol Schtam senator asked.

"The mine was recently under the control of the Sha'ghol, Caspol li'Moren, who was in league with the Daer Sorcery…"

"That is not proven," a Daer senator interjected.

The Charren senator glared at the man interrupting him, then continued. "They'd yet to export any of the nethrin to Daereneth, so there is an extensive cache available for our use."

"And where is this monstrosity to be crafted?" the same dwarf asked.

"To save time, it would be prudent to craft it where the material was mined."

"The centaurs and ogres of Ogren would not agree to such a wretched thing being made on their homeland," Oreniel said.

"Castle Mavarre is hardly their homeland; it is under Charren's dominion," a Daer senator replied.

"They would not agree, especially when the Daer Sorcery has been *mining* Ogren for anadel. While this chamber might have good intentions for the talisman, it is an evil thing. I can assure you, it will not be permitted on Ogren soil. Nor do I like the idea of it reaching Eklean's shores. Do know, if it is brought near the Illumined Wood, the centaurs will kill all who accompany it," Oreniel said.

"Well, let's avoid that," Aorinol said. "Is there any objection to it being crafted in Daereneth?" A flurry of protests followed.

"Can it be crafted enroute to Eklean?" a Sorenth senator asked. "We hardly have the luxury to delay."

"We'd have to verify if that's possible with the Sorcery. Do know they will not do this for free. They will either expect compensation or negotiate the continued existence of their order," Aorinol said.

"You mean you don't know their price?" asked a Charrenese senator.

"I have neither dabbled nor am I interested in the Sorcery, Senator. Despite this body's assumption, the Daer Senate has no authority over the Sorcery, just as Krysenthiel has no authority over Septyl," Aorinol replied impatiently. Devlyn felt Ellendren stiffen at the comparison between sorcerers and ei'ana.

"Either way, Ja'horan ships will sail it to Eklean with ei'ana and mages aboard."

"And when it arrives? We can't exactly march into Ramiel's fortress, let alone get anywhere near the Shadow Mountains without being attacked by the Erynien Empire. Need I remind this chamber, even if Tolvenol is defeated and the Void beasts are no longer a threat, it was the Erynien Empire that brought Krysenthiel low. Sha'ghol, Deurghol, Void beasts, shadow elves, dragons, Erynien legions, and their allies will command the battlefield. They will not forfeit a path to Mount Cyngol," said a Luminari senator representing Eandyl.

The chamber quieted; the reminder of the Erynien Empire's strength had been forgotten considering Ramiel's return. "Would the Guardian Senate formally declare war on the Erynien Empire and Ramiel?" Ellendren asked. As prelates, their role in the Guardian Senate was minimal, more one of mediation than participation in the debates.

"We're already at war," a Thellish senator said brusquely.

"Eklean is at war and Qien is divided by civil war. The world must come together to confront and put an end to both the Erynien Empire and Ramiel," Ellendren said.

"I propose a vote to make it official," said an Eldinari senator, followed by a series of agreements.

The voting mechanism was nearly identical to what the Krysenthien aryls used in their chamber. Since it was a simple vote to declare war or not, only two globes lowered from the ceiling. The globe representing affirmative rapidly filled with light. An overwhelming, almost unanimous, vote.

"Jeanne Darkel, as First of the Guardian knights, you are tasked by the Guardian Senate to renew our war effort against the Erynien Empire and Ramiel. Teraeniel's soldiers and wielders will answer to you in our unified assault," Ellendren said.

"I accept this charge," Jeanne replied, eager to see the wrongs from long ago righted.

"How will we keep the talisman from Ramiel's knowledge?" asked a Dwonian senator. "Light forsake, but what if the unit guarding it falls?"

"I have a suggestion," a dwarf standing beside the Oern Schtam senator spoke up. Devlyn recognized Oma. "Open the way between Jopht and Nunstol." At once, shouts rose from the dwarven senators, all yelling in Schtach so whatever they said was lost to everyone else in the room. Oma, who was not a senator and technically did not have a right to speak in the Guardian Senate unless invited, stood firm. "Our ways are not a secret," she said in the Common Tongue.

"What are you talking about?" a Jadien senator asked.

"Is it possible?" Devlyn asked, familiar with the Great Dwarven Tunnel, connecting every dwarven Schtam, including those that had been cut off from the Schtamite.

"We blocked it so we can also unblock it," Oma said.

"You do not have the matriarchs and patriarchs' permission to speak of this, and only they can grant permission," chided the Brunst Schtam senator.

"Then get it and stop wasting our time." Oma remained unmoved.

DECIMATED

Devlyn and Ellendren stood on their balcony, all Arenthyl spilling out before them. Without the sun shining on them, the lumaryl structures had a consistent tone. Devlyn hadn't realized how much he'd enjoyed the slight variations in color and luminosity throughout the day, and how much he had depended on them. The elves had always been drawn to the changes of the sun and had even dedicated themselves to a certain time of day. Already he was beginning to forget the simple magic of a sunrise and how it could transform the entire world and touch every heart.

That's what Teraeniel needed now more than anything—the sun. He felt his reserves were low, and his motivation dwindling. The opening session of the Guardian Senate had drained him. He had known bringing Teraeniel's nations together was not going to be an easy endeavor, but now he and Ellendren found themselves mediating between them. Having to defend the Daer after seeing what they were capable of with the Sorcery had left him unsettled. Yet at the moment, he couldn't see any other path to defeat Ramiel. How could they defeat someone who fashioned himself a god? It's not like they could kill him. Could anadel even be killed or unmade?

Gripping the balustrade for support, he felt himself fraying at the edges from the stress. Devlyn was more likely to become undone than Ramiel. Ellendren placed her hand over his. She was aware of all that went through his mind, just as he felt her own doubts and anxieties. "If we find another way, we'll do it," she said.

"We don't have time. The Seven Chairs have readied their delegation and a message has already been sent to Charren, Ja'horan and the Daer Senate."

"What do you think the Sorcery will demand?"

"Likely sanction to practice their *art*."

"We cannot grant it."

"And if they refuse to help us? How else will we defeat Ramiel?" Devlyn didn't mean to shout. "I'm sorry, Elle."

"We're all anxious," Ellendren said, her voice noticeably calm. Her other hand touched her growing belly. "I hope the sun returns before we bring our twins into the world."

"As do I." Devlyn wrapped his arm around her; her head nestled against his chest. A messenger came onto their balcony, holding a rolled-up message, its seal already broken. Their moment of solitude ended. They knew it wouldn't last.

"The First of the Guardians asked me to bring this to you," the messenger said, noting Devlyn eying the broken seal. "She asked that you join her in the Guardian Citadel."

Devlyn read the message quickly, lost for words after he did. "New Castle has fallen." The city had long stood as a stronghold between northern and southern Eklean, both Mindale and Yanil holding a claim to it. Dozens of wars had been fought over its control, each conflict contributing to stronger fortifications. Most recently, the city belonged to Mindale. While its nobles had been quick to support the emerging Erynien Empire, New Castle was now part of Thellion and was the first Mindalean city to pay the cost for crossing its former emperor.

After the shock had settled, Devlyn and Ellendren moved quickly through Aerodhal, then through Arenthyl's upper tiers, trailed by Viren, Abbie, Danielle, and Fyona and a score of knights. The Guardian Citadel was abustle with knights and recruits rushing to perform their duties, awaiting their orders in light of New Castle's fall.

In the crowded map room, a dozen generals from several nations stood around the lumaryl map table. The generals had come from different countries, sent to assist Jeanne in wake of the Guardian Senate formally declaring war. Among them were Karl, Tye, and an Arantiulyn ei'ana; Sorenthil, Gestoria, Ja'mare and the dwarves had also sent generals and admirals.

"What happened?" Ellendren asked. There had been no warning of an army descending on New Castle.

As the room echoed with greetings, Devlyn took note of a young woman with an ashen expression. "They came at night. No alarms bells rang. Most of the city's population were asleep and woke to die painfully. Only a few of us escaped," she said.

"Escaped what?" Ellendren asked before the generals could control the narrative.

"Monsters. They moved in the darkness as we would in the light. Even with all our fortifications, New Castle didn't stand a chance. They came over the high stone walls unimpeded."

"What about the city and everyone who lived there?" Ellendren asked.

"The only lights came from the fires. The flames clung to stone and melted it as though it was glass. Forgive me, Ei'terel, but New Castle and anyone who couldn't escape are gone. The ruins are doubtless flooded with ghosts now."

"Can nothing be done?" Devlyn asked, wrapping his head around a city and all its inhabitants being snuffed out in a single night.

"Not for New Castle," Jeanne said, her voice heavy.

"Is there no way to defend ourselves against these Void beasts?" Devlyn's shoulders tensed.

"Wielders and dragons will have more success than any knight with a sword against those monsters," Jeanne said.

"Has Septyl been informed?" Ellendren asked.

"A messenger should be presenting the report to the Seven Chairs as we speak."

"The only people still alive who have fought Void beasts are draelyn and dragons. Perhaps they will know how to best defend our cities," Devlyn said, knowing full well that Tenethyl had fallen when Ramiel had set his eyes on the bejeweled city that had attracted dragons.

"I've already sent word to the Ealyn of Tenethyl," said a man whom Devlyn had assumed was a Luminari elf, as his hair was a golden sheen, but as Devlyn looked more closely, the man's eyes held a golden light not derived from a bond with a phoenix. No, he was a draelyn of the Gold House, descended from Galithinol the Gold, and Devlyn's distant relation.

"And?" another general asked.

"You already know the draelyn and dragons of ancient Tenethyl could not stand against Ramiel and his Void beasts. Much of our population fought off the invading horde, knowing they wouldn't survive so the rest might escape to the Valley of Saeryndol," the draelyn said.

"So, we're back to what the Guardian Senate has already asked? Where are we to go if fleeing is our only option?" asked a Sorenth general.

Again, Devlyn didn't know. Krysenthiel was likely the best suited to withstand an enemy capable of melting stone. But he had no idea how lumaryl would resist fire laced with tenebrys.

"What about the villages surrounding New Castle? Do we have any idea if they're still standing? Can we help them evacuate? If New Castle couldn't resist the Void beasts, what hope will villages have?" Ellendren asked.

"Ramiel might target them, but I doubt it. He focused on larger communities or places of note in the Elder Days. He expects villages to fall into line after the greater places are brought low or destroyed," the draelyn general said.

"We can't just abandon them to be absorbed by Ramiel's influence," Ellendren said.

"I'm afraid we have more pressing matters, Ei'terel," Jeanne said apologetically. She didn't want to abandon anyone to the whims of monsters either. "We don't know where they will strike next."

Everyone gathered around the map table looked anew at the illumined representation of New Castle on the border of Mindale and Yanil. Would the monsters continue east and set flame to the now abandoned Freiton Wood or would they strike north? Mindale was a powerful kingdom, even after the political upheavals of passing from the Maroven king who had sold his kingdom to the Erynien Empire, to the Dwonian chief-king, and now to the Ashtons.

"Jeanne, how soon would you recommend we take the offensive, if anything to occupy the Void beasts and prevent them from decimating another city?" Devlyn asked, sharing Ellendren's concern for the vulnerable scattered across Eklean and beyond.

"We'll only be able to use that tactic once. While I dislike the idea of using the Sorcery to defeat Ramiel, I believe it most prudent to hold off our offensive engagement until the talisman is ready," Jeanne said.

"Going too soon would end in a slaughter. It's not like we'd have a keep or castle to defend from. We'd be camped in valleys around the Shadow Mountains, vulnerable. Dynthol Mirk is no welcoming forest," a Sorenth general said.

"Not that any keep would ensure our safety from Void beasts," a Guardian knight said.

"So, we do nothing?" Devlyn asked, alarmed.

"No. Now that we know the Void beasts are on the move, we monitor their path. They'll make their next destination clear soon enough, and when they do, we evacuate whoever is in their line of sight," Jeanne said.

"Will the dragons help us?" a dwarven general asked.

"I cannot speak for the dragons. We can only beseech them," the draelyn general said.

Devlyn had only met a few of the dragon primuses. Lyvenol, Aerinol, and Caephenol, primuses of the Gold, White, and Blue Flights, had already pledged to help the free peoples of Teraeniel resist Ramiel and his horde. Devlyn wondered if he would have to fly to Phroenthyl to tell Lyvenol what was happening in Eklean. Even now, shifting to Phroenthyl felt wrong. That place was sacred to Phaedryn and the Gold Flight.

We will not abandon you. The dragon flights stand with you, young Lorenthien, Lyvenol's deep voice echoed in Devlyn's mind mixed with images of the seven dragon flights fighting alongside the Guardian army. Judging by the startled expressions of the others around the map table, they too had heard Lyvenol.

Thank you, Devlyn shared back. He then looked back to the map. While he couldn't know Ramiel's intentions, he did know Erynor envisioned himself as the rightful emperor of the continent and would not want all Eklean's cities to be destroyed. "Do we know where the Erynien legions have positioned themselves?"

Jeanne expanded the map so it showed more of the continent. "We know most of the legions were summoned to Mount Cyngol, likely to greet Ramiel when he returned. There's been whispers of a legion in Daerinth, supporting its prince who is caught between Sorenthil and Gestoria. I've asked both kingdoms to monitor their movements and to engage only if the Cyndinari move against them. As for the legion responsible for mining Lake Saeryndol and felling Verakryl, their location remains a mystery. They likely fled to Torsil after their task was complete, assuming they were able to escape the icy shafts."

"Do you expect them to join forces with the Void beasts?" Devlyn asked.

"Possibly, but I don't know the enemy's strategy. This is also new to me." Hearing Jeanne, a confident woman, admit to doubt or ignorance was as likely as Alex wanting to learn how to wield and a bit disturbing.

"How do you mean?" Ellendren asked.

"Ramiel just had New Castle obliterated in a span of hours. I can't say whether he plans to allow any anacordel not vowed to him to live. For all we know, he might very well intend to purge Teraeniel of creation, slaughtering us all to achieve his goal. Our only option is to stop him before he can," Jeanne said, causing everyone in the room to look at Devlyn.

The prophesy hung in their stares. They all believed he was the key to defeating Ramiel. The blasted prophecy weighed him down, reminding him of his inability to do whatever was expected of him. Was dying the only way he could save the world?

"I'll be meeting with the Daer senators tomorrow to discuss how to approach the Daer Sorcery. If everything goes well, we'll travel to Daereneth to negotiate with the Sorcery." Devlyn saw the unasked question on their faces—what would they do if the Daer Sorcery refused to help? Based on the Sorcery's reputation, they could already be pledged to Ramiel.

SORCERY

Devlyn once again found himself waiting outside the Daer senators' palace. His honor guard was just as large as it had been the first time, only this time, Ellendren and her ever-constant companions had joined in. He wondered if the two wielders who greeted him were only wielders or if they also dabbled in the Sorcery. His recent visit to Charren had given him the impression that it was widely practiced among the Daer. Their elongated limbs and platinum white hair marked every Daer's ties to the Sorcery from ancient days.

Abbie scowled as the two wielders took them into the palace, the honor guard left at the entry. This time, they weren't taken to a lush balcony and provided with an assortment of fruits and tea, but rather to a formal chamber with a long table, where many Daer senators occupied most of the available chairs. Two chairs waited for him and Ellendren near the center of the long table, leaving Viren, Abbie, Danielle, and Fyona to stand behind them.

Aorinol stood. "Welcome, Prelates. You warm our halls with your presence and your phoenix bring a light we all desperately want returned."

"Thank you, Senator Aorinol," Ellendren said as she took her seat. "I believe you are aware of this meeting's intent. Deterring action will be detrimental to us all."

"Agreed. I couldn't have said it better." Aorinol smiled like many other senators and representatives Devlyn had met. Their practiced grins weren't necessarily fake, but they were shallow.

"You mentioned in the senate chamber that the Daer Sorcery would expect something in return for helping us. Is not ensuring our world's survival enough?" Ellendren asked.

"They would not see it that way. The Daer Sorcery feel as though their heritage was dismantled by the previous Guardian Senate, having bowed to Septyl's overreach. They would argue for the decriminalization of their art," Aorinol said.

"And what of the anadel they enslave for their *art?*"

"What difference does it make if they float around in a valley or in a talisman?" a Daer senator asked.

"Anadel are sentient beings; they are not meant to be caged. Daereneth is in upheaval because the Balance has been nearly destroyed there. The anadel are active forces in maintaining that Balance. By cutting them off from their charges, unspeakable things might happen," Devlyn replied. Doubtless, such events had already occurred. He had never been to Daereneth; he couldn't say what sort of upheaval had occurred in its long history.

"Daereneth is not for the weak. It has always had irregular weather patterns and tremors."

"Not always." Devlyn might be young, but the elves remembered what Daereneth was like before the Sorcery took hold of the continent. He had seen it through Kien and Kiara's visits, before the Sorcery existed—before they had had the heinous idea to ensnare anadel.

"We are only intermediaries here and merely expressing what the Sorcery will argue," Aorinol interjected, taking control of the Daer's position. None of us can decide what the Sorcery will demand in return for their services."

"Then we should go to the source," Devlyn said.

"Now?" a Daer senator asked.

"The longer we wait, the longer it will take to reach a solution,"

Devlyn said, Ellendren's hand over his. They had been of the same mind before this meeting; they couldn't wait for a prolonged negotiation with the Daer Sorcery.

"Are you certain?" Aorinol asked. Devlyn couldn't help but note the senator's nervousness. He clearly hadn't expected to return to Daereneth so soon.

"Is that a problem? The negotiations need to begin with the Sorcery. The Guardian Senate will have to weigh in on the final decision," Devlyn said.

"Do you think one of their members could be persuaded to come here? It would save precious time if they could address the Guardian Senate directly," Ellendren said.

"We could recommend it, but they might perceive it as a trap," Aorinol said.

"In what way would we ensnare them?" Ellendren asked.

"Remember, the Guardian Senate outlaws their practice. They might not trust an elf's intentions," one of the senators said.

Devlyn didn't see an alternative to going to the Daer Sorcery. He doubted he'd be able to persuade any of them to speak before the senate, but he would encourage it. "When would you be ready to leave?" he asked Aorinol.

"Whenever it pleases you."

"Wonderful." Devlyn bonded with Aliel, the flash of light causing the senators to gasp.

"Forgive me, I did not anticipate that. Must I do anything to… what do you call this form of travel?"

"Shifting. I need you to show me where we are going, then you just need to maintain contact with me."

"I'll meet you back at Aerodhal," Ellendren said, once again bound by their promise to the aryls. Only one of them could leave Arenthyl and the aryls had made it clear they preferred that it not be their pregnant ei'terel. She kissed his cheek and she and Abbie, Danielle, and Fyona excused themselves as the remaining senators stayed to observe what a Phaedryn was capable of.

Aorinol described where the Daer Sorcery leadership could be found, a place called Mahl Havn. His description did little for Devlyn and the senator only mildly objected to Devlyn peering through his mind. Aorinol's mind was a series of locked boxes, compartmentalized in a way that suited him. Aorinol opened the one that held Mahl Havn's location and only its location. Devlyn couldn't even perceive Aorinol's opinion of the place.

Now clear on where they had to go, he held out a hand for Viren and Aorinol. The walls of the palace vanished, replaced by a towering ziggurat with many tiers, reminding Devlyn of Arenthyl's tiered terraces. But the ziggurat was not a city; it was an impressive complex set within an untamed jungle. Nothing about the jungle felt safe or friendly. This place had been stripped of its anadel—a jungle long out of Balance.

The ziggurat rose from the jungle's roots and Devlyn sensed the wild trees wanted it brought down and for every stone to be cast away and tossed into the deepest ocean. The Daer Sorcery did not respect the natural order and as he felt the ire of the jungle, he considered shifting back to Arenthyl. No good would come from this place.

Aorinol moved toward the ziggurat. There was an opening a third of the way up with many stairs between them and the first tier. "I don't like this," Viren said, hanging back with Devlyn.

"Neither do I, but what other option do we have?" Devlyn reluctantly followed Aorinol.

Let's stay bonded, Aliel conveyed. *We've been warned the Daer Sorcery are no friends to my kind.*

Agreed, Devlyn shared back.

They went up the ziggurat's steps, pausing briefly before passing through its unobstructed entry portal. A line of braziers lit the interior, their flames casting long shadows.

"A stranger from a stranger land enters Mahl Havn under the guise of friendship," a voice echoed down the long stone corridor.

"I do come to you in friendship," Devlyn answered the voice, whose owner he could neither see nor sense.

"Would a friend treat us as his ancestors had?" another voice called.

"Or would he too deem us evil as they? We lost much because of that *friendship*," a new voice whispered.

"My ancestors care for the anadel. They are not slaves to be imprisoned and abused for their power," Devlyn said.

"Bold for one who does the same."

"Bold," the other voices echoed in agreement.

"Our bond is not forced, but mutual." Devlyn was tired of defending his connection with Aliel to the Daer. It was not the same. "We freely chose each other."

"Either they are the slave, or we are enslaved to them. Who is the master?"

"That is not how the relationship between anadel and anacordel works," Devlyn argued. How could the Daer not understand that?

"Yet we treat cordel as subservient. By composing body, soul, and spirit, we have a right to be masters over those less perfect. The anadel are ours to use as we desire."

"Neither is more perfect than the other," Devlyn said, fists clenched.

"So, you let yourself be the slave to others, choosing weakness over power."

"I am no slave."

"Not if you don't want to be."

"We can help you."

"We can show you."

"Let us teach you."

"Enough!" Devlyn said, frustrated. "I came here for your help."

"Yes, to enslave a great anadel."

"We know why you came to us, Devlyn Lorenthien."

"To do what you supposedly stand against."

"If there were another way, I would see it done," Devlyn said through gritted teeth.

"But you can't see another path. You only see imprisonment and slavery as the solution yet would shun us for doing the same."

"Our world is cast in darkness because of him," Devlyn said.

"Yet he did not kill the Tree."

"An elf did that."

"A corruptible, imperfect elf."

"No more perfect than the rest of us anacordel."

"They too are slaves."

"They chose to submit and serve."

"They did so willingly, believing they would become powerful."

"Erynor and the Sha'ghol chose their lot. Will you help us stop Ramiel or not?" Devlyn's voice was low, nearly a growl.

"We are not slaves."

"We do not bow to anadel, great or small."

"A contract for a price."

"What price?" Devlyn asked, dreading the answer.

"Part is already paid. You took away the elf who pretended to belong to our Sorcery. He would have betrayed us once he learned all he could from us. We thank you."

"And the rest?" Devlyn was glad locking Caspol away had come with some thanks from his supposed allies in the Sorcery.

"Your ei'ana are not welcome in Daereneth. Our art is our own. They subjugate the erendinth to their will yet in the same breath condemn us for doing the same with anadel."

"That is not the same," Devlyn protested.

"Are you so sure? Are the erendinth not also alive?"

"While you ponder, our last demand is once the great anadel is captured, the talisman be returned to us."

"I can promise none of that as they are not mine to promise. I doubt the Guardian Senate will find your terms agreeable. The rest of our world has come together to stand against Ramiel and his forces while you demand payment. If we succeed without your help, the world and all its people will know that you did not stand with us. You will be left behind and condemned." Devlyn turned away, trailed by Viren and Aorinol, went out the ziggurat, and shifted to Arenthyl.

Alone, save for Viren and Aliel's constant presence, Devlyn mulled over his interaction with the Sorcery. He'd presented their demands to the Guardian Senate, receiving a swift refusal, which he wholeheartedly supported. Even the Daer senators, most familiar with the Sorcery, had issue with supporting their demands. As the Guardian Senate refused the Sorcery, Ja'horan ships already sailed with ei'ana to Charren. Time was not a luxury they could waste for a decision to be made. Should the ships be called back to Eklean?

Was it relief he felt now that the Guardian Senate wouldn't agree to the Sorcery's high price in exchange for their help in creating a talisman to capture Ramiel? The sense of wrongness at bringing such an instrument into existence had left him uneasy. But handing a talisman containing Ramiel over to the Daer Sorcery would lead to a grim future. The unspeakable terrors the Sorcery would commit with so much power would leave creation to grovel at their feet. But without the talisman, they were no nearer to defeating Ramiel. Killing an anadel wasn't possible, let alone one who had once been counted among the seven irythil.

With no options to consider, he found himself walking away from the senate chambers, but he didn't go back to Aerodhal. He wasn't interested in lingering around the senators and descended through the complex until he reached the Guardian Citadel on the tier below. He found himself moving toward the cells in the keep's foundations. Viren didn't question his motives, despite knowing his destination.

"Ei'denai?" Caspol li'Moren intoned from his cell. "To what do I owe the pleasure?"

"Clearly not the pleasure from your own presence," Yloran eth Gnashar purred from the shadows nearby. "I heard a rumor that you were here, but had to see for myself, and Devlyn conveniently thought to accompany me."

Devlyn stared, wondering what game Yloran was playing as she stepped out of the shadows. Had she been waiting for him? He didn't believe anything Yloran did was coincidental.

"I see murdering Jaris wasn't enough for you. Must you also torment me?"

"You heard about that?" She flicked something off her cuff.

"Not much gets past Oduin dur Sethara."

"I suppose not." Yloran paced in front of the cell, then turned to Devlyn. "Would you like to ask your prisoner your question first, or shall I ask my own?"

"And how would you know what I want to ask him?" Devlyn didn't know what he wanted from the Sha'ghol who had played at being a sorcerer, so how could Yloran?

"What happens in the senate chamber is no secret in Arenthyl, darling; it never has been."

"Then, by all means," Devlyn gestured Yloran toward Caspol.

"Such a kind elf. You see, Caspol, manners and integrity are possible."

"Save that blather for your attendants," Caspol said.

"You wound me." Yloran touched her heart as though pierced.

"I doubt that's possible. Not even Jaris could scratch the ice over your heart."

"No." Yloran reflected and for a moment seemed as though she wasn't going to ask anything of Caspol. "I am curious. Why did you dabble with the Sorcery? Surely you don't think it more powerful than our former Master's gifts."

"Likely the same reason you stopped using his *gifts*."

"Which is?" Yloran wouldn't offer him any clues to her own motives.

"Neither our former Master nor the other Sha'ghol can track us if we don't touch what was given to us."

"You meant to hide, and let me guess, attempt a coup to become Charren's next king." Yloran crossed her arms. "How long did you envision that charade would last? Even if you had managed to usurp Charren's throne, you could not escape him. None of us can while he's free."

"And what would you suggest, oh wise Yloran eth Gnashar? The woman who'd rather kill her lover than speak with him. You didn't deserve him."

"Even after all these years, you still vie for Jaris' affection. Well, you can have him. Enjoy sharing a bed with a ghost." Yloran spun about. "I believe it's your turn to ask your question."

Devlyn could only blink at the exchange. His question had only been half formed when he had left the senate chamber. How had Yloran known that the unformed intent nesting in the back of his head wasn't something he wanted to dwell on. "Did you learn how to make talismans when you were with the Sorcery?"

"It's simple enough, so long as you have the right mineral," Caspol said.

"Could one be made to hold the Evil One?" Even in the apparent safety of Arenthyl, it was never wise to speak Ramiel's name in the presence of a Sha'ghol who wanted to remain hidden.

"In theory, yes. You'd need a mountain of it, which I suppose you now have since I went through the trouble of having it mined from beneath Castle Mavarre." Caspol tapped a finger against his cheekbone. "And you would have me do this for you in exchange for what?"

"In exchange for you being able to sleep with both eyes closed once our former Master is ensnared and unable to reach us ever again." Yloran clearly didn't think much of Devlyn's ability to negotiate. Considering the result of his visit to Mahl Havn, he couldn't fault her.

"And I'm to believe I'll be free to create this talisman for you?" Caspol asked.

"You'll be on a Ja'horan ship with the required nethrin, supervised by its crew, ei'ana, and Kilnae Del mages," Devlyn replied.

"Ei'denai, if I might. The ei'ana of this age are no match for a Sha'ghol. Let me and my attendants ensure Caspol behaves himself," Yloran said.

"You know that decision is not mine to make," Devlyn said.

"Then take it to the Guardian Senate—if there's time."

SERPENTINE

The Emerald's Kiss rocked as a tumultuous wave crashed against its side yet again. The Tempestien Sea was not for weak stomachs, and even Jaerol, who had never once felt queasy when on water, now retched into a bucket. There weren't enough buckets aboard as the ship rose and plummeted with the huge waves. If not for the wielders aboard, Jaerol doubted the ship would have stayed afloat, even as it plowed through another wave.

Irritated and exhausted, he considered never stepping on a ship again. What need did he have to sail when bonded with Rusyl? But they all needed to conserve their strength.

Sea drakes would attack once they reached the Misty Sea. They wouldn't be alone though; merpeople swam below the waves and the dragons who'd remained at Aldinare had promised to join them. Other than the Qien, no one wanted the jade dragons to awaken more than their cousins of the other dragon flights.

After a long and tumultuous journey, the water finally settled. Fog rolled out to greet them. They'd arrived. No ship had survived crossing the Misty Sea since the sea drakes had betrayed their own flight. The dense fog was treacherous to navigate at the best of times, but with the Void blocking out the sun, they could only rely on torchlight.

Empress Qien Wei came out of the captain's cabin, Qien Fei, imperial sister and illustrious pirate captain, beside her. Fei looked around as though it might be the last time she saw her ship. Whether it was because she feared she wouldn't survive the day or the ship wouldn't was unclear.

Even as the mist closed in, Wei stood resolute. A moment later, a high-pitched screech came from the watery depths. More shrieks followed until all anyone could hear were ear-piercing, bestial screams. Cautionary orders were called out and the dragons prepared to transform into their larger forms, ready to carry their riders into battle.

Jaerol waited for the first drake to ram the ship. Everyone on the ship held their breath, knowing there was little they could do while the sea drakes stayed beneath the waves. The sea drakes did not entertain ships passing through their domain. Jaerol strained his eyes looking for the screeching drakes, until someone yelled, "Portside!"

Jaerol spun about to see a vertical column shoot out of the water. It vaguely reminded him of the frozen jade dragons in the imperial throne room, but where the jade dragons sported brilliant scales, this creature's were faded, nearly white and translucent from living in the sea so long. Like the jade dragons, the drake had a long, sinuous body but its legs were significantly smaller from lack of use, making the creature appear more like a great snake than a dragon.

The first sea drake was followed by others leaping out of the water then arching to dive back in. Jaerol wondered if they could fly like other dragons. Even as Fei ordered the harpoons prepared, the wielders readied themselves. A large part of this battle would be fought beneath the waves, led by the merpeople. Fortunately, Rusyl belonged to the Blue Flight and had a certain affinity with aquaeys. Not that he would be diving below the water to battle drakes. And Rusyl and Kanastil wouldn't be the only dragons in the sky today. Jaerol looked toward the rear of the ship and skyward, searching for the other dragons who'd promised to help. If not for the mist and Void, he might have seen them in the distance.

But he couldn't let their absence distract him. His full attention was needed. Pressing into the elemental erendinth, Jaerol sent his senses beneath the waves to find out what was happening. A score of merpeople surrounded the belly of the ship while the rest charged the sea drakes.

Ferinn gripped his trident, swimming hard toward the nearest drake. Its girth was wider than he was tall, fin included. The merpeople loathed the sea drakes, having lost many of their kind to the monsters who perpetually tried to expand their control over the seas. The sea drakes had never been content with having dominion over the Misty Sea, bestowed on them by Erynor, not that he'd had any right to do so. The seas belonged to an elf just as much as the Skylands belonged to a merperson. The Meridean Conclave had never forgiven the Cyndinari for poisoning their waters with the sea drakes by promising the foul beasts even more of the sea if they remained loyal.

While the merpeople had always wanted to expel the sea drakes, they had also known they could not accomplish it on their own. The sea drake Ferinn approached was three times as large as the Qien ship. This creature was ancient and had never stopped growing, but there were still larger and more ancient ones in the depths.

A score of merpeople carrying tridents and wielding aquaeys swam with Ferinn toward the beast. Despite its gargantuan size, the sea drake moved just as quickly as the merpeople did, its sinuous body having adapted to moving in the water over the centuries. The drake contorted, easily avoiding the merpeople's tridents, even as its sharp fangs snapped at them.

Ferinn's unit fought as one, fanning out to surround the drake. Every part of the monster's long body acted independently. Its head snapped at them, the long torso contorted to avoid their tridents while its tail swatted at them. The tail did more than swat; Ferinn's eyes widened as it coiled around a merperson, squeezing the life from her. How could its tail be so strong?

Dashing forward, Ferinn dodged its midsection as he tried to reach the tail, lashing violently as it crushed another merperson. No one could maintain consciousness under that duress. The drake moved too quickly for Ferinn to drive his trident into it, so he took a chance he knew he might regret. He didn't have the time to consider it though and launched his trident with as much muscle as he could, knowing it would be lost if he missed his mark. He laced aquaeys along the shaft, providing more force than his own strength could muster.

The trident struck true and the sea drake screamed angrily. Black blood poisoned the water around the wound and the beast released its prisoner as it flailed about, unable to dislodge the weapon. The now free but unconscious merperson floated in the water and before Ferinn or anyone could swim to her aid, the sea drake's head darted around, its teeth snapping down hard on the defenseless merperson.

Ferinn's heart ached as he saw dismembered body parts sink to the depths. Enraged, he sped forward, overcome with unexpected adrenaline at seeing a merperson under his charge killed in such a gruesome manner. He'd known there would be casualties, but nothing could have prepared him for seeing one of his people broken in two.

Grabbing his trident, he pulled it free from the beast's torso, the jagged spear points causing as much damage coming out as when they had gone in. Ferinn focused anew, now on its monstrous and vicious head. The drake licked its lips with its forked tongue, enjoying the blood and gore of his latest victim. Her ghost lingered where her body had floated a moment before, her features showing her confusion at her unexpected change in state.

Ferinn dodged the drake's maw as it tried to break him too. He would not give this beast the pleasure of tasting any more blood but its own. Darting around the beast, he threw his trident a second time, taking a moment to properly aim at the drake's eye. Again propelling the trident with aquaeys, he held his breath as he watched it—guiding it forward as he wielded and hitting his target.

The sea drake screamed in agony, half-blinded. Ferinn reached the impaled trident and pushed it deeper into the drake's eye until the monster stopped moving. Its lifeless body sank just as the merperson's had, its ghost also left behind.

The other sea drakes, although occupied with their own battles against merpeople, took note of their fellow drake's death. They responded, enraged, their fight now fueled by the death of one of their own. In their berserk state, Ferinn realized that the merpeople could not defeat them alone. More drakes swam up from the depths, some as small as a dolphin but much skinnier, others even larger than the one Ferinn had slain.

Ferinn had yet to see the one fabled to be of disastrous proportions, the one who played at being primus of the sea drakes, thinking themselves equal to the other dragon flights. Ferinn dreaded that beast, but if they were to wake the jade dragons, Faoxi had to stir.

Pressed into aquaeys, Jaerol wielded darts of ice and launched them at the sea drakes when they breached the surface. The ice darts had yet to kill a single drake, but they did distract them long enough for the merpeople to take advantage of the situation.

Another wave of sea drakes joined the battle and Jaerol's heart sank as a particularly large one breached the surface. The monster had twice the girth of any of the other drakes seen so far and its whole body never fully cleared the water, too large to manage what the smaller drakes could. Its head remained below the surface as its exposed scales bristled in the mist.

"That's the one. That's Faoxi." Empress Qien Wei stared at the serpentine beast as though she intended to slay it herself. Jaerol paled. How were they supposed to kill that monster? She could easily coil around the ship and snap it, leaving everyone aboard in the water as fodder for the drakes. Rusyl and Kanastil couldn't carry everyone to safety, especially not in water infested with sea drakes.

Still pressed into the erendinth, Jaerol formed another wield as the large monster angled toward the ship. Aware that there was nothing he could do to stop the drake, he still pressed all his strength and being into the elemental erendinth, simultaneously embracing umbrys and animys. Working his wield, he felt a flutter of hope come from Rusyl. Jaerol spared an upward glance and saw the first of many dragons dive from the clouds, some alone, others carrying draelyn or elves.

Having impatiently awaited their arrival, Rusyl and Kanastil leapt, transforming into their larger forms in midair. They refused to allow their fellow dragons to confront the drakes in their larger forms without doing so themselves. Rusyl sent images to Jaerol, giving him just enough warning for him and Liam to leap onto his back to join the charge of dragons flying toward the monstrous sea drake, still angling toward the ship. Jaerol wondered if the monster knew the Qien empress was aboard or if it just wanted to destroy the ship that had dared to sail its sea.

The dragons raced toward Faoxi, their riders gripping weapons and wielding the erendinth. Jaerol gripped his replacement sword despite knowing it would do little against this serpent. The first wave of dragons swooped down, blasting fire imbued with erendinth according to their flight. Faoxi's exposed scales singed under the inferno, and her undulating body dove into the water.

The dragons formed up again, waiting for Faoxi to return to the surface. Too much time passed. No drakes breached the water. Something was wrong. "What are they doing?" Liam asked, voicing Jaerol's thoughts, even as they both repeatedly checked to see if the ship remained whole.

Then the sea's current warped and the waves swirled into a whirlpool, the Emerald's Kiss caught in a devastating eddy. Jaerol feared for the merpeople under the surface. Could they resist a whirlpool? Surely, they wouldn't escape it if a much larger ship couldn't. As the eddy strengthened and the ship was pulled closer to the whirlpool's eye, the massive sea drake brought her head above the water for the first time. Faoxi glared hungrily at the ship. None of the dragons here rivaled the drake for she was ancient—a relic from the Elder Days.

Too distracted by the beast's head, Jaerol missed the jade loop in the drake's ear. Empress Qien Wei, however, did not. She refused to let the monstrous appearance distract her from her goal nor did she let the ship being caught in the whirlpool paralyze her. Faoxi smirked as the ship drew near her maw, the ship too near the large head for any of the dragons to swoop down to rescue its passengers. But as Jaerol watched the events unfold, he saw that none of the passengers were frantic. The imperial sisters stood poised, staring down the monster, waiting.

Too late, Jaerol realized their intention. The two women leapt from the ship, vaulting impossibly far based on the strength of their legs alone. But the imperial sisters were wielders and they fueled aerys into their jump so that they flew over the sea to the top of the drake's head. It all happened quickly. Jaerol didn't have a chance to blink and saw Wei wrench the jade loop from Faoxi's ear and shatter it. An explosion of jade light bloomed from the ruined loop.

The serpent lost its haughty demeanor, its eyes sharpened, and it dove, sucking the sisters under with it. Impossibly, the ship stayed afloat, no doubt due to the crew's wielders.

Thunder rippled across the sky and the mist parted as a regal jade dragon as large as Faoxi dove toward them, its mere presence scattering the mist. Jaerol had only seen this dragon once, frozen in the imperial throne room—Guanxi. The jade dragon dove into the sea without a splash despite his size, headed after the clutch mate who had betrayed him and the rest of the Jade Flight.

Everyone above the surface anxiously waited. The whirlpool stilled and the waves slowly resumed their natural current. The sea reminded Jaerol of a graveyard after the violence that had ensued. He feared it would be the imperial sisters' resting place too, and as his fear deepened, a vibrant head broke the surface, its sanguine body weaving up and out of the sea behind it. Jaerol breathed a sigh of relief when he saw the imperial sisters clinging to Guanxi's long mane.

EMPTYING

The palace was quiet but Devlyn couldn't sleep. His conversation with Yloran and Caspol played through his mind. He hadn't taken Yloran's recommendation to the Guardian Senate yet. She might have saved his life in Lankor, but could he really trust her and another Sha'ghol to create a talisman capable of trapping Ramiel? The possibility of them misusing it was far greater than them handing it over once completed. Worse, would they try to capture one of the irythil and take their power for themselves? No one should have that sort of power.

Not wanting to disturb Ellendren, he walked through the palace, trailed by a silent Viren. He reached the ambulatory behind the throne room where seven shrines held the lucilliae forming Ceurendol, the Jewel of Life. Only one was sealed; it contained the final jewel, the only one he had yet to see. The jewel of love would bind the others, returning Life Immortal to the Luminari. He'd been told the jewel of love had been corrupted, but not how or why or even to what extent. Nor did he know who had corrupted it. How was he supposed to remove that corruption if he didn't know any of the details? It's not like he could go to the Sophillium and delve into a sophilliae to find the lost knowledge. Septyl had fallen long before Arenthyl's final days.

The only people who'd been in Arenthyl at that time and who were still alive were the Cyndinari, possessed by the Deurghol, and the Aldinari. Devlyn certainly wasn't going to ask the former what they had done to Ceurendol to bring about the Shroud. And the Aldinari who had long been trapped in Arenthyl had already shared what they knew.

Then Devlyn remembered there was one Aldinari elf who had been there who hadn't told his account of those dreadful days. Before Devlyn could shift to Ceurenyl, Alethea and Wyn appeared behind him. "We're coming with you," Alethea said.

Devlyn smiled, not bothering to ask how they knew he intended to go anywhere. *I'll be quick*, he shared with Ellendren, feeling her stirring in his mind at his absence.

Give Therril my love, she returned drowsily. Abbie, Danielle, or Fyona would be checking on her soon.

He and Aliel bonded and the four elves clasped hands before the spacious halls of Aerodhal were replaced with a cramped tunnel beneath Ceurenyl, the one connecting the Temple of Ceur with Gwilnor Academy. Devlyn had brought them as near to the temple as he dared. Not that it mattered anymore now that the Light in the Chamber of Light had gone out, and with it the temple's wards that prevented wielding.

Before Devlyn could decide whether to walk toward the temple or to Gwilnor, a deep belly laugh followed by a "ho-oh" echoed down the tunnel. "I knew letting you know about my secret passage was a mistake! There isn't a soul in the temple or Gwilnor who doesn't know about it now," Therril said with a laugh still in his voice.

Devlyn withdrew from Aliel and embraced his old theoreticals magister and distant ancestor who had fallen in love with Lucillia, fathering the twins, Roendryn and Feolyn.

"I've missed you too," Therril said gently before his more robust tone returned. "And you, getting yourself lost in the Void!" he said, looking at Alethea.

"I was never lost, and neither did the Void touch me," Alethea said.

"If only we were both so lucky," Wyn added.

"As long as you don't steal any souls to become a shadow elf, I think you'll be just fine," Therril said. "And it's good to see you too, Viren. Keeping Devlyn and Ellendren safe I see."

"Despite their best efforts." Viren smirked at Devlyn's offended look.

"Shall we get out of this cramped tunnel? Not that my office is much roomier, seeing that there's five of us, and Devlyn is no longer the small boy he was when he first snuck through this tunnel." Therril winked at him. Devlyn had noticed the positive effects jienzu had had on his body over the past years. Viren remained an imposing figure beside him, but his own muscles had developed definition. He was no longer the timid child from Cor'lera.

They went through the window that was not a window and into Therril's temple office. Aliel perched on the back of a chair, his lighted form illuminating the room just enough to make everyone forget the Tree of Life had died and a perpetual darkness now blanketed the world. That could only last a moment though. They could not afford to ignore the state of the world.

"Aside from solving all the wretched things happening across Ter-aeniel these days, what brings you to me?" Therril asked.

"Unless you know how to bring low a mountain, so we can revive Verakryl..." Devlyn left the question unfinished, hoping Therril did know how to bring Mount Verinien and Mount Saecrien low so the Waters could revive the Tree.

"As you might imagine, my study of theoreticals never branched to physical mountains."

"I was afraid of that." Devlyn grimaced, no closer to correcting the great imbalance in the world. "Then I wanted to ask you about Ceurendol and those last days before Krysenthiel fell to the Erynien Empire and how the Shroud had come about."

"Not the most joyous of topics." Therril mulled over his memories. "Let's see, those last days of the war were dreadful. Erynor had every Luminari city under siege; he left Ceurenyl alone because Ceurtriarch

Daeryn had made it impossible to wield the erendinth, preventing Erynor's wielders from taking the city.

"Arenthyl was a dark place though. Despite knowing we were losing the war, no one had imagined Arenthyl could fall. The city's wards and defenses had ever ensured its protection, even with the Erynien Empire's war barges surrounding us on every side. Ithendryl did her best to reassure her people while mourning her husband and her imprisoned heir. She cared deeply for the Luminari and even the Aldinari who were given refuge there."

"What about Ceurendol?" Devlyn asked.

"Ah, yes. Well, as you know, she and Faerndryn had successfully secreted five of the lucilliae out of Arenthyl. Even if Erynor managed to take the city he would not have all the jewels—he would not have Ceurendol. The last lucilliae, the jewel of love, was kept in Aerodhal. Some say removing the jewel from its shrine is impossible. I do not know how it was corrupted and the Luminari severed from their Life Immortal. But I do know that on that fateful day the Cyndinari who would become Deathless went into Aerodhal and Ithendryl was never seen again. The Shroud spilled out from the palace like a fog of death; it could not stay in the city, since the lumaryl repelled it, but we all fled in the panic. The barges were our only option and the war was lost. The Cyndinari forced the Aldinari back into the city to be its caretakers. But most shocking of all, before the Shroud could spill out, Lake Saeryndol began to freeze, as did all Krysenthiel."

"The Shroud didn't cause the lake to freeze?" Devlyn asked, having always assumed the Shroud was responsible for it.

"My hunch is that Ithendryl knew the Shroud would corrupt anything it touched and she could not bear the trees and flowers saved from Luminare to fall to the Shroud's corruption."

"And once Krysenthiel was entirely thawed, the Void was released into the world," Wyn said, looking down at his hands.

"You've wielded it." Therril's eyes widened at the realization.

Wyn nodded.

"We wouldn't have captured Caspol if you hadn't," Devlyn said to encourage Wyn. He'd done nothing wrong in Devlyn's mind. Wyn offered a weak smile in return.

"Where do we go from here?" Therril asked and Devlyn had a hunch he wasn't referring to Wyn wielding tenebrys.

Devlyn clutched the back of his neck, feeling panicked and at a loss for options. There was so much he had to do but he didn't know how to see any of it through. Even if Yloran and Caspol managed to create a talisman capable of containing Ramiel, Devlyn's problems wouldn't end. The Void beasts and Tolvenol and the Dark Flight were still free to wreak havoc across Teraeniel. The Erynien Empire hadn't needed Ramiel or Tolvenol to destroy Krysenthiel and divide the nations during Erynor's last reign. The Guardian Senate had been better poised to defeat the Erynien Empire and they too had failed. There was nothing stopping Erynor from doing the same again. Even if they managed to stop all the forces of evil trying to destroy the world, the Void would still consume Teraeniel and Somnaeniel if Devlyn couldn't fulfill the prophecy.

Pressing his palms against his head, the tides of his responsibilities and emotions weighed heavily. Aliel cooed gently, a reminder that he was not alone. These challenges weren't only his.

"Despair is never the solution." Therril wielded a globe of brilliant light. The lumenys globe was different from what Devlyn could wield. He knew ei'ceuril had a special connection with the Creating Light. "The Tree might be dead, but Anaweh lives. All corporeal beings must taste death; even elves must transition at some point. But Life does not end when we die, and neither has it for the Tree."

"And what about the Void—what about the Evil One?" Devlyn asked, voicing his anxieties. Therril's wielded globe mingled with Aliel's light.

"Neither are stronger than creation. Even as we speak, new life is quickening in Ellendren's belly. Ramiel cannot stop life from beginning.

He might fashion himself as an enemy of creation, but even he is part of its cycle. He cannot escape it or pull a single creature out of it. His corrupted touch can only graze the surface."

"What of the Void beasts and the Dark Flight? They seem to have been corrupted to the very core," Devlyn grumbled.

"Death is likely their only escape from their burden in this life, having too long been bent on chaos and destruction," Therril said.

"A diseased branch must be removed from the tree, lest the rest of the tree die with it," Alethea added.

"Can the branches be cured?" Devlyn asked.

"The Deurghol, Dark Flight, and Void beasts have been under the Evil One's corruptive touch for eons. We can only hope there is a way to reach through to them and let the Light that had created them cleanse them," Alethea said.

"But that's not likely to happen on a battlefield, is it?"

"It isn't," Alethea admitted.

Devlyn's thoughts went back to Mount Saecrien and the Waters that were supposed to revive Verakryl. How was he supposed to bring low the two tallest mountains in the world?

And then there was the prophecy. How was he to give of himself entirely? The world had already turned to shadow when the Tree of Life had been killed, and the Void loosed on Teraeniel. Had he missed something? Was he too late? The thought taunted him—what if they had already lost? Both Children were confident that the Tree was supposed to die. But what if they'd been mistaken? They could have misinterpreted Anaweh's message from the Elder Days.

The thought struck him. He didn't want to believe hope was lost. Panic took hold as his anxiety built up. His heart pounded frantically, and his breath came in quick intervals. There were too many people in the small office. He wanted to get away—had to get away. He didn't hear what the others said. Viren would be furious with him, but in that moment he didn't care. He bonded with Aliel before he fully knew his intent, and shifted out of the temple, alone.

The weight of his responsibilities was crushing him. He needed to be away from them—away from Krysenthiel.

A statue stood before him under an emerald canopy with traces of silver and gold hanging above. A still pool surrounded the statue, just as it always had. Devlyn didn't know what had brought him here. Lucillia's palace had once stood here, before it and the rest of the city had been returned to the forest. The statue of Lucillia was all that remained. Behind it rested the Roendryn monarchs, tree roots cradling their graves. Ellendren's parents shared the resting spot of her ancestors behind the place where their palace once stood. Her family had shaped her to be perfect, and to him, she was.

Thinking back to his first visit to Lucillia, he understood why he had come here. The prophecy had been interpreted in such a way that he could either join the ei'ceuril or die. How else could he give of himself entirely? Having shunned the first option, was death his answer now? Would the world be in a better place if he had joined the ei'ceuril? He wanted to scream at the unfairness of it all. He'd fallen in love and was expecting twins as fruits of that love. Devlyn wasn't ready to die.

He sat on the ground and crossed his legs, facing the statue, just as he'd done with Alethea and Therril countless times. The only difference was they weren't here to guide him. His mind reflected on those early lessons. Silencing his mind, he focused inward, his trepidation more of a storm than he'd realized. Hesitantly, he pulled open the lid holding back his anxiety, and allowed his emotions to wash over him, tumultuous as they were.

A memory of Therril whispered to go deeper—past the surface of his heart, deep within. The erendinth pulsed around him, echoing what was happening inside. Power radiated off his body in response as he sifted through his feelings. He couldn't let his emotions and fears control him, but neither could he ignore them. He'd been so occupied with his responsibilities that he couldn't remember the last time he'd sat with his interior self. No wonder it was so chaotic. When had he last practiced steadying his breath or allowing his awareness to open to the created world around him, and not just as a defensive measure?

He sensed the imbalance within himself. Everything felt wobbly as he tried to steady his breathing and not allow the panic to take hold. The wind built, swirling like a cyclone, but it didn't affect the pool. No ripples disturbed the still water. Yet he felt as though he were a ship caught in a storm as waves crashed against him and tossed him about.

He screamed, the sound rising from a place deep inside his being—a well of spiritual energy he'd unknowingly clogged. It found its release through his lungs, shaking his vocal cords. His throat ached and his skin tingled, electrified from whatever was pouring out of him in waves.

The birds above fled in the thrashing wind; Devlyn couldn't stop to think if he was causing the tempest. But as the birds took flight, he felt Aliel's approval reach through him. He'd finally allowed himself to be honest and to sit with his emotions and they were larger than any mountain. Still bonded with Aliel, his wings fluttered as he rose off the ground. With his emotions thrumming through his entire being, he connected to Teraeniel and all its creatures and the Light that could not be killed. He reached out to the two mountains—Mount Saecrien where the girl and the River were, and Mount Verinien where the boy and the wilted Tree of Life dwelt.

Entrenched, he pulled at their peaks as though he were a giant and ripped them open. Teraeniel shook in the violent motion. Mountains were not supposed to move. Teraeniel sighed and groaned, having long awaited this promised moment. Every creature would have felt the ground quake. Stone rolled down the mountain sides, returning to where it had come from before Anaweh had raised the mountains to protect the Tree and the River.

Whatever ice remained in Lake Saeryndol shattered under the avalanche of rock and snow. Water was pushed out from the lake, resurrecting long dormant riverbeds. Lake Saeryndol spilled more of its waters as more rock tumbled into the lake, but one river struck a new path from the Illumined Wood. A great waterfall spurred from where Mount Saecrien had been brought low and snaked across Sorenthil in a River, finding the least resistant route to its preordained destination, one determined before the elves had been given their Skylands.

The River shone brilliantly and the Void could not touch it or even remain above it. The light coming from the River was like a star and it pierced through the Void until the sun's rays reached Teraeniel again in its first dawn since the Tree had been killed.

Ellendren felt the tremors before she heard people screaming. One moment, she had sensed Devlyn in Ceurenyl. He'd been terribly distressed, feeling overwhelmed. She had been angry at him for not telling her how he was feeling—for hiding how he felt even from himself. They were married and were to share each other's burdens. Then she felt him shift to the Illumined Wood, pouring out all of who he was. She sensed the massive well of cathartic energy pulsing through him—it was going to pull him apart if he didn't channel it. Then the ground quaked. Many things fell from her desk and shelves and Abbie, Danielle, and Fyona were in a fright like the rest of the elves in the palace. Only Evellyn remained calm.

Ellendren heard Devlyn scream, his pain ricocheting through her and she wanted nothing more than to go to him and hold him. And if she hadn't been with Evellyn, she just might have. But his mother held out a hand to Ellendren, encouraging her to stay, leading her to the balcony, scared for her husband and people, and they watched Mount Verinien's peak crumble in a landslide. The mountain was coming down too fast. Ellendren bonded with Tariel and embraced terys, forming a wedge to guide the avalanche around Arenthyl. She strained under the massive weight of rock and snow rushing toward the city until Evellyn, Abbie, Danielle, and Fyona offered their strength, and together they diverted the rockfall around the city.

Exhausted, Ellendren leaned on the balustrade and looked around to see Arenthyl whole and unscathed. Relieved, she turned to where Mount Verinien had towered moments before. The wilted Tree was visible, even as the mountain continued to come down, rocks falling until the Tree was entirely exposed. To the east, there was a bright light, stark against the Void. She realized it was the sun, its rays pouring down in a sinuous line cutting across the landscape. Through her connection with Devlyn, she realized that it was the River from Mount Saecrien. It emptied into Lake Saeryndol, turning the entire lake a brilliant hue and cutting through the Void suffocating Krysenthiel. Verakryl's dead roots, still exposed in the lake, drank in the new water.

Unhindered tears fell down her cheeks as Light issued from the Tree, more resplendent than she remembered. The Tree of Life grew and its luminosity dwarfed the newly visible sun.

The ground stopped shaking and where Arenthyl had been filled with petrified screams, now only bells could be heard as the elves celebrated what had happened. Horns joined the bells, and the elves added their own voices and sang joyously. The lake reflected the wondrous light, both from its own properties and from the Tree and Arenthyl glowing in golden hues as morning light touched lumaryl once more.

STOLEN HOPE

Devlyn decided to fly back to Arenthyl rather than shift there. He was curious about the effects of Verakryl's revival and hoped the Void had been banished. But the sun breaking through the Void was limited to the River's path. Only there did dawn brighten Eklean. A perpetual gloom covered the land beyond that trace of light. The ghosts who were near the River recognized it as a path to Lumaeniel, and as he flew, he saw hundreds of ghosts drifting toward it. He hoped they would make it to Lumaeniel, that whatever the River had done in Teraeniel, it had also done in Somnaeniel.

Krysenthien cities glimmered as he flew over them, as did Lake Saeryndol. He soared above the thawed waters, gleaming in the sunlight. Arenthyl shone like a beacon with the Tree of Life towering behind it. Tears fell freely at the sight. That a mountain had been capable of containing Verakryl now seemed impossible.

Flying over Arenthyl's golden spires, Devlyn landed on his palace balcony. His wings relaxed after the long flight from the Illumined Wood, drinking in the sunlight as it kissed his skin. Too many months had passed since he'd been able to enjoy the sun, returned but limited to Lake Saeryndol and the River. How was he supposed to extend Anaweh's Light across the entire world to banish the Void? Instinctively, he knew defeating Ramiel was the answer. But would defeating Ramiel destroy the Void? Was Devlyn expected to seal it off in its own pocket of existence as Anaweh had done during the Elder Days?

"Heavy thoughts for so early," Ellendren said, placing her hand on his back.

"I'm afraid it's become a habit, Elle," he replied and brought his arms around her.

"Krysenthiel lauds your name for bringing Verakryl back to life." Pride flowed from her. He accepted her warmth. For the first time in a long while, he had done something to return Balance to the world. The Tree was alive again.

Devlyn turned to look north and around the spire where Verakryl rose from the roots of the mountain, a brilliance Devlyn had only seen in the Empyrean Sphere. That it somehow existed in Teraeniel seemed impossible.

The base of Mount Verinien had widened to expose the Tree. The center of Lake Saeryndol now felt like a proper island and not just the base of a mountain. Trees and flowers would take root there.

"We should plant trees of every Skyland there," Ellendren said.

"That would be lovely." Devlyn imagined a forest of gold, silver, bronze, and green leaves. "Do you think a miervae would grow there?"

"I'm sure many will. The settlings are likely eager to take root after their long absence from Krysenthiel."

"We'll have to ask a faun how to encourage them to migrate back. Any idea how to get them to cross the lake? Would they travel in a boat?" Devlyn envisioned a barge full of the tiny creatures crossing Lake Saeryndol.

"We could shift with them or ask a minum to open a seguian."

"I kind of like the image of them sailing." Devlyn smiled just as bells pealed throughout the city. He wanted to spend more time alone with Ellendren, but these bells were a warning, not for a joyous occasion. "How urgent do you think it is?"

"Is anything not urgent these days?" She rubbed her stomach. Abbie, Danielle, and Fyona would not permit her to engage the threat in her condition, not after she had diverted a mountain from crashing into Arenthyl. "I do hope the twins come soon."

"I can't wait to meet them," Devlyn said before launching off the balcony just as he heard Viren curse from the bed chamber. In Devlyn's absence, he must have returned from Ceurenyl through a seguian portal with Alethea and Wyn.

He flew around the spire, seeking the reason for the alarm. His heart sank when he caught sight of a monstrous beast, its wingspan darkening a great swath of the lake below as he flew toward Arenthyl. He hadn't taken the alarm seriously and didn't have his verathn in hand.

He shared the sight with Ellendren and then with Viren and Jeanne. He had been terribly outmatched the first and only time he had confronted Tolvenol. They had known the dragon would make his way to Eklean, but Devlyn had hoped they would have more time to prepare.

Petrified, he watched the beast pour its tenebrys-laced fire on Arenthyl's docks, burning the ships moored there. Devlyn hoped the dockhands and workers on the docks had heard the warning bells and had fled behind the city's walls. Would those walls save them? Devlyn fretted as the Dark Primus sought out the second of Arenthyl's three docks, obliterating the ships and anything that wasn't wrought of lumaryl in black flames, darker than the darkest nights, clinging to the lumaryl. Once the third dock was engulfed in flames, Tolvenol flew skyward, his heavy torso held aloft by his equally massive wings. Devlyn watched as the dragon flew over the city and toward its center and highest tier where Aerodhal rose. Horror and adrenaline surged through him. Ellendren was there. He hurried to place himself between the monstrous dragon and the palace.

Devlyn hung between the two and miraculously, Tolvenol halted his advance. The dragon's mouth snarled into a dangerous grin. "Ah, young Lorenthien; the boy-king. We meet again."

"You're not welcome here, wyrm!"

"Where are your manners? Do you forget with whom you speak?"

"I'm well aware; now begone from Krysenthiel."

"I see you're emboldened by the Tree's resurrection. But beyond your borders, the Void thrives. Even with the Tree returned, I can still pass into your aryldom and burn it," Tolvenol said.

"You've made your point; now leave." Devlyn stayed firm, despite his rapid heartbeat.

"And let you elves believe you have a shred of hope? I think not. You will never be safe." Tolvenol flapped his wings, carrying him up and over Devlyn. Fire poured down on the aryl's spire where Ellendren still was.

Devlyn screamed as he wielded every erendinth possible, trying to redirect the flames. The torrent of fire felt as though it had the entire force of an ocean behind it and Devlyn buckled under its strength. The gold spire darkened, charred by tenebrys and fire. Devlyn knew he wasn't the only one wielding to thwart the attack, but in that moment, it certainly felt like it. He watched in horror as he wielded; the erendinth was no match for Tolvenol's fiery breath as it enveloped the spire.

Ellendren held her belly, as though she already nestled her children in her arms. She watched Devlyn dive over the balcony, his fear and trepidation passing through their bond. That fear escalated the moment he saw Tolvenol. Her heart jolted with his.

Arenthyl's wards should have barred Tolvenol. They had been assured the wards would hold. This wasn't just any enemy though. This was the Primus of the Dark Flight and Ramiel's general. She couldn't waste thoughts on how Tolvenol had broken through the wards. The monstrous dragon was here and she needed to do something. Arenthyl would burn if they didn't lure him away from the city. Already she could hear civilians screaming.

As she moved toward the balcony, she was stopped by another scream, not outside but in the palace. From its proximity, it was within her residence. She spun, torn between helping Devlyn or investigating the scream. "Elle!" the scream came again. She knew that voice—Fyona!

The balcony and the burning city beyond held her for only a moment before she dashed toward Fyona's cry, Abbie following on her heels. She couldn't leave her friend to suffer. Fyona had sacrificed so much to be with Ellendren during her pregnancy.

Ellendren and Abbie rushed down the spiral stairs, freezing when they reached the salon. Blood pooled around Fyona's limp body. *Don't be dead*, Ellendren pleaded. There was no ghost, but with the Void pushed from Krysenthiel, Fyona's specter wouldn't be visible. A woman she didn't know battled Danielle. Trethien, blood in his hair, slumped against the far wall, unconscious or dead.

How did an assassin not only enter the palace, but the Exalted Aryl's residence? The spire was the most secure place in the entire city. What had happened to the guards?

Ellendren bonded with Tariel in a flash of brilliant light. She didn't have time to mourn Fyona and possibly Trethien. She would not lose another friend to the intruder. Ellendren and Abbie wielded aerys and flung the woman across the salon to slam against the wall.

"Who are you?" Ellendren demanded.

The woman straightened herself, ignoring the demand.

"Answer her," a bruised and bloodied Danielle said.

"An Aerquin, I presume. Granddaughter of the Aryl of Ostyl, yes?" The stranger casually stepped over Fyona's corpse, barely registering her.

Danielle poised herself to attack, Ellendren and Abbie ready to assist. The intruder reached out to stroke a fingernail down Danielle's neck. "Step away from her," Ellendren warned.

"Ah, the Lorenthien bitch. Child to Vernal and Harnyl Roendryn. Eager to join your dead parents are you?"

"Who are you?" Ellendren had a firm grip on the erendinth, ready to counter whatever deadly wield this woman would unleash. She had already proven she wasn't above killing on sight. Ellendren had no doubt that the guards outside the residence were also dead.

"A recruiter of sorts. Gwilnor was ever my home. I sought out the strongest women in those halls, offering them power beyond measure." Shadowy lightning prickled at her fingertips. Tenebrys.

Bile rose in Ellendren's throat. She knew all she needed to about this woman who had betrayed her counsels as an ei'ana. "The Tenebrae failed to hold Gwilnor. Septyl proved to be stronger than your power-hungry school."

"You think the other Chairs expelled all my sisters?" She laughed. Other Chairs? Did this woman play at being the Chair of Tenebrae? "Catching on, are you? The Seven Chairs of Septyl couldn't chase me away from what is rightfully mine. I was in their midst the entire time and they never realized. How do you imagine I got into your palace? The library is conveniently close to your golden spire."

The seguian portal from the Sophillium to Aerodhal's library. Of course. Still, someone intending harm to any of Arenthyl's residents shouldn't be able to pass through.

"I am Nadia Desuani and Septyl will be mine."

"Ei'ana won't fall for your lies again, not with the Sophillium and all its knowledge at their disposal."

"Foolish girl. Every ei'ana who joined me knowingly betrayed their original School. The Sophillium and Gwilnor's library will be pruned so girls like you won't live in a fantasy that values weakness over power. Nor will Gwilnor's students have to tolerate their current magisters much longer."

"You've failed to hold Gwilnor once and you'll fail again," Ellendren said.

"And you've failed to grasp your predicament. I've found stronger allies than Erynor—I've gone to the source of power!" Nadia threw a bolt of tenebrys at Danielle. Ellendren deflected the wield with lumenys. Nadia wasn't to be underestimated. She might be outnumbered but she was powerful. What source of power did she mean? Did she mean Ramiel? Tenebrys shot across the salon, each bolt more deadly than the last.

Together, the three women subdued the reckless wields. It was taxing though. Ellendren knew she shouldn't strain herself as much as she was doing now. The extra weight she carried was a constant reminder of her pregnancy. She should be resting. What choice did she have though? Nadia had already killed Fyona and she wouldn't stop there.

The three women heaved as Nadia paused between wields.

"You're outnumbered," Abbie yelled. "Surrender!"

A dangerous look crossed Nadia's face. "Am I?" As though on cue, Tolvenol roared outside the palace. Nadia dashed out the salon and toward the tower's stair.

Ellendren's thoughts spun to Devlyn. She saw through his eyes. Tolvenol raced toward Aerodhal, maw opened. "Run!" she screamed.

Danielle rushed to Trethien, who moved with difficulty. Ellendren and Abbie checked Fyona, but she was gone. Abbie placed a comforting hand on Ellendren. "We have to go," Abbie spoke urgently.

Ellendren nodded, a tear escaping her eye. Abbie helped Danielle with Trethien. Ahead of them, Nadia laughed as they fled down the spire's steps. Another roar filled Ellendren's ears. She ducked as intense heat seared her back and neck. Nadia must have known what would happen.

"Keep moving," Abbie ordered. The four of them trudged on, but the heat was unbearable. Ellendren coughed from the tenebrys-laced fire as smoke consumed the spire. She could feel the power Tolvenol unleashed on the palace—her home. Nothing would survive that. Fyona's body would be cremated in the inferno. Ellendren hoped Fyona had transitioned to Lumaeniel. The way might not be open everywhere, but it was in Krysenthiel.

Then smoke and fire blocked their path. Ellendren froze. "Nowhere to go," Nadia taunted, hidden in the smoke. The fire was too hot.

"Fly!" Abbie ordered. "Get out of here—we'll be fine."

Ellendren glanced at the window. The fire, smoke, and heat were too much to bear. Her head felt light. Maintaining consciousness was proving difficult. She couldn't stay here, doing so would only risk her pregnancy. She didn't have the luxury to think twice.

As Devlyn despaired at the sight of the burning spire, Ellendren flew out a window from a level noticeably lower than their bedchamber, likely now destroyed.

"Ah, there's the one my Master desires," Tolvenol purred.

"You can't have her," Devlyn screamed but couldn't reach her in time.

The dragon's claw snatched Ellendren out of the sky. "Hello, precious. Sleep now." A gas poured out Tolvenol's nostrils. Ellendren slackened and fell unconscious, still bound with Tariel. The beast swatted at the spire, roaring in agony as the lumaryl didn't break, injuring the beast's free arm. Enraged, Tolvenol poured more fire down on Arenthyl. Holding the one he had come for, he turned and flew southwest.

Unwilling to let him escape with Ellendren, Devlyn followed. The dragon gained speed as his enormous wings beat steadily, propelling him faster than Devlyn could fly, leaving him with the realization he'd never catch up. He pursued Tolvenol anyway, following him across the lake as the distance between them grew. By the time Devlyn reached Krysenthiel's southern border, Tolvenol had such a commanding lead that he appeared the size of normal dragon.

Devlyn kept flying.

He crossed into Mindale and was approaching Yanil when Alethea finally breached his mind, which he had unknowingly walled off. He'd faintly heard her trying to reach out to him the moment Ellendren had been captured but wouldn't allow anyone to divert him from saving his pregnant wife. Finally, Alethea had managed. *Devlyn.* The mental voice was soft, compassionate, but also tired. *Devlyn, you must come back.*

He stopped then and hung in the sky, realizing that he was sobbing. When had he started? Was it from the moment Tolvenol had caught Ellendren? Hours had passed since he'd left Arenthyl, chasing in vain after a dragon he could never catch or defeat.

Devlyn sank to the ground, his emotions uncontrolled now that he could no longer see Tolvenol nor sense Ellendren. Her light had been swallowed by Tolvenol's shadow.

He withdrew from Aliel, his knees slamming into the dirt, naked, and sobbed, defeated.

He lost track of time as his mind blanked, uncaring that he knelt for hours near Yanil's border, naked and alone. Alethea's gentle touch came to him again. Believing he didn't have any more tears to shed, he sought out Aliel, who'd remained by his side the entire time.

Should we go back? Devlyn conveyed, his mind feeling weak and defeated.

We can't rescue Ellendren and Tariel without help.

No. He conceded as he stood and turned to find Viren standing guard with Falthion beside him. "Viren," Devlyn choked, unaware his protector had been there.

"Forgive me, Ei'denai. I've failed you. I could not keep her safe."

Devlyn found more tears and collapsed into Viren's arms. Viren held him firmly.

"We need to go back," Viren said. Devlyn nodded and followed Viren onto Falthion's back like a slack puppet.

TAKEN

Ellendren woke in a dark, prison-like room. The walls were dorthl and her reflection gleamed back at her only because she'd remained bonded with Tariel. She would be in complete darkness otherwise and resolved to stay bonded. She would not give Ramiel and his servants the opportunity to separate her from Tariel. She well remembered when Devlyn had been taken and the effect the separation from Aliel had had on them. She also feared she would never find Tariel again if she withdrew from her in this desolate place.

I'm alive, she tried passing to Devlyn. She had dreamt of his torment and knew it was real. While she doubted she could reach out to him, he had somehow managed to pass his anguish through the dorthl, at least in her dreams. How dark must his thoughts be to breach Ramiel's fortress? There was no doubt that was where she was. Dreams, she remembered, could not be contained. She had only been able to reach out to Devlyn through his dreams when he had been locked in a dorthl box. Perhaps her own rescue would come similarly. But Somnaeniel, the World-in-Between, was lost to the Void. Abbie and the other druids could not traverse it safely.

Feeling Devlyn's anguish, Ellendren feared for him. There was nothing she could do for him now, not from here. She would try to reach out to him while they slept tonight. Distinguishing night from day would be difficult from the windowless cell.

Despite knowing she wouldn't be able to, she tried to shift out of the fortress. Nothing happened. Her connection with Tariel was all that reminded her that she could wield. She couldn't sense the erendinth in the halls of dorthl. She wondered if this was how the Void had felt before Anaweh had sent the seven irythil into it to bring about creation.

"Ah, you're awake," said a woman. Ellendren had been certain she was alone. She hadn't heard the door open, a footstep, or an exhale. A ghostly woman stood by the door, her legs fading into shadow. She wasn't just ghostly; she was a specter.

"Erynel Meriden."

"I see you remember me."

"You're not an easy elf to forget and neither was your Shroud."

"My Master has yet to forgive me for its loss. Especially now that your wretched husband has managed to bring back the Tree. It matters not; he escaped his prison and brought his Void back to its rightful place. The small pocket of Light around the Tree will not endure."

Ellendren didn't reply but studied the ghost. What power did Erynel have without her Shroud to give her form?

"Come; the Master awaits." Erynel turned to leave, expecting Ellendren to follow.

"What does Ramiel want with me?"

Erynel froze, then threatened, "You will *not* use the Master's name. You are *not* worthy." Her posture suggested she would strike Ellendren but she couldn't—she was no more than a ghost.

Assuming she wasn't going to get an answer as to why she had been brought here, she followed Erynel out of the dorthl chamber and into a long and twisting corridor. The onyx-like stone had the same polished finish throughout the fortress. She doubted she would have been able to see any of it without being bonded with Tariel. While the dorthl had a sheen, it did not reflect any of the light issuing off Ellendren's body. Rather, it drank in the light, trying to consume it, as though to prevent it from ever shining life into the world again. Most curious about the citadel though was the evident lack of windows. This place was so unlike anything she had ever seen. The fact that it was not designed for anacordel was abundantly clear. She wondered then what had so attracted the Cyndinari who had become Sha'ghol to even step foot in this place.

What sort of power was tempting enough to draw someone here?

Erynel took her into what could only be a throne room. The space had the form of a square, but eight jagged apses equally distributed made it appear round. The dark walls stretched high, terminating in a point, reminding her of a spear. And indeed, she remembered it was a weapon that had broken through the veil and loosed the Void on Teraeniel.

Her feet padded on the onyx-colored floor, so dark it seemed it would swallow her. She looked around for the anadel responsible for bringing her here—and responsible for so much more. All the pain and darkness in the world had sprung from Ramiel. Ellendren wondered what would have become of the many creatures he had corrupted over the eons had he not interfered. Would the Children who had first woken ever desire to age? Would the various races have come about if there hadn't been a division? Would the elves have lost their Skylands if the Sha'ghol had not gone into Mount Cyngol?

"You place much blame on me, young Lorenthien," Ramiel said. His form appeared as shadow and smoke, somehow darker than the surrounding dorthl. He hung in the air like a god one should bow before and worship, which was precisely what Erynel did. Ellendren could sense her disdain as Ellendren refused to replicate the oblation.

"You know my thoughts?" Ellendren had always believed herself capable of guarding her mind. Then again, this was Ramiel, the fallen irythil who had brought umbrys, the first erendinth into the Void.

"Your mind is not stronger than I, elf."

"You address her, but not my son?" Erynel asked, looking up from her bowed posture.

"Your son has placed his empire above my interests. He is not worthy of hearing my voice." Erynel shied away at the rebuke. Ramiel's attention remained on Ellendren. "Ah, and Tariel. I admit I never thought Anaweh would allow the favored pets to leave Lumaeniel. Did you tire of its unending sterility? Did you long for the world I've sought to return to its previous perfection?"

"This world is not yours," Ellendren said, voicing Tariel's mind.

"Look around you, elf. You've lost. Whatever hope you envision still exists is gone. Your husband might have resurrected the Tree, but its power is limited to the River that was hidden away. The Light will never find you here in my halls. Only death awaits you here."

"Death is only a single step in our lives."

"Strong words for one who has experienced so little of life."

Ellendren squared her shoulders and straightened her posture. The act always made her feel more confident. It didn't matter if she was standing before the Luminari aryls, the Guardian Senate, or even Ramiel. She stood defiantly before him, just as she remembered her mother doing to the Tieli queen when she'd visited Lucillia. "Is that why you had me brought here? To kill me?"

"My dear, vain elf. Whatever made you think Tolvenol brought you here for your sake?" Ellendren felt his gaze on her belly, to her children forming there. "The prophecy named the youngest Lorenthien—and you will soon give birth and the title will no longer be your husband's. The fate of the Light's place in Teraeniel will be under my care. That child will be raised in my likeness and will never wonder what the Light might hold but will relish in the Void's Darkness."

Ramiel laughed as the reality of the situation fell on Ellendren. Her hand went to her belly and she held the roundness of it. She'd never been pregnant before, but based on her size, she imagined she would give birth in a month or two.

Her children could not be born here. Their lives should be blessed. As much as Ellendren feared the implications of Ramiel's words, she feared more for her children. What was worse was that he only cared for the younger one. What would he do to the twin that came first? She wanted them to grow and laugh and play in Arenthyl's gardens, safe from all threats.

Ramiel's slow, throaty laughter mocked her. He didn't have to say her children would be deprived of her hopes and dreams.

The burnt-out shell of the aryl's spire felt wrong without Ellendren. His first memory here was waking to her. She had feared he wouldn't survive his bout with a Deurghol. The spire had since become their home. Already they dreamt of children running through it, giggling in delight. Devlyn still thought they were too young to start a family, but Ellendren had assured him they were ready. She was ready and her resolve and surety in herself made Devlyn ready.

Those memories and dreams turned to ash, perfectly reflected by the spire's scorched interior. Wood and fabric furnishings and the many books and scrolls in Ellendren's study had been destroyed. Only lumaryl and lierathnil artifacts remained; they were singed and damaged but could be restored. The portraits, landscapes, and statues would see a second life. The bed frame had survived, but the feathered mattress and blankets were gone.

Everything in the bedchamber reminded him of Ellendren. Her vanity stood, charred, but only his sooty reflection looked back. *I'll find you.* He tried to send the thought to her but there was only silence, their bond blocked. He refused to believe the silence was a result of her death. Tolvenol would have killed her if Ramiel had wanted her dead. He would have killed Devlyn too if that was the intent. No, the dorthl of Ramiel's fortress had to be blocking their bond.

Devlyn felt a tug pulling him toward Vasknir, the Void fortress many leagues away. He looked out the southwest window. Despite it being too far to see, he imagined a point on the horizon darker than its surroundings. Remembering Wyn's description, he visualized the jagged towers that had cut through and into Teraeniel. Ellendren was its prisoner now, that place's only light.

Guilt assaulted him when he envisioned Ellendren locked in Vasknir. He should never have turned back. He should have chased Tolvenol all the way to Mount Cyngol. He should be beating down the fortress gates to rescue her. Deep down, he knew confronting Ramiel alone would be both reckless and a death sentence. He wasn't strong enough—not alone.

Her life hung in the balance. What would Ramiel do to her? He felt powerless and he hated it. He wanted—no, needed to act. In that moment, Devlyn wanted nothing more than for his word to be law. He wanted to direct all the Guardian Senate's resources to Ellendren's rescue. It shouldn't be a debate. He didn't have the luxury to sit in endless meetings—Elle couldn't afford their inaction. She wasn't just the senate's prelate; she was the Exalted Aryl and High Queen of Eklean. She had kept the Luminari aryls united and led them to the Shroud when Lucillia had returned to the Illumined Wood, believing they could reclaim Krysenthiel. She had united Teraeniel to reestablish the Guardian Senate. Former enemies had come together under her leadership. The full force of the Guardian army should be marching for Mount Cyngol to rescue her. They hadn't even come to a decision on whether to permit Caspol to create the talisman.

Frustrated, he slammed his fist on the window casing. They didn't have time for this.

Aliel cooed, then perched on his shoulder. The warmth comforted him and broke through his anguish. *She would not want you to throw away everything you both built*, Aliel conveyed.

The Guardian Senate had already agreed on a plan of action. There was nothing they could do to speed it up. Marching to Mount Cyngol without a means of entrapping Ramiel would end in their defeat. Ellendren knew this and she had worked tirelessly to ensure that the world came together to confront the threat to all creation. Countless meetings since retaking Arenthyl had resulted in their current plan of action to see Ramiel and his forces conquered, and the Erynien Empire toppled. And now she was that threat's captive.

The phoenix sang softly. Devlyn scratched the side of Aliel's head. Warmth spilled through his fingers, comforting him. *What would I do without you?*

Walk to Mount Cyngol and likely perish, Aliel conveyed, mirth in his sentiment.

A smile crossed Devlyn's lips, the first since Ellendren had been taken. *We'll get her and Tariel back.* Devlyn realized he wasn't alone in losing a companion. *I didn't realize,* Devlyn admitted. Looking inward and staying with his own suffering had been too easy.

Tariel is a light I never expected.

We'll save them, together.

The Guardian Senate would not entertain Ellendren remaining Ramiel's captive. He prayed their allies would join them as promised. They stood little chance alone. The dragon flights would be key to shifting the tides.

Quiet footsteps alerted Devlyn to someone joining him in the burnt-out spire. "Not now, Viren." Devlyn didn't bother to turn around to dismiss his protector, come to comfort him.

"Would you have me leave too?" his mother asked.

"Mother." Devlyn had thought he was finished with tears. He turned away from the window and went into her arms. In that moment, he felt like a child again and his vulnerabilities spilled forward like a ruptured dam, impossible to restrain.

"I'm here, my Devlyn." Evellyn rubbed his back, making him feel more vulnerable as he cried into her shoulder. He had dreamt of his mother comforting him as a child. So many lonely nights had gone by at the abbey school in Cor'lera following the abbot's cruelty. But now, the worst thing imaginable had happened to him.

"We'll get her back, Devlyn; Ellendren and the children."

Devlyn believed her. Something in her voice inspired confidence. He nodded and stepped back, wiping his tears away. He would bring her home. The whole world had banded together to do so. Strength and determination blossomed inside. "We'll get them back." The despair he had been carrying lifted a bit as he repeated the mantra in his head, strengthening his resolve.

That resolve was tied to the reminder of how easily Tolvenol had taken Ellendren. They hadn't stood a fighting chance against the Dark Primus. They were only two Phaedryn against the ancient dragon. While the world's forces were to descend on Mount Cyngol, he still feared it wouldn't be enough. Deep in his heart, he knew they needed more. And then it struck him.

"Mother, when you were Erynor's prisoner, did you know where his dragon stayed?"

"Ythinor had a lair below the imperial complex. He might fly Erynor and fight with him, but as you know, dragons are not pets. And as Erynor's half-brother, he enjoyed the luxuries offered him."

Devlyn's mind churned. Inside Ythinor were the phoenix he'd consumed in the Ceurendol War, their cycle of death and rebirth in a perpetual state in the dragon's fiery belly. If Devlyn could find a way to kill the dragon, he could free the phoenix and they could find someone to bond with. At the very least, he could remove Ythinor from the battlefield and replace him with the promise of future generations of Phaedryn. He well remembered the harrowing flight on Yelaris to escape the beast only a few months after he'd first arrived at Gwilnor. The dragon was terrifying, dwarfing Yelaris. He might not be as large as his father, but Devlyn doubted many other creatures could reach such colossal proportions. But neither was Devlyn the boy who had fled Gwilnor Academy so long ago. Resolve built inside him. After losing Ellendren, he had to do something. He couldn't sit in Arenthyl until the armies were ready to march south.

"Tell me you're not thinking of confronting that dragon alone,"

Evellyn said, worried.

"Not alone. But I think I must confront him. Imagine the advantage we would have if the phoenix were freed."

"There won't be time to train new Phaedryn before this war is over." She didn't say Ellendren couldn't afford to wait that long, but Devlyn unintentionally caught it from her thoughts. Ellendren's pregnancy was nearing its end.

"No, but at least we'll right the wrongs Ythinor has committed against the world by freeing the phoenix. If we fail to defeat Ramiel, there will be phoenix to help future generations. Ithendryl did that when she ensured the protection of Aliel's egg. I have to do this."

Evellyn considered his words, then surprised him by saying, "I'm coming with you."

"You can't."

"Just as you don't see an alternate path, neither do I." She smiled encouragingly.

"But you only just escaped Erynor," Devlyn pleaded.

"Ah, but I am not entirely defenseless. Auriel revealed much to me while I was his host."

Devlyn couldn't see a way of dissuading his mother from what promised to be a foolish endeavor. He also didn't know where they'd find Ythinor. The dragon would likely be with Erynor but that wasn't much help. Were they attending Ramiel in Vasknir or were they personally directing the Erynien legions on the battlefields? The dragon could even be in his lair at the heart of the Erynien Empire.

"Go to Jeanne; see if she has any insight about this plan." Evellyn turned to leave.

"I'll do that." He felt resolved. Having a course of action—something he could do rather than wait inspired him. But there was something he had to do first.

Viren must have caught the recklessness coursing through Devlyn's mind, first from thinking about killing a dragon, and then this new intention. Viren replaced Evellyn in the doorway. "Are you certain about this?"

"There isn't time for deliberations. Elle can't afford the Guardian Senate to squabble about specifics. The Ja'horan ship already sails for the Skrein Sea. We're running out of time."

"The Guardian Senate could hold this against you." Viren was patient, but patience was not what the world needed just now.

"I know, but they did consent to having the talisman created."

"Not by a Sha'ghol."

"What other option do we have?" Devlyn spat, becoming frantic. His chest heaved at the questioning. He felt threadbare, as though he would tear apart. "I'm sorry. I must do this."

"Very well." Viren offered his hand. Devlyn took it and together they shifted to Yloran's mansion. Water bubbled in the fountain while she lounged in the sun, as though expecting Devlyn.

"Are you ready?" she casually asked. Had she known Devlyn would come to this decision?

"Yes."

"Good." Yloran stood and two of her attendants came out into the garden. "Clovis, Raelinth, I doubt we'll be home soon, so do put someone in charge in your stead."

"Of course, Yloran." They disappeared into the mansion, returning with luggage.

"Shall we?" Yloran offered a hand to Devlyn, as her attendants followed. "Do be careful when positioning us on the ship. I'd rather not get seawater on my belongings. Dreadfully salty."

"Let me locate the ship first," he said, and she nodded and waited while he did so. Focusing on the Ja'horan ship, he visualized it sailing up Ogren's coast. He doubted it had reached Glacien before sailing back south after passing the northern pole. He shifted alone to find the ship first. A chilled wind blasted his face, saltwater spraying as treacherous waves rose and fell. How any ship could sail these waves was beyond him. But the Ja'horans were confident in their ability.

His eyes were little help in locating the ship. Coupled with the lack of sunlight and stinging mist, the waves were too erratic. Opening his awareness, he sought lifeforms. The ship would be full of sailors, ei'ana, and mages charged with transporting the already mined nethrin to create the talisman. He reached out, searching for them. Sea creatures swam beneath the waves, but no people were nearby. Locating the ship on his first try would be impossible. He knew that.

He shifted further north. Nothing. Again, and again, and again he shifted. At last, a flicker of consciousness came to him. People were yelling and arguing as they battled the treacherous sea. He shifted to them, the place firm in his mind. The people aboard saw him at once, his lit form impossible to miss, especially on the dark and stormy seas.

He swept down to the deck, where the captain, ei'ana, and mages greeted him. The rest of the Ja'horans were too busy keeping the ship afloat. "Is the Sorcery ready to cooperate?" the captain asked, disdain thick in her voice.

"Not quite," Devlyn admitted, and returned to Arenthyl to bring Yloran, her attendants, and Caspol to the ship.

BELLY OF A DRAGON

Devlyn sat opposite Jeanne in her study. She held him in her gaze, hands folded. Whether she was digesting his intent to kill Ythinor or weighing its stupidity, he couldn't tell. A single look had never made him feel so foolish before, although it didn't change how he felt. The phoenix trapped inside Ythinor had to be freed.

That he had also confessed to taking Caspol and Yloran to create the talisman was another point of contention between them. She had simply commented that there was nothing left to do on that front and moved on. Her disapproval was thick—she hadn't disguised it. That two Sha'ghol were creating it rather than the Daer Sorcery mattered little. Neither were to be trusted. At least Yloran had saved Devlyn's life and had proven a true ally. Yloran had also secreted Evellyn out of the Erynien Empire, after Jaerol, Liam, and Rusyl had rescued her from Broid.

"Do you know where he is?" Devlyn asked. Until he knew where Ythinor was, he could only speculate what the best course of action would be. Confronting Ythinor alone was an entirely different situation than if Ythinor was with Erynor or the Dark Flight.

For all Jeanne moved, she could have been a statue. "Suppose I told you where our intelligence suggests Ythinor is." She paused, holding his gaze as though to see how he reacted. "How would you envision killing him to free the phoenix?"

"I suppose it would depend on the situation."

"No. It doesn't. Ythinor is one of the most powerful creatures on Teraeniel, fueled by phoenix caged in his stomach. Even if the dragon is alone and the opportunity to slay the beast presents itself, how would you manage it? Your verathn is not a sword; slicing its stomach open isn't an option. There are wields capable of such carnage, but could you bring yourself to do it?"

Devlyn was no warrior. He'd rarely carried a sword and had only killed shadow elves by unworking the prisons within them to free the captured spirits. Their deaths had only come about because they no longer had another's soul to sustain their cursed life. He'd never brought a blade to someone's throat with the intent to kill.

An image of Ellendren, alone in a dark cell, flashed across his mind. He would do anything to rescue her; even killing a dragon. "I have to—*we* have to," Devlyn said, determined.

"How will you kill the dragon?" Jeanne pressed. "Forgive me, Ei'denai, but I cannot simply allow you to go off to needlessly risk your life again, especially as Ellendren is already Ramiel's prisoner and your heir has yet to be born. What would happen if you don't return? Our armies march for New Castle as we speak. How do you think we'll fare without you? Ramiel isn't Erynor, he won't keep your house alive to parade around like pets. He *will* kill you." Jeanne planted her palms on her desk and looked him squarely in the eyes. "Do understand, I'm not trying to dissuade you but neither will I entertain reckless actions that could result in your certain death."

Devlyn held onto his resolve. Caving to Jeanne would be easy. This was important though and he knew Ellendren, who always looked ahead, would agree. Ramiel was too powerful not to take advantage of every possible resource. Devlyn didn't want to consider the alternative reason for freeing the phoenix before facing Ramiel. The thought was unavoidable though—there was a very real chance Ramiel would win this war. He'd spent eons in the Void plotting the seizure of Teraeniel and Somnaeniel. The creatures he'd corrupted in the Elder Days had only grown larger and more vicious since they had been trapped with their Master.

"Help me devise a plan then. We have to do this…" he choked, "in case we don't succeed, and Ramiel defeats us." There would be no hope of defeating Ramiel if he and Ellendren were killed and Aliel and Tariel were consumed and prevented from bonding with another in the future. All the hard-fought hope they had won would mean nothing. The world would know only misery without any potential for escape. Even death would not lead to freedom as Ramiel sought to extend the Void over all existence.

Jeanne leaned back in her chair, her gaze steady. "You will need to subdue the beast first. Then you will need a sword. I don't know if you'll be able to sense the phoenix inside his stomach, but if you can, use that to your advantage."

"How do you envision we subdue Ythinor?" Devlyn was about to voice more doubts, but a thought occurred. "The Jade Flight! Are they awake? Did the Qien empress and merpeople succeed in defeating the sea drakes?" He hadn't heard any reports from Qien.

"They did. Not all the sea drakes are dead, but their leader who held the jade dragons in a stasis is. Empress Qien Wei and Guanxi are currently on an imperial tour to unify the continent and put to rest any notion of rebellion."

"We don't have time for that," Devlyn interrupted.

"Let me finish." She glared at him. "While they unite the hundred kingdoms and keep them from tearing the empire asunder during their soon-to-be absence, most of the Jade Flight and Qien monks are enroute to Arenthyl as we speak. They, and the other dragon flights will be our best defense against the Dark Flight. But do know, Guanxi has forbidden the jade dragons from engaging Tolvenol until he and the empress reach Eklean."

"But not Ythinor." Devlyn smiled.

"Not Ythinor."

"And a sword. What weapon should I take?"

"You will need a sword, but I do not think it wise for it to be in your hands. I was thinking Toryn, who will ever be Krysenthiel's sharpest weapon."

Devlyn nodded. Other than Viren, there were few others he would entrust to slay Ythinor. "Has she returned?"

Jeanne stood and silently led Devlyn out of her office and into the map room. The large lumaryl map table was currently focused on New Castle and the surrounding area. The lumaryl features shifted once Jeanne placed her hand on it. The edge of a great forest rose on the eastern part, a familiar village beside it. The abbey school stood outside the village, but the distance between them was much less as the village had expanded since Devlyn had last been there. The Illumined Wood kept it from expanding east, so Cor'lera had swelled north, west, and south.

"Why is Ythinor in Cor'lera?" Devlyn asked, his voice cold.

"Our assumption is Erynor still fears a weapon is hidden there."

"There never was a weapon there."

"Reports suggest Erynor has been acting erratically."

"Is he with Ythinor?"

"No. Ythinor is with a small group of dragons terrorizing the village."

"Why wasn't I informed of this?" Devlyn had not meant to let his anger spill out.

"I understand you're upset; you were born there, Ei'denai, but Cor'lera is part of Parendior, and by extension, Thellion. Thellish forces are defending the village and its people. Forgive me saying this, but we've had larger concerns of late."

"When can the jade dragons reach Cor'lera?" Knowing that the village of his birth was threatened, urgency sprang inside him. He knew so many there—people who had cared for him despite the false rumors about his family.

"I'll inform them of our plan. Kanastil and Rusyl will stay with them and bring Elayne, Jaerol, Liam, and Toryn there too. Aside from Viren and Falthion, who else in Arenthyl will be accompanying you?"

"My mother has insisted on joining us. I'll also ask Alethea and Wyn. Perhaps Abbie and Danielle. They are distraught over Ellendren's abduction. I think they feel the need to act too."

"Then Andrew and Trethien will doubtless join you. I also suggest you reach out to Velaria and Yelaris. The ei'ana and Septyl knights might prove invaluable, especially since I cannot spare more Guardian knights."

"I'll ask her." Devlyn turned to leave, realizing that this battle would be determined by dragons. There was no telling who else Erynor had sent to Cor'lera.

"And Devlyn, don't do anything stupid. We need you alive." Her glare told him she might kill him herself twice over if he didn't return.

"I promise." He hurried out of the map room, then paused. He didn't have to return to the palace. Instead, he sent a mental note to Evellyn, Alethea, Wyn, Abbie, and Danielle, sharing what he and Jeanne had conspired, then asking them to meet him in Septyl. They all agreed before he bonded with Aliel. "Ready?" he asked Viren.

"If you're certain. Falthion will meet us in Septyl." They shifted.

The Azurelle's capacious entry atrium surrounded them. The fountain with a life-like statue of Cyrelle Azurelle stood in the center beneath a crystalline dome. Curled beside the fountain was Yelaris, a paw in the water. The blue dragon blinked at their sudden appearance.

Images of greetings passed from Yelaris to Devlyn and back. He tried to maintain a level of calm, but must have failed, for Velaria rushed out of her palatial residence at Yelaris' behest.

"Devlyn, what are you doing here? Has there been a change of plans? And Devlyn—Ellendren—I'm so sorry. We'll get her back," Velaria said in a single breath.

"Our plans haven't changed, but there's something I—we need to do first." He fought back the urgency to go to Ellendren at once. Only death would result from that sort of rashness.

"What could be more important?"

"Killing Ythinor." Devlyn told her the plan and how the dragon was terrorizing Cor'lera.

"And Erynor isn't with him?" Yelaris growled in what Devlyn could only interpret as eagerness. Did the blue dragon want to face Ythinor again?

"Will you come?"

Velaria looked past Devlyn to Yelaris. They must have shared a private communication, for she replied, "Of course, we'll come. To see the world unburdened of that beast and the phoenix freed will be a service to Teraeniel."

"Thank you." Devlyn could hug her.

"Cor'lera holds a special place in my heart too." Devlyn had been a toddler when Velaria had first visited the village. That was before Lex had killed Devlyn's father and abducted Evellyn and Liam and sent so many more relatives to Gneal's dungeons, never to be seen again.

"Cor'lera deserves a long rest after this."

"You said Ythinor is not alone. Do we know who accompanies him?"

"Afraid not. How many ei'ana and Septyl knights would you recommend we bring to fight against unknown odds?" Devlyn asked.

"Against unknown odds? None. If not for the Jade Flight joining us, I wouldn't support this plan, not if it puts the lives of my fellow ei'ana in danger. Septyl already feels empty after so many have left for New Castle with the Arantiulyn Chair. We cannot leave Septyl entirely defenseless. Still, I recommend we take twenty ei'ana. I'll bring the proposal before the Chairs at once."

"Thank you, Velaria."

"Of course." Her lips softened into her small smile. "While you wait, you should visit Kevn. He's rarely left the Sophillium in recent months."

Devlyn turned to Viren as though to ask permission. "You did lay a heavy charge on him when you last saw him," Viren reminded.

"I'll send someone for you when we're ready to leave," Velaria said before turning to go back into her palace to call a meeting with the other Chairs.

"Velaria." She paused at Devlyn's call. "You should know, Abbie and Danielle claim Nadia Desuani used the Sophillium's seguian to Aerodhal to confront Ellendren and kill Fyona."

"I had feared that the Chair of the Tenebrae was among us all along." She frowned, lost in thought. "Thank you for telling me. That wretched woman will answer for the pain she's caused Septyl." Yelaris growled, sharing Velaria's feelings toward Nadia.

Devlyn and Viren walked Septyl's street-like corridors, Aliel flying above. The crystalline roof, a form of lumaryl, allowed the sun to pass through and warm the interiors of the palace-city. He didn't want to recall how eerie this place had felt when the Void had encompassed Krysenthiel. He didn't need the reminder that only a small portion of Teraeniel was free of the Void. Most of the world remained in darkness.

As they moved through Septyl, the city reminded him of a military camp. The ei'ana and knights here busied themselves with preparations to leave for the Shadow Mountains. No one walked alone, moving about in units, as though they were already dependent on the units for their own survival.

At the Sophillium at the center of the city, Devlyn, Viren, and Aliel went inside unchallenged. The interior was dark as usual, the only lights being the variously sized sophilliae floating throughout the space. Devlyn considered calling out for Kevn but knew he wouldn't appreciate the disruption. There was no saying what critical subject someone was researching here. Disturbing an Albien ei'ana was never advisable. Instead, Devlyn reached out mentally, finding Kevn absorbed in a sophilliae. He let Kevn know he was there and withdrew to wait.

A red-eyed Kevn soon greeted them, his entire face drooping from fatigue.

"Are you sleeping?" Devlyn blurted out, surprised at Kevn's appearance.

"I'm forcing myself to sleep four hours a night. Well, that is, I'm lying in bed."

"You can't do that to yourself—our bodies can't function on so little sleep," Devlyn said, concern for his friend fueling his words.

"Not now. I do hope you manage to untangle whatever is blocking Ceurendol from granting us our Life Immortal. Sleep was rarely needed then; elves simply rested occasionally. No wonder they were so productive in all they accomplished," Kevn said.

"But they didn't exclude leisure. Life Immortal does not exempt burn out," Viren said.

"Right. Anyway, I'm happy you figured out how to restore the Tree of Life. I can't tell you how many sophilliae I delved into only to find nothing relevant. There was some bit about being emotionally sensitive to the Tree and having to connect with it…"

"That's kind of how I managed it," Devlyn interrupted. "All my emotions and vulnerabilities poured out of me."

"Really? I didn't think it was pertinent, so I didn't mention it," Kevn admitted with a shrug.

"How long did you know?"

"Months now. It was from one of the first sophilliae I tapped into." Kevn scratched his head. "Perhaps you should try that with Ceurendol."

"I doubt I could manage it without Ellendren."

"Was she with you when you brought the mountains down and revived Verakryl?"

"No, but…" he trailed off.

"It's worth a try. Again, I could use our lost constitution."

"I suppose I'll try after Cor'lera."

"Cor'lera? What could possibly make you go there now?"

"Ythinor."

"Will the Jade Flight be there?" Kevn asked.

"Yes."

"Good. Happy to hear they're awake. Did you know that if not for their kin betraying them, Erynor wouldn't have won the First Ceurendol War? That's what I'm calling it now since we're clearly in the Second Ceurendol War. Anyway, the jade dragons would have defeated the Dark Flight. I'm not saying it would've been easy, but we would have never been without Phaedryn if Ythinor and the rest of the Dark Flight had been subdued."

"That's good to know. Have you found anything that might help us defeat the Evil One? It won't be long until we march to Mount Cyngol."

"The only useful thing I could find regarding defeating him involved an empty vessel."

"So, the Sorcery's talisman is the only way?" Devlyn had held out a small reserve of hope that there was another solution. That Kevn would have found something—anything so they wouldn't have to create the talisman, thereby legitimizing the Daer Sorcery. The Sorcery would prove an unending thorn in his side. They had already named him a hypocrite. How much worse would they become if Ramiel was trapped in the talisman?

"Perhaps. I don't know what else it could refer to. Will it reach Mount Cyngol in time?"

"It's hard to say. It's not only a matter of sailing it across half the world, but it has to be crafted."

"Hm. I doubt the irythil would sanction its creation. Imagine if it fell into the wrong hands. The ramifications of it being used against the irythil are insurmountable. Teraeniel is already out of Balance; we don't need something that could further destabilize the world."

"Could the empty vessel refer to something else?" Devlyn asked.

"I'm not sure—what else could hold the Evil One?" Kevn looked off distantly as though lost in thought, likely considering alternatives before shaking his head. "Does it give any credence to Lucillia's prophecy?"

Those words had been etched on Devlyn's mind. "It only says that the lesser brother shall give his life. What if we were wrong? What if there was nothing to interpret—what if Lucillia spoke directly?" Devlyn's heart quickened in panic, an all too familiar episode in recent months. He steadied his breath to calm his nerves, to no avail.

He didn't want to die, but neither did he want to doom the world and every creature to Ramiel and the Void.

"Perhaps; perhaps not. Prophecy is hard to be certain about. Naturally, I'd rather you didn't die," Kevn said with a tired grin.

"I'd recommend you stay on the path you already set yourself on," Viren said, helping to stabilize Devlyn. "Come, you should get some rest before we leave for Cor'lera. I would recommend you do the same, Kevn."

SWALLOWED LIGHT

Devlyn feared for Cor'lera and its people. His memories of the small village might be tainted by his cruel childhood, but it had still been his family's home for over a thousand years. House Lorenthien was thought to have perished during the First Ceurendol War, but Gwendolyn Lorenthien had survived and started a family with Feolyn in Cor'lera.

No one regretted House Lorenthien's survival more than Erynor. He would see the village that had given them refuge eradicated. Devlyn didn't even know if it still stood. How long had Ythinor been free to terrorize Cor'lera? Had other dark dragons joined him? Familiar faces flashed through his mind. Walei and his daughter in their shop, and Brother Bernard holed away at the Cor Inn. Alex's oldest brother and his small family had a vineyard to protect, while his uncle, Abbot Entiel, was likely assisting the dragons and giving shadow elves shelter in the abbey school.

"Are we ready?" Devlyn bonded with Aliel in a flash of golden light. Evellyn and Viren stood to either side of him, while everyone else formed concentric rings, either holding hands, or placing their hands on shoulders to form a link to Devlyn.

They would have to move swiftly once they reached the village. They couldn't have Ythinor fleeing once he realized they had come to slay him. Without another thought, Devlyn shifted everyone, griffins and dragons included, to the market square.

Dozens screamed at the sudden appearance of a small army in the now very crowded area that looked like a field hospital. Devlyn remembered the space being much larger. The shock lasted only until the residents recognized Evellyn. For many, especially the elves and lethien in Cor'lera, she had been wrongly accused and imprisoned with most of her family in Gneal. But the humans of Cor'lera had believed the allegations against her for killing her husband. Now, there wasn't a soul in Cor'lera who didn't know that Lex had murdered his adoptive brother, Dolan.

The startled screams shifted to repetitions of Evellyn's name. But they didn't have time for the entirety of Cor'lera to apologize for how they'd condemned her. Devlyn looked to the sky, searching for signs of the Dark Flight. The Void consumed the sky here and Devlyn had difficulty seeing anything. "Where are the dragons?" he asked.

"Waiting at the abbey school," said a familiar voice.

"Why?" Devlyn asked, trying to identify the face.

"I believe I'm to blame for that." Impossibly, Aaron came through the crowd which readily parted for the Ceurtriarch.

Devlyn blinked. "Aaron? How—*why* are you here?" A wave of questions bubbled over, each more outlandish than the last at seeing Ellendren's brother in Cor'lera.

"Initially, I came to investigate the Thellish king's uncle."

"Lex is dead."

"The other one. I suspect Abbot Entiel has been providing a haven for fellow stewards of shadow. He's handed the abbey school over to the Erynien legion, dragons, and shadow elves to stage their assault on Cor'lera."

"Then it's confirmed—Entiel is a steward of shadow."

"I don't think it was ever in doubt. Sadly, we just didn't have the resources to investigate."

"So, you've decided to take it upon yourself?" Devlyn arched a brow. Typically, he was the one receiving admonishing looks from Jeanne and Viren for his rashness.

"Well, not alone. I've brought some of my most trusted temple knights, and several ei'ceuril to purify Cor'lera of Entiel's corruption, including Clara and Lillianna. Lillianna has agreed to become the abbess of the abbey school here once Entiel is deposed."

"Is Entiel still at the abbey school?" Evellyn asked.

"Unfortunately, yes. He's squirreled himself and his stewards of shadow away, all capable of wielding tenebrys. We came back to the village to regroup after being denied entry to the abbey school—then the dragons arrived. I'm presuming that's why you're here."

"It is—Ythinor is among them. We're going to free the phoenix," Devlyn said.

"How will you manage that? When we first met, you told me how you and Yelaris barely escaped him and Erynor," Aaron said, getting a low, threatening growl from Yelaris.

"Jade dragons are on their way," Devlyn said.

Aaron looked confused, not having been part of the talks with Qien or awakening the Jade Flight. Devlyn filled Aaron in as briefly as he could manage. While he was anxious about defeating Ythinor, there was little he could do until the jade dragons arrived. Aaron nodded, taking it all in.

"Do you know when they'll be here?"

"Within the hour," Devlyn said.

"You'll have the ei'ceuril and temple knights at your disposal. Ythinor might be the target, but the more of those monsters we rid Teraeniel of, the better. Oh, and there's one other person here you might want to see." Aaron's face lit up.

"I imagine there's quite a few. I did grow up here, you know."

"Come, she's with Clara. You'll want to see her too, Evellyn."

Before following Aaron, Devlyn turned to Wyn. "Get everyone in place. Ask the village guard how we can best defend Cor'lera. We must be ready before the jade dragons arrive."

"Of course."

Velaria tagged along, having been caught in a conversation with Evellyn. The ei'ana and Septyl knights were heading to where they were needed. Aaron took them through the original village limits to the Cor Inn, its wooden defensive wall gone, returned to the forest. Devlyn looked at his mother, who had had so many happy times here and saw her features darken with memories of her last moments when Dolan had been murdered in front of her, and her children torn away. Whatever she felt at seeing their old home, she didn't express it.

They entered the crowded common room filled with ei'ceuril, temple knights, and many recognizable people from Cor'lera, Bernard and Walei among them. Devlyn had never imagined the inn was large enough to house so many people. He tried smiling back at everyone, but it was almost impossible. One person stood out in the crowd. Her back was to them but Devlyn and Evellyn knew her by her hair. Only she and Devlyn had golden-brown hair, mixed with strands of silvery-blond, ebony-black, and coppery-red, the hair of every elven Skyland.

"Leilyn," Evellyn gasped; she hadn't seen her since that fateful night at this very inn.

"Mother." Leilyn turned, her all-blue eyes looking back at them, seeing more than anyone else could because of them. Evellyn ran to her as quickly as the crowded room allowed.

"Oh, my Leilyn—my precious, strong Leilyn." They held each other tightly. Evellyn pulled Devlyn in once he was close enough. "Oh, my hearts." Evellyn cried as she squeezed her two children for the first time together since their family was torn apart. "Now all we're missing is Liam."

"He's close," Devlyn said. As much as he wanted to stay in this moment, he couldn't. They had dragons and corrupt ei'ceuril to deal with. And wherever there were dragons of the Dark Flight, there would also be shadow elves and possibly Deurghol. Devlyn hoped none of them would be here today, let alone one of the Sha'ghol. But the dragons were likely here at Erynor's bidding, not Ramiel's. Sha'ghol and Deurghol only answered to their Master. Then Devlyn felt Liam reach out before his voice filled his mind.

We're flying into the region now. We've been spotted by enemy scouts—the Dark Flight is flying from the abbey school toward Cor'lera, Liam shared.

We'll be ready, Devlyn sent back before saying aloud, "They're coming. It's time we freed the phoenix. For Ellendren." He said the last part almost as a whisper, but everyone heard. They knew Ellendren was Ramiel's prisoner and they turned it into a chant, unfolding into a war cry.

"For Ellendren," they cried as they filed out of the inn.

As Devlyn followed, Aaron caught his arm and gripped it tight. "For Elle," he said staring hard into Devlyn's eyes.

"For Elle," Devlyn repeated. Her face flashed in his mind—her soft voice calling out to him, as though in a dream.

Outside, the streets bustled with ei'ana, ei'ceuril, and knights. The Cor'leran watch wearing tabards proudly displaying Parendior's purple doe filled in the ranks. The village's original wooden wall was gone and the new outer stone wall and castle, not wrought from the Illumined Wood's magic, could not stop dragon fire.

Devlyn and Aliel bonded, and he could see Velaria on Yelaris flying up and out of Cor'lera. The castle housed most of the defenders and he could sense Alethea wielding defensive shields, assisted by Wyn and Danielle. Eager to see the field, Devlyn launched himself into the air, Viren trailing behind on Falthion. They flew to the top of a stout tower—like at Gneal's castle, this one wasn't particularly tall. From there, Devlyn saw a host marching from the abbey school beneath the shadow of wings. Even without the sun, the dragons still cast a dark presence.

The host was significantly larger than a spattering of stewards of shadow. Cinnamon-haired armored elves marched with them. Jeanne had been fretting over the unaccounted Erynien legion. Devlyn sent her a quick mental note that he had found it. There wasn't time for her to plan a proper defense for Cor'lera, nor for her to send more reinforcements. Besides, their armies were needed in New Castle. Their forces, including Thellion's army, were already marching south. Jeanne sent back a startled curse and a warning to be safe.

The approaching legion far outnumbered Cor'lera's defense. Meeting the Cyndinari elves in the field would be disastrous, so the defenders stayed behind the stone walls. The dragons must have expected that, for they soared ahead of the legion, Ythinor leading some twenty dragons.

On any other day, seeing so many dragons flying toward Cor'lera would have been enough to give Devlyn nightmares for a month, but Ythinor was more terrifying than all the rest combined. His massive form dwarfed the others. He flew with a haughty confidence that said no one could bring him down. Leaving the rest of his flight behind, Ythinor sped over the defensive walls, quickly unleashing fire and tenebrys on the village below.

Before Devlyn could launch into the sky, he felt Evellyn link to Alethea and Leilyn. Alethea shifted her control over the wield to Evellyn, who had a much stronger connection to Cor'lera. Aaron and the ei'ceuril also joined the wield. As fire rained down on the buildings, Evellyn shielded them. Ythinor roared in frustration as none of the village caught aflame.

The first specks of jade appeared in the distance. Ythinor must have seen them too, for he roared in their direction. The dark dragons continued to pour fire down on the city; if the jade dragons and their riders intended to bring them down, they would have to do so over the village. Now that the jade dragons were visible, the Erynien legion hurried their march toward the defensive walls.

Enraged at the unfolding events, Ythinor veered away from the village, then angled toward the nearest gate. The Erynien legion hadn't brought any siege equipment but with a dragon as large as Ythinor, a spawn of the Dark Primus, they didn't need to. Ythinor thumped down, ignoring the multitude of arrows raining down on his black scales. Fire spewed out his maw; the gate didn't stand a chance. Ythinor rumbled, laughing at Cor'lera's defenses as the gate burned away under the flames. He'd destroyed the gate so those on foot could swarm the city.

Ythinor's massive body turned away and he joined the rest of his flight, all determined to break through the wielded shields and burn the city. The jade dragons had reached Cor'lera, immediately engaging the Dark Flight while a different battle unfolded at the gate where Septyl and temple knights fought the Erynien legion. Evellyn continued directing her wield to protect the village from dragon fire.

Devlyn looked at Viren riding Falthion, ensuring he was ready before launching into the sky where dragons snapped and clawed at each other. He spotted the only blue and white dragons, Rusyl, Yelaris, and Kanastil, assisting the jade dragons. Despite being immobilized for fourteen hundred years, the jade dragons fought with a mind-dizzying speed and aggression.

Animys and all four elemental erendinth issued from the jade dragons, also wielded by the Qien monks riding them. Devlyn tried to replicate the wields, but they gained their strength from the jade dragons' sinuous bodies. The movement reminded him of jienzu in a way, but rather than balancing one's own self, the jade dragons were trying to bring Balance back into the world.

The dragons fought tooth and claw above as the rest of the battle raged on below. The wings of the smaller dark dragons grew sluggish, their movements no longer sharp as though they could no longer support the weight of their bodies. A mixture of relief and concern suddenly tugged at Devlyn. The entire aerial battle was happening over Cor'lera. Even the smallest of the dragons would destroy the buildings below if they fell on them.

Devlyn pressed into aerys and hurled a strong gale at the descending dragon, pushing it past the defensive walls to crash to the ground. He sent a frantic mental note to Viren, Liam, Velaria, and Elayne. They too were limited in this fight. While they could certainly fight the dark dragons, they couldn't do what the Jade Flight was born to do, assisted by the Qien monks. As more dragons fell, they too were pushed out of the city by a rush of wind.

Ythinor roared in fury when he realized his flight was dropping out of the fight. He was far from the only dark dragon left, but he must have realized his peril as he filled his chest to unleash an explosion of fire and tenebrys. Devlyn felt the intensity of Evellyn's wield waver. Still airborne, he quickly lent his own strength to her, hoping to halt the great torrent from destroying the village.

Evellyn harnessed his power and added it to those she was already linked to, channeling their strength and control in her wield. Together, they pushed Ythinor's fire and tenebrys back down his throat, filling the unprepared dragon with his own destructive force. Before Devlyn could even consider a plan, he saw a small jade dragon carrying someone wearing a Guardian knight's tabard and not a Qien monk's robes.

Toryn held fast to the dragon with one hand, gripping Shrouds-bane with the other. Ythinor either didn't notice or didn't consider someone on such a small dragon a threat. He had larger jade dragons to contend with. But the world crackled all the same when Toryn's sword caught the underside of his belly and sliced along its length. During the entire battle, violent and hate-filled images had spewed from Ythinor, now replaced by an abrupt fear. His terror was sharp and sudden, but the realization came too late, even as Ythinor's belly opened and spilled down on Cor'lera. Fiery gore and bright light spewed out the dragon's open wound in a golden explosion.

Phoenix. Dozens—hundreds of phoenix erupted from their draconic prison and Erynor's greatest fear of Cor'lera concealing a weapon that could destroy him was fulfilled. His malice and paranoia had brought Toryn and Shroudsbane to Cor'lera to free the phoenix from Ythinor's belly. Erynor's dragon half-brother could only fly a short distance before crashing to the ground.

GOLD WINGS

The inn was quiet after the battle. Patrons sipped their drinks, not interested in sharing what they had seen that day. Too focused on the dragons, Devlyn had missed what had unfolded between Cor'lera's defenders on the ground and their attackers. The Erynien legion were ruthless killers, known for their butchery throughout Teraeniel. And making them an even fiercer army was that shadow elves and stewards of shadow had accompanied them.

Many Septyl and temple knights and much of the Cor'leran watch had died. When Ythinor had fallen from the sky, the battle below had fallen apart. The shadow elves had been the first to flee, knowing they would meet the dragons' fate when the spirits they had stolen would be torn from them. And while the stewards of shadow had control over tenebrys, they were not warriors. They sought to corrupt people's hearts, something Entiel had been very accomplished at. While many of the stewards of shadow had been captured following the battle, Entiel was still free. The Erynien legion had been last to retreat, fracturing when they realized they stood leaderless.

Despite this tremendous cost, the phoenix Ythinor had swallowed were free. Most of them had fled Cor'lera, presumably to search for a Luminari counterpart to bond with. Those who had remained had already chosen their elf. Toryn had barely pulled her sword out of Ythinor's belly when she had been engulfed in a brilliant light, wings springing from her back.

Evellyn and Leilyn too had been chosen by the phoenix, as were many other elves in Cor'lera. Evellyn told Devlyn that many were distant cousins, removed enough that they had not been rounded up and taken to Gneal's dungeons to die. Feolyn and Gwendolyn Lorenthien's blood ran through their veins just as much as it did through Devlyn's.

But his time in Cor'lera was growing short. After the battle, the jade dragons and Qien monks had almost immediately flown south to New Castle where another battle awaited them, as it also awaited Devlyn. Leaving the common room, he went into the innkeeper's quarters to find Evellyn, Leilyn, Liam, Jaerol, and Velaria sitting on the couches and chairs, their cups suggesting something stronger than tea. Only Dolan and Arlyn were missing from the occasion when Evellyn had served Velaria tea so long ago, Devlyn only a toddler at the time.

Evellyn patted the vacant cushion beside her in invitation to Devlyn. Aliel joined the other two phoenix in the room and their quiet song filled the space. Devlyn recognized it as one of longing; Aliel missed Tariel just as deeply as Devlyn missed Ellendren. Not for the first time, he wondered if the two phoenix were more than simple companions. "It's a miracle, isn't it?" Evellyn smiled at Mariel, the phoenix who had chosen her.

"It really is," Devlyn said, trying to sound optimistic. As happy as he was about freeing the phoenix, the fact that Ellendren was still Ramiel's prisoner weighed on him. "We might actually have a chance against Ramiel now." He had hoped the phoenix would bond with elves quickly, but never dared hope they would do so as fast as they had.

"Phaedryn have ever had a singular purpose, but I trust you already know this," Velaria said with a small smile.

"And me?" Devlyn couldn't stop himself from thinking about the prophecy that loomed over him like a storm cloud. Was his purpose in life to die?

"Our fates are ever in our own hands," Alethea said as she and

Wyn came into the room. She smiled at the cozy scene. "Leienya would be happy to know Dolan had lived here, surrounded by love."

"I would like to meet my grandmother," Liam said.

"She would very much welcome meeting all of you. It would certainly give her new life to see this family," Alethea said.

"That might have to wait," Devlyn said with a sad smile.

"Only for a little while, I think. Whether we head to victory or not, Teraeniel's fate will soon be decided," Alethea said. With those words, the conversation shifted from what was to come and the challenges before them, and they spent the evening telling stories, both new and old. They all had remarkable tales to share with each other, some happy and others sad.

They were all laughing hard following Jaerol's story of Liam wielding for the first time when Aaron came into the room. He greeted them briefly, then added, "You'll want to come with me. We caught Entiel."

"Where?" Devlyn asked.

"Looting Ythinor's corpse, likely hoping he could use some of the foul beast for a ritual," Aaron said.

"Where is he now?" Devlyn asked.

"In the castle dungeon. Clara is with him."

Devlyn and Viren rose and followed Aaron through the common room, where the mood had lightened. Patrons were laughing, crying, some singing for the fallen, honoring their memories. Devlyn overheard a discussion about a monument. It was much the same outside. Even the humans who had once hated the elves in Cor'lera spoke fondly of them now, no longer seeing a divide between them. In time, Cor'lera would be a village of lethiens, as the two races continued to join.

At the dungeon, Devlyn recognized the man he had once believed to be his uncle. Entiel looked miserable on the other side of the bars, sitting on a wooden stool. Clara watched him, not speaking, just humming what Devlyn thought sounded like a hymn.

"Nephew," Entiel spat. "Come to gloat? Eager to treat me as I treated you when our positions were reversed, and you were my prisoner?"

"I should have realized that that was my station back then. That even when we thought we were family, you had no love in your heart for me."

"You've become even more insufferable. Natures such as yours make me sick. At least the Cyndinari elves don't waste their breath on weakness."

"Some do." Devlyn didn't elaborate. "Care to share anything before you're sent to live the rest of your days as a prisoner in the Temple of Ceur?"

"You think I will be there long?" Entiel laughed. "Ramiel's Void has already claimed Teraeniel. His Darkness is the new faith of this land. Your silent and absent Anaweh has no recourse into this world. Teraeniel's first god has sanctified the Darkness and it will never belong to the Light again." Entiel's eyes gleamed, his laughter unhinged.

"I understand that you've been holed away in the abbey school for a long time. Rightly too afraid of facing the consequences of your actions. But Verakryl lives once more, and the Void has been pushed out in a broad radius. Sun rays fall on Krysenthiel and that Light will not stop at its borders. Ramiel and his Void will be defeated. The Erynien Empire will crumble again, its foundations too weak to support the weight of its fall."

Entiel threw himself at the bars, a sharpened tool in his hand as he reached to stab Devlyn, but quick as he was, Viren was quicker. Entiel let out a startled exhale. He looked down to see Viren's sword reddening with blood. When he died, his ghost lingered, snarling at his corpse before dashing away as though on a mission.

Devlyn blinked in surprise. He had not expected this. "Even if he had been brought to the temple and knelt every day in the Light, I'm afraid only death would have released him from his hatred. Perhaps now he can begin his pilgrimage on the Great Transition," Clara said.

"I doubt it will be a quick journey," Aaron added.

"But it will be his journey, nonetheless. Just as so many souls were ensnared by the Void since Ramiel was first shut away there, their pilgrimage to Lumaeniel may finally begin anew," Clara said.

"How do you mean?" Devlyn was lost. "Did Anaweh intend for the Void to claim Teraeniel?"

"You know the Creating Light foresaw the Tree of Life's death. Anaweh sealed Ramiel and the Void away beneath the Tree. But now that the Tree is resurrected and the Void is no longer a realm unto itself, the lost souls who had been trapped there can finally find peace. Even if we fail and Ramiel becomes a god in this realm, the dead will ever have a path to Lumaeniel. The Void is no longer a prison." Clara smiled then resumed humming her hymn.

The morning after the battle, Devlyn joined the village in mourning the dead. Aaron led the funerary rites, requesting that the attackers be laid beside the city's defenders. He explained that the path in death was the same for all, whether that person was great or small, performed good deeds or ill. The choices people made in life might make the transition easier for some, but in death, the path remained the same. Whether to follow that path to Lumaeniel was a choice only the individual could make. Aaron would not curse the dead who had had little choice in serving the Erynien Empire.

Listening to Aaron's sermon stirred something inside Devlyn. He couldn't tell how he felt about the Ceurtriarch's words. Did that also apply to Ythinor and Entiel? Did Aaron pray for them to find Anaweh's blessed realm of Lumaeniel? What of the shadow elves and stewards of shadow? Their crimes weren't an accident of their birth as Cyndinari elves. They had dedicated their lives to horrendous deeds, opposing Anaweh at every turn, hurting people—killing and torturing them. Shadow elves lived an elongated life at the expense of others.

As Aaron prayed, he invoked Anaweh and the special form of lumenys embraced the dead. The Light fell on their bodies like a blanket, then seeped through. Many of the bodies vanished at the touch, but others disintegrated into ash. Devlyn wondered what it meant, for there was a clear divide between the defenders and attackers. Had there been soldiers loyal to Erynor who still held Anaweh in their hearts?

The Light dimmed as Clara's soft voice led a dirge. When only the grey darkness of the Void remained, the bodies of the fallen were gone, only their belongings left behind.

Following the ceremony, those who had come from Krysenthiel gathered, ready to return, including Aaron and many of the ei'ceuril and temple knights. Some would stay to cleanse the abbey school and return it to its original purpose, Lillianna leading the efforts as the new abbess. The new Phaedryn would also go to Krysenthiel. Devlyn hoped the phoenix that had sought out others beyond Cor'lera were already at Arenthyl. He worried about the new Phaedryn receiving instruction even knowing it was not his place to do so. They had to learn first from their phoenix and then from Elyse on Phroenthyl. But they did not have the time for that.

The Guardian army was marching to New Castle, and from there to Mount Cyngol.

Once certain everyone was holding hands, Devlyn shifted them all to Arenthyl. Bright blue skies replaced the grey dull of Cor'lera. His mood immediately improved with the sunlight, but the reminder of the Void claiming the rest of Teraeniel nagged at him. And what had Clara meant about the Void being freed? Had Anaweh always wanted that to happen? Was it to remain part of Teraeniel, darkening the skies and blocking out the sun? Was it to remain a source of fear and nightmares all their days?

Velaria was quick to bid farewell. She had to return to Septyl with the ei'ana and Septyl knights. They still had a part to play in Jeanne's scheme in winning this war. Aaron and the ei'ceuril and temple knights quickly took the seguian portal back to Ceurenyl. How long had the Ceurtriarch been away from Ceurenyl? Aaron's elderly assistant was going to be furious.

Devlyn led the Phaedryn to their new home in Arenthyl. While they didn't have to live there, he wanted to make sure they had the option if they wanted to. Until today, Aren had been alone in Parenhal. Devlyn had always thought the place entirely too empty. The Phaedryn were not as large an order as the ei'ana or ei'ceuril, but they had once been a sizable force, capable of incredible power.

The new Phaedryn from Cor'lera had never left their village before. They had witnessed its rapid growth in recent years, but nothing could have prepared them for the stark change that Arenthyl presented. The walk through the city was slow as they repeatedly gawked or got distracted by the grandeur, their phoenix swooping about above them in delight. Devlyn had to stop several times to ensure he didn't lose anyone. He explained many of the city's curiosities and pointed out the various places of interest. Their interest in Arenthyl wasn't the only reason for the slow trek though, for the residents of Arenthyl were also excited about the new arrivals. Elves and humans alike swarmed the column of Phaedryn walking through Arenthyl, and for the first time since Tolvenol had attacked the city, the people sounded hopeful as they cheered them on.

Parenhal, the Phaedryn's citadel, was the only structure that rose from the sixth tier to the seventh and highest tier where Aerodhal was. Its spire was fully integrated into the seventh tier's defensive lumaryl walls and terracing, while the rest of the citadel was grounded in the sixth tier.

As Devlyn and the new Phaedryn approached, they were greeted by Aren waiting at an unimpressive gate, hands clasped behind his back. "There's more," he said, and turned to walk inside. Phaedryn rarely had need of walking through gates.

Devlyn and the others followed, elf and phoenix alike. Aren must have reached out to the others already inside for there were easily over a hundred elves and phoenix gathered in the great hall. Devlyn recognized Aren's phoenix, Tyiel, reborn at last and again with Aren.

"I didn't realize there were so many." Devlyn shuddered as he took in the Phaedryn.

"It's been a long time since these halls were filled. Let us hope it's a precursor of the days ahead of us," Aren said.

"Is there time to train them?" Devlyn asked, carefully not mentioning Phroenthyl. He knew not to speak of Elyse and the ancient home of the Gold Flight.

"Not to the degree that you and Ellendren were trained, nor those before. They will learn our ways in time, and we will help prepare them for when that time comes," Aren said.

"You don't intend to keep us locked up in this spire like a precious keepsake, do you? We intend to fight," Toryn said to a round of cheering. Apparently, she wasn't the only one thinking it.

"You want to fight?" Aren asked. "Do you know the first thing about fighting as a Phaedryn?" He unsheathed his long, crystalline sword and pointed it at Toryn in invitation to duel. Eager to prove herself, she responded by unsheathing her sword, a glint in her eye.

"The sky is ours." Toryn bonded with her phoenix in a flash of light before leaping into the air. The hall had soaring vaults, providing plenty of space to fly unhindered.

Aren smiled at her response. "You learn quickly." Aren bonded with Tyiel. Together they had accomplished deeds remembered in legends and worthy of having a city named after them. Aren joined Toryn aloft. "Your first lesson is that your sword will ever be your weakest weapon."

Devlyn smiled at that. His lack of a sword had always made him feel weak in some way, as though he needed a sword to prove himself. But Aren—this legendary Phaedryn who'd always worn a sword—now claimed to one of the Guardian knight's best and most famous recent recruits that she was so much more than her sword.

Devlyn saw Aren's wield before he released it, hurling Toryn backward, her wings unstable. "You have much to learn before fighting as a Phaedryn," Aren said.

"We don't have time to learn how to wield," Toryn growled in protest.

"Fortunately, not all of you need to learn. Many of you have already wielded the erendinth." Aren's eyes locked with Evellyn.

Evellyn bonded with Mariel and she too flew into the air, already embracing the erendinth, her only weapon her control over it as a wielder. "I do not think this is wise indoors," she said.

"Our halls weren't built of lumaryl just to look pretty," Aren said. He unleashed a wield of ignys and terys. Evellyn easily intercepted the wield as startled yelps came from the elves.

Devlyn's heart raced. He knew his mother was a skilled wielder, but seeing Aren duel with her was another thing entirely. Despite now trusting Aren, Devlyn had still witnessed him committing terrible crimes before he remembered himself. Aren was no longer shrouded in shadow and darkness, but resplendent in light.

The mock airborne duel continued, Devlyn watching in awe as his mother expertly parried Aren's wields. She managed to press the legendary Phaedryn and push the offensive against him.

"Surprised?" Leilyn asked from beside Devlyn.

"I probably shouldn't be." He had never doubted his mother's strength. Few could survive being Erynor's prisoner for so long while also sharing a bond with Auriel. Ellendren came to his thoughts then. She was just as strong as Evellyn. *Be strong my love*, he sent along their bond.

HEARKENED BALANCE

Ellendren hugged her stomach, cradling the nearly fully grown babies within her. Twins. Just like Lucillia, Ellendren would deliver twins into the world at the dawn of a new age. She prayed that she would not face the same end Lucillia did, even though she would embrace it if it meant protecting her children and people. Lucillia had died at Erynor's touch, but in her dying breath an incredible light had issued from her body, searing Erynor in the process. Only the twins, Feolyn and Roendryn were left when the light had faded.

Alone in the room given her, Ellendren shied away from the dark walls, drinking in the light her Phaedryn form gave off, her wings folded against her back. "He won't have you," she said, mostly for herself. Abbie had told her she should talk to her children while she still carried them, that they would recognize her voice and be comforted by it.

They might not be fully formed yet, but your voice will resonate with them, Tariel conveyed.

How can we protect them once they're born? Ellendren pleaded. Ramiel had promised to steal them away and twist them to his purpose. Was it possible to extend a pregnancy, just until they were safe? Knowing that it was drawing to an end and she could not keep them inside her made it all the more difficult.

Ellendren, you must face…

No. The phoenix bristled; her emotions quelled as though she hid herself away. *I'm sorry, Tariel. I can't.*

I will ever be with you. Ellendren felt Tariel withdraw without ceding their bond. Given their captivity in the Void fortress, she had no idea if they'd be able to reconnect. The entire structure was built of dorthl and Ellendren could barely sense the erendinth as it was. They felt distant, as though an ocean lay between her and them. That wasn't possible though; the erendinth were everywhere. Nothing could exist in the er-endinth's absence. She wouldn't be able to breath without aerys, and neither could she be hydrated without aquaeys. The dorthl fortress might be solid, but it was so only because of terys.

It might feel that an ocean stood between her and the erendinth, but she knew all seven were still here. Dorthl couldn't negate the erend-inth, especially since she still lived, as did others in this fortress. What she couldn't figure out was why she couldn't sense them.

Looking around the darkened room, she tried to grasp anything familiar. She had a bed and a table for a waterglass, but little else. Ramiel certainly hadn't provided any comforts. What would an anadel bent on creation's destruction know of consoling an anacordel? The mattress felt like a stone slab and no blankets or pillows had been provided. A chair sat next to the bed, the only other piece of furniture. She dearly wished for a book to pass the time, particularly something that would provide directions on defeating Ramiel before he could steal her children.

Even practicing jienzu felt risky. The exercise often left her drained and dehydrated. While water was provided, she doubted more would be brought to her room if she asked outside the allotted time. Instead, she spent her time meditating. She wished she go to the Tree of Life and ask for guidance. The Tree might have been revived, but Vasknir was absent of Anaweh.

Remember what your brother said, Tariel conveyed.

The Creating Light resides in us all. Ellendren remembered that the *ana* of every anacordel and anadel was a drop of the Creating Light. Her spirit was creative light, but that reminder felt shallow while locked away in Vasknir. Her door was locked from the other side; she didn't think a guard kept watch. What need was there if she couldn't wield in this wretched place?

She spent hours alone, Tariel her only contact. The days dragged on endlessly. Unable to tell night from day, she forgot how many had passed since she'd been captured.

She sat on the dorthl chair. Dorthl might surround her on every side but sitting directly on it added a layer of wrongness. This stone did not belong in Teraeniel—it didn't belong anywhere. One of Ramiel's corruptions. She wondered what it had been before. For all she knew the only mines were in the Shadow Mountains. The thought of more dorthl mines scattered across Teraeniel made her pause. Would Ramiel encase the world in dorthl just as he had with his Void?

A vision of trees dying under the burden of corruption filled her mind, just as flowery meadows turned to ash after a wildfire. Suddenly afraid, she squeezed the armrest, feeling the corruption in the dorthl. It didn't surge or weave like the erendinth but rather was frozen in stasis. She again wondered what this stone had once been. Closing her eyes, she pressed herself into it as though she intended to wield one of the transcendental erendinth. She delved deeper, reaching. It felt like something lay dormant in the stone, locked away and encased in time.

Was this how the phoenix trapped in Ythinor's fiery belly felt? Hundreds of bright lights in a perpetual state of death and rebirth. She hadn't seen Erynor or his dragon here in Ramiel's dark court, but she doubted there was anything she could do to them here.

Eyes closed, she continued examining the dorthl chair until she felt something different. A dim ember, barely burning, hid deep inside the casing of its prison. The dorthl wasn't just corrupted stone, but a thick, multi-layered scab that had encased something completely other. Reaching again, her hold expanded to the entire structure, finding that the dorthl's essence wasn't dorthl at all. Neither was it terys—it was something else. Something that belonged to the mountains that Ramiel had corrupted or tried to kill to replace with a stone infused with tenebrys.

Its essence hadn't died though. Weakened and choked by tenebrys, it lay there, dormant. Ellendren felt a spark that yearned to reach out to the corruption. Hesitant, she feared doing so. Would the corruption seep into her if she delved into the dorthl? What if it had the same effects on her as it had on whatever this stone once was? She couldn't bring that corruption into herself; she had her children to think of. Still, something urged her forward. Something pained and tortured reached out to her. It wasn't the dorthl, but the dormant ember in the stone.

Ellendren didn't quite know what happened next. Instinct drove her, and something deep within awakened. It reminded her of the erendinth, and she thought it originated from the same place, but it was more. She didn't wield, for whatever this power was, its rules weren't the same as the erendinth's. This power somehow encompassed all the erendinth, or rather it was the purpose of the erendinth, to harness life and creation. Just as the irythil had brought the erendinth to create Teraeniel, they were merely a tool for something greater. Ellendren realized the elves had once known this, or rather the Children had, before they began to age. The two remaining Children did not wield as Ellendren knew it, but neither were they blind to the erendinth. That deeper, older power was theirs to control.

As Ellendren felt that spark of Life—Creation—she also felt it leap from her heart, the place where her spirit resided, and link with the dormant essence buried in the dorthl. She had to stand in a hurry then, as the dorthl forming the chair turned to dust, returning to the nothingness it had come from. That corruption had no place in Teraeniel or anywhere. In the chair's place was the something she had felt encased in the dorthl. It looked like a gemstone emitting a brilliant light.

Devlyn fell into another jienzu form, leading the new Phaedryn in a few of the forms Elyse had taught him and Ellendren on Phroenthyl. While jienzu typically calmed him, it also brought his emotions to the surface. Anger mixed with grief were plain. He blamed himself for Ellendren's abduction. How could he not? He was there when Tolvenol had snatched her out of the sky.

He switched to another form, too quickly, and another after that. He didn't hold any of the forms long, passing from one to another in rapid succession. His back was to the other Phaedryn, so he couldn't see if they had difficulty keeping up. Dwelling on any form for too long meant he had to sit with his triggered emotions. However, rest was a crucial component to jienzu. Rushing through the forms provided little benefit, only exhaustion.

Skin slick with sweat, Devlyn heaved as he tried to switch to a new form. He nearly collapsed when someone gripped his shoulder. "I'll take it from here. You need to rest."

"I'm fine, Aren." Devlyn shrugged off his hand.

"You're in an impossible situation. You don't have to pretend at being fine—not among fellow Phaedryn, many of us also being your family."

Devlyn pursed his lips, holding back a scream. His body felt as though it would crumble if he allowed it. If he stopped now, he would never pull himself back up. "I'm needed here."

"The new Phaedryn will spend the rest of the day learning to wield. Ei'ana magisters from Gwilnor have arrived," Aren said. His patience was in stark contrast to Devlyn's stubbornness.

Devlyn turned to see the new Phaedryn in various poses as they caught their breaths. He didn't want to admit it, but his instruction had been more of a detriment to them in his current condition. No one could properly learn jienzu without pausing to hold each form. But to do so, he would have to sit with his erratic emotions. He told himself he didn't need to. He knew how he felt. Still, rather than argue with Aren's sound judgement, Devlyn gave a curt nod then walked off, leaving Parenhal. He stalked across the seventh tier's gardens, debating whether to go into

Aerodhal. The aryl's spire was still uninhabitable and the memory of El-lendren being taken was too strong. He didn't need to see the aryl's spire from inside to be reminded. There wasn't a place in Arenthyl where the burnt spire wasn't visible.

Entering the palace, trailed by the ever-present Viren, Devlyn found himself drawn to the blessedly vacant throne room. His and El-lendren's crowns sat on the Crystal Throne, their verathn hovering over them. The scepters stood vertically and hovered on their own, waiting for their owners to claim them. Devlyn had never made it a habit of carrying his verathn. He couldn't help but wonder if it would have made a difference when Tolvenol had attacked. It hadn't been enough to slay the beast in his lair in Qien, but that didn't stop Devlyn from finding new ways to blame himself. Now that he was home, he had all the time in the world to do so.

He took his verathn, determined not to be caught without it again. Tolvenol had come to Arenthyl and passed through its wards as though they were a thin sheet of water. There was no telling what other enemies might manage the same. He walked past the Crystal Throne and to the ambulatory behind the throne room, where seven shrines radiated in an arc.

Pausing at the only sealed shrine, he gripped its handle and tried to force the door open. Shoulders and arms strained at the effort. His feet slid as the handles dug into his palms. It wouldn't even rattle as he use-lessly pushed and pulled. The only lucilliae unaccounted for was behind this door and until Devlyn could unseal this shrine, Ceurendol was out of his reach. The Luminari elves and all the other races would still be cut off from the promise of Life Immortal.

He pressed his head to the door, again wanting to scream.

"That might be the heart of Ceurendol, but it's not wise to forget the others. Love was not your ancestors' only virtue."

Devlyn turned to find Gael, one of the eight aldarchs of Aldinare. "Gael, when did you arrive?" Devlyn pressed his fist to his chest in greeting—acknowledging and respecting his elder.

"Not an hour past, Ei'denai." She mirrored his courtesy, but to Devlyn's surprise, she acknowledged him as her equal.

"You honor me." Devlyn might be the Exalted Aryl of the elves, but Gael was a draelyn from the Elder Days, daughter to the fallen Queen of Tenethyl.

"The dragons and draelyn who came to Aldinare told me much of what my people have missed since the Darkness took hold of the Skylands. Most curious among their tales was the Luminari pouring their Life Immortal into a jewel."

"Do you think it a folly?"

"Kien and Kiara would not have thought so, and neither would Thien and Loren." Gael's emerald eyes twinkled. "You remind me of them. Thien held the weight of the world on his shoulders. The fall of Tenethyl haunted him, even after he went to Luminare. Loren insisted he share that burden with her. He could deny her nothing."

"I would have liked to meet them." The memories of Thien, Kien, and Kiara flashed through his mind. He had no recollection of Loren, yet she was as pivotal to his house as Thien.

"They would be so proud of you and Ellendren." Gael looked from Devlyn to the sealed door. "Would you show me the lucilliae that form Ceurendol? I've heard so much about them, it would be a shame to visit Arenthyl and not see them before leaving."

Devlyn took Gael to the first shrine, where a violet glow emitted. "The jewel of faith. The smallest of the seven."

"But with the greatest effect." Gael smiled as they both took in the small violet jewel. A small spark struck inside Devlyn's chest, covered in shadows and doubt.

They went to the next shrine, glowing indigo from the jewel of prudence. The wisdom of the Luminari elves brightened his mind and it felt balanced, allowing him to better weigh his actions. A blue lucilliae, the jewel of justice, was next. A fervor rushed through his core, demanding he right the wrongs Ramiel had committed. Next, they stopped at the green shrine, where the Luminari elves of old had placed their hope in a green lucilliae. The promise of expectant joy flooded into him. The hopes of the Luminari brought tears to his eyes. They envisioned a bright future and never doubted whether it was achievable. The yellow shrine beside it held the jewel of temperance. Calm washed over him, smoothing the wrinkles and creases of his impatience and anxiety. Passing to the orange shrine, Devlyn took in the most recently acquired lucilliae, the jewel of fortitude. He still felt its strength of resolve coursing through his veins.

In seeing the other lucilliae, he realized he had allowed the last to take precedence over the others in recent weeks. He had told himself that all he needed was to be brave and face his enemies. He was convinced that was the only way he would rescue Ellendren and defeat Ramiel. But courage in isolation of the other virtues had blinded him, just as any of the other jewels would. They were never meant to be observed in isolation, but together as one. And the jewel that held them all together was love. Devlyn stopped again at the sealed door where the red lucilliae was kept. He placed his hand on the surface.

"The lucilliae might contain the embodiment of the virtues most prized by your ancestors, but it would be a mistake to think they didn't also dwell in your heart. Ceurendol might hold the Luminari's Life Immortal, but it could never deprive the Luminari of the virtues it contains. Those have ever nestled in your heart, growing more excellent with every passing year." Gael stood beside Devlyn, hands clasped.

A surety stirred inside him. Devlyn couldn't recall when he had last felt so stable. His love for Ellendren blossomed in his chest, mingling with the Luminari virtues. "Thank you, Gael. I fear I was on the verge of losing my way."

"You weren't. Your heart would not allow it." The aldarch shared a warm, confident smile. "If you don't believe me, ask Viren or Aliel here, or any of the countless people who love and follow you. I assure you, the list is not small."

Various faces and names flashed through his mind, all those who had helped him in his journey from Cor'lera to Arenthyl and who would continue to support him all the way to Ramiel's fortress on the slopes of Mount Cyngol.

"Ei'denai." Devlyn turned at Jeanne's voice. "It's time. Our armies have reached New Castle."

# DEAD HALLS

Devlyn stood beside Jeanne outside the command tent, where they were surrounded by many more Guardian knights and peoples of every race and nation from across Teraeniel. Althea and Wyn had their griffins nearby, ready to fly into battle at a moment's notice. Viren and Falthion stood protectively behind Devlyn. The battle for New Castle had begun and Devlyn could hear it in the distance. The Void made it almost impossible to see anything. He had to trust Jeanne's reports.

The fortified city was largely defended by humans of the Erynien Empire, but Jeanne seemed uneasy about how quickly they were gaining ground. Void beasts had yet to join the fight, but that wouldn't last. What were they waiting for? Why retreat from the city and allow the Guardians to seize it? And Jeanne's scouts had no idea where they had vanished to. Devlyn didn't like it—it felt like a trap waiting to spring.

Jeanne must have sensed his unease, for she broke the tense silence as they awaited the next report. "I've been meaning to ask how Toryn has transitioned to being a Phaedryn?"

Caught off guard, Devlyn stuttered, "Fine. She's still dependent on her sword."

"As expected for the bearer of Shroundsbane and now Dragonsbane. When I sent her to Cor'lera, I expected her to return as my squire. She was one of my most promising recruits."

"Understandable that a phoenix chose her, though," Devlyn said warily, uncertain whether Jeanne expected an apology for her lost recruit.

"Agreed." Jeanne clearly wasn't thrilled about losing Toryn as her squire. "Ithendryl would be proud of you. She dreamt of the day when the phoenix would be freed from Ythinor's fiery belly. She saw them as our only chance to defeat Ramiel."

"She knew Ramiel would be freed?" Devlyn asked, unable to hide his frustration. How many people simply knew the Evil One would be freed?

"She feared he would be. After all, that was why the Guardian Senate was initiated. Many of the Phaedryn before the First Ceurendol War believed they had a greater purpose, only to die fighting Erynor—a peon of the Evil One."

"That peon has made our lives plenty difficult."

Jeanne grunted in agreement. Despite her upset about losing Toryn, Devlyn had never seen her in such high spirits. He liked this side of her. She still held herself in stern authority, but something about her was more relaxed and confident. Had freeing the phoenix really done that?

"Remember what my mission was," Jeanne said, not hiding her awareness of Devlyn's inner musings. "Ithendryl charged me and the other Guardian knights to safeguard a single phoenix egg because she hoped that the other phoenix might be freed."

That Jeanne had heard his thoughts barely registered to Devlyn. He had grown quite accustomed to elves doing so. The absence of Ellendren's consciousness was far more disturbing. Their minds and hearts had been intertwined since they had entered the Empyrean Sphere and he felt incomplete without her.

Focusing anew on the battle, he kept his eyes peeled for shadow elves who were destined to be here. New Castle was much closer to the Shadow Mountains than Krysenthiel. It would serve as a strategic stronghold for the Guardian armies if they could win it. Surely Ramiel and Erynor understood that. Without it, the Guardians had a stronger position to launch their campaign against the Shadow Mountains. What were Ramiel and Erynor playing at?

Liara and Prya swooped out of the sky to land near the command tent. They'd been scouting the battle from above. "Anything to report?" Jeanne asked.

"New Castle's defenses will fall soon," Prya said.

"You think New Castle stands alone?" Jeanne asked.

"I do. But why, I cannot imagine."

"Why would Ramiel unleash his Void beasts on New Castle, devastating the city and its people only to abandon it?" Devlyn asked.

"A nefarious reason, I'm sure," Jeanne said as a horn blew from the city walls. A white flag was lifted over its gates. She peered through the grey Void and toward the city, as though she expected something else to happen.

"Should we enter the city?" Devlyn asked.

"This was too easy. The Guardian knights bonded with white dragons should have been needed to take a city like New Castle." Jeanne waited as though she anticipated a trap of some sort.

"What do you suspect?" Devlyn asked.

"I can't say. We need to be ready for anything though. Alert the dragon flights to be on guard. If Ramiel intends to catch us in a snare, we'll be ready," Jeanne said, before moving forward. She led the way through the battlefield, largely muddied from soldiers marching, not fighting. Ramiel had left a meager defense and the battle had been quick.

The gates were open when Jeanne and Devlyn reached them, Alethea, Viren, Wyn, and Prya behind, griffins and dragons ready to fight. The surrendering army was composed of Yanileans, but none belonged to the elite force, the Sons of Yanil. Devlyn didn't see any nobles and neither did any present themselves in surrender for ransom. Their weapons had been stripped of them and they sat under guard in orderly rows outside the city walls.

Once through the gates, Devlyn could not see any residents. None of the buildings were barricaded. Broken doors hung open to the elements, but only ghosts passed through. Viren kept close to Devlyn, not trusting that the buildings were truly empty as they moved through the city. Most of the structures were damaged, and some had collapsed entirely. Nothing had been repaired since the attack and Devlyn felt sick when he realized the reason. "There aren't any survivors here. Everyone who lived here was slaughtered."

"If that's the case, where are their corpses and ghosts?" Prya asked.

"I shudder to consider it," Alethea said.

Shadow elves had likely scoured the city's dead, stealing the lingering souls to elongate their own cursed lives. He wanted to hold out hope that someone, anyone, had survived the attack. Perhaps someone had.

New Castle was known for its formidable keep that Mindale and Yanil had long fought to claim. What little hope of finding survivors dwindled the closer they came to the sturdy structure. A wide, stout tower stood partially collapsed, and based on the amount of rubble, it would have doubled the height of the castle.

Jeanne led them through the castle gates and into an entry hall. The eerie quiet of the interior was unnerving. Devlyn didn't have to tap his inner senses to know that no one was alive here. "Search the castle, but take a wielder with you," Jeanne instructed the knights.

"Do you expect a trap?" Devlyn asked.

"It's possible, but I'm more concerned about the structure's integrity. That being the case, I don't expect we'll find anyone alive."

"In the castle?"

"The whole city." Jeanne clenched her jaw as she took in the vacant hall. "Erynor might value slaves, but Ramiel has no use for the living."

"Life in all its forms is a reminder of Anaweh, and Ramiel wants to purge that memory from Teraeniel," Alethea said.

"So, Ramiel intends to kill everyone?"

"That's my fear, which is why it's important we defeat him first."

Jeanne stared at a hole in the vaulted ceiling. If not for the Void, sunlight would have poured through it. But now, only the grey Void and its darker shadows fell through the violent storm clouds above.

Following her eyes to the hole in the vault, Devlyn asked, "Is it safe to stay here?"

"It's here or out in the open, and to be honest, I don't know which is preferable. We'll have the erendinth architects fortify the castle and city walls, to ensure they won't collapse."

"Could New Castle withstand a second siege if required?" Devlyn asked, hesitant about placing his trust in a fortress that had already fallen to enemy control.

"Perhaps from the Erynien Empire, but I doubt it would stand against Void beasts or dragons." Before Jeanne could elaborate further, a knight rushed into the hall.

"First Guardian, Ei'denai, we found someone alive—a child."

"Where?" Jeanne said.

"Here in the castle—the undercroft. He's alone and looks as though he hasn't eaten in weeks, maybe longer."

"Bring him to us," Jeanne said.

"We tried. He won't budge. The poor thing is too petrified to move."

"Very well. Take us to him." They followed the knight deeper into the castle. Scorch marks and signs of battle adorned every surface. If any art had hung on the walls, it was now gone, likely burned to a crisp. A heavy sense of loss—agony and sorrow—permeated the castle, seeping out of the walls like sludge. Devlyn stopped himself from delving into his inner sense—it was too painful to brush against what had happened here.

The deeper into the bowels of the castle they went, the darker and drearier it became. Aliel's illumined presence did little to brighten the space. The Void fought against the intrusion, as though it was alive and wanted to swallow it.

They reached an opening in the undercroft and the knight point-ed into a dark chamber. They had to duck into the space and remained hunched over as they approached a trembling child. If not for Aliel, Devlyn wouldn't have noticed the boy. He sat on the floor, knobby knees tight against his chest.

Jeanne crept over to him then squatted to his level. "Hello, there. My name is Jeanne Darkel. I'm a Guardian knight. We're here to help."

The child didn't respond, just crouched there, eyes fixed on the blank space before him.

"And here is Devlyn Lorenthien. He's the Exalted Aryl of Krysen-thiel, High King of Eklean, and Prelate of the Guardian Senate." Jeanne gestured to Devlyn.

Devlyn drew closer, imitating Jeanne's careful approach. "You look like a brave boy. I'd be very scared if I was here alone."

"I'm not brave," the boy choked out.

Jeanne sent a mental note as sharp as an elbow to Devlyn's ribs. *Keep talking.* He nearly winced at the unexpected jab.

"Of course, you are. It's scary to be alone when strangers and monsters bring war to your home," Devlyn said.

"I heard them scream. I can still hear them screaming and see them. How do I know you're alive? How do I know I'm alive?"

Devlyn extended his hand, palm up, to the boy in invitation. "You can trust your senses. Touch my hand. You can tell I'm alive."

The boy looked up, taking in the added light. "What's that?" He pointed to Aliel.

"This is Aliel, a phoenix. Together, with many other good people, we're trying to make our world safe again. We're trying to defeat the Evil One and the monsters that did this to your home. Do you know who the Evil One is?" Devlyn asked.

"Papa said he wasn't real. Just a story to scare poor people into working. Papa said the Light was only a story too."

"What about your mother?"

"Papa was mean to her whenever he caught her praying. I think he's dead now; I think she is too." The boy started to cry, covering his ears with his hands and rocking back and forth. "So much screaming."

"It's okay. You're safe now. Would you like to come upstairs?"

"Not safe. Bad things up there." The boy hugged his knees again and lay his head on them.

"They're not here now. Only people who want to defeat them are here," Devlyn said.

"They'll come back. They always come back."

Jeanne tensed at that. "Ei'denai," she said urgently. They had to be ready if the Void beasts returned. They couldn't linger here any longer.

"You'll be safe with us. We can take you where the sun still shines. Would you like to feel sunshine again?" Devlyn asked.

"Are there dead people there too?"

"No. The way is open for them to pass to Lumaeniel there." Devlyn offered his hand again, and this time, the boy took it. He stood, his legs wobbling.

"Did you hear that, Mama? You can leave Papa and find the Light. You don't have to stay with him anymore." Devlyn's heart ached for all those who had been killed here.

Jeanne hurriedly led the way back up through the castle. The boy clung to Devlyn's side, especially once they reached a crowded room where some knights had spread maps on a table. They were a far cry from the lumaryl map table in Arenthyl, but this would have to do.

"The city is vulnerable at every gate. The defensive walls didn't stop the Void beasts from entering the city before and they won't do so this time either," Jeanne said.

"Do we stand a chance?" Devlyn asked. The castle barely stood in its current condition.

"Only if the dragon flights join the defense." Jeanne glared pointedly at Prya, one of the few draelyn who had been part of the siege of New Castle.

"Draelyn have no authority over dragons. And you already know the dragons will not fight anacordel untouched by Ramiel's corruption," Prya said.

"Well, we just learned that the Void beasts are coming," Jeanne replied sharply.

"I can only relay the message," Prya said and stepped away.

"We'll need ei'ana to strengthen our fortifications at once. If they direct their efforts where the beasts try to force their way into the city again, we might be able to stop them at the city walls." A horn blew outside, cutting Jeanne off. She cursed under her breath, having hoped they would have more time. "Ei'denai…"

"I will fight," he said, resolved, assuming she was going to insist he return to Arenthyl for his own safety.

"You are not allowed to die today." She locked gazes with him, then looked severely at Viren. "Our forces are largely centralized by the north gate. We'll go there first and find out what the situation is."

They quickly left the castle. Even though ei'ana had been reinforcing the structure, it still looked as though a strong wind would topple it. The army soon surrounded them.

"What's the situation?" Jeanne asked the first knight she came across.

"Four Void beasts approach from the east. One of them is airborne."

"A dragon?" Jeanne asked.

"It appears to be feathered and more bird-like."

"Right." Jeanne didn't remind Prya of their situation again but speedily rolled out a series of commands. The Guardian knights quickly moved to their designated stations where the ei'ana were busy strengthening the compromised stone walls. Devlyn doubted the wall would stop the Void beasts. He wondered if the ei'ana should invest their energy in defense or offense.

"Where do you want us?" Devlyn asked.

"Until more dragons arrive, you're our best chance at defeating these monsters. Take the Eldinari star wardens and focus on the avian one. The city walls won't stop it," Jeanne said, hurrying off.

Devlyn bonded with Aliel, their light pushing against the Void, but to anyone else, it looked as though the Void was swallowing them. Viren climbed on Falthion, while Alethea and Wyn mounted their griffins, joining the other star wardens. He chanced a look at the unending Void storm above. No one should risk flying in that.

Devlyn followed them up, catching sight of the Void beasts the moment he was above the city walls. They were even larger, more gruesome, than those he had seen in Thien's memories. The avian one's feathers dripped a black ooze that suffocated everything it fell on. Its crooked beak and talons looked just as deadly as any dragon's.

The three beasts on the ground moved slowly, their claws tearing at the already ruined terrain, eradicating any remaining vegetation. While Devlyn's sight was limited in the Void, he could see their tough hides, although none of them were the same. One had sharp horns, another had fangs jutting out of its mouth, and the last stood on its hind legs. The Guardian knights bonded to white dragons would have to deal with them until the dragon flights arrived.

Devlyn could feel his heart pounding in his chest. The star wardens flew into formation then toward the avian beast. Devlyn, Viren, Alethea, and Wyn followed.

The beast screeched as its attackers neared—the loud pitch destabilized them and their mounts alike. The star wardens quickly rebalanced then divided into two groups flying to either side of the monstrous beast. Its beak was large enough to sever Falthion's head from his torso if given the chance. As the elves maneuvered around the beast, they fired wielded enhanced arrows at it but that only made it angrier. Knowing the star wardens couldn't bring the monster down on their own, Devlyn pressed into ignys and embraced lumenys.

Fire and light struck the vulture-like beast. Its wing caught fire and it spun in the air to put it out. Viren stayed so close to Devlyn that he could feel his protector's anxiety. Devlyn launched another bright, fiery attack, and Alethea and Wyn wielded aerys to slow the nimble bird.

The beast screeched again, destabilizing the elves and griffins anew. Alethea and Wyn lost control over their wield and the beast plunged after Devlyn. He and Viren dove away, but his ears rang from the beast's beak snapping shut too close to him.

DECONSTRUCT

Dodging the beast's beak again, Devlyn felt its claws strike his chest. He saw the blood before he felt the strike, but when he did, it exploded in pain.

"Devlyn!" Viren yelled as Devlyn spun through the air.

He forced himself to maintain consciousness, despite his sight going in and out. The slash burned and he could feel something digging into the wound. The star wardens had seen the strike and rained a volley of arrows at the avian beast's eye.

Enraged, the Void beast spun about, allowing Viren on Falthion to catch Devlyn as he clutched his chest. His vision faded again and without realizing it, he released his bond with Aliel. Alethea joined them while the star wardens drew the beast further away and quickly wielded the erendinth to heal Devlyn. It poured into his open wound as his vision darkened. He felt Alethea try to extract something from the wound, the pain making him scream anew.

"What is it?" a frantic Viren shouted.

"The beast's talons must be laced with dorthl. The wound is festering with tenebrys." Alethea turned to Wyn. "Quick, you need to pull it out. The erendinth can't heal him otherwise."

Wyn didn't need to be told twice. His eyes turned into oily pools as he reached for the tenebrys burrowing in Devlyn's chest. Holding onto his consciousness as best he could, Devlyn fought to stay awake, but each moment only became more painful. The process of withdrawing the tenebrys was excruciating, the shadowy power tearing at his wound like a thousand knives.

Still slackly slouched in Viren's arms on Falthion, Devlyn pointed despite his pain. The others were too preoccupied with trying to defeat the Void beast, but Devlyn could see it coming for him as he lay weakly in Viren's arms. Its beak opened, greedily longing to crush them in it.

Viren couldn't dive away, not with Devlyn in his condition, and even if Alethea and Wyn had tried to construct a defensive wield, it was too late. Black blood oozed from its injured eye, the other narrowed on them. Devlyn said a prayer, then apologized, thinking this was the end.

Just as the beast came within snapping distance, a burst of light and color crashed against the avian beast. Devlyn blinked, trying to make sense of the situation. He should be dead. Then he saw dragons diving from above. Scales of every color representing eight dragon flights surrounded them. The dragons and their riders divided and struck out toward the Void beasts.

Devlyn winced when Wyn renewed the arduous process of drawing tenebrys from his chest. He could feel it trying to spread to the rest of his body. But Wyn had a grasp on it and sucked the corruption out. Once the burning stopped, Wyn wheezing in exhaustion, Alethea quickly resumed her healing wield. Where Wyn's wield had felt like fire coupled with salt, Alethea's was like a cool spring. His skin stitched back together, leaving slick blood all over his chest.

"Are you okay?" Viren asked, holding Devlyn firmly lest he fall.

"I think so." Devlyn leaned forward and saw the blood. It had spilled down to the dragon's white scales and smeared on Viren as well. "Sorry for the mess."

"The mess can be cleaned; I'd rather you not lose another drop of blood."

"I doubt the avian beast was the only one laced with dorthl, Wyn. There will be others in need of having tenebrys drawn out before they can be healed," Alethea said.

Wyn nodded and dove away on Eolwn, following the destructive path of the Void beasts. Devlyn tracked them to the monsters, outnumbered and overwhelmed by dragons and their riders.

The dragons poured fire mixed with their flight's erendinth down onto the three remaining Void beasts, keeping their distance. From the Elder Days, they knew the dangers of fighting these monsters. When the last beast collapsed, its flesh swiftly set aflame, Viren took Devlyn down to where the dragons and draelyn had gathered.

A wielded pavilion was already rising from the ground, vines and leaves twisted together in wondrous display. Flowers bloomed from the vines, preserving the draelyns' reputation of crafting everything with attention to the beautiful, even for temporary structures that would return to the ground. In the pavilion, Devlyn recognized the seven Ealyn who governed Tenethyl, one from each of their houses, Vivien's golden hair and eyes standing out. She smiled at Devlyn as he joined the Ealyn, avoiding the furnishings springing from the ground. A table of the same vines formed in the center, surrounded by woven chairs.

"It's good to see you, Devlyn," Vivien said. "Please, have a seat. You must be exhausted. From the stains and tattered state of your clothing, I see you lost a lot of blood." She gestured to a chair, and an attendant offered him a cup of water and a vaer.

"Thank you," Devlyn said as the Ealyn and the dragons who had shifted into their smaller forms took seats around the table. Devlyn did not have the energy for a meeting. Ellendren might be able to pull off a battle and immediately follow that by meeting with the Ealyn of Tenethyl, but Devlyn wasn't sure he could manage it. He hoped someone would tell Jeanne. She'd be much more useful in this setting than him just now.

He bit into the vaer, surprised at the energy that rejuvenated him. He hadn't realized how hungry he'd been and quickly consumed the rest of the fruit.

"I trust your verathn has been treating you well," Vivien said.

"Quite well, so long as I remember to carry it, thank you."

"That is good," Vivien said. He could see the other Ealyn eying him curiously.

"Is something wrong?" he asked. The leaders of Tenethyl had been much more welcoming when he had visited their city.

"That has yet to be decided," Niron said, Ealyn of the Sapphire House.

"What has to be decided?"

"Whether you allow this talisman of the Sorcery to be completed," Torik said, his onyx eyes and hair matching his house.

"Ramiel is a menace and deserves the worst of imaginable fates, but surely you can see the risks in crafting a talisman powerful enough to contain an irythil," Daela said.

"Ramiel is an anadel. He can't be killed, not physically. How else do you imagine we defeat him?" Devlyn asked.

"The irythil accepted your presence amid their thrones, and this is how you would repay them—crafting a talisman that could imprison them if it fell into the wrong hands?" Mellory asked, her ruby eyes flaming.

"You cannot allow that talisman to be made," Helen echoed.

"If you do nothing, we will ensure the ship carrying it is destroyed. We make no promises for survivors," Niron said.

"How are we supposed to defeat Ramiel without something capable of imprisoning him?" Devlyn had gone through endless alternatives with the Guardian Senate. There weren't any good options. Even ancient records alluded to a vessel of some sort to hold Ramiel. Devlyn doubted a vase would be sufficient for a being of Ramiel's caliber. "I trust the Daer Sorcery's devices as little as you do, but what option do we have?"

"Ramiel was locked away before and the prison did not stop his evil from seeping out. He will continue to corrupt our world if merely confined to a prison," Vivien said.

Devlyn had left the Ealyn unresolved. He knew they were right in fearing the existence of a talisman capable of holding an irythil, but neither had they provided solutions.

Frustrated, he fell into another jienzu form. The exercise calmed him. His back strained as he flowed from one form into the next, just as he felt the erendinth flowing through him. With his senses open, he felt another join him on the semi-private terrace in the ruined keep. New Castle's keep might be largely destroyed but Jeanne had found him adequate and stable rooms.

When he realized his guest was Galithinol the Gold, he moved to end his exercise. "I was hoping to join you," the gold dragon said, his voice deep and ancient.

"I doubt I'll be able to keep up with you."

"I might have seen the first Children wake, but this body feels the eons pressing on it," Galithinol replied. He was already in his smaller form, wearing loose black trousers and a matching tunic that made his golden hair and eyes stand out. Despite his comment about his age, he easily fell into a jienzu form, following where Devlyn had left off, then shifted to a form Devlyn didn't know. He followed the dragon's lead, pushing and twisting in new and unimaginable postures.

They continued like that for a while. The lead passed between them, until Galithinol straightened and exhaled deeply. Devlyn too eased out of the jienzu form.

"Thank you. It's always more desirable to practice jienzu with another."

"But you didn't just come for jienzu."

"No. The Ealyn are concerned. They spoke harshly with you because they believed you needed it. This talisman cannot be permitted to exist."

"It's already under construction on a Ja'horan ship sailing for Eklean. It could very well be completed."

"By Sha'ghol, no less."

"They would see Ramiel defeated."

"And after? Do you imagine they'll forfeit the power of their former master?"

Devlyn hadn't considered that. He trusted Yloran, but could he trust her to release a shred of power if it was in her control? The Sha'ghol had a history of harnessing power without concern. "What else can we do?" he asked.

"If the solution rested with the dragon flights, we would have shared it with you. But alas, our wisdom is not so infinite or creative. Remember, it was not dragons who first learned to wield the erendinth, but the Luminari elves. We only knew how to harness the erendinth connected to our flight. Our purpose has ever been to assist the anadel as their physical guardians, a charge we have failed in Daereneth. The land there is all but stripped of its anadel, forced into confined baubles, their powers forcibly used at another's whim."

"If we do the same to Ramiel, we are no better." Devlyn understood the Ealyn's perspective.

"Worse is that your actions would sanction it and the Sorcery would spread. People will see you defeat Ramiel with the talisman. History will not forget and people will emulate those actions. The Sorcery could take root in Eklean, usurping the ei'ana. How long do you think it would be before the anadel in Eklean are farmed? How long until the Illumined Wood shrinks further?"

"What if they have already completed it?"

"Then you'll have to unmake it."

One more thing to do. Time was short, time that Ellendren didn't have. How many days until she gave birth? Devlyn couldn't afford to destroy the talisman sailing for Eklean. "And if I can't?"

"Last I checked, there were many more Phaedryn now than there were at the last moon."

"Right. I'll speak with Jeanne. Doubtless, this will change her strategy."

Galithinol followed Devlyn and Viren, who'd been standing guard at the entry. Jeanne was easy to find. She'd made the largest hall, crumbling as it was, her war chamber since her maps were already spread out there. A dozen generals spoke almost simultaneously, all leaning over the maps.

Jeanne spotted Devlyn. "Ei'denai, I was just about to send for you. We have great news."

"Oh?" He needed some good news.

"The Ja'horan ship has exceeded our expectations and has docked near Vorn Schtam along the Skrein Sea. The talisman, along with those who created it and supervised the undertaking are travelling through the Great Dwarven Tunnel as we speak. I've been assured they will make impeccable time, and if we don't begin our march for Mount Cyngol at once, they'll beat us there."

Devlyn groaned. Not only was the talisman complete but it had already reached Eklean.

"I assumed that would've pleased you." Jeanne leveled a glare.

"Before today, it would have."

"What's changed?" she asked, her generals silenced. Her tone could slice through stone.

"We have to destroy it."

Jeanne sucked in her breath and pursed her lips. "Are you able to?" She didn't question or argue. She had never supported the talisman's creation. And she hated that it had been done without the Guardian Senate's explicit consent. They might have agreed to have it crafted, but not by Sha'ghol.

TALISMAN

Armies from across the world had answered the call of the Guardian Senate and now swarmed the Shadow Mountains. There wasn't a child in Eklean who didn't know to stay clear of that mountain range—it was to be avoided at any cost. Children heard stories of the Evil One claiming those mountains before they learned Anaweh's name. The volcano and mountains' sinister presence marred the landscape. Even those aligned with the Erynien Empire were leery of them.

Now, the Guardian armies surrounded the Shadow Mountains on every side, intent on keeping the evil lingering there from oozing out. Jeanne wasted little time in mobilizing the forces at New Castle following the deadly encounter with Void beasts. A reserve force remained to hold New Castle, but the bulk of the army now marched toward the ever-darkening horizon.

The arid land shifted from the first hints of the desert expanding past Dwota's Gap as they marched south and west. The vegetation and fauna hadn't just dried out but had died at the Void's corruptive touch. Dead stalks lined the route, trampled flat by the marching army. The Void was much stronger here, condensing around the fount of its corruption.

The horizon darkened where Mount Cyngol's jagged peaks threatened the heavens above—a hole in the fabric of their realm where Vasknir's spear-like spires had released the Void on Teraeniel. Devlyn's imagination and Alethea and Wyn's description painted a horrific image of Ramiel's fortress, too distant to see. He knew what he looked at. Nowhere else had such dense darkness claimed the land. The horizon to the north and south appeared warm grey in contrast.

Devlyn kept his gaze toward the dark, jagged fortress in the distance. *We're coming, Elle,* he sent even knowing the fortress wrought of dorthl prevented it from reaching her.

The caravan slowed to a stop, and a series of commands originating from Jeanne came from generals and captains. But it was too early to stop. They hadn't even reached Dynthol Mirk yet. As everyone began setting up camp, Devlyn went to find Jeanne to find out why they had stopped so soon. They had marched only half the distance they had in previous days. They'd even covered more ground when crossing the River Eindol, a feat made considerably easier due to the draelyn having wielded bridges across the watery span.

Jeanne's command tent was already pitched and easy to locate in the mass of people. She stood over a folding table where maps had been unfurled. "Ei'denai, what can I do for you?"

"Is there a reason we're stopping so early?"

"We must wait for all the reinforcements before crossing into Dynthol Mirk." She placed figurines on the map, positioning some on top of the Shadow Mountains, more surrounding them, and still more figurines farther away. "We travelled faster than I'd anticipated from New Castle."

"Shouldn't we take advantage of the momentum?"

"I wouldn't call our swift march momentum. And no, we need to wait for all our reinforcements. Not so much for our sake—we'll be fine navigating through the corruption of what was once a forest. But I can't say the same for a smaller force lagging behind."

It made sense, even though it meant they'd be waiting. Again, he wondered whether Ellendren could afford the delay. "What should we do in the meantime?" He needed to distract himself. He couldn't charge into Vasknir before their forces were fully prepared. Still, every second

Ellendren was Ramiel's prisoner was a chance their twins would be born in darkness.

"The soldiers will practice drills, set up watches, and scout the safest route to Mount Cyngol." She paused and placed another figurine on the map, this one in the Vespien Mountains. "While I wouldn't presume to issue an order to the Exalted Aryl of Krysenthiel, I might suggest you fulfill your oath to the Ealyn. The talisman will be reaching the dwarven front soon and I would not trust the Sha'ghol to destroy it in your absence."

Although it would take Devlyn further away from Ellendren, Jeanne was right; he had to see the talisman destroyed. The Daer Sorcery would take advantage of the Guardian Senate using the talisman as justification for farming anadel. The continent of Daereneth was dying due to the imbalance the Daer had imposed on it. The irythil had brought Devlyn to their thrones, expecting him to protect the Balance in Teraeniel. The Ealyn and dragon flights also expected it and would assist the Guardians only if the talisman was destroyed. They trusted him to see it done, even if that meant abandoning their best chance at defeating Ramiel. "Is there anything you need before I go?"

"Promise to come back."

"Of course." Devlyn bowed out of the command tent, Viren and Falthion joining him. He paused before shifting to the Great Dwarven Tunnel. How was he to destroy this talisman? His experience with the Daer Sorcery was limited. He didn't trust them enough to ask how to unmake their artifacts. The Ja'horan and Charrenese had fought against Daer invasions for centuries. No one knew how to better defend against the Daer.

"We should ask a mage of the Kilnae Del to join us." Mages were already accompanying the talisman, but uneasiness nagged at the back of Devlyn's mind. He didn't want to think of Caspol or Yloran betraying them, but neither could he afford to fully trust their intentions. Devlyn extended his hand to Viren.

In a flash of light, they traded one military camp for another, this one situated on the coast. Tall ships were moored where the sea was still deep.

Hundreds of colorful banners, largely from Ja'horan, filled the camp. Seeing the Charren flags flapping in the breeze, Devlyn, Viren, Aliel, and Falthion headed toward them, easily identifying the command tent. He was delighted yet surprised to find Sanjin inside, surrounded by his generals. He hadn't expected Sanjin to cross the sea, considering the instability in Charren due to Caspol's interference.

"Devlyn, what a surprise! What brings you here?" Sanjin asked with a broad smile.

"The Daer Sorcery."

Sanjin's grin vanished. "What have they done now?"

"It's about the talisman."

"The one that was never made?" Sanjin arced a brow.

"Yes, that one," Devlyn admitted. "There wasn't time to request a formal session before the Guardian Senate."

"That sounds like a mistake."

"Agreed. We have to destroy it before it can be used."

"I don't understand." Sanjin blinked. "While I don't like such a talisman existing, especially without the senate's approval, I thought we needed it to defeat the Evil One."

Devlyn told him about his meeting with the Ealyn and their perspective. "I figured the Kilnae Del would have the most experience in destroying Sorcery artifacts."

"Certainly more than others. But we've all come here to see the Evil One defeated. What chance do we have without it?"

"If we're united, we'll find a way. Ramiel is not stronger than the whole of creation."

Sanjin paused and nodded to himself. "Cali," he called, "Go with Devlyn and help him destroy that wretched talisman."

"With pleasure." Cali bowed her head, partly to conceal her smile.

"Will we be flying to the ship carrying it?"

"It's already in the dwarven tunnels. I mean for us to intercept and destroy it before it reaches the Shadow Mountains."

"So, how are we getting to these tunnels?" she asked.

Devlyn closed his eyes and reached out. His awareness blossomed as though a bubble had expanded over him. Many individuals came to the front of his mind. The talisman was likely far to the north, still somewhere in the Vespien Mountains. He had no idea when Jeanne had received the report of its arrival in Eklean, but the dwarves travelled swiftly through their tunnels. For all Devlyn knew, the talisman could already be at the southernmost roots of the Vespien Mountains. Broadening his awareness further, assisted by Aliel, he felt as though he was in the tunnel, surrounded by thousands of dwarven warriors ready for battle. The way between the Schtamite and the exiled dwarves in the Shadow Mountains was still sealed but would not remain so for long.

Searching, he did not sense Yloran. Wherever the talisman was, she too would be. Striking north, Devlyn kept his awareness limited to the tunnels. The dwarves would never permit Sha'ghol to enter their Schtams. They hadn't even extended such an offer to Devlyn or Ellendren. Allowing the Sha'ghol to enter their tunnels at all had been a stretch for them.

Devlyn then sensed Yloran, her essence unmissable. She might know ways to change and conceal her appearance, but she could never hide her spirit from someone who knew it.

Devlyn offered his hand to Cali, Viren already gripping his shoulder, Falthion gripping Viren. "Oh, I do love this part," Sanjin said as a flash of light took them away. The gloomy military camp was replaced with a wide tunnel. Rivers of gold and silver ran along the stone's surface. The precious metals didn't just sparkle in Devlyn and Aliel's light but flowed on their own. While it had been some time since Devlyn had visited the dwarven wonder, he thought the gold and silver veins had diminished somehow, as though sickness had sapped some of the life from the mountains.

"Is this the right place?" Cali asked, taking in the tunnel.

Knowing how quickly the dwarves could move through the tunnel, Devlyn had shifted the small group south of Yloran's location.

Devlyn heard the low hum before seeing the approaching boulders, rolling along at a dizzying speed. The people inside those rocks would be disoriented. But whatever dwarf had been tasked with bringing the outsiders to the Shadow Mountains must have sensed the new arrivals, for the rumbling of the tumbling rocks slowed, then stopped altogether. Pebbles dripped from the mass, revealing the elves and humans, along with the talisman in their charge.

Devlyn had expected more dwarves to accompany the outsiders, but only one stood at the front of the group. "The Patriarchs and Matriarchs will see you banished from the Schtamite for entering uninvited," Oma warned.

"I had to—before we make an even graver mistake," Devlyn said.

"Ah. The stones also feel its wrongness. They don't want it here. The mountains are already sickened by the Void. They would see the talisman destroyed if they had the strength to do so. They threaten to collapse on us all," Oma said.

Caspol reoriented himself, overhearing the discussion. "You can't. Nothing will stop him. Only this." He staggered, placing himself in front of the talisman. For all the nethrin the talisman required, it was surprisingly small. Granted, it still stood just as tall as Caspol and was a perfect silvery sphere of interlocking rings with a hollow core, undeniably a prison.

"We must. It's too dangerous—we should never have created it. If we permit this, others will follow." Devlyn didn't want to consider a Daer Sorcery that felt they had the right to abduct anadel.

"No!" Caspol flung his arms wide, deterring others from approaching the talisman.

"Caspol, don't be a child. Step away," Yloran said calmly. Devlyn let out a silent sigh of relief. He hadn't been sure where Yloran stood on the matter.

"We can't defeat him. You of all people should know this, Yloran." The air in the tunnel changed. Devlyn didn't feel Caspol wielding and the erendinth were passive around them, but the talisman hummed, awakening. It tugged at Devlyn, still bonded with Aliel. The others didn't seem to notice.

The talisman drew the light from his Phaedryn form, pulling it toward itself. The light warped around the talisman, turning into a vortex that yanked anadel from the stone and sucked them in.

Resist it, Aliel! he screamed through their bond.

"You will not stop me," Caspol hissed, twisting the captured anadel's power against them. The tunnel shook and Devlyn could only just hold himself up as he and Aliel strained to resist the talisman's pull but managed to throw a wielded dart of ignys at Caspol, who easily swatted it away. Off balance, Devlyn sought to find his footing. The talisman's pull was powerful. Yloran, her attendants, and the ei'ana fought Caspol, who only grew stronger as more anadel were pulled into the talisman. The mountain quaked and rocks fell from the arched tunnel, crashing around them.

Oma extended her arms, her body rigid. Her focus wasn't on Caspol, but on the tunnel. Devlyn could sense her wielding a special form of terys, unique to the dwarves, just as the ei'ceuril could wield a special form of lumenys. Reinforcing the tunnel and strengthening the mountain required her full attention.

Cali too was consumed in a magic foreign to Devlyn. He had thought destroying the talisman would have been a simple endeavor, but whatever Cali was doing required all her effort, leaving the others to fight Caspol. The ei'ana, mages, and Yloran, distrustful of each other, pressed their own disunified attacks against Caspol. Devlyn tried to contribute, but it took all his and Aliel's focus to resist being pulled into the talisman.

A powerful surge exploded from Caspol, knocking Devlyn and

the others off their feet. When Devlyn stood, the pull was gone. Caspol hadn't been defeated but lashed out with reckless attacks. Then Devlyn realized light no longer issued off his body and his wings were gone.

Aliel—Aliel! he screamed aloud and through their bond. "Caspol. Release Aliel at once!"

"You can have your pet bird after I rid this world of the Master."

"Release him now!" Unlike dorthl, the talisman didn't block Devlyn's connection with Aliel. He reached out for the phoenix trapped inside the massive orb. He could feel the Sorcery's device sapping Aliel's power and twisting it as Caspol used it against him. Devlyn had sworn they would never be separated again after Queen Alesei had locked him in a dorthl cage, and later a tenebrys bolt struck them in the sky over Lankor, locking Aliel in Devlyn's twisted wound. It had taken months before their bond was healed. The reminder of that wound flashed through him.

Not again. Never again, he conveyed to a shrieking Aliel.

No longer fighting the talisman's pull, he pressed into the elemental erendinth and embraced the transcendental erendinth. He wielded a lance of aquaeys and aerys laced with umbrys. An icy spear struck at Caspol who stopped it with ignys. Devlyn wielded more vinelike lances, none of the same erendinth combinations, but Caspol effortlessly swatted them away. He grew more powerful with every anadel he sucked into the talisman, seemingly endless. He was draining the mountain of its anadel faster than the Daer had farmed their own continent.

Knowing he wasn't going to defeat Caspol on his own, he tapped his interior sense and reached out to Yloran and the ei'ana. *Link with me—we can't defeat him divided.* They might not trust each other, but they did trust Devlyn. He felt the immense power swell inside him, and pressing into terys, he wielded the rubblestone to lash Caspol's hands and feet in place. He would not escape. Devlyn swung his verathn, directing his wields through it, strengthening them.

As Caspol reverted to tenebrys laced with terys, Devlyn responded by wielding lumenys to engulf and halt the wield. The mountain rumbled again, but not because of Caspol.

"Child of Luminare, favored of Uriel." The voice was slow and mighty. Oma fell prostrate, her face pressed to the stone. "I grant you my strength. Free the anadel of my mountains and destroy what ought never have been wrought."

A surge of energy opened to Devlyn. He had not bonded with whoever spoke, but it was clear that the dwarves worshiped him based on Oma's reaction. As Devlyn tapped that new power, he became aware of the entire mountain range. Every tunnel, cavern, and the carefully guarded Schtams lay open to him. He gasped as he took them in. They were just as remarkable as Arenthyl. They thrummed with living stone—stone that had not fallen asleep as much of Teraeniel's had. Veins of true gold and true silver pulsed through the remarkable subterranean structures, set deep within the mountains, deeper than Devlyn had thought possible.

He realized the tunnel was the same living stone, and the gold and silver veins were as blood to the mountains. They surged hotter than the fiercest forges, their heat preserved within the metallic shell, for the gold and silver were not solid, but flowed like rivers through the stone.

Tapping the mountain's power, Devlyn wielded the living gold and silver and directed their path toward Caspol. The molten metal swelled off the wall like an ocean wave and with just as much force. Unable to stop the torrent, a screaming Caspol was swallowed in the molten metals flowing in an unbroken stream. When Devlyn released his hold over it and it returned to the tunnel wall, Caspol's ghost was all that remained in its wake, his body completely disintegrated.

Devlyn turned to Cali holding an arcane gem, glowing a brilliant orange. The talisman had stopped pulling anadel in, but those Caspol had caught, including Aliel, were still trapped inside. With Caspol gone, Cali approached the talisman and pressed the gem to its spherical surface. Nothing happened at first, but she held it there and it continued to brighten as tiny fissures danced across the woven surface, penetrating from shell to core.

Green light seeped out of the fissures; most of the anadel trapped inside were those of terys. The talisman shattered, not into shards, but into a metallic dust and a wave of hundreds of terys anadel poured out. No one would use any piece of it again to rework its foul purpose. So many anadel had been caught in so short a time! He bonded with Aliel at once, caught in the explosion of light. His panic eased as they nestled back into their shared bond.

Aliel's brief experience in the talisman swept through Devlyn's mind. It had been nothing less than torture. Caspol had forcibly pulled at Aliel and the other anadel's powers, twisting them and forcing them to act against their purpose and stripping them of their autonomy.

Are you okay? Devlyn embraced Aliel in a spiritual hug.

It's over. Thank you for destroying it. The Ealyn were right; it was wrong to bring that abomination into the world.

A Prince to Die

In the aftermath of the talisman's destruction, knowing that it had been the right thing to do, Devlyn couldn't stop the pang of dread. The talisman might not have been their best option, but they could have defeated Ramiel with it.

Now, that weapon was gone. What hope did they have of defeating Ramiel without it? Countless meetings had taken place to devise a plan to bring down Ramiel. The Guardian Senate had not formally agreed on how the talisman should be created, but for better or worse, he had acted alone in destroying it. They were going to be furious with him. He couldn't deal with the senate just now, though. The Guardian forces were closing in on the Shadow Mountains.

Yloran noticed Devlyn slumped against the tunnel wall and came over to join him. "Do you believe you did the right thing?" She remained standing, not one to sit on the ground, but neither had Devlyn thought her the sort of elf to offer encouragement.

He stared at the glimmering dust, still hanging in the air where the talisman had exploded. Aliel's lingering agony was all the reassurance he needed to be confident in his choice. "Positive."

"Then you have nothing to worry about. And certainly, no reason to look as defeated as you do," Yloran said, offering him a hand. He accepted it and pulled himself to his feet.

"Hmph. We should have never brought it into the mountains."

Oma was still wielding terys to soothe the fissures Caspol had caused.

"Will the mountain recover?" Devlyn asked, deciding not to comment on it being Oma's recommendation to the Guardian Senate to bring the talisman into the Great Dwarven Tunnel. Granted, that was before he received express approval from the senate to allow Caspol to create it.

"These mountains are made of strong stuff. They'll be just fine, especially with Mundi tending them," Oma said.

"Is that who reached out to me?"

"Hmph. Doesn't even recognize our Great Father when he bestows his power on you. Hmph!" Oma focused anew on mending the tunnel.

"Your *Great Father*?" Yloran asked, cocking an eyebrow.

"Do you elves know of anything but yourselves?" Oma stared them down from behind her crossed arms. Neither replied and Viren, Cali, and all the others took decisive steps away, pretending they hadn't heard. "Hmph. I bet you believe your enthiel were the only ones to lead you somewhere special after the Great Blessing, as though only the elves deserved such privilege." Oma waited for them to answer, tapping her foot.

"Mundi brought the dwarves to the mountains?" Devlyn asked, skirting the accusation.

"Are those pointed ears filled with clay and rocks? Of course, he did. He also showed us how to work the stone. Do not forget, our stone seers were singing to the stone long before your ei'ana learned how to wield terys," Oma said.

"Is that why so few dwarves attend Gwilnor Academy to become ei'ana?" Devlyn asked carefully.

"We don't need to throw fireballs or ice darts to protect our Schtams. It's a shame there's only a fraction of us stone seers today. Erynor never dreamt of invading our Schtams when he last rose to power. Now if I'm not mistaken, you lot have overstayed your welcome. You won't be defeating the Evil One from here." Oma renewed her focus on fortifying the tunnel.

She was right. They had to rejoin their forces. Unsurprisingly, the others had gathered around at Oma's dismissal, having overheard the entire conversation. *Ready, Aliel?*

Aliel sang a soft tune as he fluttered to Devlyn before bonding. Only Oma stayed behind, the others shifting to the main military camp, east of the Shadow Mountains.

"You were meant to bring me the talisman, not let it be destroyed!" Ramiel thundered at the ghost.

"Forgive me, Master." The ghost shrank before Ramiel's berating.

"I've already forgiven you once for your hubris in plotting to imprison me. Why should I forgive you again? You not only betrayed me, but worse, you failed me!"

"Yes, why indeed, Caspol?" Erynel said with a purr. "In what way are you deserving of a third chance?"

Ellendren watched in horror as Ramiel chastised the dead Sha'ghol. As scared as she was, she couldn't help but wonder what Devlyn was doing. Had the Guardian Senate allowed Caspol—a Sha'ghol— to create the talisman? What had happened to the plan to have the Sorcery create it? And once it had been created, why destroy it? Had Devlyn discovered Caspol's duplicity? Perhaps there was another reason. Ellendren couldn't consider Devlyn going behind the Guardian Senate. The institution could crumble, dividing the world anew if Devlyn didn't respect their authority.

Being trapped here with the enemy was driving her mad. She wanted—needed—to help her people. They depended on her and all she could do was let others plan and fight in her absence.

"Do not forget, Erynel, you too have failed me." Ramiel turned on her specter.

"Master, my Shroud accomplished what you wanted. We killed the

Tree."

"And yet the Tree lives once more. Anaweh's presence is returned to Teraeniel."

"Your Void is stronger. Look how it contains the Light to a single lake."

"And how long until it spreads like the disease it is? I was there when the Light first came to the Void. It will scatter my Void if left unchecked."

"I also bore you a draelyn, sired by Tolvenol, for you. I died for you," Erynel said.

"You did it for your own vanity," an ethereal figure said. It was not a ghost, but Ellendren had seen him with a physical body before, when he had required a host to be in Teraeniel. His host was dead, killed by Devlyn when they had won back Arenthyl. But now that the Void encompassed Teraeniel, the Deurghol could move about Teraeniel as they had in the Elder Days.

"Erynor has proven useful," Ramiel said, slowly and deliberately. "But he's been a disappointment. He might be a draelyn, but his so-called empire crumbles at the fringes, not that it will matter. Yes, your son, for whom you sacrificed yourself to bring into this world, has been useful, Erynel, but you promised more from him. You were better suited for his mantle than he."

"Then grant me my body back," Erynel said, risking Ramiel's wrath.

"You know I cannot."

"Then give me hers!" Erynel pointed ravenously at Ellendren.

"No. I still have my uses for her as she is."

Ellendren quivered. She wanted to run—to shift out of this wretched place and never return. But she couldn't so much as wield a spark with all the dorthl here.

"You'll be done with her soon though, yes? By the looks of her belly, she'll be ready to give birth any day," Erynel said.

"Yes, he's nearly ready." Ramiel's smile was sinister.

Ellendren held her midsection in defense. These monsters would not have her children. Ramiel had suggested one might not make it to birth, but she refused to entertain that outcome. No. They would both live.

The thought of Ramiel using one or both for his own schemes to turn the world to his Darkness petrified her. What sort of mother would she be if their first breath was in Ramiel's clutches? She had to either find a way to escape Vasknir or vanquish Ramiel before he could lay a finger on her children. Even as she thought it, a wave of exhaustion swept over her. She stumbled back a few steps and looked for something to steady herself.

"Return her to her chambers. Her weak mortal frame needs its rest." Ramiel's ethereal form flew through the room to whisper in her ear. "Death would free you of your frailty. You could be as perfect as we anadel are. The constraints of sleep, pain, and disease would never touch you again. Shed your fragile body and be perfect."

"You do not understand what it is to be an anacordel. How could you?" Ellendren had no idea where her sudden strength had come from, but she pressed on. "Our perfection lies in our complexity and finding Balance within ourselves."

"Teraeniel was a mistake. You anacordel were Anaweh's great accident. One I intend to remedy. My Void will swallow you all until not even a memory of light lingers. If you die quickly, perhaps your specter can reach Lumaeniel before I sever the way again," he threatened.

Ellendren's breath caught in her throat as she stepped away. As much as she feared Ramiel, she understood him even less. What had driven him to hate anacordel and the Light so much? "I thought you said the Light would spread again?"

"Take her away," Ramiel repeated, his voice low and dangerous.

Few in Ramiel's court were capable of physically supporting Ellendren back to her chambers. They were either dead or bodiless Deurghol.

Someone sheathed in black approached, offering an arm for support, an unexpected kindness. "Come, I'll take you back so you might rest."

"Thank you."

They walked in silence, only the padding of their feet on the black dorthl floor making any sound. While Ellendren could not wield in this place, she had maintained her Phaedryn form since Tolvenol had snatched her out of the sky. Tariel was her one recourse in this prison. Being able to communicate with her phoenix was all that kept her mind stable. The dorthl suffocated the light emitting off her though, seeking to abolish it.

Reaching her chambers, she thanked her escort and asked, "Might I know your name?"

"Erethien." He lowered his black hood, revealing the cinnamon hair and bronze skin of the Cyndinari elves. A scar stretched from above his eye and down to his chin, his black eyes a gift from his draconic grandfather.

"Erynor's son. I thought you were a Deathless."

"The Deurghol who had claimed me when we corrupted Ceurendol and brought about the Shroud no longer requires me as a host. I had prepared myself for death, thinking the Deurghol was all that kept me alive these fourteen hundred years."

"What will you do now?"

"My father would have me become a shadow elf. But I have no interest in lingering in this world with my crimes. They're too heavy to bear without the Deurghol," Erethien said.

"So, redeem yourself. The Deurghol's sins are not yours to bear. Only the corruption of Ceurendol is yours."

"You do not know the sort of elf I was before the Ceurendol War. I was a prince and heir to the Erynien Empire, with pride equal to my draconic grandfather. I do not deserve a second chance."

"Then help us." Ellendren considered whether she could trust Erethien.

"I cannot get you out of this place, if that's what you seek."

"You were there when Ceurendol was corrupted. The central jewel remains unreachable, locked in its chamber."

"We might have corrupted the jewel, but to my father's wrath, we were not the ones to seal it away. He had tasked us to return with the jewel for his crown."

"Then how was it locked away?" Ellendren blinked. She hadn't expected that.

"Ithendryl. She didn't want us taking it after what we'd done. In a fit of unprecedented power, she caught our weakened and distracted selves off guard when the Deurghol claimed us as hosts, making us Deathless. Ithendryl expelled us from the chamber in a powerful wield as the Shroud fell over Krysenthiel. In that moment, she sealed herself and the jewel away."

"She's still there?" Ellendren's mind whirled at the revelation.

"I imagine. Whether she's a skeleton or alive is the true question. It's possible that if you reach out to her, she'll open the way."

This was news. Ellendren's eyes sharpened with determination. "I have to tell Devlyn. Find me a way out."

"I already told you, I cannot."

"You must. If you want any redemption for your crimes, you must help me. And I need to be away from this place. Ramiel cannot have my children."

"Child," Erethien corrected.

Ellendren's heart skipped a beat. "They're twins."

"They were. Surely you can sense only one will come into this world breathing."

She'd feared this truth. She hadn't delved into her being to discover the truth of it. She couldn't bring herself to see if she had lost a child. She shook her head, still in denial. "The day Tolvenol stole me from Arenthyl, an assailant attacked me and my companions in Aerodhal."

"Nadia Desuani," Erethien supplied.

"You too managed to slip past Arenthyl's wards, intending to cause harm to its inhabitants. I trust you told Nadia how to do so. How?"

"The wards only stop those who intend to do harm to the city's residents."

"But you and she did intend to harm its residents and did just that. She killed Fyona."

"You have to lie to yourself and believe the lie."

"That's not possible."

"I assure you, it is," Erethien said, giving Ellendren time to consider the implications. She couldn't fathom how someone could believe a lie of their own making. "There might be one opportunity to get you away from here."

"When?" Ellendren didn't want to dwell on her loss, didn't want to consider it.

"When your armies bring the fight to Mount Cyngol. They're close. Ramiel might not engage in the battle but he will not hide in his darkened halls. Watching anacordel kill each other will be a spectacle to him," Erethien said. Ellendren flinched at the thought. Murder was not entertainment. "We could use the distraction to get you away."

"Won't you be required to fight?"

"I'm no longer useful to Ramiel since I no longer host a Deurghol. He'll throw as many mortals as he can against your allies, but he cares not for their victory."

"How do you mean?"

"He already revealed to you the victory he seeks. He wants all anacordel to be eradicated and only the shapeless Void to remain. The living have no place in his Void, only the dead."

FANGED IRE

Devlyn had never been inclined to visit Dynthol Mirk. Was anyone? Thick vines with fang-like thorns strangled other vegetation and what animal life dwelt there was just as friendly to outsiders. When he reached Jeanne and the Guardian army, Devlyn was not greeted with a tent or warm bath. Rather, he'd found the army marching west through the strangled wood for Mount Cyngol.

The ei'ana wielded ignys to fight off the prickly vines and clear a path for the army. Alethea, Wyn, Viren, and Falthion accompanied Devlyn to Jeanne near the center of the column. Despite her lofty position, the First of the Guardians looked like any other knight. Nothing in her bearing or dress distinguished her. Jeanne might be leading the Guardian army against the forces of evil, but she still saw herself as a regular soldier with a job to do.

"Is it done?" she asked as Devlyn approached her.

"It's destroyed. Caspol betrayed us in the process."

"And Yloran?"

"She and her attendants helped us defeat him. Caspol's dead."

"I suppose that's one less threat we need to worry about."

Devlyn didn't like her phrasing. What other threats did she anticipate? "What's the situation here?"

"We're being watched. I'd hoped to reach Mount Cyngol unseen, or at least with some element of surprise. But we've sensed an unseen eye monitoring us the moment we crossed into Dynthol Mirk."

"Should the ei'ana stop burning the thorns to create a path?" Devlyn asked. The fire and smoke had to be a beacon to anyone who was looking.

"I only set them to the task after we discovered our presence was known. Haste is now our best option. I don't intend to linger here to find out whether the Evil One or some other sinister being watches us in this marshy dead land. Whoever it is does so hungrily, as though they will descend on us at their first chance."

It sounded like a beast was prepared to pounce on them. "Is there anything you require of me?"

"Stay close to your phoenix—preferably bonded with your verathn in hand." Jeanne paused, then added, "I don't like how this place feels. There's a wrongness here. It's ancient. I've no doubt it's connected to the Evil One, but I cannot say how."

"I feel it too." His skin prickled; Aliel nestled on his shoulder, just as uncomfortable, both wanting to be away from this place. They didn't need to be physically close to bond, but Devlyn sensed the phoenix's discomfort following his entrapment.

They marched on and Devlyn stayed near the central command. Their forces moved in relative silence with only the sound of boots sloshing though the marshy land, few comfortable enough for idle conversation. The sun's absence made tracking the time impossible. And the smoke from the burning vines made his vision worse, despite the ei'ana mitigating the smoke so the army wouldn't breathe in toxic fumes of the burned vines.

A runner found Jeanne, sending a nervous look at Devlyn who was too far off to hear. After receiving the scout's report, Jeanne frowned then said, "Well, you might as well tell him."

The scout bowed, a quaver in his voice. "Ei'denai."

"Is something wrong?"

"While scouting, I was set upon by a small unit of legionnaires.

They took me to a pavilion where the Erynien emperor waited. He requests an audience."

"Erynor is here?" Devlyn said, aghast.

"Yes, and he's expecting you."

Devlyn turned to Jeanne. "What would we gain from this?"

"It's impossible to know. Erynor could be scheming something. It sounds like he has a modest guard with him, but it could also be a trap," Jeanne advised.

"You don't think he means to help us, do you?"

"Not likely. He has nothing to gain from helping us, but everything to lose. It's odd though; our intelligence had placed him in Broid, which makes me wonder if he came here without his Master's knowledge," Jeanne said, turning back to the scout. "Did Erynor place any limitations on Devlyn coming to him, such as to come alone?"

"No."

"Curious. Aside from the small contingent and Erynor, was anyone else there?"

"A handful of servants were attending the emperor, and no more than fifteen guards."

"That's a small honor guard for an emperor. Our best chance to learn anything useful would be to match it. Fourteen Guardian knights and a wielder will join you. Jaerol should accompany you, as he'll be the most familiar with Erynor, but I worry how Erynor would receive a Cyndinari who's betrayed him."

"What about Yloran?" Devlyn asked. "She never expressly betrayed Erynor."

"Can we really trust her?" Jeanne asked.

"She's proven herself time and time again."

"Do I understand someone is looking for me?" Yloran joined Devlyn and Jeanne as though summoned.

"We were about to." Jeanne glared at Devlyn, as though asking if he was sure. She clearly wasn't fond of Yloran's sudden appearance.

"Erynor is near and has requested an audience with Devlyn."

"You realize it's a trap, yes?" Yloran said as though there was nothing more obvious.

"Naturally, but we cannot ignore it." Jeanne's lips thinned to a narrow line.

"Whyever not? I've found ignoring the petulant emperor always preferable."

"What if he takes it as an insult and does something rash?" Devlyn asked.

"You killed his dragon half-brother, so we're far beyond him coming from a place of reason. I recommend ensuring he never learns of Liam's whereabouts. Erynor has a certain fondness for symmetry when it comes to revenge," Yloran said.

"Jeanne, can you ensure that Liam is protected?" Devlyn asked.

"You'll be hard pressed to find a better protector than Jaerol and Rusyl, but I'll make sure they're aware of the danger," Jeanne said.

"Please do; I'd rather Jaerol not suffer any more than he already has," Yloran said with an unexpected softness. The slightest hint of Jeanne's eyes widening gave away her shock, causing Yloran to add softly, "I am not a monster."

Jeanne nodded curtly. Her grievance with Yloran would not dissipate in one day, but her disdain for the former Sha'ghol did seem to lessen. Three knights jogged off at her instructions.

"Now, about Erynor," Devlyn said.

"You intend to spring his trap? I thought we were past that, darling," Yloran complained.

"We need to know where he stands in this," Devlyn said.

"Do we? He's the son of Erynel and Tolvenol; you won't find a more wretched pairing to spawn a child. But if you insist, let it be remembered that I, Yloran eth Gnashar, called the Exalted Aryl a fool for following this path." She eyed Jeanne as though expecting her to write it down.

"But you haven't," Devlyn said, bewildered.

"Oh darling, I just did. Do keep up." Yloran had a glint in her eye, one surprisingly shared by Jeanne. "I'll be bringing two of my attendants, Clovis and Raelinth. I have zero interest in meeting that worm of an emperor without my own protection."

"We were intending on meeting him on level ground, evenly numbered," Devlyn said.

"The battlefield is never fair where Erynor Meriden is involved, trust me," Yloran said.

At the Erynien camp, an opulent tent had been erected. Auxiliary tents on either side reminded Devlyn of an entry court. But where he expected the imperial palace to be furnished in stone and rare metals, the camp was garnished with silks and gems.

Jeanne's scouts had reported a small force of legionnaires. While the numbers were accurate from what Devlyn could see, Yloran was quick to note they weren't regular soldiers. The emperor's personal guard was composed of the most elite fighters in the empire. The guard greeted Devlyn, insisting the Guardian knights, including Viren, remain in the open with them.

"I won't be far," Devlyn said to Viren's unvoiced complaint.

A scantily dressed servant led Devlyn and Yloran into the tent. Devlyn's eyes widened. A roof of crimson silks soared above, supported by magically floating columns. Cables linked them in an extravagant structural system. Four bubbling fountains demarked the tent's corners in the otherwise round space. Exotic plants, flowers, and trophies lined every wall. It felt more like a garden or greenhouse than a war tent. In the center was a raised dais with a throne wrought of a reddish bronze stone that could only be cyndaryl and where sat an elf—no, a draelyn—that Devlyn had only seen once before, on dragon back.

Emperor Erynor Meriden was imposing. His imperial robes of

rich crimson and bronze parted on his chest. His eyes were not silver like other elves' but oily black like Tolvenol's. He did share the cinnamon hair of the elves he ruled over, although specks of onyx laced the strands. Adorning the emperor were gold chains and rings set with immaculate rubies, diminished by the imperial circlet set on his brow. A hole was at its center, presumably intended for a missing jewel.

"Devlyn Lorenthien." Erynor spat the name like a curse. "And Yloran eth Gnashar. Dare I ask how a Sha'ghol has curried the favor of Luminare's golden house?"

"In a way your dear Alesei would find most unrecognizable." Yloran shared a vicious smile with the Tieli queen, who Devlyn had entirely overlooked, having mistaken her for one of Erynor's servants. Apart from her jewelry that had to equal her weight, she wasn't dressed all that differently from the servants standing behind the throne.

"We know how Yloran eth Gnashar curries favor," Alesei bit back. "I'm surprised the pious aryl allowed a common whore into his wedding bed. Granted, I did tell him he would tire of the girl when he needed a woman."

"Thank you for proving my point, Alesei. A shame your alliances can't be born of anything more…" she coughed, eying the queen up and down, "enduring." A wicked smile lingered where she had feigned sincerity.

"A shame, indeed," Erynor said. Alesei blanched, mouth agape. She grew smaller as the emperor's words struck her like a spear to the heart.

"Why did you ask to see me?" Devlyn asked. As irritated as he was over Alesei's insinuation, he had to focus on the emperor. He couldn't let the Tieli queen distract him.

"You've grown since we last met."

"Need I remind you I was thirteen when you tried to kill me in Ceurenyl."

"Had I succeeded, we could have been spared the disaster we now find ourselves in."

"You would blame me for Verakryl's death and the release of Ramiel and the Void?" Devlyn said, fists clenched. The presumptive accusation stung. He held himself responsible for more than Erynor could know. Ellendren in a dark, windowless cell flashed through his mind. But he wouldn't stand for being blamed by the very man who had set it all in motion.

"So much like Faerndryn. You Lorenthiens are all the same. Your ancestors left me no choice. I never wanted to slay elves or wage a war against Krysenthiel. But you made yourselves weak and sought to make the lesser races our equal. You who would flaunt Balance destroyed it! As the Sha'ghol have ever known and feared, elves would invite Death unto us. By crafting Ceurendol, you sacrificed your Life Immortal and welcomed Death into your people's hearts."

Devlyn blinked. How could anyone be so deranged as to hold that twisted opinion, least of all the emperor responsible for starting the Ceurendol War that led to the slaughter of tens of thousands of elves, their eventual enslavement, and corruption of the Jewel of the Life?

"We elves were—*are* gods to the lesser races; it's our right to rule over them. But you Lorenthiens sought to diminish us by lifting them up to our level and destroying Balance. Had your ancestors left the state of the world alone, the Master would have never been released from his Void."

"You're blaming us for his release? Need I remind you who killed the Tree of Life?" Devlyn said, exasperated.

"The Deurghol were never mine to control. They only answer to their Master. The Sha'ghol were the same, other than the few who deigned to betray him." Erynor glanced at Yloran.

"The Deurghol were only given access to Teraeniel when you ordered Cyndinari to corrupt Ceurendol, thereby granting them access to Teraeniel, not my ancestors."

"The stage was already set and your people already weak. Your precious Phaedryn couldn't even stand against Ythinor or me. One by one, the elves died, and the phoenix were swallowed, dying to be reborn, again and again and again." Erynor sneered as he spoke, as though he relished the pain he had caused the Luminari and phoenix.

"The cycle is broken." Devlyn struggled to control his anger.

"Yes, I heard you had some part in murdering my half-brother. Do remember, the jade dragons were only ever able to contain my father. If your people were smart, you would have garnered stronger allies, not wasted your time with mortals in the Guardian Senate."

"The draelyn and dragon flights stand with us."

"Tenethyl was reduced to rubble when my Master last walked these lands. You think they'll be able to stand against Void beasts, the Dark Flight, and my empire?" Erynor laughed, echoed hollowly by Alesei.

"Aside from trying to justify your actions, why ask to see me?" Devlyn had tired of this. Erynor's mind was unsalvageable. He was convinced that his actions having been the right choice. He even claimed Ramiel's presence was Devlyn's fault. "What do you want?"

"To be honest, I haven't decided yet. While I very much desire to see your dead eyes gaze into the nothingness that awaits you, killing you would offer little benefit. My Master cares not if you live or die. You are inconsequential to him. Your heir is to be born soon, and with that child will Lucillia's prophecy pass on to the next generation. Having you bow to me as the lawful emperor of elves and all Eklean would be a good place for you to start your next chapter though."

Devlyn tucked what Erynor had said about his soon-to-be-born child away for later. He couldn't dwell on that just now; he couldn't let his trepidation for Ellendren distract him. "Uriel named Ellendren and me the Exalted Aryl of the four Skylands. Even the aldarchs have pledged themselves to us. Our reign has only just begun."

"I am the Erynien Emperor! My empire was bestowed on me by my Master!"

"Ramiel is a disgraced anadel who was stripped of his irythil throne."

"You *dare* speak his name." Erynor snarled.

"Ramiel," Devlyn repeated, holding firm, "has no authority over the elves or any corner of Teraeniel. Not even the deepest, darkest caverns that the sun will never see are his domain."

"Everyone will die if you hold to this course. Everything you love will burn. Only the Void will remain. How can you not realize that I alone can preserve our world? Only I can prevent my Master from annihilating Teraeniel. Only my empire was promised to remain untouched by his Void."

"Oh, Erynor darling, you dolt. Your Master does not share nor concede power. He does not care for you or anyone. Whatever is left of your empire will suffer the Void just as the rest of the world will if your Mas…" Yloran cut herself off before continuing, "…if Ramiel is the victor in this struggle." Devlyn had never heard her speak the Evil One's name before. The consequences of being found were too high. She must have felt the stakes couldn't possibly get higher. That, or she was goading Erynor.

"You promised Tiel would be protected—that *I* would live forever young and beautiful," Alesei screeched, her eyes bulging.

"I promised you nothing. You will die like every other human is destined to; only death awaits your kind." Erynor didn't turn to acknowledge Alesei, but if he had, he would have seen what Devlyn and Yloran saw. Something snapped inside her. She pulled a slender knife from her sleeve and slashed Erynor's throat, quick as a viper and deep as a snake's fangs might bite. Alesei was much quicker than Devlyn would have expected, especially with all the jewelry weighing her down.

Erynor gurgled, surprised. He had never needed to prepare for death, so when his body staggered, then collapsed and his specter remained, he could only blink in silence.

"You killed him." Devlyn was as shocked as Erynor's ghost, the suddenness startling. He had tormented Eklean for centuries, causing immeasurable suffering. Now, he was dead.

"You should go. I won't ask for mercy for my part in this war. All I ask is you destroy that fiend so my people can live another day. You have nothing to fear from my house. I was promised immortality, so I never bothered to bear an heir. House Ziera will die with me," Alesei said.

It took the servants a moment to realize what had happened, and when they did, shouts arose. The next moments were a whirl of confusion as the imperial guard and Guardian knights rushed in, not knowing who had been harmed. The imperial guard saw the body of their emperor and fought to surround their charges, while Viren lashed his crystalline sword dangerously at anyone who came too near Devlyn. Raelinth and Clovis lazily went over to Yloran, who made it clear how unnecessary their concern was. The knights and guards fought and threw punches. The tent, while large, wasn't large enough to house thirty dueling elves.

The Cyndinari in command unsheathed his sword and pointed it at Yloran, whose attendants did little to defend her. They were both wielders and could likely kill most of the elves in the tent without a second thought.

"Explain yourselves," the guard demanded, risking Raelinth and Clovis' ire over Viren's.

"You're pointing those at the wrong perpetrator. Your emperor's assassin still holds her bejeweled knife with his still-wet blood on it," Yloran said, unconcerned.

"He lied to us all. We were fools to believe him—to love him, thinking he would love us back," Alesei said, coming to terms with what she had done.

"Then we are finally free of him." The guard lowered his sword, took a deep breath and exhaled, shoulders slackening as he did. The rest of the imperial guard lowered their swords as well.

Devlyn felt a whirlwind of emotions and thoughts coursing

through his mind and could sense that the other elves of the imperial guard experienced it too. Their world had irrevocably shifted with their emperor's death, and Devlyn realized they had not loved or respected their emperor but feared him.

The guard turned to Devlyn. "The Erynien legions are full of good elves. They followed their emperor's orders, as any soldier should. They are not lost or twisted like the shadow elves. It's likely too late to stop them from engaging your forces in the battle ahead. The emperor's orders have already been issued. All I ask is that you remember who the real enemy is when your Guardian knights and allies level their swords on the battlefield."

"And what will you do?" Devlyn asked.

"We remain imperial guards. We will take Alesei to Broid and await the next emperor to deliver his judgment."

"Or you can come with us," Devlyn offered. "We can't avoid engaging the Erynien legions on the battlefield, but perhaps if they see the emperor's own guard, we can limit the bloodshed."

"We won't be able to save them all; many will refuse to believe their emperor did anything wrong. But if we could spare some Cyndinari, I would see us try," Yloran said.

The guard turned to the scantily dressed servants. "You are free. Do as you wish."

"We cannot survive on our own in this forsaken, thorn-infested marsh."

"We cannot escort you to Broid. You can stay with us if you wish. The Exalted Aryl might have granted us leniency, but I doubt the First of the Guardians will. We'll be kept under constant watch, like prisoners, once we join their camp. The choice is yours."

"I suppose it's better than being swallowed by one of those vines."

"And Alesei?" Devlyn asked. He turned to inquire what the guards intended for her.

"Oh, she's already gone. Her fangs are clipped, she won't hurt anyone else," Yloran said, seeming to hold a growing respect for the woman who had killed Erynor.

AN ACCORD

Jeanne leveled a hard glare at Devlyn, seething in anger. "Will you ever cease making my job more difficult? What were you thinking bringing *them* here?" she said.

"I was thinking of Teraeniel's future. When better to neutralize the Erynien Empire than now?" Devlyn replied. It's what Ellendren would have done. That alone had assured him.

"After we've dealt with our enemy. I don't have knights to spare to guard Erynor's most elite fighters. And who knows what the former servants are capable of, especially if they're anything like Yloran's attendants."

"They seem harmless. They commented on not being able to survive in the wilderness."

"That doesn't give them free rein in my camp. I trust them as far as I could toss a giant."

"Understood. We can make sure they return to Broid after this."

"About that." Jeanne paused, letting the silence fill the space between them. "I still wonder if the battlefield is the best place for you. You must remember, there is much more at stake if we lose you to a stray arrow then simply finding a new Exalted Aryl."

"My part in the prophecy won't matter much longer as it is."

"Ei'denai, how could you say that?"

Devlyn hadn't had the chance to digest Erynor's revelation. Ramiel wouldn't need Devlyn to foil the prophecy after his children were born. Would the prophecy's fate really transfer to the youngest of his line after their birth? The thought terrified him. He didn't want the burden to pass to another, especially not to an infant born as Ramiel's prisoner.

"The Evil One still has Ellendren. It's only a matter of time before she gives birth…" he choked as he spoke, the thought too terrible to verbalize. He blinked the moisture from his eyes. "We have to get her back—before Ramiel can use our children for his own devices."

"No Lorenthien will be born in this Darkness," Jeanne vowed.

"We're running out of time—I doubt we have days to spare."

Oddly, Jeanne smiled. "Have you looked to the western sky since returning to camp?"

He hadn't, making it a priority to inform Jeanne about the Cyndinari he'd brought back. Their force had stopped marching for the day and tents had been pitched for the night.

"The urgency has not been lost on me or anyone who marches with us. Come." Jeanne stood, inviting Devlyn to do the same. The night sky was dark as they left the tent, darker than it should be with the Void and its unnatural storm blocking the light from the moon and stars. Devlyn longed for the quiet lights. Jeanne pointed west to where the jagged hills and winding paths stopped at a black gate. It swallowed any remaining light, not that there was much beyond flecks of firelight. Beyond the gate rose Vasknir. Its spires were sharp and jagged like broken spears. The whole structure had the appearance of a dangerous beast, prepared to pounce. The fortress had already torn a hole into Teraeniel; what more was it capable of?

"When do we strike?" Devlyn asked.

"In two days, assuming Ramiel doesn't attack first. The soldiers need to rest following the march. A whole Void city stands between us and the fortress."

"Tosk."

The city was not a place for the living. Its streets and alleys were littered with lost souls who had feared death in life. They had clung to the World-Below rather than transition to the World-Beyond. Devlyn knew to expect monsters and legions beyond the gates, but wondered if the dead would take part in the battle. Could the dead harm the living? Ellendren would have found the answer before they charged the gates.

Curiously, Ramiel hadn't attacked during the Guardian armies' treacherous march through the corrupted Dynthol Mirk. Now that the armies had reached the gates, Devlyn grew suspicious. Why had Ramiel allowed the Guardian armies to reach Mount Cyngol without at least trying to reduce their numbers? Had he kept his forces behind the dorthl walls because he wanted a siege? Ramiel could have dealt a defining blow before the siege even began. But thinking further about Ramiel's strategy would do no good at this hour.

"What can I do until then?" he asked.

"Rest. You are not immune to the temporal needs of this army. Spend time with your friends. I understand you're anxious about Ellendren—we all are—but I don't need to remind you there are no guarantees on the battlefield."

"Thank you, Jeanne."

"Of course, Ei'denai. I would not see our people fall into Darkness again."

Devlyn left Jeanne, Viren trailing him to his tent. As he neared his tent, he saw a soft glow inside. His instincts turned to caution—who would go into his tent without permission? Other than Viren, the list was terribly limited.

Devlyn tapped his bond with Aliel. The phoenix flew high above, one of the few specks of light in the sky where the stars should be. Alarm pervaded them both, ready to bond if needed.

Sucking in a breath, Devlyn pushed the tent flap aside. His anxiety seeped out and his shoulders slackened. He smiled. Liam, Jaerol, Rusyl, Wyn and Alethea, and even Abbie, Andrew, Danielle, and Trethien were there. "What are you all doing here?" He felt weak at the sight.

"Jeanne didn't trust you to get the rest you require, so she imparted the responsibility on us," Jaerol said, filling a cup with Cor'leran Blue and passing it to Devlyn. "The ice wine was Liam's idea of course. It might have a fine taste, but I'm afraid I still can't get past its color."

"Not every wine has to be a rich burgundy from Cynethol," Liam teased.

"But can you name even one from there you'd let spill?" Jaerol swirled his own glass.

"As Erynor grows richer off the taxes collected from the exports, all of which go directly to his army." Abbie gave Jaerol a side eye.

"She has a point," Trethien said. Devlyn had never imagined Trethien agreeing with Abbie. Flashes of their days at Gwilnor came to mind. Trethien was not the same elf Devlyn had known. Glancing around, he realized none of them were. Even the much older Alethea and Viren could not claim consistency since they had first met Devlyn and Erynor had thrown the world into chaos.

They wouldn't know what had befallen the Erynien Emperor. How could they? It's not like a public declaration had been yelled throughout the camp. "He won't be taxing anyone ever again. He's dead." The jibes and teasing came to an abrupt stop.

"How?" Jaerol asked for them all. He was the only Cyndinari here, one of the dead emperor's former subjects.

"Alesei slit his throat once she realized her alliance was built on empty promises."

"Queen Alesei of Tiel?" Andrew asked, exasperated. "By the Light, I've imagined a lot of things, but never that."

"A vain woman, but she had her principles. Deceiving her was Erynor's greatest mistake, his pride notwithstanding," Alethea said.

Jaerol lifted his cup. "To Alesei, the viper queen who slashed the emperor's throat!" The tent erupted in cheers to a woman Devlyn had despised from the first moment he'd met her. He didn't know if he'd forgiven her for abducting him, but her recent actions had cast a new light on her. In the end, all she truly cared about was her people. She understood the threat Teraeniel would face and had placed her trust in Erynor, believing he could save her people from the Void.

Even Viren accepted a cup to celebrate the tyrant's death. No one else here had lost as much on Erynor's behalf. His loved ones had either been slaughtered or perished at Erynor's behest while enslaved. Everything he had known had been stripped from him because of Erynor's actions. The only Luminari elves still alive from his time, other than Aren, Elyse, and the Saecrien monks, were the Guardian knights who had protected the phoenix egg at Ithendryl's command.

"A long overdue justice, finally served," Alethea said to Viren, noting his tears.

"I expected his death to be more, as though it would require an elaborate battle and the entire world would pause with bated breath as he breathed his last. But in the end, a dagger from someone he underestimated was his downfall," Viren mused.

"Cairn died similarly. A knife from the woman he had abused," Devlyn reminded.

"A fitting end for men who thought they were great, only to be reminded how small and fragile they truly are," Abbie said with a smirk. "Still, those women could have at least prolonged their suffering. Light knows they deserved it."

"Perhaps. But both are gone now. They can't hurt anyone ever again," Liam said, to which Jaerol wrapped his arm around him, holding Liam close.

"What of the Erynien legions and shadow elves?" Trethien asked.

"Regrettably, they already have their orders," Devlyn said.

"The shadow elves are irredeemably lost, but we might have a chance to win over some of the legion. Erynor ruled through fear and brutality. I won't be the only Cyndinari happy to hear of his death," Jaerol said.

"I still can't quite believe he's gone." Devlyn stared into his cup, swishing the blue wine around in a tiny whirlpool. Erynor's tyranny had left many scars on Eklean and her inhabitants. His sudden death was jarring.

"He was only ever a pawn in Ramiel's plot," Alethea said, gleaning his thoughts.

"Erynor believed if we hadn't interfered, Ramiel would have never been set free." Devlyn considered the state of the world and how much worse off they were now because of Ramiel's Void suffocating Teraeniel. Worse, they had had a plan to defeat Ramiel and Devlyn had helped destroy the talisman that would have accomplished it. Now, their allies converged on Mount Cyngol without any real plan to defeat him. What hope did they have in defeating an ethereal being who had existed before Teraeniel? It's not like Ramiel had a body to kill.

"We do not walk blindly," Alethea said, hearing his overly loud thoughts. Her eyes seemed to look right through him and into his heart, an all too familiar occurrence when it came to the wizened elf. She knew his state of mind. "You and Ellendren have brought the world together in the Guardian Senate, finding long lost peoples believed to have perished. We do not stand defenseless or directionless against this evil. All creation has risen against this threat. If not for the Exalted Aryl of Krysenthiel, we would remain divided to fight the Darkness on our own. One by one, scattered nations would have fallen, but united, we have hope. The world believes in you, Devlyn Lorenthien, and the hope you bear for a brighter future. Do not despair at this late hour."

Viren lifted his cup. "To the Exalted Aryl of Krysenthiel." A round of cheers to Devlyn and Ellendren followed, bringing a blush to his cheeks. Whether it was from the wine or the attention, he didn't care to find out.

Alex sat at a table with the other human monarchs of Eklean, all descended from Thellish nobility and provinces from a time long past. Velaria had requested they meet before sieging the Void fortress. Myranda sat poised and regal, wearing her crown more comfortably than Alex ever would. It was as much a part of her as his sword was to him.

Beside Myranda was her betrothed, Prince Donovan Orithil. His sister, Princess Victoria, and his father, King Leonard of Gestoria were also present. Hard lines etched Leonard's face. This was not a man who had been born into fineries but one who knew hardships while rebuilding his kingdom. Alex wouldn't have been surprised to learn that the Gestorian king had spent his younger days beneath the sun as a mason, rebuilding his capital city.

King Lawrence of Briel and Duke Paolo Farneis sat with the eastern block of Eklean. Queen Lara of Evellion and the newly raised Queen Daphne and King Henry of Mindale sat by Alex and Diana, representing Thellion. Among the sovereigns were two that Alex had not expected, King Gordon of Torsil and the Yanilean, reputed to be staunch allies of the Erynien Empire. Prince Rezeki of Jadien, having recently assumed his father's crown, also sat at the table. Alex had never planned on sitting on the eve of battle in the same tent with all Eklean's human monarchs, save one: Queen Alesei of Tiel. Her absence wasn't surprising, but it was noticeable. The Prince of Daerinth was also absent, but Myranda had ensured no one at the table recognized his independence from Sorenthil.

Velaria was determined to see this gathering take place. For whatever reason, she was convinced that the humans of Eklean who had once formed Thellion before it had fallen had to be bound as one to overcome these dark days and the days to follow. How she had managed to convince the Yanilean and the Torsillian king to attend was beyond Alex's imaginings. But neither did he think it beyond her ability, all too familiar with Velaria's machinations.

"Thank you all for agreeing to meet tonight," Velaria started, acknowledging the various sovereigns.

"Mother Velaria, I know you have the best intentions, but I pray you do not intend for us to kiss Alexander's ring in fealty," Myranda said before the proceedings could go too far.

"If this were another age, perhaps. My hope today is for an alliance of the kingdoms that rose from Thellion's ashes. Not just for the coming battle, but for the days after when it will be easy to point fingers at those we believe were in the wrong. Eklean has ever been a divided continent, home to many cultures and races. I do not ask you to form an empire under Thellion's banners, but to sign an accord—a pact. For my fear, fueled by prophecy and warnings, is that a greater evil, one of annihilation, will arise if humans continue their wars in Eklean. Your ancestors knew the path they were heading toward when they named the Luminari Exalted Aryl as Eklean's High King and High Queen."

"We are already bound in purpose to defeat Ramiel," Paolo said.

"And if we succeed and there is a tomorrow without Ramiel, how long will that peace last? A generation or two? Will your grandchildren remember that you came together without a formal accord holding the peace?" Velaria posed.

"This treaty is moot without Alesei," Lawrence said.

A brush of wind blew through, bringing in a cloaked woman, her jewelry jangling. "I did not realize you so admired my company, Lawrence." Alesei pushed back her hood. "Fear not, I received your message, Chair of Azurelle. I confess I did not consider answering your summons until after I slit Erynor's throat and watched his blood pour out, no different than anyone else's."

"You killed him?" the Yanilean asked, his tone shocked behind his bronze mask.

"And watched his ghost leave his corpse," Alesei assured.

"How can we trust your word?" Leonard asked.

"Devlyn Lorenthien was present. He answered Erynor's summons and came with a small host of Guardian knights and the Sha'ghol, Yloran eth Gnashar. I still haven't determined if the golden elf is a fool or the best thing to ever happen to this continent."

"Why did you do it?" The Yanilean's features were unreadable behind his bronze mask. Unlike other monarchs, he did not wear a crown, but instead wore a mask molded from the first Yanilean, passed on every twenty years to the favored heir.

"He deceived me. And I finally saw through his lie, or rather, Ramiel's deception. The same, I trust, has happened with you."

"Yes, the Judges of Yanil have brought much to light since they have come out of hiding. Fortunately, they waited for me to bear the Yanilean's mask and not the man before."

"The Yanilean is eternal, but is it not almost time for you to pass the mask?" Alesei asked.

"My successor is of the same mind. The Yanilean will uphold this treaty."

"And what precisely will it entail?" Myranda looked from Alesei to Gordon. Both had lain siege to Myrium in the events that saw Aren kill her mother. She had little reason to trust them.

Velaria withdrew a scroll and unrolled it on the table. Alex blinked at its length. "I invite you all to read it, but in essence, this treaty is to stand as a peace alliance. I've titled it the Thellish Accord, not because of the kingdom's revival, but the shared history your nations stem from. A sibling rivalry divided that ancient kingdom and the continent with it. This treaty is to remind future sovereigns that we remain brothers and sisters and to prevent our sons and daughters from dying an early death due to their sovereigns' pride. Should any nation break the peace, the rest of the continent, elves, dwarves, and merpeople included, will pacify the aggressor."

Velaria waited while the assembled monarchs reviewed the document and when they had done so, asked, "Do we have an accord?" Alex was the first to sign, Lara, Daphne, and Henry signing below his name in smaller print. The other sovereigns followed, Myranda ensuring her signature was slightly larger than Alex's, which made him smile.

VOID GATES

Black dorthl gates separated the Guardian armies from Tosk and the Void fortress beyond. All Devlyn knew of Tosk was that it was a city of the dead made entirely of dorthl. The tall gates, coupled with the Void storm, prevented him from seeing what awaited them on the other side. Only Vasknir was visible in the distance, rising on Mount Cyngol's jagged crags. But what waited for them between the gates and the fortress? Were Tosk's streets lined with legionnaires, shadow elves, Deurghol, Void beasts, and dragons?

The enemy forces weren't all the Guardian army had to worry about though, especially for those who would fight airborne. The Void storm was strongest here. While its tumultuous clouds had blanketed all Teraeniel, its effects were limited to the slopes on Mount Cyngol. Strong winds stung Devlyn's face as he squinted at the Void fortress. Tenebrys lightning cracked above the city as thunder threatened to unravel the world. Flying through that storm would be difficult. Avoiding bolts of tenebrys from shadow elves and other enemy wielders was challenge enough; now, anyone who flew would also have to avoid the storm's lightning.

"Is everyone in place?" Devlyn asked Jeanne, shielding his eyes from the wind.

"They are. Nunstol Schtam has fallen to the dwarves; their reserves have retreated while the Schtamite wait to press their attack on Vasknir from below the mountain. To the west, the Dwonians, Aldinari, and Qien siege a gate similar to this one. And to the south are the Ja'horan, Charren, Daer, and merpeople. Guardian knights and the dragon flights have divided into three groups, since they cannot assist the dwarves below the mountain. With us stand all the kingdoms east of Dwota's Gap, the Eldinari elves, the Ei'ana of Septyl and the draelyn. We believe we'll face the greatest resistance here at the eastern gate."

"And if we're wrong? What if the others are overwhelmed?" Devlyn asked.

"The dragons and the Eldinari on their griffins can fly where needed, this wretched storm notwithstanding. Qien Wei and the Jade Flight will remain at the western front until Tolvenol reveals himself."

"Are we certain the Daer won't betray Ja'horan and Charren again?"

"Of course not, but contingencies are in place if they attempt it. Besides, the Daer only devoted a small force, easily contained if necessary."

Devlyn gripped his verathn, feeling the power course through it. "And what about the dorthl? The erendinth can't touch it." It didn't matter how powerful he was as a wielder, he couldn't bring the gate down. And he wouldn't be able to wield once inside the fortress.

"We might not be able to affect it, but we can alter its surroundings. After all, a wall is only as strong as its foundations," Jeanne said.

"Could Wyn or Aren wield tenebrys to undermine it?" Devlyn hadn't taken his eyes from the massive gate. Even if it had been solid stone rather than dorthl, it would have been a gargantuan undertaking to wield an opening in it.

"Aren has confided that very few understand the secrets behind working dorthl. He assumes only the dwarves of Nunstol and Zorik understand it," Jeanne said. They stood there, Devlyn second guessing the decision to have the new Phaedryn stay in Arenthyl. Aren was the only other Phaedryn to join the Guardian armies.

The phoenix had been freed only a month ago, a month spent in intense training between the bonded elf and phoenix, nowhere near enough time. Devlyn had required years before he stood a fighting chance to survive; years that he often hadn't had, to his detriment. If anything went sour today, the new Phaedryn would at least have a chance to defend Krysenthiel. They couldn't risk losing any of them while they weren't properly trained.

"Let's get on with it then." Devlyn lifted his verathn and a great beam of light shot forth. Already bonded with Aliel, he flew up, hovering over the Guardian forces. Harsh wind whipped his hair and clothes. Individual faces came into view as he looked across the masses. Representatives from the entire world had gathered to fight the evil unleashed by Ramiel. What was there to say? Everyone knew their goal and what was on the line.

But he also saw terror in their eyes. Monsters awaited them behind the gates. The Erynien legions were the least of their concerns when dragons, Void beasts, and Deurghol waited to tear them apart.

"Guardians of Light." Devlyn's voice echoed across the battlefield, supplemented by aerys on the air currents. "We stand against a being who would see us vanish from Teraeniel—who would rather see the ground crumble to dust than for trees and flowers to bloom. Ramiel would have our experiences diminished until we are hollow ghosts without a voice, and for our skin to never feel the soft kiss of the sun or a lover again. He'd see mighty mountains brought down and fields and farms set to flame. Rivers and oceans would dry up as their basins crumbled. As part of Teraeniel's creation, we stand today to defend our homes and to ensure the sun will dawn tomorrow, and for the Light to sweep away the Darkness that grips our world."

He lifted his verathn and spun about to point it at the dorthl gate, challenging it. Thunder and tenebrys lightning answered him. Undeterred, the Guardian army blew horns from below and behind, signaling the charge. From above, Devlyn watched the army march forward. The ei'ana wielded immense power as they sought to destabilize the gate and bring it crashing down. A dragon flew beside him, gold scales shimmering with a light of their own.

"We fly together," Vivien said from Galithinol's back.

More dragons carrying draelyn came from the rearguard. The Green Flight broke away and dove toward the ei'ana to help bring down the gate, digging their claws into the ground. Terys pulsed through the battlefield and the ground quaked but the gate stood firm. Pressing into terys, Devlyn delved into the stones beneath it. The foundations shook violently, yet the dorthl held.

He added more of his own strength to weaken the foundations, thrilling when he saw movement in the gate. But just as quickly, his excitement plummeted when he realized the gate's movement had not been caused by their efforts. It had moved at Ramiel's will.

"Jeanne!" Devlyn yelled both vocally and mentally.

She had seen but was too busy issuing orders to respond. Soldiers with lances readied themselves as ei'ana fell back.

The gate slowly and steadily creaked open. Devlyn's heart raced, anticipating large numbers of enemies. As the opening widened, it appeared as though nothing stood beyond. But then he saw that the lack of identifiable forms wasn't just the indeterminable blackness of the city beyond the gates, but an army, composed of large and small foes. The Erynien legions marched with shadow elves as Deurghol and the Dark Flight hovered over the army, while monstrous Void beasts of many forms filled the gaps, towering over the others. They appeared as a curtain of death.

Amidst them, Devlyn spotted a pair of massive eyes, so dark that they stood out as though alight. Tolvenol. Devlyn's arms electrified at seeing the dragon again. The Dark Primus led Ramiel's armies and was said to command the Void beasts. He did not follow the army out the gates; instead, he gazed across the field, watching. Ramiel's forces spilled out, taunting them, seeming to say their siege was of no consequence to those within.

Devlyn understood then why Ramiel hadn't attacked before. He didn't care—nor did he consider the Guardian armies a threat. All creation had come together to oppose him, but he only saw them as an annoying bug to be swatted away.

As people fought and died, Devlyn swooped down to the front lines, joined by Galithinol and Vivien, Viren on Falthion, and Wyn and Alethea on their griffins. Galithinol and Falthion thumped onto the ground, sending shockwaves across the dead stone. Devlyn gripped his verathn, ready to unleash a wield of all seven erendinth against the Void beast whose path they'd obstructed. Standing taller than both dragons, the beast walked on its hind legs, its arms as long and thick as tree trunks. It looked as though it could split stone in half. *We're coming, Elle.*

The Void fortress was quiet. No one had come to summon Ellendren to Ramiel's court. Had they forgotten her? The days bled together, her concept of time all but obliterated. For all she knew, it was night and she ought to be sleeping. Even if the sun managed to breach the Void, her room had no windows; no part of the fortress did. Not that it mattered; she had no interest in looking upon the dead mountainside. All life here had been suffocated by Ramiel's Void, as Vasknir and Tosk had taken root. Were other Void cities scattered across Teraeniel?

Another reason for being left alone gnawed at her. She cradled her stomach. Her time was near. How long before her twins were ready to enter the world? Would they care for their mother and enter Teraeniel gracefully or would they claw out of her and leave her body too weak to live? These thoughts wouldn't have tortured her if she'd had a Crimsyn ei'ana at her side. But she was Ramiel's captive and he cared not whether she survived giving birth.

If she'd still been in Arenthyl, Ellendren would have been confined to bed rest at this stage of her pregnancy. Instead, she'd been summoned daily to Ramiel's court where she'd recently been startled to see Erynor's ghost. Erynel had rebuked him when he'd arrived, calling him weak and a disappointment. Dread filled her. Ellendren couldn't imagine her children being raised around such hatred. Ramiel would twist them to his own design if he got his hands on them, ensuring the prophecy ended how he desired.

Refusing to let that happen, Ellendren pushed herself to her feet, something that had become increasingly difficult in the past weeks. She knew she shouldn't strain herself, but her twins were coming and she had to get them away from this place. Waiting for Erethien to secret her out of the fortress was no longer an option. Tariel comforted her as best she could, unable to diminish Ellendren's pain and discomfort.

Shuffling to the door, she leaned against it, one hand pressed to the dorthl, and the other gripping the small golden orb that had once been covered by a dorthl husk. She didn't think she could use it as a weapon but held it as a reminder of what she could do. Ellendren Lorenthien was not a weak woman. Daughter to Vernal and Harnyl Roendryn, descendant of Lucillia, now the Exalted Aryl of Krysenthiel, High Queen of Eklean, Prelate of the Guardian Senate, and a Phaedryn—Ellendren knew her strength.

The dorthl hummed at her touch, its dormant heart aware of her previous accomplishment and yearning to be freed of its corruptive husk. Ellendren tapped her innermost spirit, that spark of Life where Tariel bonded with her and brushed it against the dorthl, delving into it until she found the heart. It bloomed at her touch and the dorthl fell away to dust, the door now an opening—her way out.

Her stomach heaved as she walked out. The process of opening the way had left her exhausted. She let the wall support her as she moved forward, one careful step at a time. Her feet and all her joints ached. Short of breath, she kept on.

"What are you doing?" someone called after her. "And how did you get out?"

Too weak to turn around, Ellendren's heart quickened. She couldn't waste her energy on anything but escaping.

A bolt of tenebrys flew dangerously close to Velaria. Her group of Azurelle ei'ana had to switch tactics from sieging the gate to defending themselves. Septyl knights surrounded them and took the brunt of the attack coming from the Erynien legion. Embracing the elemental erendinth, Velaria wielded ignys and terys, sending arcs through the enemy lines, all of them intercepted by their wielders. Her lips tightened to a thin line as she drew more strength from her sister ei'ana.

Another bolt of tenebrys forked toward her. Velaria embraced terys, lifting a solid stone to block the lightning. The stone exploded into hundreds of pebbles, forcing Velaria to protect her eyes from the dust and debris. An offshoot of the tenebrys bolt had forked away from the boulder and shot uncontrollably to the side. A sharp scream, quickly ended, pierced Velaria's ears, and she felt her strength dim as the bolt pierced one of her linked sisters. It had barely grazed the ei'ana, but it killed her just as fast. Yelaris roared beneath her, ready to tear the enemy wielder apart.

The blue dragon clawed at the dirt as her wings bristled, eager to launch after the wielder. Yelaris cared for the Azurelles just as deeply as Velaria did. Seeing even one ei'ana perish was too many. Velaria knew they would suffer casualties today—avoiding so would be impossible. Still, Velaria had been linked to that ei'ana and had felt her heart stop and her ghost depart.

"May Anaweh's Light reach you, sister," she prayed.

Another torrent of wields came at her and Velaria wondered why the wielder targeted her exclusively. Sure, Velaria was atop a dragon, but none of the other enemy wielders were targeting individuals. Most of the enemy wielders were shadow elves, and Velaria knew their minds would not be sound enough for a cohesive attack. Crazed and dangerous, sure, but they had no reason to target Velaria specifically. Unless of course, this wasn't a shadow elf.

Other wielders were capable of wielding tenebrys. The Sha'ghol had never shown any vendetta against Velaria and neither had the Deurghol. No, this wielder held a grudge, her wields filled with rage and hatred. Whoever it was, they knew Velaria, abhorred her, and wanted her to suffer.

A barrage of tenebrys lightning struck out again from behind the enemy lines. Velaria could only wield so many boulders to protect her group. The ei'ana tried to defend themselves, but few were as strong as Velaria. Two more ei'ana were caught by the assault—dead.

"Enough!" Velaria couldn't stay here. She was putting her sisters in jeopardy. She dug her knees into Yelaris, and the blue dragon stretched out her wings and carried them over and away from the ei'ana. Velaria barely heard their protests as thunder cracked across the battlefield. Yelaris spun through the sky to avoid the Void storm's tenebrys lightning.

Keeping her eyes peeled, Velaria watched for the guaranteed bolt of tenebrys that would launch from below. She didn't have to wait long; the promised lightning cascaded up. Avoiding it, Yelaris dove toward its origin. The enemy ranks scattered as Yelaris landed, breathing fire laced with aquaeys at them. Only one woman remained, fighting off the erendinth-enhanced inferno. Velaria recognized Nadia Desuani, the woman who played at being the Chair of Tenebrae.

"Hello, Velaria."

"Nadia." Velaria held the erendinth, any number of wields ready to be unleashed.

"Crossing battle lines to see the Chair of Tenebrae reduced to a common soldier?"

"Haven't you realized yet? Ramiel cares not for any of us. Your death would mean nothing to him. The Erynien Emperor is dead and Ramiel didn't even bat an eye."

"Ever the foolish girl who lost her parents."

"Because you killed them." Velaria had trusted this woman once. Nadia had recruited her at a young age to attend Gwilnor, all the while manipulating her to join the Tenebrae School. That the wretched woman had gone to great lengths to kill Velaria's parents in hopes of finalizing the deal had set Velaria beyond sympathy.

"Yet you are stronger for it. The first Azurelle in fourteen hundred years to tame a dragon, becoming Chair in the process. Ei'ana have killed for your position." Tenebrys licked at Nadia's fingers. "But you'll always be the scared and foolish girl I found in Lucillia."

Velaria then saw that Nadia was not alone. Several women she recognized stepped forward, all having broken their ei'ana counsels, throwing their lot in with the Tenebrae School. She knew they hadn't all been accounted for when the Seven Chairs tried to root them out. The former ei'ana, stripped of their position by Cyrelle Azurelle, formed a link with Nadia. The lightning continued to crackle, growing more dangerous as Nadia fed more power into it.

She hated to admit it, but she had been a fool for coming here alone. She couldn't fight ten wielders by herself. Yelaris dug her claws into the ground, sending images and thoughts to communicate that she was not alone. They linked together and steadied themselves.

"You aren't even going to try to run away? How noble," Nadia taunted, weaving a wield, dark sparks humming off her fingers. "Good." Tenebrys lightning barreled toward Velaria. She was too close to wield terys to obstruct the negating erendinth—too close to consider a proper defense. Her only chance was to contain the deadly wield and overpower it. She didn't want to consider the alternative.

Velaria pressed into animys and umbrys and caught the lightning in her wield, but the chaotic energy lashed about as Nadia fed more power into it. The tenebrys wield fought for freedom, punching against the walls Velaria had created to hold it in. She didn't have to subvert it entirely, only enough to redirect it away from the battlefield. Pressing more of herself into her wield, she angled the lightning up, feeling her control slipping. There were too many wielders fueling Nadia's wield; they were overpowering her.

"You are not alone," the yell came as Rusyl crashed down beside Yelaris. Jaerol, Liam, and Rusyl linked with her at once. Strengthened by their added support, Velaria threw the tenebrys lightning skyward.

"Another Cyndinari who chose weakness over power," Nadia taunted.

"You betrayed your people for a lie," Jaerol yelled back.

"You betrayed Septyl when we needed you most," Velaria said, disgusted that this woman had insinuated she and Jaerol were the ones who had forsaken their people.

"Septyl will ever be weak when cracked and broken into Seven Schools," Nadia said.

"You mistake our differences for division. Even at our weakest, when the rot of Tenebrae infected Septyl, we managed to cut you out like the disease you are. You failed at taking Septyl because you've yet to realize that the Seven Schools are stronger than your Tenebrae School. We are not fractured, we are a unified Septyl," Velaria pronounced. A well of energy not originating here on the slopes of Mount Cyngol, but from the palace-city of Septyl, swept through her.

Velaria didn't quite understand what she had done, but she knew better than to waste her chance. While Nadia wielded another barrage of tenebrys, Velaria wielded a torrent of power that easily swallowed Nadia's wield, shocking her.

"Impossible," Nadia screeched, terror lacing her voice.

Velaria felt the power from Septyl channeling through her. She had never learned to wield lumenys, yet her wield somehow encompassed it and the other six erendinth. The wield engulfed and nullified Nadia's wield, careening forward to consume her and the others linked to her.

Velaria felt each of them and saw their crimes against Septyl and others in their lust for power. They had tortured and mutilated people, all to gain access to tenebrys. The cultish rites sickened her. The women screamed as she held them, exposing their crimes. Velaria knew these weren't the last who'd betrayed Septyl. Having dedicated her life to serving Septyl, Velaria would not allow the Tenebrae to threaten it again. Nadia was the key, and Velaria pulled names and faces from the would-be Chair of Tenebrae, seeing those who had come before Nadia to undermine Septyl, many of them high ranking and respected ei'ana.

As the wield exposed their crimes, Velaria felt its deciding judgment. Death would be too kind for these women. This wield was not meant for executions, but something worse. It overpowered the ten women, searing into their hearts and burning the piece of them that linked all anacordel to the erendinth, leaving only a withered thread.

The wield ended. Her shoulders slackened.

"What have you done?" Nadia's scream was feeble. She sprawled on the ground, too weak to stand.

"You've escaped Septyl's justice long enough. You were stripped of being an ei'ana by Cyrelle Azurelle's decree through me. Now, you will never pretend at being an ei'ana again. First year students at Gwilnor will have a stronger link to the erendinth than you."

Nadia crawled back, trembling. Velaria couldn't imagine experiencing the sentence she had just delivered. To be stripped of the erendinth was unfathomable. Her entire identity was linked to being an ei'ana. What would become of her if the same was done to her?

"Velaria," Jaerol said, pointing to the Void beasts, flanked by the Erynien legion. "We can't stay here." She nodded and both Yelaris and Rusyl took to the sky to return to their posts, leaving the Tenebrae defenseless.

They Come

Devlyn wielded terys to pull the Void beast's legs into the ground as though it was quicksand. He dashed around the monster as Falthion and Galithinol, carrying Viren and Vivien, wove around it in turn. Vivien and Galithinol had a commanding control over lumenys, forming wields Devlyn had never envisioned possible with the transcendental erendinth. They laced the other erendinth into their wields, but since Galithinol was of the Gold Flight and Vivien was a draelyn of the Gold House, lumenys dominated their every wield.

Diving beneath the beast, Devlyn landed beside one of its legs. He braced himself and wielding terys, pulled the massive leg, three times the girth of his torso, deeper into the ground. Unbalanced, the beast's other legs buckled. As it toppled, Viren sliced his verathn sword down an exposed tendon, taking advantage of its compromised state to further weaken it.

Close behind, Wyn and Alethea wielded aerys about the beast's massive head, sucking the air out of its lungs to incapacitate it. Galithinol and Vivien wielded lumenys and ignys, setting the beast's insides aflame, washing away the tenebrys that had corrupted it since the Elder Days. It mystified Devlyn that this creature had existed when the world was young. Cordel weren't meant to live forever. But Ramiel had twisted whatever animal this Void beast had once been to not only give it unending life to serve him, but to cause as much destruction and chaos as possible.

The creature's husk crumpled, its colossal weight snapping its leg bones as gravity brought it crashing down. Even as this Void beast collapsed, another tore a path through the army, its hooved feet trampling humans and elves. Devlyn glimpsed the destruction it and other Void beasts had already caused. He couldn't stop them. There were too many. They'd managed to kill three of the monsters, but there were still dozens on the battlefield. Worse, they had no idea how many remained behind the dorthl gate with Tolvenol directing their every move.

Devlyn knew Viren would discourage his next move and could hear his protector cursing after him as he flew toward the gate. Tenebrys and volleys of arrows followed him. To avoid them, Devlyn practically danced through the Void storm in an acrobatic display. Not trusting the opening in the gate, he angled himself parallel to the gate and flew up its tall height.

He reached out to Empress Qien Wei. Devlyn couldn't defeat Tolvenol without Guanxi and the other jade dragons.

The Qien empress bloomed in his mind, ready. He hoped they would be enough. Their armies might have a chance to successfully siege Vasknir with Tolvenol removed from the field. What would the Void beasts do if their leashes were severed? Devlyn stopped himself from considering potential outcomes and focused on his task at hand.

Cresting the top of the gate, he faltered at the sight of Ramiel's host. How did he have such a massive force? Only a fraction had engaged the Guardian armies. The Erynien Empire had been dwindling over the past years and the Dwonian deserters had suffered a major defeat with Cairn as their brief chief-king. Devlyn locked eyes with Tolvenol. The Dark Primus looked back hungrily. Viren topped the gate after Devlyn, aerys propelling Falthion, Vivien close behind on Galithinol, Alethea and Wyn following. Together they flew over the enemy, dodging wields and arrows.

Overpowering thoughts flooded Devlyn's mind, luring him to ac-

cept defeat and death. Images of Ythinor and the phoenix he had consumed followed. Tolvenol delighted in that image, sharing his intent to
swallow Aliel after killing Devlyn. The images promised to do the same
to the other phoenix Devlyn had recently freed.

Devlyn pushed the overpowering images from his mind, trying to
purge the dragon from his thoughts. Pressing into the elemental erendinth while also embracing the transcendental erendinth, Devlyn formed
a lance of all seven erendinth and launched it at Tolvenol. A low rumble
of laughter followed as the wield was deflected off the dragon's black
scales.

Tolvenol's eyes gleamed as Devlyn drew closer, fire and tenebrys
swimming in the dragon's maw. Devlyn wondered how much the dragon
cared for his own forces and how much caution he would exercise. While
there was little Devlyn could do to pacify the gargantuan dragon until
the Jade Flight arrived, he wondered if he could thin the enemy ranks.

"I have an idea," Devlyn said. "Split up and draw Tolvenol's attention—perhaps we can get him to thin Ramiel's forces for us."

"Fly too low and the dragon won't be the only enemy you'll have
to dodge," Viren growled, his displeasure evident.

"We can't just wait up here until the jade dragons arrive," Devlyn
said. Did Ellendren have any time to waste? She could have already giv-
en birth for all he knew. What would Ramiel do with their children in his
grasp? The thought jolted Devlyn into action, even as tenebrys lightning
forked through the storm.

He dove over the wall, his golden form stark against the black gate.
Tenebrys lashed toward him, hitting the gate instead. Levelling off, he
flew over the enemy, Viren on Falthion close behind. The others had split
off, following Devlyn's plan to stir Tolvenol to action. With any luck, they
just might get the dragon to kill his own allies.

Reaching the massive dragon, Devlyn paled. Tolvenol was so large
that Devlyn had stood atop him in his volcano prison not realizing the
onyx ground was his scaled back. Tolvenol could swallow Devlyn whole

without even registering him. Remembering why he was here, Devlyn directed another wield at Tolvenol, again easily deflected by the scales.

Tolvenol ignored Devlyn, unconcerned by the meager attacks. Devlyn was like an annoying gnat to the dragon who hadn't even bothered to stand. Irritating the Dark Primus wasn't going to see Devlyn's plan through. He had to anger the dragon, encouraging it to attack recklessly.

Flying up and over, he spotted a glint of metal against the dark scales. Jaerol's sword! It was still wedged between the scales. Embracing lumenys, Devlyn launched a wield at it, hoping it would act as a conductor. Pouring his strength into the wield, Devlyn clipped it as Tolvenol snapped at him, barely moving his head, unfazed by the attack. Devlyn's jaw dropped. Had the dragon felt any of it? Was the sword only a splinter to him?

As he reassessed the situation, the sword gave him an idea. It might not have any effect on Tolvenol's hide, but that was hardly the only point of attack. Devlyn spun closely about Tolvenol's head, reptilian eyes following him as though he was a tempting snack. As he readied his primary wield, he released a second wield at the dragon's neck as a diversion. Tolvenol rumbled, amused, until Devlyn released a needle-like spear of aerys and terys at the dragon's eye, too tiny for the large eye to notice. If a sword was like a splinter, he would never see the threat of a needle.

Tolvenol roared in fury when the wield struck true. His scaled eyelids clamped shut, blood oozing out the pierced eye. His teeth snapped at Devlyn, already zooming away. Tolvenol lifted his massive torso, finally moving to stand. Half-blinded, the dragon had to turn his head to see where Devlyn had gone. Wanting Tolvenol to chase him, Devlyn wielded another spear at the dragon. Tolvenol walked several steps, sparing no concern for Ramiel's forces surrounding him, trampling his screaming allies. Unfortunately, only the closest ones were crushed before his wings lifted him.

Viren's concern flooded his thoughts as Devlyn felt the dragon's murderous intent narrow on him. Tolvenol was by no means the only enemy on this side of the gate who could kill Devlyn. The dragon's massive wingspan brought him upon Devlyn swiftly. Still enraged, he roared, fire and tenebrys pouring out his maw like a volcanic eruption. There was no getting around that.

With little choice, Devlyn shifted at the last moment, avoiding the blast. More screams followed as Tolvenol's fiery onslaught burned through his army. Dozens of soldiers in the direct blast died at once; they hadn't had the chance to escape. Screams rose from the hundreds on the edges of the blast, crying out from the burns that would eventually kill them.

As he took in the damage, Devlyn sensed something was wrong or missing. Viren had been cursing the foolish plan only a moment ago, but now he was silent. Scanning the sky, Devlyn sought the white dragon. Falthion shouldn't be difficult to spot, not here. Not seeing him, Devlyn's heart plummeted. How close had Viren and Falthion been when Tolvenol unleashed his fire?

He looked below again at the enemy lines lying in disarray, many of them burned. Viren was on Falthion, they had to be safe. Dragon fire couldn't kill a dragon. Devlyn willed it to be true. He just couldn't see them yet. Tolvenol's laugh rumbled below—something held his attention.

Devlyn looked to where Tolvenol focused. Bloodied and blackened by the fires, Falthion stood defiantly, barely recognizable. By no means a small or young dragon, he still didn't compare to Tolvenol, being only twice the size of Tolvenol's head.

"No. No. Noooo," Devlyn screamed as Tolvenol's jaw snapped Falthion in two.

As Falthion died, Devlyn screamed out mentally for Viren, only to be met with silence.

Alex's sword reverberated in his grip as he fought a Dwonian deserter. "I thought we were done with you," he cursed, using his shield to push back the deserter's spear.

"We aren't so easily defeated."

Alex ground his teeth, pressed the attack, and was startled when an arrow buried itself in the man's chest. The white feathers told Alex that Diana, mounted on Dennion, had fired it.

"I almost had him," he complained.

"He got past your defense. That he had breached the lines to this point at all warranted a quick death. He was too dangerous to be left alive any longer," Diana said resolutely.

"Well, he's dead now." Alex watched the ghost's confused look. He hadn't expected to die.

"How'd he get past your honor guard?" Aen asked.

"Overwhelmed, most likely," Alex said. A horrendous roar echoed across the battlefield, shaking the ground with its intensity. "Did that come from *behind* the gates?"

"What sort of monster can make the ground quake with a roar?" Aen asked.

"Likely the sort that my cousin is busying himself with," Alex said, considering whether he should follow Jeanne's orders and remain with his army or fly after Devlyn.

"You don't think he's going after Tolvenol, do you?" Diana asked.

"Can't imagine what else it could be. Whatever it is, it's angry," Alex responded.

"Has he lost his mind? He won't have any support from the army. We're nowhere near to breaching the gate," countered Diana.

Alex sucked in a breath as the colossal dragon lifted into the sky, its torso so massive that it shouldn't be able to fly. Tolvenol hovered above Tosk, then fire and darkness rained down from its maw. Why would Devlyn provoke Tolvenol? Surely he couldn't defeat the dragon on his own.

"We have our instructions. Jeanne wants us here," Diana said, clearly knowing what her husband was considering.

"Devlyn must be desperate if he's already confronting Tolvenol," Aen said.

"The Evil One has his pregnant wife. War is not a time for bearing children. Ellendren should have known this," Diana said.

Alex bit back a remark about her mother bearing a child during the same war, knowing it would only end in a fight he had no chance of winning. Challenging Tolvenol alone with a stick had better odds.

"Erethien," Ellendren gasped. Her heartbeat stabilized some, but adrenaline coursed through her veins. It was all that kept her moving.

"How did you get out of your room?" he asked.

"I returned the door to its original state—dorthl is a corrupted form of what I think is the mountain's heart."

"And you managed to remove the corruption without wielding? How?"

"I freed it of its tenebrys husk. I don't entirely understand how."

Erethien nodded, seeming to consider something that he kept to himself. "Come then, we should get you away from here."

"Has the battle started?" Ellendren asked.

"Yes. I fear for your allies. Ramiel opened Tosk's gates and loosed a fraction of his horde at each front though it's miniscule compared to what stands between the gates and the fortress."

"How are we to escape when there are so many?"

"They will not be looking toward the fortress, but outward." Erethien gently took her hand and led her away from the chamber that had been her prison. They hurried as fast as Ellendren's condition permitted, notably slower than they both cared for and especially worrisome should they pass anyone; Ellendren's lighted Phaedryn form was not easily missed. It would only take one servant or ghost, or worse, a Deurghol or Sha'ghol to alert Ramiel. They would know Ellendren was not permitted outside her chamber without their Master's express permission.

They went deeper into the fortress, descending when they came to stairs. Ellendren had no concept of where she was in relation to the volcano Vasknir sat on. Without windows or balconies, she couldn't determine whether her chamber had been on the ground level or in the highest tower. She now knew that she had not been in a deep crypt due to the many stairs Erethien led her down.

Turning into a long and tall hall, Ellendren and Erethien froze. A Cyndinari stood in the center of the space that could have easily been a throne room or great hall given its generous proportions, blocking the way forward.

"Kynol." Erethien breathed. Kynol min Othstrin—Ramiel's Mouthpiece.

"Going somewhere with our Master's prize, Erethien?" Kynol's back was to them as he examined the hall's architecture; he didn't need to turn around to know who'd joined him. The dorthl was uniform throughout, not even the floors were different. Every edge felt like a sharpened weapon. Ellendren feared what further destruction Ramiel intended to use it for.

"I am no one's prize," Ellendren bit back. Had Kynol been expecting them? Why else would he be here? And if he knew she had escaped her chamber, others would too. She had to get away before it was too late.

"Not you. He cares not for you—" Kynol turned then and closed some of the distance between them and looked at her stomach. "—but what you carry."

"He will not have them," Ellendren said sharply.

"You still think both will come out of you alive?" He smiled haughtily. "It matters not, you have no power to stop him from taking the one he desires."

"She has more power than you know, Kynol," Erethien said.

"I told your grandmother she was a fool to pursue a child with

Tolvenol. Ever arrogant, she thought she would survive giving birth to a dragon's spawn. Now, both she and her precious draelyn son are dead."

"And Teraeniel is already the better for it," countered Erethien.

Kynol chuckled, his sly smirk irking Ellendren. "In that, I agree with you, *Your Highness*. Enlighten me; how many children did your father spawn? Five? Ten? A hundred? All pure Cyndinari and draelyn."

Ellendren gulped at the thought of so many children having been sired by Erynor, passing down Tolvenol's corruption. "Most died when he lost his empire the first time," Erethien said.

"But not all. And you think to take your father's place with the other heirs cementing their place in Broid?" Kynol laughed again. "Even if the Master cared to let the Erynien Empire survive, you are in for a rude homecoming if you think stealing the Master's prize will grant you a place on the Guardian Senate in a vain hope to preserve your father's crumbling empire. The Cyndinari will spurn you."

"You do not know them. Not every Cyndinari was as easily twisted by Ramiel's deception as you were."

A lash of tenebrys punched Erethien hard in the face. "You are not worthy to utter a syllable of the Master's name." Tenebrys electrified at Erethien's fingers, bringing a grin to Kynol's smug face. "Eager to join your father and grandmother in death's cold embrace?"

Erethien responded with a bolt of tenebrys aimed at Kynol who easily deflected it. He laughed again and his own power lifted him aloft, tenebrys clinging to his body like a shroud.

Ellendren wanted to help. But even bonded with Tariel, she was still cut off from the erendinth because of the dorthl. She didn't even have a weapon, her verathn back in Aerodhal.

"Run!" Erethien yelled.

"I won't leave you," she said, weighing her options.

"Like you'd get far. But I would rather you didn't flee and ruin my fun with the prince. I'd hate to end it prematurely to chase after you," Kynol taunted.

Erethien launched another bolt at Kynol. The Sha'ghol caught it in his own wield, poured more tenebrys into it then directed it back at Erethien who tried to catch it like Kynol had but was easily overpowered and thrown against the far wall, smacking hard against it. The impact would have cracked any other stone, but not the dorthl. Truly, Erethien was lucky to have crashed against one of the few flat surfaces. Most of the hall's architecture would have skewered him.

Ellendren took in the hall anew. She might not be able to wield the erendinth, but she wasn't completely deprived of her strength. The vaults above were inverted in the middle, with lance-like pinnacles pointing down. Kynol hovered in place, having little need to chase after his prey. Given how many lances were above, Ellendren didn't have to worry about his placement.

The vaulted ceiling was far above and while she could fly up there, it would only alert Kynol to her intent. Reaching out, straining herself as she did so, she felt the dorthl in the spiked ceiling, reaching though the corrupted husk above the spikes. It was foolish, considering how close she was to giving birth, but determined to deliver her children away from Ramiel's clutches, she did it anyway. The highest part of the vaults turned to dust, leaving the mountain's heart exposed. Ellendren carefully kept her unworking from the spikes—they needed to remain intact and sharp.

The first spike crashed to the floor with an explosive clatter. Neither floor nor spike were damaged. Kynol spun in alarm at the noise. His eyes shot open. "Impossible," he said, unable to wrap his mind around the fortress being unmade. More of the inverted pinnacles fell, too fast for the stunned Kynol to register. One caught him in the chest, impaling him. Ellendren withdrew from the dorthl, but now the ceiling and many floors above that had relied on this hall's vaulting for support were compromised. Mixed small and massive pieces of rubble began to fall.

"We have to go or we'll be buried." Erethien coughed blood.

"Can you stand?" Ellendren asked, concerned. Kynol's attack had left him bleeding and he moved with difficulty.

"I'll manage." His eyes widened at the puddle under Ellendren as her water broke.

"Not yet," she breathed, looking down.

"Come, let's get you away from here. The tunnels aren't much further."

Heart racing and too scared to breathe, she nodded. "Please, hold on, my dear ones."

They left the collapsing hall as more dorthl fell around them. Erethien led the way down a smaller corridor, then down more stairs. Soon, Ellendren heard voices ahead, gruff and angry. She didn't have time to stop and neither could she afford another confrontation. Erethien kept moving toward the voices. Ellendren prayed Anaweh would hear her and get her away from this place.

Turning a corner, Ellendren groaned as they came upon a battle in the lowest parts of the fortress. A dwarf holding a bloodied axe came up at them, ready to strike but stopped at the last moment. He said something in a rough, guttural language that had to be Schtach, then saw the fear and confusion in their faces. "Golden haired elf with wings," he said. "You're Luminari."

"Do you fight for the Schtamite?" Ellendren gasped, her eyes watering.

"Aye."

"Thank the Light! Please, I need to get away from here. Is there a safe passage out?"

"Ei'terel?" a rough female voice called. "What in the stones are you doing down here?" The dwarf with the axe recognized the elven title and quickly sketched a bow. "Get out of the way, brute." Oma stopped before Ellendren, surmising her condition at once. "They're coming then?"

"We have the enemy on the retreat," the other dwarf said.

"Not them, you bull-headed ox!" Oma snapped. "We'll take you away from here, Ellendren. Do you trust the Cyndinari prince?" Oma appraised Erethien, knowing who he was.

"He helped me escape and brought me to you."

"One that was Deathless?" Oma eyed Erethien, distrustful.

"Please, there's no time," Ellendren said.

"Tie me up if you must."

"Hmph. As though rope would stop you." The stone shifted beneath Ellendren, forming perfectly to her body and taking on the shape of a chair. It was surprisingly comfortable, relieving her various aches and pressures, particularly in her lower back. As she was about to complain she didn't have time to rest, the chair moved at Oma's behest. The stone seer took Ellendren into the tunnels, Erethien and a clutch of armored dwarves protecting the Exalted Aryl. Ellendren felt the pressure of the dorthl lessen—the thick sludge that blocked her from grasping the erendinth diminished as they went further out of Vasknir.

"The dorthl," Ellendren said weakly, her exhaustion having finally caught up with her.

"We're almost away from it. Save your strength, Ei'terel. Another sort of battle awaits you. You'll need all your energy then," Oma said.

"It's corrupted. It's something else—a stone I've never seen before."

"Ah, you wouldn't have. It's only found where the dwarves have established Schtams. That stone is alive, just as the trees above are. The dwarves of the Shadow Mountains offered it to the Evil One as tribute, killing the living stone and letting it twist into dorthl. We cut them off from the Schtamite for that sin."

Ellendren pulled the hot sphere from her pocket. It glowed softly, as though an ember burned inside. "It's not dead; only trapped in the dorthl shell." Ellendren offered it to Oma.

"There's hope yet. How'd you manage it?" Oma asked in wonder.

"I don't know," Ellendren felt her consciousness weaken.

"Rest now; you hold onto that. We'll get you to safety."

FLIGHT

Devlyn hung in the blustery sky as the battle raged below. Great swaths of the enemy had burned under Tolvenol's fury as he tried to incinerate Devlyn. Despite being incredibly powerful, the Dark Primus was too slow to catch Devlyn in his flames. Devlyn didn't have the chance to look for Viren before shifting out of the inferno's path. Could he have reached out for him and Falthion? Could he have saved them?

He fought back tears as he shifted yet again. Viren had been his protector since he had fled the Temple of Ceur with Ellendren. That role had intensified when Viren had learned Devlyn was a Lorenthien, descended from Faerndryn and Ithendryl, the last Exalted Aryl of Krysenthiel. Viren had saved Devlyn from certain death on more occasions than any guardian should have to. He'd devoted this new chapter in his life entirely to Devlyn, and by extension to Ellendren. And now their Guardian knight was dead.

Wyn flew to Devlyn's side. "We'll mourn his passing when the way to Lumaeniel is opened for all Teraeniel. Let's not despair now and risk joining him."

Devlyn clenched his teeth, cradling his grief for later. Would he even be able to find Viren's corpse after the battle? Had any part of Viren's body survived Tolvenol's fires?

Don't despair. What awaits him in Lumaeniel will leave him never wanting, Aliel conveyed.

Right. Despite the abject sense of loss he felt, Aliel brought a shimmer of hope back into his chest. This fight was not over. Viren Dekenurel and Falthion would not have died in vain.

"Look!" Wyn pointed west.

Devlyn spun to see, feeling renewed hope when he caught sight of a score of jade dragons flying over Tosk, Guanxi and Empress Qien Wei in the lead. Qien monks rode the serpentine dragons, intent on forever defeating the monster who had ravaged their home in ancient times.

Devlyn sensed Kai and Di among the monks flying on either side of their empress. Images of hatred from Tolvenol toward the Jade Flight flashed through Devlyn's mind. Tolvenol had not forgotten who had kept him entombed in a mountain for tens of thousands of years. They had already killed dozens of dragons of the Dark Flight, Tolvenol's son, Ythinor, among them.

The jade dragons were soon upon Tolvenol, gliding through the sky as though swimming through the clouds. Their bodies wove the elemental erendinth, not as wielders, but as dragons naturally attuned to their erendinth.

Tolvenol knew their ways though and did not intend to succumb to them again. The Dark Primus roared fiercely, sending an explosion of fire and tenebrys toward the jade dragons. Some of the younger ones were not strong enough to resist and perished. Tolvenol was not done yet, summoning his flight to his defense. The dark dragons responded, overwhelming the jade dragons.

With Tolvenol occupied, Devlyn flew to Vivien and Galithinol. "We need the other dragon flights. The jade dragons can't defeat the Dark Flight alone," Devlyn said, pointing to the approaching dark dragons, bound to also be carrying shadow elves. They easily flew through the Void storm.

"What about the Void beasts?" Vivien asked, sadness in her eyes for Viren and Falthion but not mentioning them. It would have to wait.

"They will be freed from their compulsion once Tolvenol is defeated. We don't need every dragon to join us here, but we must defeat Tolvenol and quickly," Devlyn said, hoping the battle would sway to their advantage once the Dark Primus was dead.

"Very well," Vivien said, and Galithinol sent images of the Dark Flight to the other dragons, requesting help. A series of roars echoed across the battlefield, including from above. Devlyn hadn't realized there were dragons waiting in reserve there.

Dragons of every flight answered Galithinol's summons, united in their desire to see the Dark Flight eradicated. The sky above Tosk was awash in color as dragons of every flight dove from the tumultuous clouds to harness the erendinth, supplemented by wielders on their backs. Devlyn felt Velaria riding Yelaris, Jaerol and Liam on Rusyl, and Prya with Liara. Devlyn also fought against the dark dragons and shadow elves, focusing on freeing as many enslaved spirits as possible from the shadow elves. Embracing animys and lumenys, he delved into those he came across, turning them to dust and releasing scores of spirits, the ghosts quickly discovering there was no clear path to Lumaeniel.

As dark dragons fell from the sky, victory seemed possible. But Tolvenol refused to bend and wrapped himself in a cocoon of power, a sphere of tenebrys and fire forming around him, like a dark sun, constricting then exploding outward. Guanxi tried to stop the expanding fiery tenebrys ball, larger than most villages. But the Jade Primus wasn't strong enough to do it on his own. As Devlyn worried that the dark powers would overpower Guanxi, a red dragon dove from the sky; Fyrinol, the Red Primus. The other primuses followed and the eight dragons circled Tolvenol and his terrible power that fought to expand. The jade dragons abandoned their fight with the smaller dark dragons and formed a sphere around Tolvenol, joining the primuses.

Together, they pushed the tenebrys and fiery sphere inward, constricting it by pouring dragon fire mixed with every erendinth down on Tolvenol.

Devlyn saw the flash of light that came before the explosion hurled him back. He couldn't stop himself, blinking in confusion in the rush of black smoke surrounding him, his ears ringing with a steady high-pitched tone. It was impossible to see anything as he careened through the sky, finally crashing against a dorthl wall. His body screamed in agony. How far would he have been thrown if he hadn't crashed there? Gathering his senses as the smoke dissipated, he finally managed to see the eight primuses still in a ring, but no dragon in the center.

The dragons roared triumphantly.

"Is it done?" Devlyn asked, although there was no one to answer him. Below, the Void beasts had stopped fighting, the compulsion to attack now gone. They were cordel—animals not meant to fight as war machines. Once their minds were freed, they stampeded out the gates from every side of Tosk and away from Vasknir. They wanted to be as far as possible, fleeing so they would never be caught in the Void's trappings again.

The stampede crushed through enemy lines. Fearing for the Guardian army, Devlyn reached out to Jeanne, showing her what was coming her way. He was preparing to shift to her when Oma spoke urgently into his mind.

You must come at once, she said.

We're a little busy up here, Devlyn shared back, more clipped than he'd intended.

Unless you want your wife to give birth inside the Shadow Mountains... Oma didn't have the chance to finish; the Void storm and battlefield vanished, replaced by a tunnel crowded with armored dwarves. Devlyn knelt in front of Ellendren, holding her hands. He cried then, not hearing Oma or noticing that a familiar-looking Cyndinari was among them.

"I knew you would come," Ellendren said weakly.

"You've never needed me to rescue you—that's always been your job with me," Devlyn said, half laughing, half crying. "How did you escape?"

"Later, my love. You should know, Ithendryl sealed the last lucilliae away." Ellendren coughed, tired and in pain. "I'm too weak to shift on my own. Take us away from here."

"Well, hold hands, you brutes," Oma instructed. "You too, Your Highness. Your fate won't be kind to you if you remain here."

Devlyn had no idea which highness Oma meant, because all that mattered was Ellendren. He didn't shift them to the military camp where a stampede of Void beasts would stomp them, or even to New Castle. Instead, he shifted them all the way back to Arenthyl, to the safety of Aerodhal where the Void storm around Mount Cyngol was replaced with light pouring through the palace's tall windows and crystalline dome. Not knowing whether their residence in the palace had been restored, he brought them to the throne room.

"Is anyone here?" he yelled. Several of the palace's attendants appeared, surprised by the new arrivals. "Quickly, Ellendren's in labor." He didn't need to explain further; they hurried away at once. Aerodhal was far from empty and many Luminari were soon rushing about to make Ellendren as comfortable as possible, having decided not to move her from the throne room. Kaela quickly came to her sister's side. News spread from the palace through the city that the Exalted Aryl had returned, and that Ellendren was giving birth. People flocked to the seventh tier's gates, excited and hopeful, not knowing what was happening on the slopes of Mount Cyngol.

Oma ordered the armored dwarves to secure the throne room. Only those who Ellendren wanted here were permitted. Servants hurried in and out, carrying pitchers of water, blankets, towels, cushions, and even a chaise for Ellendren to lie on.

Slightly panicked and greatly worried, Devlyn ignored the thoughts people were sending him about his abandonment of the battlefield. Then Jeanne pushed through. *Ei'denai*, she yelled, finally getting his attention.

I'm back in Arenthyl with Ellendren.

He's coming for you. Ramiel is coming. Be ready, Ei'denai. Aren is organizing a force to shift back. We might not make it in time.

Devlyn's heart stopped. Ellendren must have seen the color drain from his face, for even in her exhaustion and agony, she said, "He's coming for us, isn't he?" She didn't have to say who.

"He'll be here soon."

"The Phaedryn will protect us," Ellendren said, finally withdrawing from Tariel, seeming to have forgotten she still had her wings. Tariel flew directly to Parenhal and Devlyn felt the Phaedryn respond at once. Evellyn and Leilyn quickly rushed to the palace, intent on ensuring Ellendren was properly cared for. Bonded with their phoenix, they wielded to soothe Ellendren's pain.

Toryn arrived on their heels. She bowed to Devlyn, Shroudsbane in hand. "Jeanne has placed Arenthyl's defense under me," Toryn said.

"Thank you. Protect the city but know that Ramiel will come for the palace. I don't know if we can stop him," Devlyn said.

"We can try. We will not abandon you." Toryn left as quickly as she had come. A shadow fell over the palace, the sun snuffed out and Ellendren screamed. Ramiel had come.

"I'm here, Elle." Devlyn held her hand as she squeezed his.

"Don't leave me," she said, her face contorted with pain.

"I promise." Arenthyl would burn to the ground before he left her side.

Despite the impossible odds, Toryn prepared the Phaedryn against their incorporeal foe. She could see the enemy coming from the south, darkness clinging to the Evil One as he crossed over Krysenthiel and Lake Saeryndol. Ramiel had not come alone, but they were still too far off for Toryn to identify individual beings. She imagined Deurghol and dragons carrying shadow elves flying with their Master, all bent and twisted, seeking to unmake the physical world and return it to the Void.

Although still new to her Phaedryn powers, Toryn wasted little time in organizing the other Phaedryn to defend the city. Aren had ensured that the new Phaedryn mastered bonding with their phoenix. She might have only had a month to train with Aren, but she had spent years under Jeanne's tutelage. Toryn still saw herself as a pupil of the Guardian knights, now with the advantage of wings.

Communicating with a phoenix was still a work in progress; learning a new language had to be easier. This was an entirely different way of thinking. While her phoenix understood her just fine, it wasn't mutual. Nor had she fully mastered telepathic communication with other elves. Both would have made today's task simpler; instead, she yelled commands over the noise of fighting.

She'd already had someone fly to the cathedral. The newly trained Phaedryn might eventually be able form a shield around the palace to protect the Exalted Aryl, but none of them had reached that level yet, so the ei'ceuril would have to do it. Aside from Evellyn, years would likely pass before the new Phaedryn could wield lumenys.

When a shield of light bloomed around Aerodhal, Toryn let out a breath she hadn't realized she was holding. At least the Exalted Aryl was safe. She'd seen the state Ellendren was in, and she had felt the anxiety in the room. She was not in for an easy delivery and any interruptions could mean the life of the mother and child—had Toryn heard someone mention twins?

Elven nobles and senators from across the world rushed to Aerodhal for safety. They'd heard the alarm bells ring. The Phaedryn couldn't protect the entire city; they were too few and untrained. But they would try. If the ei'ceuril could keep their shield around the palace, they might just have a chance. A meager defense had remained in the city, but what good would it do against this enemy? Still, she had archers posted along the terraced walls and watchtowers as the elves who called Arenthyl their home fled into the many keeps positioned across the city. Aerodhal was not the only building capable of withstanding an attack here. The entire city had been wielded from lumaryl; it would not bend easily to Ramiel's Void, as he would soon discover, and neither would the Luminari elves defending their home.

Darkness poured over the city walls, bypassing whatever defensive wards those walls contained. Ramiel's Void swept across the lowest tier, swallowing it in darkness. Toryn couldn't see anything through it. It reminded her of smoke and storm clouds, but its density deprived it of the variation she would expect. Sunlight still reached Arenthyl, but Ramiel clearly intended to thwart it as his Void rose like the tide to swallow the second tier.

It clawed up the city on all sides, slowly and deliberately. Toryn could only hope that the people in the lowest tiers had managed to find safety. Arenthyl had been built to protect all its residents, not just the aryls. Tunnels led into the mountain the city had been built on. Toryn hoped they had had enough time to reach them. As the Void continued to roll through the city and up the tiers, Toryn saw formless creatures that belonged in nightmares.

Deurghol led the strike against Phaedryn. Some of the Phaedryn were already capable wielders and fought the twisted anadel with the erendinth. Toryn had to rely on her sword. It had pierced the Shroud and had sliced through Ythinor's belly to free the phoenix, ending his reign of terror. She trusted her weapon more than anything she couldn't see, so she flew toward the first Deurghol who threatened her post and flung herself at him.

He laughed as she challenged him. "You *will* feel my blade," Toryn yelled, willing her physical blade to harm this bodiless being. Shadows clung to him as the Deurghol taunted her, inviting her to try her hand against him, amused that she threatened him with a sword. Toryn hated his gaudy confidence and swung her sword in an arc, then swiped it up.

It caught.

The Deurghol flew back in a whirl of smoke, grasping his side. "How?" he asked as a sword of tenebrys formed in his own hand.

Toryn smiled. In truth, she had no idea how her sword had connected to the Deurghol as though he had flesh and bones. She didn't care either. All that mattered was that she could kill it.

Steadying her wings to launch herself at the Deurghol again, her breath caught as a being seemed to form from the Darkness that encased the city. When had it reached the upper tiers?

A creature larger than most palaces stepped out of the Void, its form somehow even darker, the antithesis of light. Toryn gulped; this could only be Ramiel. How were they supposed to defend against this? It wouldn't matter if the Phaedryn had centuries of experience. This being was beyond them. Could anyone equal this creature? Could Anaweh? The Tree of Life, perched above the city, stood in stark contrast to this being. Ramiel smiled at her, seeming to know her thoughts. Had he placed them there? Toryn couldn't say, all she knew is that she was terri-fied.

Ramiel ignored Toryn and stepped toward the palace. He seemed to study the shield around the palace for a moment, then laughed and brought a shadowed fist down on it. Hairline cracks splintered across it. He brought his fist down again. The shield rippled under the duress.

Whipping her sword, Toryn renewed her fight against the Deurghol. She couldn't hover there idly. When she saw a flash of light behind her, she feared that Ramiel had shattered the shield. She turned to see that a great host had appeared in the palace grounds and the sixth tier, making Ramiel pause at their number. It was staggering; how had so many been transported? She knew Aren had been at Mount Cyngol, but could he really shift so many people at once?

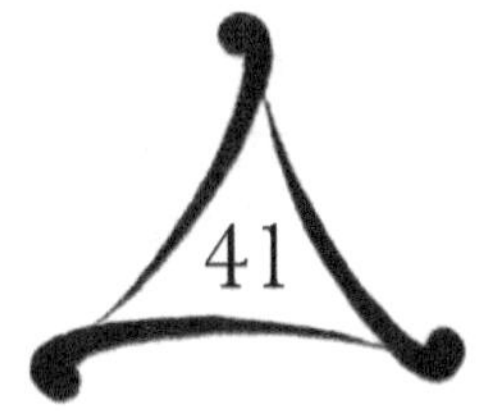

41

LIGHT UNBOUND

Ellendren screamed again. Kaela dabbed a wet cloth to her forehead and Evellyn encouraged her with soothing words. Leilyn knelt at her legs, wielding the erendinth to ease her labor.

Outside, the battle roared. Devlyn knew his place was beside Ellendren, but he feared this battle's outcome. Toryn was leading a fine defense, but Ramiel had arrived. How long could Arlyn's shield hold around the palace? He tried not to despair, tried to keep his anxiety out of his bond with Ellendren. She needed him to be strong.

He then felt more people enter the city. These weren't beings of Darkness like the others who had already come to plunge Arenthyl in darkness. Aren and a great host had come to their defense. The number was staggering. How had Aren managed it? Soldiers of every race and continent had shifted from the slopes of Mount Cyngol, abandoning the battle there to protect the Exalted Aryl. Thousands of people had come. Devlyn sensed not only the Aldarchs of Aldinare and the Ealyn of Tenethyl outside the palace, but every sovereign who had gone to Mount Cyngol was outside. Dragons of every flight, the Seven Chairs, and the Ei'ana of Septyl fought the formless beings. A perimeter formed around the palace, and those who could strengthened Arlyn's shield.

"You cannot hide in your golden halls of light. They will crumble to dust. No one will remain to remember what your people wrought," Ramiel said, a sinister whisper, both in Devlyn's mind and for the entire city to hear. "The child is mine. Return it to me and you can live and die a mortal life before I return this world shapeless to the Void—perfect."

"Never!" Devlyn yelled back, his voice echoing through the throne room, booming beyond it. Flashes of light bloomed outside as Ramiel struck the shield once more.

Ramiel laughed. "You think the erendinth can stop me? You forget I was here before they tainted the Void. I will purify all until only the Void remains and the stain of creation is forgotten."

The battle raged on; Devlyn lost track of time. He could sense the fight outside and people dying to protect the palace. But Ramiel cared only for what happened inside, leaving the fighting to his Deurghol, dragons, and shadow elves as he pounded on the shield. Devlyn again worried how long it could hold.

The present rushed back to him when Ellendren screamed and Leilyn yelled, "Push."

Ellendren screamed once more and a high-pitched wail filled the throne room. The world stopped as Devlyn saw the infant—their first-born—enter Teraeniel. His heart was awash in emotions, the strongest the urge to protect this defenseless baby.

"Braelyn," Ellendren breathed, having held the name inside during her entire pregnancy. Tears rolled down her cheeks when she saw him.

Devlyn held tiny Braelyn. Were all newborns really this small? "He's beautiful, Elle," Devlyn said, tears staining his cheeks.

"You're so strong, Ellendren, but we're not done yet," Leilyn said.

Evellyn took Braelyn from Devlyn; Ellendren needed him. His spirit fully mingled with hers and he felt her pain and suffering but could not relieve it. He begged Anaweh to pass her suffering to him. How could anyone survive such agony?

As Ellendren pushed, something in the world shattered. A second cry did not come and Ellendren collapsed; her body went limp and she wasn't breathing. To Devlyn's ears, the room fell quiet. He saw people shouting and giving orders but heard none of it. All he saw was Ellendren as Leilyn took the still infant that did not breathe or cry. The world stood frozen for what felt an eternity.

Then, Devlyn screamed. It came from a deep well inside him, shaking his entire being to the core. The world snapped back. Ellendren wasn't breathing.

Ramiel laughed. "You cannot win. All will return to the purity of the Void."

"No!" Devlyn wailed even as Ramiel and the Deurghol fought to break through the shield around the palace. Refusing to accept Ellendren's death, he held onto their bond, grasping at the frayed edges with all his will. He would not let her go. Kaela sobbed and tried to stop Devlyn as he lifted Ellendren, but Wyn took Kaela in an embrace.

Ellendren's body slumped in his arms as he held her. Instinct drove him now; he had no plan and neither did he care what happened outside the palace. Ramiel would break through the shield soon, but none of it would matter without Ellendren. Saving her was all that mattered now and if anything could, it was the jewel sealed away, inaccessible at Ithendryl's behest.

He cried as he carried her to the back of the throne room, to the ambulatory that housed the seven jewels forming Ceurendol. Six of the lucilliae were accessible, only one locked away.

Devlyn knelt at the sealed portal. Leilyn had followed with the stillborn babe in her arms, while Evellyn held a wailing Braelyn. Devlyn wept, Ellendren's slack body in his arms, holding her tenderly as though she were made of glass that would shatter. "Please, Ithendryl. Please let us in. Don't let Ellendren perish. Please. Let us access Ceurendol," he pleaded.

Silence fell, the sound from the battle outside the palace muted. Devlyn sensed the shield weakening as ei'ceuril keeping it in place died, overpowered by Ramiel's touch. Arlyn wouldn't be able to hold out much longer, and certainly not on his own. The world's sovereigns had come to Arenthyl to protect Ellendren as she gave birth; they knew the prophecy and the consequences if they fell to Ramiel. There would be no place to hide if they failed.

"Ceurendol is corrupted. It cannot save her or the child," a voice said at last. "Only an empty vessel can contain the corruption. The price is high and irreversible."

"Please—I'll do anything. Take my life, not theirs. I was supposed to die, not them. Take me. I give my life freely for theirs."

The door parted in the middle, unsealing as ribbons of lumaryl folded and retracted. A red jewel waited inside, dim under what looked like a film of oil coating it. A woman with the golden wings of a Phaedryn stood stoically behind the jewel—Ithendryl Lorenthien. "Come forward."

Devlyn did as commanded. Ithendryl was an imposing figure, statuesque and the model of authority. How was she alive? Devlyn didn't have the mind to be afraid of her, but if he had met her on any other occasion, he would have been. "What must I do?" he asked, eyes still damp.

"The vessel is empty—the price has already been paid."

"What do you mean? The prophecy named me. Let me be the vessel."

"You are no longer the lesser brother. Ithendryl looked at the stillborn child. "A mercy he did not live to make this choice."

"But the jewel, it can bring him back. Don't take our child."

"The youngest Lorenthien will take Ramiel and his Void within himself. Ramiel will experience what he sought to destroy. The Void will be contained and the Light will shine forth from Arenthyl once more."

"You *want* Ramiel to take our child?" Devlyn couldn't believe what Ithendryl was suggesting. His heart pounded against his chest. Ramiel had captured Ellendren for that very reason and now Ithendryl expected Devlyn to just hand him over.

"He will not know what resides within him until he matures, but a day will come when he must reconcile who he is. How you raise him will determine his choice. But Ramiel will continue his destructive path if you refuse the vessel. The choice is yours."

Devlyn stood with the impossible decision, still holding Ellendren. "What would you do?" he asked her, tears welling, then shedding unhindered as he looked at her unresponsive body. He didn't need to ask. He knew what she would choose. "Do it. Do it before I lose them both."

"Very well. What is corrupted must be broken before it is remade." Ceurendol shattered at her words. The oily film pulled away from the red glow that was the Luminari elves' most prized virtue. The shattered shards of the jewel hung in the air, surrounding the red glow finally freed of Ramiel's Void. Ithendryl waved a hand and the Void poured into the stillborn child. A horrified scream echoed outside the palace. It felt as though a cyclone formed about the city, Aerodhal at its core. A swirling mass twisted about the child, too large for such a small body to bear. Ramiel roared like a beast as he was pulled into the newborn, snarling at Devlyn.

Devlyn watched in horror as Ramiel and the entirety of the Void poured into his child. A moment of silence passed, then the infant wailed, just as his twin brother had done. Despite knowing that the child contained Ramiel, Devlyn could only see his son crying and his own tears came again; the child was alive. He would live.

The lucilliae reformed, solidifying around the red glow that was the Luminari elves' most prized virtue—their love, which had first drawn the phoenix to Teraeniel. Devlyn's heart ached with it as he clung to his tattered bond with Ellendren, refusing to let her pass to the World-Beyond. Her phoenix, Tariel, had not turned to ash, and fluttered above their heads. There was still hope.

A tearful Devlyn looked again at Ellendren. "Come back to me—to us. We need you." Various colors and light filled the ambulatory, colors of every hue and spectrum. Devlyn watched the seven jewels hover around him, then join into a single one. The Luminari elves' Life Immortal hung there. Another choice presented itself to Devlyn. He could either return it to its elven hosts or allow it to remain within the jewel for all people to benefit from. The Life Immortal of the Luminari elves could return to their hosts and never be threatened again.

An explosion of light and color filled the room. Ceurendol was whole once more, the choice made long ago. It glowed brilliantly, saturating the room and then Ellendren gasped.

Devlyn squeezed her hard, unwilling to let her go. "Elle," he cried into her hair. His voice cracked and his body convulsed, overcome with emotion and relief that she was alive.

"You never left me. I felt you holding me, all of me—body, soul, and spirit. I couldn't cross because of it. You tethered me here," she said, shocked to be alive, her body too weak to move.

The world shifted again. Devlyn and Ellendren were now surrounded by seven tall thrones occupied by the irythil.

"Ramiel is at last contained," Remiel said, umbrys cloaking him in shadow.

"A path stands before you, a decision to be made," Gwynthiel said, animys flowing from her.

"Decide what?" Ellendren asked.

"Your youngest child contains Ramiel and the Void. You do not have to raise the child. You can kill him and return Ramiel to Anaweh's Light. Be warned, if you let him live, the Void has a path to return if the child so chooses," Sariel said.

Ellendren looked at Devlyn and saw the truth in his eyes. "Tristyn is *not* Ramiel." Her eyes brimmed, resolute.

"Yet your Tristyn is the vessel that contains him," Theniel said.

"Much will be at risk if the child lives," Lereniel stressed.

"You will always know who the child contains and what he has done. The boy and the fallen anadel will be indistinguishable. Can you love the child and raise him as you will his twin with that knowledge? The rest of the world need not ever know that he lived," Kariel said.

"It is not a choice. Tristyn is our son," Ellendren said, resolved, finding strength with every word. She looked to Devlyn for support. She refused to entertain the idea of killing their son.

"Did Anaweh intend for this to happen? For Ramiel to see the world through an anacordel's eyes?" Devlyn asked without thinking. Was that possible? Why would the Creating Light put such a burden on a babe?

"I have ever loved Ramiel, just as I love all creation." A small light in the form of a child appeared. The seven irythil bowed to the Creating Light. Enthroned, they dwarfed Anaweh and appeared greater than the Creating Light, who's chosen form was a vulnerable child. "Will you raise him and love him as I love him?"

"We will," Devlyn and Ellendren said as one, overwhelmed at being in Anaweh's presence.

Anaweh smiled. "The phoenix, most precious to me, have ever been confident in their choice to come to Teraeniel and bond with the Luminari. They first saw that love shared by Kien and Kiara, and then between so many others. But none has been greater than the love shared between your hearts. Go forth knowing that only love will protect the child and all Teraeniel from returning to the Void. Your love can transform the world."

The throne room was quiet when Devlyn and Ellendren returned. It was far from empty now as the leaders of Teraeniel filled it, standing victorious, but somber. The cost had been high that day. Many friends and loved ones had died, Devlyn sharing in that loss. Viren's death weighed heavily on his chest. Aaron led the gathering in a dirge for the fallen. It rose slowly with whorls of smoke to the lumaryl dome above.

Devlyn and Ellendren sat on their crystalline throne. Each wore their crown, their verathn scepter in one hand, and a babe nestled in their free arm. The small family of four held the attention of everyone in the throne room. No one knew how Ramiel had been defeated, only that Ellendren had brought twins into the world. Ramiel might be defeated and the Void contained in Tristyn, but there remained many evils scattered across Teraeniel. What would become of the forces Ramiel had left behind? Would they renew the fight to seek revenge or would they slither into the deepest and darkest caves? Those were concerns for tomorrow. Today, the Guardians of Light were victorious. Devlyn cleared his voice as Aaron concluded the dirge.

"Our long war has finally ended," Devlyn announced to a cheer. "We all knew the cost would be great, but we came together in the Guardian Senate to be freed of the Void. Anaweh has blessed these new days ahead of us. They will be ours to live, with Life Immortal for anyone who chooses it. Ceurendol is remade. The Jewel of Life is not a prize to be won or bought. It was not just elves who fought those who would have seen creation replaced by the Void. No, all creation came together to ensure our victory. As the Exalted Aryl of Krysenthiel and the Skylands, Ellendren and I declare that the Jewel of Life belongs to all creation. None may lord it over another for wealth, influence, or power."

Ithendryl walked around the throne, receiving startled gasps at her appearance. No one had expected her to have survived for so long locked away in the shrine with the red lucilliae. She carried Ceurendol, cupped in her hands like an offering. Her phoenix, Eliel, watched from her shoulder, her long wings and tail wrapping around her like a golden garment.

"Friends, a new sun has risen," Ellendren said. "Carry this Light from Arenthyl to your homes and brighten every crevice darkened by Shadow." She gestured her verathn toward Ceurendol and light blossomed from it, pouring out of the throne room and beyond Arenthyl. Elves, humans, dwarves, centaurs, merpeople, giants, fauns, goblins, lethiens, ogres, and minums stepped forward as Evellyn sang a song Devlyn had sung himself once before. It held much of the elves' history and their woes. He listened as his mother sang the last stanza.

"Thrones blossomed beneath to reign, whilst budding city was sung from tree.

Where Lucillia passed, her likeness gazed west, the wooded city off'ring rest.

Roendryn now Aryl with his wife, the Erynien Empire brought to broken knee.

North, Feolyn went in peace, beneath the forest eaves he stayed, a pilgrim like the rest.

Feolyn, Feolyn, oh father mine, ever shall Cor'lera's treasure be, cradle of an unborn king."

But Evellyn didn't finish there. She added to the song.

"The unborn king, birthed at long last, to bond with a phoenix free.

The Shroud defeated, Arenthyl's frozen shores restored.

The elven city beside the wood, returned at last as to tree.

The Tree did die to live again as the Void was vanquished evermore.

Devlyn, Devlyn, and Ellendren too, who gave the Jewel anew.

With the song of Ceurendol upon thy hearts,

Light and love will ever mark your start."

EPILOGUE

Seven years had passed since the Guardians of Light had gathered on the slopes of Mount Cyngol. Few understood how Ramiel had been defeated. If Lucillia had not given birth to twins twelve hundred years prior and scattered the Erynien Empire by that delivery, there would have been more questions. Even the Ei'ana of Septyl did not press the issue. Devlyn and Ellendren knew questions would arise as their twin sons matured. But with Ceurendol whole once more and Life Immortal returned to the Luminari elves and anyone else who sought it, decades would pass before the differences between Braelyn and Tristyn manifested.

Devlyn already recognized a mingling of himself and Ellendren in both children. Their faces were identical. But where Braelyn's hair was golden-brown, mixed with threads of onyx-black, silvery-blond, and cinnamon-bronze, Tristyn's hair was like oil and his skin was paler than other elves'. Not even the Aldinari had skin so light. Those present at their birth knew Tristyn had not breathed when he was first born, and that only the restoration of Ceurendol had brought life back to his tiny lungs. Devlyn and Ellendren had kept the full truth to themselves.

The boy was too young for them to know whether he was their son or Ramiel. They feared the day when he would have to grapple with who he was. Until then, they resolved to give him a loving and affirming childhood. Despite knowing what was inside the child, Devlyn and Ellendren kissed their son on the forehead every night before bed, treating him no differently from his brother.

Devlyn smiled at his sons as they splashed in a garden fountain, squealing with laughter. Devlyn couldn't stop his own laugh from joining theirs. Ellendren joined them in the palace garden, but unlike her sons and husband, she wasn't smiling.

"Devlyn, you know how important today is."

"I'll be ready."

"Your lierathnil is soaking wet. We had to coordinate our outfits. I'll have to change if yours doesn't dry in time."

Braelyn and Tristyn stopped splashing at their mother's tone but giggled when Devlyn bonded with Aliel. The transformation would have disintegrated normal fabric, but only the dampness was banished from his yellow and white lierathnil. The boys squealed in delight when Devlyn withdrew from his bond and they both repeatedly called out for Aliel.

Clothes dry, Devlyn splayed his arms, offering an innocent smile. Ellendren rolled her eyes, but Devlyn caught the grin she tried to hide. An older elf drew up behind Ellendren, offering her hands to the twins. "Come inside, boys." They went with their nanny into the palace.

"Is today a crown day?" Devlyn asked, noticing Ellendren already wore hers.

"You know it is."

He offered a playful smirk in response before kissing her. "Care to join me while I retrieve mine?"

"I suppose. Don't want you getting sidetracked again." They crossed the gardens before going into the palace.

"I still can't believe the Eldin Wood is gone."

"Every last Stellendae Tree returned to Eldinare, except for those growing on the Isle of Life here. The settlings are delighted at the new forest surrounding the Tree of Life. Some have even settled already and will become miervae," Ellendren said.

"It'll be a wondrous forest. It's hard to believe the Skylands are habitable once more."

"Eklean will feel empty with so many elves returning to the Sky-lands."

"Perhaps. Thanks to the Time Wardens agreeing to open more seguian portals, the Skylands won't feel as far and cut off from the rest of Teraeniel. Many Luminari will divide their time between Luminare and Krysenthiel. And a good portion of the Eldinari and Aldinari elves will remain here too."

"And Cyndinari."

"Them too. I'm glad they agreed to relinquish their island, Cynethol, back to the goblins. What we agreed on will be an interesting experiment for the elves."

"We won't be the only elves with mixed hair colors in a few generations." He winked, knowing Ellendren was more concerned about infighting between Cyndinari and other elves.

"Likely only those who remain here in Krysenthiel. And I have nothing against our decision. I'm simply concerned about violence and division breaking out in our cities. This has never been attempted before."

Devlyn placed his crown on his head, feeling its subtle weight despite its lightness. "We did not come to this decision alone. Every aryl voted in chamber, even the remnants of those Erynor left among the Cyndinari. We're embarking on this great elven experiment together."

Ellendren nodded, then extended her hand. "Shall we?"

Devlyn took her hand in his and together they left the throne room, crossed the lumaryl halls and out the grand entry to find hundreds of Luminari elves gathered in the plaza. These elves were destined to go to Mar'anathyl, Aren and Ithendryl among them. Minums and Time Wardens were already with the other Luminari in their respective cities, waiting to take some of those elves to their sister cities on Luminare.

Ithendryl and Aren stood to one side, Evellyn, Leilyn, Arlyn, Kaela, and Aaron on the other. A minum stood at the center of the dais, a small key dangling from her belt. Devlyn's eyes widened as he took in the Keeper of the Time Wardens, the mysterious and secret leader of the minums. Her identity had been kept a secret lest Erynor take advantage of her authority over time and space. Erynor could have rewritten history had he discovered the Keeper's identity.

"Are you ready?" the Keeper asked.

Devlyn and Ellendren nodded. A small reflective orb appeared between the Keeper's hands. The orb didn't reflect the plaza they stood on but was a window to the destination beyond: Luminare. The Keeper widened the portal to a city of golden light. Devlyn had only visited Mar'anathyl in shared memories. He had never physically been there himself. No one had since the Darkness had descended on the Skylands. The past seven years had been devoted to preparing trees, plants, and animals native to Luminare for the return. While Krysenthiel would be for all elvenkind, the Skylands would remain the ancestral homes of the various elves. Luminare would ever belong to the elves of the dawning sun.

Hand in hand, Devlyn and Ellendren stepped through the seguian portal and into Mar'anathyl, where Loren and Thien had made their home on Luminare.

Alex sat across from a very pregnant Diana. He couldn't believe it had happened again so quickly. Well, he supposed he could. There were already four children running around Elothkar's palace. He had known Diana intended to have many children, but he had not expected her to begin the moment they had returned following Ramiel's defeat.

Two of their children sprinted across the room, chasing each other with wooden swords. "Thellion will end in a civil war if we keep having children like those two," Alex quipped.

"That's not amusing." Diana held their youngest, asleep in her lap. "Besides, they won't be scattered across Eklean with their own provinces.

We'll keep them home."

"With Life Immortal? How long until we're all grown adults with only a couple decades between us in the span of thousands of years?"

"I'm sure you'll adjust." Diana smiled as she brushed her fingers through her daughter's hair. "How are the trade negotiations with the dwarves faring?"

"Unending. We should have hammered out an agreement when the world was on the brink of destruction. We might have gotten a better deal."

"I do believe I suggested just that." Diana smiled triumphantly.

"Fine. You were right, as always," he grumbled.

"Isn't the Goblin Guild helping?"

"I haven't determined who they're advocating for yet. You'd think with one of their islands returned they'd be more agreeable, but this trade treaty will fill their guild's pockets just as much as the dwarves'."

"The treaty will benefit us all."

"We should've asked the minums to open portals for us to bypass the mountains."

"That still wouldn't have provided trade with the dwarves. Bypassing their mountains would have left us poorer. Thellion would fall behind the other kingdoms benefiting from the ore and jewels in their mountains. Besides, Devlyn and Ellendren were quite clear on a more open and transparent Eklean."

"The High King can be a pain in my royal…"

Diana hushed him before he could finish. "Not in front of the children." The two older boys giggled. Alex frowned at how observant they were. He wouldn't be able to get away with anything with them watching. "Speaking of Devlyn and Ellendren, did they say how long they would be gone?"

"Six months, but we'll see if they stick to that time frame. They claim the Guardian Senate is more than capable of functioning without its prelates."

"I'm sure it is," Diana said.

"Until the Daer senators try to take advantage of their absence and demand more territory in Eklean," Alex complained.

"Malind Koth's colony on the Skrein Sea's coast has flourished into a bustling city that no Perrien sovereign had ever thought possible."

"It thrives because he made it a dedicated seaport for the Daer Empire—no one cared to trade along the Skrein Sea before."

"But even Qien uses it now to trade with us."

"Despite our efforts to make our own ports more popular. Our new city is on an inlet to the River Arvil. Once our treaty is signed with the dwarves, we'll have direct water passage from the Skrein Sea to Lake Saeryndol to the Erynien Bay and the Tempestien Sea beyond."

"Then you'd better finalize that treaty." Diana unconcernedly combed her daughter's hair. "Will you stop at Gwilnor to visit Aen?"

"I sent word for him to meet me at an inn. I'm not stepping foot near that school. Velaria has made it clear the ei'ana intend to teach me how to control the erendinth."

"You can't deny them forever. Especially once you receive Life Immortal from Ceurendol." Diana glared at him. She didn't have to comment on him not yet doing so.

He still refused to behold the Jewel of Life, a point of contention with Diana. It's not that he didn't want Life Immortal; he just didn't want to look like a teenager for hundreds of years like Wyn. The elf's age still boggled Alex. No, he wanted to wait until his third decade so no one could mistake him for a child. Being a king was hard enough without the added prejudice of his youth. That he also wanted to grow a full beard was a reason he kept secret. Diana would never forgive him if she learned that was part of his reasoning.

"They can send an ei'ana here if they so desire," Alex said, avoiding further comment on Life Immortal. "I won't have them trap me in Gwilnor again."

"You're almost believable when you say that."

The sun warmed Jaerol's skin. Liam lay beside him, and they relaxed in each other's presence. Rusyl was nearby, but far enough away to not intrude.

"I knew you would like Cynethol's beaches," Jaerol teased.

"It's not Cynethol anymore," Liam replied.

"It'll take some getting used to that. It was nice of the goblins to let my uncle reinstate his vineyard and winery."

"How much longer until the vines are matured for a real harvest? I'm dying to try his wine again. Yloran insists on keeping her reserves for special occasions until his winery is up and running."

"Hopefully by the end of next year. He's determined to rival the Cor'leran Blue."

"We'll see," Liam said.

"You're just biased."

"And you're not?" Liam tickled Jaerol's side which quickly devolved into them wrestling on the sandy beach. Rusyl growled as he moved further away.

"Have you decided what School you'll choose yet?" Jaerol asked as the sun lowered.

"I had considered Azurelle for the longest time, that way we could share a home in the same district in Septyl."

"We don't have to live in Septyl. Our home will ever be where we are together. And if we have separate apartments in Septyl, I will personally tear down every wall between us."

"Sounds spacious, but perhaps too public." Liam winked. "Then I suppose Emradiel. I am quarter Eldinari after all. Alethea mentioned my grandmother would be delighted to see me."

"You'll have to travel a lot further now."

"It could be fun, assuming we're permitted to leave Gwilnor once we start classes again."

"Then perhaps we should go before."

A comfortable quiet fell between them. Jaerol felt they could do anything with the return of the Jewel of Life and Ramiel and his Void vanquished. Even the nightmares of his history with the Erynien Empire had faded. That Erynor was dead and the shadow elves defeated, their trapped spirits freed to pass to the World-Beyond was something Jaerol had never thought he would live to see. Hope had never been valued in Broid. The Imperium and its malicious magisters, at least, those who weren't shadow elves, were answering to the Guardian Senate.

Despite the Cyndinari elves being freed from the Erynien Empire, Jaerol wasn't ready to be around them yet. Many had willingly complied with Erynor's schemes and gladly partook in the evils the empire was known for. An image of Broid's arena flashed through his mind. He remembered how crowded the stands had been. Elves had exuberantly cheered for the next class of shadow elves to join their empire as they fought their classmates to the death. As far as he knew, he was the first to refuse to steal his classmate's spirit and live.

Liam squeezed his hand. He knew whenever Jaerol's thoughts moved to Kiron.

Wyn had hoped and prayed that when the Void was defeated, his connection to tenebrys would have severed. With every day that followed, he woke, pleading for his control over it to diminish. But just as he could feel the erendinth move about Teraeniel, so too could he sense tenebrys. It seemed that while tenebrys had been wrought in the Void, it was still accessible without it.

He ensured the Chairs of Septyl were aware of it. If Wyn still had access to tenebrys, so would others. There would always be people who lusted for more power. To say nothing of those who had escaped the Guardians of Light. A shadow elf or Tenebrae ei'ana could still be out there, biding their time before they thought to challenge the new world order.

Aren and Yloran had become invaluable mentors. They had thousands of years of experience with the forbidden power. While it certainly had the ability to corrupt the person wielding it, they had also made it clear that the better one remained firm in their identity, the less likely they would become lost. Neither had seemed particularly concerned about Wyn losing himself to that corruptive power. Still, he had devoted more time to meditation and jienzu to balance himself. And whenever he lost himself in his thoughts and doubts, Kaela was quick to bring him back to the present.

She had regained her people's Life Immortal, and they would live all their years together. Like the others who had recently regained the benefits of Ceurendol, Kaela too felt a need to move fast. She had mentioned marriage on many occasions despite Wyn saying that he was too young to marry. Most elves typically lived centuries, nearing a thousand years before marriage. Wyn hoped the Luminari and Cyndinari would ease into their longer lives, remembering who they had once been as elves. Still, he doubted Kaela would allow him to follow that custom and wait several centuries, let alone a decade, before they exchanged oaths.

Kaela came up beside him and shrugged into his arms. He held her as they looked north and west toward Eldinare, too far in the horizon to see. "Do you miss them?"

"I do." There was no need for her to say who. The Eldin Wood was gone from Eklean, as were the majority of the Eldinari elves, Alethea among them. Eldinare was freed from the Darkness. They had spent the years since Ramiel's defeat preparing it for their return. Wyn knew his place was beside Kaela here in Arenthyl, but he did miss the quiet songs among the Stellendae trees under starlight. That life felt so distant to him now.

"We can visit whenever you want. But only after we make a quick trip to New Lankor."

"Why New Lankor?"

"To congratulate the new Yanilean, of course. I would also like to see Ange again. A shame her husband inheriting the Yanilean Mask meant she couldn't remain a Guardian senator."

"Has New Lankor been completed?"

"No, but I've heard the masons from Gestoria are outdoing themselves."

"I'm happy the dorthl is gone—returned to its natural state." Wyn shuddered at the memory of being surrounded by the stone that had severed his connection to the erendinth. Balance was returning to Teraeniel. He exhaled in relief.

———————

Velaria sat across Evellyn and Arlyn, an old tea pot and cups between them. They shared each other's silence, a mixture of gratitude and sorrow for those lost. It felt like an eternity had passed since Evellyn had first spoken Lucillia's prophecy, passed down from parent to youngest child, all the way back to Feolyn.

The Void was gone—defeated. The Erynien Empire had been brought low once more. Its heir acknowledged the Cyndinari aryls. Erethien and the aryls in turn recognized Devlyn and Ellendren as their Exalted Aryl, as Uriel had ordained. Velaria knew dissent among the Cyndinari would linger, especially after they had been forced to abandon their stolen island home of Cynethol. While the goblins were grateful for the return of their island, the elves remaining in Eklean were to live together in Krysenthiel. Velaria was excited to see how those cities of lumaryl would change over the years to reflect the blend of elves living there.

Velaria relished the hope that sat comfortably in her chest. She felt as though she could finally put her guard down and devote her attention to Septyl and Gwilnor. Student wielders were flocking to the school in numbers that Velaria had only heard rumored about in Gwilnor's illustrious history. At the current enrollment rate, they would have to expand the castle. The alternative was to open new schools on the other continents, but that didn't sit well with her. Seguian portals made travelling from Gwilnor to other continents easy.

The students were still limited to elves and humans, but dwarves, centaurs, and merpeople no longer distanced themselves from ei'ana, in fear they would steal their secrets or force them to become ei'ana. She had come to accept that the various races preferred to interact differently with the erendinth, it did make her wonder how humans would have interacted with them if they had been left to their own devices.

Of course, humans had uncovered magic without the elves. Druids could be found on every continent, the Kilnae Del mages had unlocked magic in arcane gems, and Qien monks had learned to wield from jade dragons. While Septyl supported the druids, mages, and monks, they had reaffirmed their rejection of the Daer Sorcery.

"Tea with friends is meant for relaxing," Arlyn said, acknowledging her thoughts.

"An old habit." A small smile tugged at the corner of her lips.

"A habit which saw Eklean's human sovereigns sign the Thellish Accord," Evellyn added.

"Queen Myranda offered a dozen different names when I first brought the proposal to her. I chose not to comment on the treaty originating in Alexandria; she would have outright refused if it was called the Alexandrian Accord," Velaria said.

"If the accord is successful, Devlyn and Ellendren will be able to renounce their titles as High King and High Queen of Eklean," Arlyn said.

"And centaurs, dwarves, fauns, giants, goblins, merpeople, and minums will exhale a great sigh, seeing as they never agreed to it." Velaria sipped her tea, wondering how else the world might change in the new age. While humans counted the passing of time in ages, the elves counted it in much longer eras, remembering ages long forgotten by humans. All creation agreed that a new page had turned. Human records would call it the fifth age, while elves would sing of the fourth era, but with the Tree of Life revealed for the first time since the Elder Days, all creation had agreed they now lived in the Days of the Tree. The Verakryl Epoch promised to be a time of peace and prosperity, where people of every race and nation exchanged knowledge freely. The Guardian Senate had become the rule of the land and its judgments were respected given its coordinated triumph over Ramiel and the Void.

The Days of the Tree were brighter than even before the Void had drowned Teraeniel, for Verakryl's light reached farther now that Mount Verinien had been brought down. Velaria smiled into her teacup as that same light brightened Evellyn's sitting room, warming Velaria's skin even as her cinnamon-bronze hair caught its rays. Verakryl's light was different from the sun and stars. It was neither harsh, nor gentle, nor distant. Velaria could walk up to its base and touch its bark without being burned, but it was overwhelming—all-consuming. She had only approached the Tree once. Its light had singed her to the core. Her body, soul, and spirit had bloomed like an inferno at the touch. So much power should have consumed her like a leaf set to flame. The opposite had happened though, and she had felt strengthened and invigorated from the experience. From all accounts, it was the same experience for everyone who approached the Tree.

A new day had come, and Velaria knew her and Yelaris' roles in it were far from over. The Days of the Tree had only just begun and like so many others, she had received the benefits of Ceurendol being whole once more. The Jewel of Life had returned Life Immortal to the elves and anyone who desired its gifts. Once again, the Creating Light gave all creatures the choice of self-determination, whether their lives were long or short, they would be theirs to live.

Here ends the Seventh Part of

The Jewel of Life

Acknowledgements

In the winter months of 2012, a silly and outlandish idea sprang within me—that I could write a book series. The dream took root and every time I told myself I couldn't, this magical world became more defined and real. The characters soon had faces and unique personalities, while the world they lived in continued to expand. After thirteen years, I can hardly believe the Jewel of Life series has reached its end.

Devlyn, the elf-boy who didn't know he was an elf, is all grown up and affirmed in his identity. I've learned so much about myself through writing his character and bringing him to life on the pages. But I wouldn't have been able to bring Devlyn and the many other characters to life without the help and support of so many people. As my first dedications went to my parents and sister, I again extend my deep gratitude to you. I could not have done any of this without your encouragement. To my husband, Nick, who met a grad student with a dream of publishing his stories, thank you for believing in me and being beside me for every publication. I also need to thank my extended family for being the best cheerleaders a guy could ask for.

To my early readers and friends who saw the books in their nascent stages, thank you so much for your incredible critiques and insights to each story. To my cover artist, Fiona Jayde, who has stuck with me throughout the series, thank you for sharing your incredible artistry and bringing these special scenes to life for each cover. Lastly, but certainly not least, to my editor, friend, and often teacher, Micheline Brodeur, who this book is dedicated to. This series would have been a shadow of itself if not for your constant guidance and attention to detail. I had no idea what to expect when you took me on as a client in 2018 when you were supposed to be retiring, but I am so grateful that you did. I feel so fortunate to have worked with and learned from you. You've taught me so much in this craft with each and every book.

From Wilmington, DE to Philadelphia, PA, Victoria, KS, Santa

Ynez, CA, Pittsburgh, PA, Middletown, CT, Madison, WI, and back to Washington, DC, this series has been written across the country and I am so grateful for all the friends I've made while writing it and being able to share this story with you.

402

Ryan D Gebhart
Washington DC
2 May 2025

Appendix A

Glossary of Terms

Abbey School

The preferred system of education for children throughout Eklean. Those deemed capable are sent to higher studies, preferably at Gwilnor Academy.

Aelish

Native language of the elves.

Aelith

Group of Aldinari elves who have been corrupted by the Darkness on Aldinare and live in the cities.

Aerethyn

Orb holding the lived memories of Kien and Kiara.

Aerodhal

Royal Palace in Arenthyl. Residence of the Exalted Aryl of Krysenthiel.

Aerys

An elemental erendinth. The essence of air.

Albien

One of the seven Schools of Septyl. Albiens focus on truth and care for many of Eklean's libraries. Motto: Truth is discoverable. Emblem: A naked male and female elf holding unraveled scrolls with an owl perched behind, cast in gold on a white field. The chair of Albien is known as the Seeker.

Aldarch

Draelyn rulers of Aldinare who reign from their sanctums.

Aldinare

Western Skyland of the Aldinari, one of the four elven kindreds. Lost to the Darkness. Only a hundred Aldinari escaped the Skyland with their lives.

Alicorn

A winged unicorn native to the Skyland of Aldinare.

Anadel

Spiritual creatures that predate Teraeniel and Somnaeniel. Their native home is Lumaeniel. There are four known classifications of anadel: irythil, enthiel, lorendil, and naril.

ANACORDEL

Creatures of body, soul, and spirit.

ANAWEH

The Creating Light.

ANIMYS

A transcendental erendinth. The essence of spirit.

AQUAEYS

An elemental erendinth. The essence of water.

ARANTIULYN

One of the seven Schools of Septyl. Arantiulyns focus on strength and protection and oversee the Knights of Septyl. Motto: With fortitude, we will protect. Emblem: A naked male and female elf in a fighting stance with swords in hand with a lion prowling cast in gold on an orange field. The Chair of Arantiulyn is known as the General.

ARCANE GEMS

Sources of magic used by the Mages of the Kilnae Del.

ARCHSTEWARD

Part of the Ei'ceuril hierarchy, they are elevated wise ones. Before kien wielders were restricted to the Temple of Ceur, archstewards lived in every major city of Eklean tending to those faithful to Anaweh, the Creating Light.

ARENTHYLEAN BELLS

Twenty-four bells composed of four materials that ring every hour.

ARYL

The united head of an elven house composed of an ei'denai and ei'terel.

AUBURNIS

One of the seven Schools of Septyl. Auburnises focus on inner peace. Motto: To love is our gift. Emblem: A naked male and female elf offering a garland with larks flying above, cast in gold on a brown field. The Chair of Auburnis is known as the Pilgrim.

AUREPHAEN

Feast day of the Luminari, commemorating Auriel and the dawning sun. Celebrated on the 15th of Aurenth, the spring equinox.

AZURELLE

One of the seven Schools of Septyl. Azurelles focus on the advancement and training of the erendinth. Motto: The zealous soul must be temperate. Emblem: A naked male and female elf wielding the erendinth with a dragon behind, cast in gold on a blue field. The Chair of Azurelle is known as the Blue Dragon.

Belin's Watch

An Evellion city in the Vespien Mountains comprised of humans and dwarves. Named for Belin, the dwarf who sheltered Thellion refugees in their greatest hour of need.

Borephaen

Feast day of the Eldinari, commemorating Boriel and the sleeping sun. Celebrated on the 15th of Borenth, the winter solstice.

Bowl of Theniel

Sea set apart by the merpeople as sacred. The place where Theniel brought the waters to Teraeniel.

Centaur

Anacordel dedicated to protecting the forests of Eklean, particularly the Illumined Wood. The upper body is like an elf's but broader and more rugged while the lower body looks much like a four-legged horse.

Ceurendol

The Jewel of Life. Created by the Luminari by placing their Life Immortal within seven jewels of incredible brilliance which allowed them to share their immortality with every race in 1.3a (7085.3E). Also known as the Light Diamond, the Lieben Stone, and the Heart of Hearts.

Ceurendol War, the

A cataclysmic war instigated by the Erynien Empire which began over a philosophical difference over the Jewel of Life and whether immortal life was proper for the 'lesser races.' The war divided Eklean in two factions, those faithful to the Luminari and those subjugated by the Erynien Empire. As the fate of the war grew clear, the Guardian Senate disbanded and merchants from other continents withdrew from Eklean, fearing the Erynien Empire. 322-500.3a (7407-7585.3E).

Ceurenyl

City founded by the ei'ceuril. Home of the Temple of Ceur and Gwilnor Academy. The only city not to fall into Erynor's control when Krysenthiel was lost to the Shroud.

Ceurtriarch

Leader of the ei'ceuril, known as High Archsteward and Arbiter of the Light.

Chancellor

The head of Gwilnor Academy under the authority of and appointed by the Seven Chairs.

Children

When capitalized, refers to the proto-race.

Citadel, the

Seat of the Sha'ghol on Cyndinare.

Cor'lera

A small village in eastern Parendior. The vineyards of Cor'lera produce the coveted ice wine, the Cor'leran Blue.

Crimsyn

One of the seven Schools of Septyl. Crimsyns focus on healing and run many hospitals and infirmaries throughout Eklean. Motto: Through healing, hope is given. Emblem: A naked male and female elf dancing with a dog, cast in gold on a red field. The chair of Crimsyn is known as the Physician.

Cyndinare

Southern Skyland of the Cyndinari, one of the four elven kindreds. Lost to the Darkness.

Cynethol

Home of the Cyndinari, situated among the Kinzdol Islands.

Daer

Anacordel that were once humans who evolved after experimenting with the Sorcery.

Daereneth

Continent south of Ogren and west of Ja'Horan. Tropical continent.

Dawn Age

The time frame that the Qien Dynasty refers to following the period in their history where Tolvenol ruled over the continent of Qien. The elves refer to this as the First Era.

Deathless

The Cyndinari directly responsible for the Shroud. They are neither living nor dead.

DEURGHOL

Fallen tenebrys anadel that follow Ramiel. Several took the Cyndinari who corrupted Ceurendol as hosts.

DORTHL

Substance that manifests differently in the different realms, either as a solid, a liquid, or a gas. Nullifies the erendinth and boosts tenebrys.

DRAELYN

A mixed anacordel race of dragon and elven origins.

DRAELISH

Native language of the draelyn.

DRAGON

Legendary creatures bound to the erendinth who helped shape creation.

DRUIDS OF KWEIL AITCH, THE

Secluded faction of humans who learned to walk Somnaeniel, the World-in-Between early on.

DWARF

Anacordel who sought the deep roots of the mountains.

EALYN

Leaders of the draelyn of Tenethyl.

EI'ANA

An organized group of wielders.

EI'ANA COUNSELS

A series of norms ei'ana are to follow in regards to wielding.

EI'CEURIL

A religious order, currently a majority of men, focused on serving Anaweh, the Creating Light. Because a kien wielder had not been capable of wielding with control, every male ei'ceuril capable of wielding had been confined to the Temple of Ceur.

EI'DENAI

Elven lord serving as aryl with his spouse. Head of House.

EI'ETHIL

Elven lord.

EI'LYTHEL

Elven lady.

Ei'phaenyl

Instructor of the Phaedryn on Phroenthyl.

Ei'terel

Elven lady serving as aryl with her spouse. Head of House.

Eklean

Continent where the anacordel first stirred as Children.

Elder Days

The Elder Days span from the beginning of creation until what the elves refer to as the First Era, following Ramiel being sealed away in the Void and the creation of the separate races.

Elder Ones

Anacordel that evolved from the Children before the Great Blessing, at which time the different races were solidified.

Eldin Wood, the

Home of the Eldinari.

Eldinare

Northern Skyland of the Eldinari, one of the four elven kindreds. Lost to the Darkness. The Eldinari were the first to evacuate their Skyland for the lands below.

Elemental Erendinth, the

Forces wielded to influence the elements. *See Erendinth.*

Elf

Anacordel who changed little when the different races were created. Because they remained in the Valley of Saeryndol, they retained their Life Immortal and were gifted the Skylands. There are four elven kindreds, the Luminari, Cyndinari, Aldinari, and Eldinari.

Elya

Powerful wielders born of any race who learn to wield instinctively and are not limited to the restrictions common to normal kien and kiara wielders.

Emradiel

One of the seven Schools of Septyl. Emradiels focus on beauty and life. Motto: Only the prudent thrive. Emblem: A naked male and female elf gesturing with open palms toward the beauty around them with a stag behind, cast in gold on a green field. The chair of Emradiel is known as the Tender.

ENTHIEL

Anadel dedicated to one of the seven irythil. The enthiel are very involved with the anacordel. A single enthiel guides an entire people.

ERENDINTH, THE

The erendinth are the wielded powers believed to have created Teraeniel. Tradition says that there are seven powers, three transcendental: lumenys, animys, and umbrys; and four elemental: aquaeys, aerys, terys, and ignys. Much is forgotten or unknown about the full extent of the erendinth which are dependent on inner spiritual and emotional workings.

ERENDINTH GAMES, THE

A game of wielding created at Gwilnor Academy, involving the wielding of all seven erendinth.

FAUN

Short nocturnal anacordel with the hind legs of a goat from the navel down. Some fauns have horns.

FULP

Dwonian staple that is mashed into a starchy dish.

GIANT

Anacordel that were drawn to the frozen north. During the Great Blessing, their physical features became capable of withstanding the harsh tundra of Glacien.

GLACIEN

Northern frozen continent spanning the northern pole. Connects Eklean and Ogren.

GOBLIN

Anacordel native to the Kinzdol Islands. Known for their monetary guild.

GOBLIN GUILD

Infamous bank and guild of Eklean. Regulates the majority of Eklean's currency. The Goblin Guild is based in the Kinzdol Islands with branches in every city and most villages.

GREAT BLESSING, THE

Event recorded in the Theseryn where Anaweh blessed the growing differences among the anacordel and solidified their choices by making each their own distinct race.

GRILAE

Red flowering fruit trees native to Cyndinare.

GUARDIAN KNIGHTS

Order of knights once based in Krysenthiel that served and protected all the land from injustice. The Guardian Knights were largely composed of Luminari and were defeated during the Ceurendol War.

GUARDIAN SENATE, THE

An international body, crossing countries and continents to ensure the wellbeing of Teraeniel. Disbanded toward the end of the Ceurendol War.

GWILNOR ACADEMY

The foremost school dedicated to the education of wielders, located in Ceurenyl.

HOLY TOMES

Volumes recorded by various ei'ceuril, some being prophets, and from which the ei'ceuril base their beliefs and practices.

HUMAN

Anacordel that differ among themselves more than any other race. They traveled the furthest from the Valley of Saeryndol, migrating across the entirety of Teraeniel.

IGNYS

An elemental erendinth. The essence of fire.

ILITHAE

Silver leafed trees native to Aldinare. The only ilithae trees thought to have survived the doom of Aldinare are found in the Wooded Hills of Thellion.

ILLUMINED WOOD, THE

A vast forest with mysterious qualities and inhabitants.

IMPERIUM

Selective school for Cyndinari youth. Its violent academic style educates the next generation of shadow elves.

IRYTHIL

The seven anadel who, under Anaweh's guidance, introduced the erendinth, thereby creating Teraeniel.

JADIEN

Island and city-state in the Erynien Bay.

JA'HORAN

Continent south of Eklean. Inhabited largely by nomadic peoples.

Jahro Islands

Island chain in the Unarian Sea.

Jienzu

Heart, mind, and body practice of meditation, breathing, and body positions called forms, used by the draelyn and ancient elves to achieve balance.

Judges of Yanil

An order that once ruled beside the Yanilean. The judges strive to uphold law and order with limited influence.

Keeper

Head of the time wardens and possessor of the time key.

Kiara Wielder

A female wielder. Kiara wielders learn to control the erendinth easily but require a kien wielder to reach their potential strength.

Kien Wielder

A male wielder. Kien wielders reach their potential strength easily but require a kiara wielder to learn control of the erendinth.

Kilnae Del

Order of mages native to Charren, headquartered in the Charrenese capital, Karithel.

Kinzdol Islands

An archipelago in southern Eklean, homeland to the goblins and Cyndinari.

Kirenae

Gold flowering fruit trees native to Luminare.

Kweil Aitch

Island east of the Illumined Wood. The place where the veil is thin between Teraeniel and Somnaeniel.

Lay Votary

A non-clerical class of ei'ceuril.

Lethien

A mixed anacordel race of elven and human origins. Largely extinguished by Erynor during and after the Ceurendol War.

Lorendil

Anadel that guard and protect individual anacordel. Some anacordel are known to communicate with their lorendil.

Lucillian Alliance, the

An alliance of the Eklean kingdoms established to return peace and order to Eklean following Emperor Erynor's disappearance.

Lumaeniel

The World-Beyond. Dwelling of Anaweh, the anadel, and those anacordel who have transitioned beyond.

Lumenys

A transcendental erendinth. The essence of light.

Luminare

Eastern Skyland of the Luminari, one of the four elven kindreds. Lost to the Darkness. The Luminari evacuated their Skyland for the lands below where they established Krysenthiel.

Mahl Havn

Citadel of the Daer Sorcery.

Mar'anathyl

City on the Skyland of Luminare. Governed by the Lorenthien aryls.

Masters, the (Seven Masters, the)

Vigyl Vyoletryn, Cyrelle Azurelle, Lanielle Emradiel, Lyon Arantiulyn, Mainor Auburnis, Caelyn Crimsyn, and Saeyrn Albien are the founders of the Seven Schools of Septyl and Gwilnor Academy.

Meridean Conclave

Governing council of the merpeople.

Meridephaen

Feast day of the Cyndinari, commemorating Meridiel and the noon sun. Celebrated on the 15th of Meridenth, the summer solstice.

Merpeople

Anacordel who longed for the depths of Teraeniel's oceans.

Miervae

Anacordel who longed to nurture Teraeniel's forests. Miervae are also referred to as Great Trees and begin their life as Settlings.

Minum

The least of Eklean's anacordel. A short mixed anacordel race of goblin and human origins. Before the elves migrated to Eklean, they were enslaved, sold by goblins to humans.

Naril

Anadel reminiscent of the seven erendinth. There are seven types of narils and they are commonly known as nymphs.

Neridu

Group of Aldinari elves who have been corrupted by the Darkness on Aldinare and live in the wilderness.

Nymphs

See Naril.

Observant

Non-wielders who have dedicated themselves to one of the Seven Schools of Septyl.

Ogre

Brutish anacordel covering the vast majority of Ogren. Mixed anacordel race of giant and human origins.

Ogren

Continent east of Eklean and west of Qien. Mountainous land with a mixture of forests and deserts. Inhabited by centaurs, giants, humans, and ogres.

Parenhal

Citadel of the Phaedryn in Arenthyl.

Phaedryn

A bonded elf and a phoenix.

Phoenix

Anadel who migrated to Teraeniel and bonded with the Luminari.

Phroenthyl

Small Skyland that is home to the Gold Flight and base of learning for Phaedryn.

Purged Desert of Dwonia, the

A vast wasteland in western Eklean that was rumored to have at one point been fertile. Home of the Twelve Tribes of Dwonia.

Return

The final stage of formation of an ei'ceuril toward becoming a steward. Often occurring in the Illumined Wood.

Sanctum

Expansive complexes housing the aldarchs and their courts on Aldinare.

Sand Warrior

Dwonian guardian responsible for protecting Dwonia's tribes and lands.

Schtach

Language of the dwarves.

Schtam

(1) A dwarven people. (2) The dwellings of the dwarves.

Schtamite

The eight dwarven schtams.

Seguian

A portal created to traverse space and time. Traversing time is restricted and only the keeper can use the time key to traverse time.

Septyl

(1) The order of Ei'ana composing the Seven Schools of Septyl. (2) The city of the ei'ana in Krysenthiel that was lost in the Shroud.

Septyl Knights

Order of knights dedicated to Septyl. The knights receive their training at Gwilnor Academy and vow to serve one of the Seven Schools of Septyl.

Seraph

Six winged anadel in Lumaeniel.

Servants of Shadow

Secret organization carrying out the orders of shadow elves and, in some instances, the orders of the Deurghol and Sha'ghol.

Settling

Tree-like creatures that wander about in their youth until finding an appropriate place to settle their roots and grow into a Miervae, also known as a Great Tree. Settlings have unique vitality qualities.

Seven Chairs of Septyl, the

The leaders of the Ei'ana. Each of the Seven Schools elects its own Chair who leads his or her School and participates in the leadership of Septyl. Responsible for admitting student wielders into Gwilnor Academy and selecting a chancellor.

Seven Schools of Septyl, the

The order of Ei'ana, composed of Albien, Arantiulyn, Auburnis, Azurelle, Crimsyn, Emradiel, and Vyoletryn Schools.

SHADOW ELVES

Cyndinari who consume the spirit of others to prolong their own life.

SHA'GHOL

Past rulers of the Cyndinari. First to communicate with Ramiel after her was imprisoned and wield tenebrys.

SHIFTING

(1) The ability to teleport in Somnaeniel. (2) The Phaedryn ability to teleport physically in Teraeniel.

SHROUD, THE

A diseased-looking fog placed by the Cyndinari over the entirety of Krysenthiel. It severed the Luminari from the Jewel of Life, cutting them off from their Life Immortal and making them mortal, as well as any others who had benefited from it. An unanticipated result was that the Cyndinari also lost their immortality with that placement of the Shroud over the Jewel of Life.

SKYLANDS, THE

Four island countries, Aldinare, Cyndinare, Eldinare, and Luminare, floating in the clouds thousands of feet above the ground. The dwelling places of the elves before they were forced to evacuate to the land below.

SOJOURNERS

The exiled of Dwonia who sought reentrance after forming an allegiance with the Erynien Empire.

SOMNAENIEL

The World-in-Between. A realm visited by dreamers. Gateway between Lumaeniel and Teraeniel.

SOPHILLIAE

Orbs that preserve knowledge.

SOPHILLIUM

The great library of Septyl that houses the sophilliae.

STAR WARDEN

An elven military unit, typically ensuring the protection of their lands.

STELLENDAE

Remarkably large trees native to Eldinare that now dominate the Eldin Wood and serve as dwelling places for the Eldinari elves.

STEWARD

A clerical class of ei'ceuril with the ability to wield.

STEWARDS OF SHADOW

Ei'ceuril stewards who forsook Anaweh to support Ramiel.

TEMPLE OF CEUR, THE

Home to the ei'ceuril and pilgrimage site for the faithful. It is impossible to wield within the temple walls. All kien wielders had been confined to the Temple of Ceur before Balence was restored.

TEMPLE KNIGHTS

Order of knights dedicated to protecting the Temple of Ceur and the city of Ceurenyl. Some of the temple knights are men who were brought to the temple when it was discovered that they could wield. These temple knights are prohibited from leaving the temple.

TENEBRAE

An unrecognized School of Septyl intended to replace the other seven Schools. Its adherents focus on power and dominance. Motto: Might conquers. Emblem: A naked male and female elf standing triumphantly on seven broken emblems, cast in gold on a black field. The chair of Tenebrae is known as the Conqueror.

TENEBRYS

A corrupted form of the erendinth, unrecognized by the Ei'ana of Septyl as one of the erendinth and absolutely forbidden to wield. The essence of the Void.

TENETHYL

(1) Jeweled city of the draelyn hidden in the Illumined Wood. (2) City destroyed by Ramiel's forces before the Great Blessing.

TERAENIEL

The World-Below. Composed of the continents Daereneth, Eklean, Glacien, Ja'Horan, Ogren, and Qien.

TERYS

An elemental erendinth. The essence of stone.

THESERYN

Holy tome recording the creation of Teraeniel and the anacordel, written by the first Ceurtriarch of the Ei'ceuril. The Theseryn states that seven irythil, under Anaweh's guidance, introduced the erendinth thereby creating Teraeniel.

TIME KEY

An artifact created by the Luminari to restrict the ability to traverse space and time. It was entrusted to the minums, the least of Eklean's races.

Time Wardens

A select group of minums entrusted by the Luminari with the ability to create seguians, allowing them to travel to any place and any time.

Tosk

City in the Void.

Transcendental Erendinth, the

Wielded forces to influence the ethereal realities of lumenys, animys, and umbrys.

Tree Spirits

Narils who agreed to bond with the trees under Sariel's guidance.

Umbrys

A transcendental erendinth. The essence of shadow.

Urda

Garment the Dwonians use to protect their heads from the sand, sun, and wind.

Vaer

Fruit native to the Illumined Wood.

Valley of Saeryndol

Birthplace of the Children, the first anacordel.

Vasknir

Ramiel's Void fortress, situated on the slopes of Mount Cyngol.

Verakryl

A crystalline tree within Mount Verinien which brought life to the world and is connected to Anaweh. Also known as the Tree of Life.

Verathel

Sprouts of Verakryl, the Tree of Life.

Verathn

Weapons of power.

Vespephaen

Feast day of the Aldinari, commemorating Vespiel and the setting sun. Celebrated on the 15th of Vespenth, the autumn equinox.

Void, the

A realm that existed before Teraeniel and Somnaeniel. Realm of Ramiel and the fallen anadel.

VYOLETRYN

One of the Seven Schools of Septyl. Vyoletryns focus on justice and diplomacy. Motto: With justice, peace. Emblem: A naked male and female elf holding a staff with an eagle soaring above, cast in gold on a violet field. The chair of Vyoletryn is known as the Watcher.

WIELDERS

Anacordel capable of wielding the erendinth.

WINGED HORSES OF THELLION

Ancestors of the grey coursers of Perrien.

WISE ONES

(1) Part of the Ei'ceuril hierarchy. There is no certainty how many are among the ei'ceuril. (2) Part of the Ei'ana hierarchy. There are seven wise ones for every School of Septyl.

YANILEAN, THE

The undisputed monarch of Yanil, always male. Used both as the monarch's title and as his name during his reign.

DAYS OF THE WEEK

(Based on the seven anadel involved in the creation of Teraeniel)

Gwynthaen–Thenaen–Uraen–Ramaen–Lerenaen–Saraen–Karaen

MONTHS/MOONS

(Based on the anadel attached to the elves)

Spring – Marenth, Aurenth, Delenth

Summer – Dynenth, Meridenth, Reventh

Autumn – Kyrenth, Vespenth, Orenth

Winter – Estlenth, Borenth, Lierenth

CURRENCY

Goblin Guild currency – 16 iron angots for a copper lewt. 9 copper lewts for a silver jent. 13 silver jents for a gold crown. 3 golden crowns for a lumol.

Luminari currency – 8 kenols for a narol. 4 narols for a lumol.

APPENDIX B

DRAMATIS PERSONAE

AARON LUCILLIA

Luminari. Ceurtriarch. Prince of Lucillia, brother of Ellendren and Kaela. Ei'ceuril. Formerly of House Roendryn.

ABBIE WINTYR

Human with emerald eyes. Student at Gwilnor Academy. Druid of Kweil Aitch.

AEN FINAMARC

Lethien from Cor'lera, squire to Alex Vaerin.

AGNELLE PHANSTIENNE

Luminari. Ei'ana and Chair of Auburnis.

AISA

Human from Dwonia. Member of Tribe Fendur. Sister to Chief Kodin.

ALESEI

Queen of Tiel. Of the Royal House Ziera.

ALETHEA LENWYN

Eldinari. Emradiel ei'ana and former Lenwyn aryl.

ALEXANDER (ALEX) VAERIN

Human from Perrien, whose family migrated to Cor'lera. King of Thellion. Betrothed to Diana Thellion.

ALIEL

The first phoenix born since the fall of Krysenthiel, bonded with Devlyn.

ALKESH

Human from Jadien. Prince of Jadien.

AMRY THELLION

Former king of Evellion. Married to Queen Lara. *Deceased.*

ANDREA FARNEIS

Human from Sudern. Septyl knight. Nephew to Duke Farneis. Known as Andrew.

ANGENNIA (ANGE) SORICCI

Human from Yanil. Judge of Yanil. Married to Enrico Desillio.

AORINOL

Daer Senator.

Arbol

A faun searching for settlings.

Aren Lorenthien

Luminari. Led a rescue party to Aldinare and did not return. Redeemed Dark Phaedryn.

Arlyn

Ei'ceuril steward from Cor'lera. Devlyn's uncle on his mother's side.

Bernadette Haert

Human from Briel. Princess of Briel. Sister of King Irvienne.

Bernard

Human from Perrien. Ei'ceuril, librarian, and magister at the abbey school of Cor'lera.

Bon Li

Prime Minister of the Qien Dynasty.

Byron Roendryn

Luminari. Squire with the Guardian knights. Brother to Vernal.

Cairn

Human of Tribe Laith. Brief Chief-King of Dwonia and Mindale. Son of Suin. *Deceased.*

Cali Mithr

Charren. Kilnae Del mage.

Caspol li'Moren

Cyndinari elf. Charren royal advisor. Sha'ghol

Catalina Turlan

Human from Yanil. Supreme Judge of Yanil.

Clara

Aldinari. Ei'ceuril, steward and abbess of the Monastery of the Poor Ladies in the Ashton Wood.

Clovis

Cyndinari. Attendant to Yloran.

Daeryn

Former Ceurtriarch who made wielding in the Temple of Ceur impossible.

Danielle Aerquin

Luminari of House Aerquin. Student wielder at Gwilnor Academy.

DAPHNE ASHTON

Human from Mindale. Queen of Mindale and Lady of Ashton Wood. Emradiel ei'ana.

DEOTHORIL

Centaur in Ogren.

DEVLYN LORENTHIEN

Exalted Aryl of Krysenthiel, High King of Eklean, and Prelate of the Guardian Senate. Elf of all four Skylands. Phaedryn bonded with the phoenix Aliel. Married to Ellendren.

DIANA THELLION

Princess of Evellion. Eldest daughter of Amry and Lara. Betrothed to Alexander Vaerin.

DOLAN LORENTHIEN

Father of Devlyn, Leilyn, and Liam. Husband of Evellyn. Son of Eldinari Leienya Lierafen and an unknown Cyndinari, although this is undisclosed. Raised in the human Telvin family of Cor'lera. *Deceased.*

DONOVAN ORITHIL

Human from Gestoria. Prince of Gestoria.

EAGAN WINTYR

Human. Druid of Kweil Aitch, and Abbie's brother.

EALYNDOL ROENDRYN

Luminari. Former Ceurtriarch. *Deceased.*

ELAYNE THENREL

Luminari. Guardian knight.

ELIEL

One of the first Phoenix to cross into Teraeniel. Bonded with Kiara.

ELLENDREN LORENTHIEN

Luminari. Exalted Aryl of Krysenthiel, High Queen of Eklean, and Prelate of the Guardian Senate. Phaedryn bonded with the phoenix Tariel. Married to Devlyn. Formerly of House Roendryn.

ELYSE LORENTHIEN

Luminari elf. Phaedryn. Ei'phaenyl of the Phaedryn. Daughter of Kien and Kiara.

EMDIAN

Human from Sudern. Ei'ceuril steward.

ENRICO DESILLIO

Human from Yanil. Noble in the Yanilean's court. Married to Angennia.

ENTIEL TELVIN

Human from Perrien. Ei'ceuril, steward, and abbot of the abbey school of Cor'lera. Devlyn's uncle on his father's side.

ERETHIEN MERIDEN

Cyndinari. Son of Erynor. Becomes a Deathless when the Jewel of Life is corrupted.

ERYNEL MERIDEN

Cyndinari. Former Sha'ghol and Erynor's mother. *Deceased.*

ERYNOR MERIDEN

Emperor of the Erynien Empire. Disappeared after Lucillia gave birth to the twins, Roendryn and Feolyn in 7857.3E. First Cyndinari born on Eklean, son of Erynel and Tolvenol.

ETRIEN FERNORIL

Aldinari elf.

EVELLYN LORENTHIEN

Luminari from Cor'lera. Mother of Leilyn and Devlyn. Widow of Dolan.

FALTHION

Dragon of the White Flight bonded with Viren.

FAOXI

Jade dragon who betrayed her clutch mates and became a sea drake.

FERINN

Merperson. Consort and widower of the late Queen Karina Larviere.

FORVL VIII

Dwarf and patriarch of Oern Schtam. Son of Oma and Forvl VII.

FURYK

Dwarf of Undol Schtam. Son of Matriarch Muriel IV.

FYONA ORENDI

Luminari. Student wielder at Gwilnor Academy.

FYREH GLAEDA

Eldinari. Azurelle ei'ana and magister at Gwilnor. Twin brother to Myrah, husband to Suella, and father to many children.

Galithinol

Dragon of the Gold Flight. Father to Weilyn and grandfather to Thien, Vivien, and Theseryn.

Genin

Human from Dwonia. Chief of Tribe Vadir.

Gordon Carvil

King of Torsil. Of the Royal House Carvil. Supporter of Erynor.

Hannah Torin

Human from Mindale. Azurelle ei'ana and chancellor of Gwilnor Academy. *Deceased.*

Harnyl Roendryn

Luminari. Aryl of Lucillia. Married to Queen Vernal. Father of Aaron, Kaela, and Ellendren. *Deceased.*

Henry Ashton

Human from Mindale. King of Mindale and Lord of Ashton Wood. Husband of Daphne.

Irvienne Haert

Human from Briel. King of Briel.

Ithendryl Lorenthien

Luminari elf. Former Exalted Aryl of Arenthyl.

Jaerol Solaris

Cyndinari. Former Erynien emissary. Student wielder at Gwilnor Academy. Bonded with Rusyl.

Jaris iln Desaris

Cyndinari. One of the Sha'ghol. *Deceased.*

Jax

Minum and time warden.

Jeanne Darkel

Luminari. First of the Guardians.

Jehn

Luminari elf. Ei'ceuril. Secretary to the Ceurtriarch.

Jenyd Tarneth

Daer of House Tarneth. Advisor to Senator Koth.

Kaela Lucillia

Luminari. Steward of Arenthyl. Formerly of House Roendryn. Sister to Ellendren and Aaron.

Kaelien

Elder One. Queen of Tenethyl. Aunt to Gael. *Deceased.*

Kanastil

Dragon of the White Flight bonded with Elayne.

Karina Lariviere

Former Queen of Sorenthil. Widow of the late King Dorian. Wife to Ferinn. Mother of Myranda. *Deceased.*

Karl Olney

Human from Perrien. Observant of Vyoletryn.

Kespus

Aerys anadel of the East Wind, Eurnos.

Kevn Weyvien

Luminari. Grand Librarian of the Sophillium.

Kiara Lorenthieb

Luminari. Attracted the first phoenix to Teraeniel and became the first female wielder. Married to Kien.

Kien Lorenthien

Luminari. Attracted the first phoenix to Teraeniel and became the first male wielder. Married to Kiara.

Kodin

Human from Dwonia. Chief of Tribe Fendur. *Deceased.*

Kyrendal Lorenthien

Luminari. First chancellor of Gwilnor Academy. Crafter of the verathn. Monk at the Monastery of Kyrendal. Son to Kien and Kiara.

Lara Thellion

Queen of Evellion. Widow of the late King Amry. Azurelle ei'ana.

Lawrence Maroven

King of Mindale. Of the Royal House Maroven. Supporter of Erynor. *Deceased.*

Leilyn Lorenthien

Sister of Devlyn, living in the Illumined Wood. Daughter of Evellyn and Dolan.

Lenora Hanaryld

Human from Ceurenyl. Ei'ana and Chair of Arantiulyn. *Deceased.*

Lex Telvin

General from Perrien. Leader of the renegade Perrien Militia. Brother to Entiel, Vine, and Dolan, who was adopted. Uncle to Alex. *Deceased.*

Liam Lierafen

Son of Dolan. Half-brother to Devlyn and Leilyn. Student wielder at Gwilnor Academy.

Liara

Dragon of the Red Flight bonded with Prya.

Lillianna

Human from Mindale. Ei'ceuril and formerly an Emradiel ei'ana.

Leonard Orithil

Human from Gestoria. King of Gestoria.

Loretta Javie

Human of Sorenthil. Ei'ana and Chair of Crimsyn.

Lucillia

The woman who gave birth to the twins, Roendryn and Feolyn.

Lyren Fenthyr

Luminari. Attendant, formerly in the Roendryn household before joining the Lorenthien household to attend Devlyn Lorenthien.

Malind Kotii

Daer Senator of the Upper Tier.

Melanie Birkwell

Human from Mindale. Ei'ana and deposed Chair of Arantiulyn.

Mildred Thellion

Human from Evellion. Duchess of Cyril and widow of Talyian, the late Duke.

Myrah Glaeda

Eldinari. Albien ei'ana and magister at Gwilnor Academy; twin sister to Fyreh.

Myranda Lariviere

Queen of Sorenthil. Former student wielder at Gwilnor Academy.

Nadia Desuani

Luminari. Ei'ana and Chair of the Tenebrys School; former Arantiulyn ei'ana.

NAIEL

One of the first Phoenix to cross into Teraeniel. Bonded with Kien.

ODUIN DUR SETHARA

Cyndinari. One of the Sha'ghol.

OLIVER PENAULT

Human from Perrien. Septyl knight of Vyoletryn.

OMA

Dwarf of Oern Schtam. Stone seer.

ORANNA

Luminari. Azurelle ei'ana and former chancellor of Gwilnor Academy. *Deceased.*

ORENIEL

Centaur of the Illumined Wood.

PAOLO FARNEIS

Human from Sudern. Duke of Sudern.

PAUREL ROENDRYN

Luminari. Ei'ana and Chair of Vyoletryn.

PEVREL

Luminari. Attendant to Ellendren Lorenthien.

PHENDIEN SHENDIELLE

Eldinari. Ei'ana and Chair of Emradiel.

PRYA

Draelyn of the Red House. Bonded with Liara.

QIEN DI

Human. Crowned Prince of Qien and Son of Empress Qien Wei. Monk of Beishi Monastery.

QIEN FEI

Human. Sister to Qien Wei

QIEN KAI

Human. Cousin of Empress Qien Wei. Azurelle ei'ana and magister of politics at Gwilnor Academy.

QIEN WEI

Human. Empress of the Qien Dynasty.

RAELINTH

Cyndinari. Attendant to Yloran.

RALENIEL

Elder One that lived in Tenethyl. Married to Weilyn.

RAMIRA BIR GINTHOL

Human from Yanil. Supreme Judge of Yanil at the time of Nauto's Wrath.

RAZCUL MIETHEN

Cyndinari. Shadow elf disguised as an Eldinari assistant magister at Gwilnor. Known as Danyol. *Deceased.*

REIA

Luminari. Arantiulyn ei'ana.

RENAUD LARIVIERE

Human from Sorenthil. Temple knight. Royal cousin to Queen Myranda Lariviere.

REZEKI

Human from Jadien. Son of Prince Alkesh.

RUSYL

Dragon of the Blue Flight. Bonded with Jaerol.

SAECRIEN

One of the Children who watches over the Waters of Anaweh.

SANJIN AL'SANHIR

Human from Charren. Crowned Prince of Charren of the Royal House Irithru.

SARA

Human from Briel. Auburnis ei'ana.

SELENYA WAEYN

Luminari. Ei'ana and Chair of Albien.

SKIMP

Minum and time warden. *Deceased*

SOPHIE

Luminari elf. Creator of the sophilliae and founder of the Sophillium. *Deceased.*

SUIN

Former chief of Tribe Laith. Father of Cairn. *Deceased.*

TARIEL

Phoenix bonded with Ellendren.

TERAN

Cyndinari. Uncle of Jaerol.

THAERWN

Aldinari elf.

THERRIL

Ei'ceuril magister of theoreticals at Gwilnor Academy.

THIEN

Draelyn of the Gold House. Married to Loren. Son to Weilyn and Raleniel. Grandson to Galithinol the Gold. *Deceased*.

TODRICK CORVIN.

Human from Evellion. Former Duke of Overen.

TORYN VICALEN

Luminari. Squire with the Guardian knights.

TRETHIEN NARIELLE

Luminari of House Narielle. Student knight at Gwilnor Academy.

TURA

Human from Dwonia. Member and elder of Tribe Fendur. Grandmother to Tye.

TYE

Human from Dwonia. Member of Tribe Fendur.

TYIEL

Phoenix bonded with Aren.

URSULA CORVIN

Human from Evellion. Duchess of Overen.

VELARIA TREYVEN

Cyndinari born in Lucillia. Ei'ana and Chair of Azurelle. Bonded with Yelaris.

VERINIEN

One of the Children who never aged. Protector of the Tree of Life.

VERNAL ROENDRYN

Luminari. Aryl of Lucillia. Married to King Harnyl. Mother of Aaron, Kaela, and Ellendren. Direct descendant of Lucillia. *Deceased*.

VICTORIA ORITHIL

Human from Gestoria. Crowned Princess of Gestoria.

VINE VAERIN

Human from Perrien. Self-styled Queen Mother to the King of Thellion.

Viren Dekenurel

Luminari. Guardian knight.

Vivien

Draelyn and ealyn of the Gold House. Granddaughter of Galithinol the Gold, and daughter of Weilyn.

Waleisius (Walei)

Merchant in Cor'lera.

Weilyn

Draelyn of the Gold House. Married to Raleniel. Son to Galithinol. *Deceased.*

Wyn Lierafen

Eldinari. Grandson of Dalenya and Fendryl. Star Warden. Emradiel ei'ana.

Yelaris

Dragon of the Blue Flight. Bonded with Velaria.

Yloran eth Gnashar

Cyndinari. One of the Sha'ghol. Known in Lankor as Enna.

Ythinor the Black

Dragon of the Dark Flight. Bonded with his half-brother, Erynor.

The Seven Irythil and their Associated Enthiel

Uriel – Lord of the Stars, whose name means Anaweh is my Light. Irythil who brought Anaweh's Light to Teraeniel.

    Auriel – The Dawn Star. Guardian of the elves of Luminare.

    Meridiel – The Noon Star. Guardian of the elves of Cyndinare.

    Vespiel – The Evening Star. Guardian of the elves of Aldinare.

    Boriel – The Night Star. Guardian of the elves of Eldinare.

Gwynthiel – Lady of the Lorendil, whose name means Strength of Anaweh. Irythil who brought Anaweh's spirit to Teraeniel.

Ramiel – Lord of Death, whose name means Arrogant toward Anaweh. Betrayed Anaweh and all creation. Irythil who brought shadow to Teraeniel.

Theniel – Lady of the Seas, whose name means Anaweh Heals. Irythil who brought water to Teraeniel.

    Nauto – Guardian of all humans living along the coasts.

Aquae – Guardian of the merpeople.

Sariel – Lord of the Land, whose name means Command of Anaweh. Irythil who brought substance to Teraeniel.

Tera – Patroness of harvest and nourishment. Often referred to as Mother Tera.

Mundi – Guardian of the dwarves.

Dwonia – Guardian of all humans living in the Dwonian Desert.

Lereniel – Lady of the Winds, whose name means Friend of Anaweh. Irythil who brought air to Teraeniel.

Kariel – Lord of Peace, whose name means Who is Like Anaweh. Irythil who brought fire to Teraeniel.

Seven Chairs of Septyl

Chair of Albien — Selenya Waeyn. Luminari. The White Owl.

Chair of Arantiulyn — Ira Urana. Luminari. The Orange Lion.

Chair of Auburnis — Agnelle Phanstienne. Luminari. The Brown Lark.

Chair of Azurelle — Velaria Treyven. Cyndinari born in Lucillia. The Blue Dragon.

Chair of Crimsyn — Loretta Javie. Human from Sorenthil. The Red Dog.

Chair of Emradiel — Phendien Shendielle. Eldinari. The Green Stag.

Chair of Vyoletryn — Paurel Roendryn. Luminari. The Purple Eagle.

High Luminari Houses and Aryls

Aryl of Arenthyl and Exalted Aryl of Krysenthiel — House Lorenthien

Aryl of Lucillia — Vernal (deceased) and Harnyl of House Roendryn

Aryl of Reinyl — Therrin and Zara of House Reyndien

Aryl of Ostyl — Naesiv and Valerie of House Aerquin

Aryl of Winstsyl — Toral and Silvia of House Narielle

Aryl of Tenyl — Iridil and Enoria of House Taerinior

ARYL OF DELMIRA WOOD — Ciraenth and Aegian of House Ginielle

ARYL OF EANDYL — Enithil and Binoral of House Clarion

ARYL OF VERENTHYL — Kyiel and Fyona of House Lauriel

HIGH ELDINARI HOUSES AND ARYLS

ARYL OF LIERTHYL — Fendryl and Dalenya of House Lierafen

ARYL OF VIRATHYL — Naerelle and Eohire of House Shendielle

ARYL OF DRETHYL — Vanoreh and Elialen of House Illia

ARYL OF LADRITHYL — Indryn and Diera of House Allandis

ALDARCHS OF ALDINARE

GAEL OF QUEL'ANIR – The Reverend Mother, also known as the Nurturer. Her followers dedicate themselves to nature and caring for the ilithae trees, native to Aldinare.

ORIEN OF ELN'DINAI – The Just Father, also known as the Judge. His followers focus on upholding law in Aldinare.

NIALTH OF DUR'LINOS – The Philosopher, also known as the Learned One. Her followers dedicate their life to study.

THESERYN OF THAS'THALLAS – The Faithful Servant. His followers devoted their lives to worshipping Anaweh, the Creating Light. Theseryn left his sanctum of Thas'thallas to establish the Ei'ceuril order and became the first Ceurtriarch.

LERATHEL OF VAL'QUIN – The Artisan. Sister to Nialth. Her followers are practitioners of the arts and designed the great cities and sanctums of Aldinare.

ENDRUIL OF KIR'ENON – The Shepherd. His followers are caretakers of the alicorns native to Aldinare.

AERYTH OF AI'LYR – The Rogue. Her followers prefer to hide in the shadows and wield the fabled Aldinari bows.

IRITHEL OF MEL'INOR – The Smith. His followers develop advanced weapons and tools, often forged from aldaryl.

Ealyn of Tenethyl

Vivien — Ealyn of the Gold House. Granddaughter of Galithinol of the Gold Flight.

Daela — Ealyn of the Amethyst House. Granddaughter of Myrasha of the Purple Flight.

Torik — Ealyn of the Onyx House. Grandson of Jiertha of the Grey Flight.

Mellory — Ealyn of the Ruby House. Granddaughter of Vulgath of the Red Flight.

Niron — Ealyn of the Sapphire House. Grandson of Naithos of the Blue Flight.

Allister — Ealyn of the Opal House. Grandson of Ithinol of the White Flight.

Helen — Ealyn of the Jade House. Granddaughter of Fenoral of the Green Flight.

Dragon Primus

Lyvenol — Primus of the Gold Flight. Warden of lumenys.

Eilynol — Primus of the Purple Flight. Warden of animys.

Orythnol — Primus of the Grey Flight. Warden of umbrys.

Aerinol — Primus of the White Flight. Warden of aerys.

Caephenol — Primus of the Blue Flight. Warden of aquaeys.

Thereinol — Primus of the Green Flight. Warden of terys.

Fyrinol — Primus of the Red Flight. Warden of ignys.

Tolvenol — Primus of the Dark Flight. Warden of tenebrys.

Appendix C

Civilizations of Teraeniel

Aldinare

Remnant of Aldinari rescued from the Skyland Aldinare by Aren and accompanying Phaedryn. They are considered part of Krysenthiel.

Race: Elf

House/Aryl: Avign, Eraen, Kenoril, Threilen

Audun

One of the eight schtams composing the Schtamite. Situated at the westernmost edge of the Laudien Mountains.

Head of State: Patriarch Dridn IV, son of Dridn III

Race: Dwarf

Briel

River valley kingdom situated between two rivers forming the River Reifen and the slopes of the Dead Wood.

Capital: Briel

Head of State: King Irvienne of the Royal House Haert

Motto: Seek the message

Sigil: Black raven on a yellow field

Race: Human

Brunst

One of the eight schtams composing the Schtamite. Situated within the Vespien Mountains. Close friends with the Eldinari.

Head of State: Patriarch Thraen, son of Anuun

Race: Dwarf

Charren

A kingdom spanning across two continents, Ogren and Daereneth.

Capital: Karithel

Head of State: King Sanhir of the Royal House Irithru

Race: Human

Daer Empire

Oldest continuous human empire in Teraeniel and advocate of slavery and colonialism. Situated on the continent of Daereneth.

Capital: Daer

Head of State: Body of the Daer Senate

Race: Human

DWONIA

Desert country once controlled by the Twelve Tribes of Dwonia. Only two tribes refused to ally with Erynor and remained in the desert.

Heads of State: Chief Kodin of Tribe Fendur and Chief Genin of Tribe Vadir

Capital: Nynev

Sigil: Red lion on a yellow field

Race: Human

ELDINARE

Eldinari society secreted away in the Eldin Wood.

Head of State: Aryl Fendryl and Dalenya of House Lierafen

Capital: Stellantis

Sigil: White tree on a green field

Race: Elf

ERYNIEN EMPIRE

Cyndinari empire founded by Erynor Meriden, its sole emperor. Responsible for the Ceurendol War and enslavement of the Luminari.

Capital: Broid

Head of State: Emperor Erynor Meriden

Sigil: Bronze sun on a red field

Race: Elf

EVELLION

The mountain kingdom where the Laudien and Vespien mountain ranges meet. Original inhabitants were the refugees of Thellion.

Capital: Everin

Head of State: King Amry and Queen Lara of the Royal House Thellion

Motto: The pure will soar

Sigil: White eagle on a blue field

Race: Human

FRIETON

The free city-state of Frieton. Given to the minums on their release from slavery.

Capital: Frieton

Head of State: The Keeper (identity unknown)

Race: Minum

GESTORIA

Fallen kingdom situated on the Plains of Orithil. Once great allies to Thellion and Krysenthiel. Obliterated during the Ceurendol War.
Capital: Quellion
Motto: Will triumphs pride
Sigil: White gold winged lion on a blue field
Race: Human

GLYOL

One of the eight schtams composing the Schtamite. Easternmost and only schtam in the Illumined Wood.
Head of State: Matriarch Vylma, daughter of Toreldn
Race: Dwarf

HAROL

One of the eight schtams composing the Schtamite. Situated in the Laudien Mountains.
Head of State: Matriarch Loewn, daughter of Brenola
Race: Dwarf

JA'HORAN, TRIBES OF

Nomadic civilization on the continent of Ja'horan.
Race: Human

JA'NALIHN

Short lived kingdom covering all of Ja'horan.
Race: Human

JOPHT

One of the eight schtams composing the Schtamite. Southernmost schtam in the Vespien Mountains and staunch defenders against the Shadow schtams from northern infiltration.
Head of State: Patriarch Oerth III, son of Oerth II
Race: Dwarf

KRYSENTHIEL

The kingdom of the Luminari. Currently lost within the Shroud. Translates to land of the golden flowers, named by a human trying to speak Aelish, the language of the elves, to describe the countryside.
Capital: Arenthyl
Head of State: Exalted Lorenthien Aryl

Sigil: Seven golden kryseniels blossoming from a larger central kryseniel on a white field.

Race: Elf

Lucillia

Kingdom of the Luminari after gaining their freedom from the Erynien Empire. Named after Lucillia, the woman who gave birth to the twins, Roendryn and Feolyn.

Capital: Lucillia

Head of State: Aryl Vernal and Harnyl of House Roendryn

Race: Elf

Mindale

A kingdom east of the southern Vespien Mountains.

Capital: Binton

Head of State: King Lawrence of the Royal House Maroven

Motto: Mind over body

Sigil: Brown ox on a green field

Race: Human

Nunstol

Shadow schtam that was cast off by the Schtamite for their actions in Mount Cyngol.

Head of State: Patriarch Uriden, son of Urodrn

Race: Dwarf

Oern

One of the eight schtams composing the Schtamite. Belin belonged to Oern schtam and sheltered Evellion and his people as they fled Elothkar.

Head of State: Patriarch Forvl VIII, son of Forvl VII

Race: Dwarf

Parendior

A hilly country north of the Laudien Mountains and west of the Illumined Wood. Most Parendians are farming folk, and when Perrien invaded, they had no means of defending their land.

Motto: Protect the harmony

Sigil: Purple doe on a beige field

Race: Human

Perrien

A kingdom north of the Laudien Mountains where the citizens overthrew their monarchy and replaced it with a council and doubled their territory by invading Parendior.

Capital: Gneal

Motto: Swift to action

Sigil: Grey rider and horse on a white field

Race: Human

Qien Empire, the

Empire of the Hundred Kingdoms on the continent of Qien, west of Eklean.

Capital: Zhongshi

Auxiliary Capitals: Beishi, Dongshi, Nanshi, and Xishi

Head of State: Empress Qien Wei

Race: Human

Sorenthil

A kingdom along the River Meyien.

Capital: Myrium

Head of State: Queen Karina of the Royal House Lariviere

Motto: Flow with the waters

Sigil: Blue dolphin on a light blue field

Race: Human

Sudern

A city state on the Dagger's Point peninsula. After a bloody civil war with Josque, the inhabitants declared themselves independent.

Capital: Sudern

Motto: Hidden daggers

Sigil: Red ship and dagger on a white field

Race: Human

Thellion

The fallen Eklean kingdom covering all the lands east of the Vespien Mountains. Met its downfall through a civil war relating to succession.

Capital: Elothkar

Head of State: King Alexander of House Vaerin

Motto: Eternal wisdom

Sigil: Silver winged horse on a white field

TIEL

A southern kingdom bordering the Erynien Bay and the Unarian Sea.

Capital: Josque

Head of State: Queen Alesei of the Royal House Ziera

Motto: Eternal wisdom

Sigil: Orange serpent on a blue field

Race: Human

TORSIL

A weak kingdom with little influence on its neighbors.

Capital: Trest

Head of State: King Gordon of the Royal House Carvil

Motto: Stronger together

Sigil: Grey wolf on a red field

Race: Human

UNDOL

One of the eight schtams composing the Schtamite. Deeply religious and situated in the Laudien Mountains surrounding Lake Saeryndol. They have strong ties to the Luminari.

Head of State: Matriarch Miurel IV, daughter of Miurel III

Race: Dwarf

VORN

One of the eight schtams composing the Schtamite. Situated at the northernmost edge of the Vespien Mountains.

Head of State: Matriarch Tiltha, daughter of Tilma

Race: Dwarf

YANIL

Southern kingdom along the Erynien Bay. Yanil was once jointly ruled by the Yanilean and the Judges of Yanil.

Capital: Lankor

Head of State: The Yanilean

Motto: Deep as justice

Sigil: Black castle on a blue field

Race: Human

ZORIK

Shadow schtam that was cast off by the Schtamite for their actions in Mount

Cyngol.
Head of State: Matriarch Jiora, daughter of Jiorza
Race: Dwarf

About the Author

Ryan D Gebhart first started writing the Jewel of Life series in 2012 in Philadelphia, PA, shortly after concluding his undergraduate studies in philosophy. This unexpected passion evolved over the years and has remained a constant companion, developing into new LGBTQ+ Fantasy stories he's excited to publish. Ryan lives in Washington, DC with his husband and cat, where he also works at an architecture firm. Ryan D Gebhart is originally from Wilmington, DE.

Keep up with Ryan D Gebhart at www.RyanDGebhart.com